Destini

the

Chocolate

Princess

by

J. V. Lewis

(Joan Wright Lewis)

JWANI
Productions

Printed in the United States of America.

Revised edition by JWANI Productions -- Jo-Val Publishing, LLC 2019
Revised edition by Jo-Val Publishing, LLC 2016
Avon, Indiana

ISBN: 978-0-9629832-1-4 (sc)
        0-9629832-1-7 (sc)
ISBN: 978-0-9629832-2-1 (hc)
        0-9629832-2-5 (hc)

Library of Congress Control Number: 2012916588

"Cover illustration by Joan Wright Lewis"

Questions for discussions at the end of this book

This book is printed on acid-free paper.

Published by

JWANI Productions
Jo-Val Publishing, LLC *Avon, Indiana*

www.jvpublishers.com

ACKNOWLEDGEMENTS

I would like to thank all the editors who took the time
To edit this book:

Renee Jefferson, for taking her precious time to
Revise and edit this book. I appreciate
Her love and patience--for being honest and caring.
Marlene Banton for her kindness in editing various chapters
Della Jules, first editor for this book.
I appreciate her patience and knowledgeable input

I also thank:
The late, **Amos Brown**, Director of Strategic Research, Radio
One/Indianapolis, IN and **The Amos Brown Show**, WDNI –TV
For having me on his show and promoting Destini the Chocolate Princess
The **Capital City Church & School** for their support
The **Plainfield**, and the **Avon –Washington Township Public Library**
In Indiana, for putting it on display
Carly Nation of the **Hendricks County Flyer**, Avon IN, for her lovely
article

I would also like to thank:
My wonderful husband, **Wycham Lewis** for his love, support,
encouragements and wisdom, and for believing in me
Nastassja Lewis, for her support
Julie Gbile, for her kindness, using her precious time and for her support of
my book
Gerald B. Coleman, Attorney at Law, Indianapolis, IN, for his support
Steve Jefferson, WTHR TV News Reporter Channel 13, Indianapolis, IN,
for his support
I thank the **Great God of the universe**,
Who gave me this talent and directed my path to acknowledge His
wonderful blessings

"Joan, I cannot get anything else done because I am so fascinated by Destini the Chocolate Princess!!!! *Destini the Chocolate Princess is just phenomenal!! I told my boys about it and now they want to read it. It is a great read I read 130 pages last night alone!!!! I was reading until 3:30 this morning!!! I am sooooo tired!!!!"*
Yolanda McIntosh, President/Founder/CEO, McIntosh Mo2Vations, McM,Saint Paul, MN

"I love this book! I could not put it down until I read the last page. I wanted to know what would happen next and I was not disappointed. Destini the Chocolate Princess is a very interesting book. I could identify with some of the events in it. Reading this book gave me courage to face tomorrow. I would recommend Destini the Chocolate Princess *to any young person, although, adults will love it too!"*
Zudia Williams, New York, NY

"Inspiring! The book Destini the Chocolate Princess *is one that touches the core of one's soul. It exhibits an awareness of life's inevitable challenges (socio-cultural biases, human insensitivity and cruelty) but exults in the triumph of abiding faith and love. One cannot read this book without becoming emotionally involved: You cry, you sigh, you laugh. It is a book that empowers you to go forward. You will not put this book down until you've read every word. Anyone and everyone will benefit from reading it. You'll love it!*
Pauline Evans, Teacher, New York, NY

Excellent book
"This is an incredibly moving and captivating novel, and it has something for everyone: romance, high school drama, alienation, family values, faith, and important social themes. As a ... teacher, this book is perfect for the pre-teen/ young adult audience, and it is one of the most popular books at my school. Destini the Chocolate Princess *is a fantastic read, and I can't recommend it highly enough!*
Patrick Roe, Teacher, Avon, IN

Dedicated to my lovely daughter Alexia
For inspiring me with her warmth and kindness

TABLE OF CONTENTS

1

Beautiful Baby

In the blackness of a cool spring night, a beautiful baby girl secured from her mother's womb, pressed forward into the unknown. Her precious little head appeared from its hiding place. She looked around and screamed with fright. She seemed to say desperately, *"Where am I? It's too bright out here and my face is very cold."* A nurse held the mother's hand as she pushed exhaustedly. The mid-wife helped guide the little body out from the warmth and security of her first home to begin her new journey. The baby girl trembled in the apparent cold, and her little voice quivered with fear. The shrilled sound of her cry rang through the stillness. Her mother, Mary, a gorgeous golden-brown woman having just travailed in pain, softly muttered in her Texan accent,

"Is it a boy, or girl?"

"A lovely baby girl," said the attending nurse, warmly. The new mother smiled wearily. Her rich auburn hair was tousled in all directions on her crisp, white pillow. "Has the doctor arrived yet?" she muttered again.

"Not yet dear," answered the nurse. Jeff Pearson, her tall, dark, and startlingly handsome husband rushed into their bedroom. He was by the door when he heard the wholesome cry of his newborn child. His tall stature made Mary feel protected as she laid on the king sized poster bed. After checking the vital signs of the baby, the mid-wife smiled pleasantly, congratulated the couple and left the room.

"Babe, are you all right? Is it a boy?"

"No, Mr. Pearson," said the nurse, "she is a lovely baby girl." He calmed down and the bubbling excitement he had disappeared.

"Oh, a girl," he said somberly. "Well, as long as Papa's little girl is healthy," he continued in his deep baritone voice. Mary looked sleepily at her husband, with suspicion.

"What 'a ya mean, 'Oh, a girl'?" She repeated his somber tone wearily. "I thought you'd said it didn't matter." Jeff shrugged his shoulder as he looked over to get a glimpse of his brand new little darling. "Nothing," he answered.

"Nothing?" she insisted.

"Mary," Jeff began, looking lovingly at her, "you knew I preferred a boy. But as long as she is healthy, that's all I care about." Mary looked at the nurse and yawned, tapping her mouth lightly.

"When you finish cleaning her up, please bring her so I can see my darling baby." The nurse brought the baby to Mary. Jeff smiled lovingly admiring his little girl. Mary stared for a moment, then with displeasure-complained, "Is that my baby? Goodness, she's so dark and ugly." The words evoked a sudden anger in the nurse.

"Ma'am," she said sharply, "you should thank God that you have a beautiful and healthy baby." The nurse realizing her tone and said calmly, "If you need me, I will be outside." Mary looked at the nurse, narrowing her eyes and then stared at her baby with disbelief.

"My first child and she's so dark," she thought. Mary looked at the top of the baby's ears. *"She's gonna get even darker as she gets older. Couldn't she be lighter? If she were a boy, it wouldn't be so bad. But, she's a girl. God, why?"* She looked up at the ceiling and paused for a while. She then stared at her baby. Jeff was happy to see his little girl.

"She's lovely." He said still admiring her. His wife rolled her eyes with a sad expression.

"Well little girl," she said to herself, "the name I had chosen for you won't fit you. I'll give you a name that complements you perfectly. It means luck or blessing; you're gonna need it. Jeff," she then said aloud, "what 'a ya think of the name Destini?" Jeff responded, choking back tears, "The name is beautiful, just as my little princess is beautiful."

2

Disappointments

even years later, on a bright sunny summer day,
little Destini and her cousin Crystal were
skipping around outside the front of the house. A three-foot
wooden fence surrounded the two-story gray wooden home. The
parched grass looked like it sucked up its last drop of water. Crystal
being about the same age and height as Destini, looked lovely in her
little pink dress. Her fair skin glowed in the sunlight. Destini's yellow
cotton dress and socks matched the ribbons in her soft, woolly hair.

Blessed with breath-taking beauty from her father's side of the
family, her smooth dark skin glowed like the richness of chocolate. As
Destini and Crystal skipped and played, they held hands and smiled at
each other. At times, they would stop and pretend that they were fixing
each other's hair or dusting off the other's shoulder and straightening
their dresses.

"You look lovely today dear," Destini would say to Crystal in her
most grown up imitation.

"Thank you ever so much," she responded.

"You're quite welcome." They'd both laugh heartily and continue
skipping around the yard.

Inside the living room, grandma, a very light-skinned heavyset
woman, rocked away in her rocking chair. She was darning a pair of
her son-in-law's work pants. The sun shun brightly through the
windows giving the red-carpeted living room a warm, radiant glow,
thus creating a cozy atmosphere. Mary descended the red-carpeted
stairs with Jeff right behind her, engaging her in conversation. Her
peach cotton dress complemented her light, golden-brown skin.

"Yes, I know Jeff," Mary answered, "everything is packed and
ready to go. Mama!" she called out. Grandma Harris stopped rocking.

"Mama! We're ready to go now. Where's Destini?" Grandma Harris stood up slowly.

"She outside with Crystal," she answered with a Texan drawl.

"Destini! Destini!" Mary called impatiently. Mary had her hair done at the beauty salon and she knew she looked great. She was eager to go to Mexico to show herself off.

"Yes, Mama," Destini answered in her sweet child voice, "coming!" Destini ran inside with Crystal.

"Now Destini," said Mary, "I want you to be on your best behavior. Listen to grandma and be a good girl, okay?" Destini looked up at her mother with her innocent, beautiful, radiant, sun-lit brown eyes.

"Yes mama. Can I come with you and Papa?"

"No, you can't," Mary responded pursing her lips and knitting her brow, "I have already told you that you can't come." Destini looked at her mother and wished she looked just like her.

"You look so pretty Mama." Mary smiled, and kissed her on the forehead. "Thanks baby, goodbye." Then she walked to the door. Jeff squatted and held out his hands, and little Destini ran into his open arms. He hugged her warmly and kissed her on both cheeks. *"Hmmm,"* thought little Destini, *"Papa smells so good."*

"I'm gonna miss you, my little princess," he smiled warmly with a hint of sadness in his gorgeous eyes. He hugged her again and said, "Now, my beautiful little princess, Papa loves you very much. I'll be back soon. I'm gonna miss you so . . ."

Mary, looking on, was anxious to go. "Jeff!" she shouted, "Would you hurry up before we miss our plane to Mexico!" Jeff looked up at Mary as if to say, *"Please be patient."*

"I'm coming," he said, "and we have more than enough time." He looked at his gorgeous little daughter lovingly. Her lovely face lowered and her gorgeous brown eyes looking up shyly at her papa. He admired her pretty face and noting her cotton soft hair that was styled in three braids. Her soft hair was tied with yellow ribbons that glowed against the rich blackness of each strand. Papa kissed her again and said, "Gotta go, Papa'll call." He smiled and said gently, "See you next week. You are my little heart. Your skin is so soft and beautiful."

He said touching it gently. "I love you my beautiful chocolate princess." He concluded lovingly.

Destini loved when he called her chocolate princess and touched her face ever so gently. She felt special. Papa stood up to go. He looked tall and handsome to little Destini; like a tall, dark, handsome king who would always be there to protect her.

Destini and Crystal played outside every day until the day Papa was coming home. Jeff called Destini each day during the trip until the day he was to return. On the day of his return, Destini woke up early. She planted herself in the living room and looked out of the window anxiously, while the sun pierced through at her. She couldn't bear to wait any longer to see her Papa.

In the afternoon, Crystal stopped by to see if Destini wanted to come out and play. But Destini declined, saying that she just wanted to wait for her Papa and Mama in the living room. Evening came and she did not see Papa. Destini was anxious to see her parents, so anxious, that she didn't eat much. She didn't notice that the phone rang a few times.

Grandma gently approached Destini. "Destini," she said. There was a strain in Grandma's voice.

"Yea, Gra-ma?" she answered, looking up at Grandma innocently, and noticing the tears in her eyes. "What's the matter Gra-ma?"

Grandma held Destini's little hands and said softly, "Mama and Papa won't be coming home today."

Destini stared at Grandma Harris, and then asked, "Why not? When are they coming home?"

Grandma explained that they had died in a plane crash. Little Destini was confused. She did not understand why her parents were not coming home. So, every day for the next month she woke up early, knelt on the sofa in the living room, and looked out of the window hoping to see Papa come home. Then one day reality hit her deeply. She realized that the only person who protected her, told her she was pretty, and made her feel happy was gone forever. Destini thought, *"No, no, no----o."* She cried and cried and told grandma that she wanted her Papa. She could not eat and she started to lose weight.

3

Destini's Dilemma

Summer vacation ended and the new school year arrived. Destini went back to school, but she felt different inside. She felt as if her peaceful world was taken from her, and cruelty replaced tranquility. The students behaved as they did the school year before. They continued to call her black spook, ugly duckling, tar baby, black beanpole, and darkie. But Destini didn't care anymore when the children teased her. She just wanted her father back.

At the end of each day, she ran outside hoping with all her heart that her Papa was waiting to take her home. Instead, with disappointment, she saw other children running into their father's arms, and her auntie waiting to take her home. Destini burst into tears. After a week, she gave up hope, and instead of running from her class through the front doors, she walked slowly to her auntie's car.

Destini didn't have many friends in school, except her cousin Crystal. But, Crystal thought she was better than Destini because people told her that she was better and prettier. Even so, the two spent a lot of time together, and even though Destini loved Crystal, she always felt ugly around her. The boys liked Crystal. They said she looked like the fairy princess. They liked her lovely cream-colored skin her hazel eyes and her light-brown hair.

As time passed, children constantly teased Destini. Even adults made negative remarks about her hair and her cocoa skin: "Poor girl, if you looked like your mama you'd be so pretty." "Look at that bad, nappy hair, can't do nuttin' with it." "Crystal's lucky; she'll get a lot further in life." "Girl, you's cursed, not only you too black, you got dem ugly big lips too. Good thang you's smart in school, 'cause dat's all you got goin' for ya."

Destini cried often in her room. She looked in the mirror and wished her looks would disappear. She'd put a long white or yellow skirt on her head and pretend she had long, blond hair. She'd say to herself, "Now they'll like me because I have long, blond hair." Then she'd get angry, pull off the skirt and cry. One night she begged God to turn her white or even light-skinned like her cousin, Crystal. She cried out to God and asked, "God, why did you make me so black and ugly?"

~~~~~~

The evil messages spoken by ignorant folks impacted Destini's life throughout the years.

It would take her sometime to realize that some people are unwise. They do not stop to think about what they say, and how it affects others. Destini would wonder whether they thought about how much energy is wasted and the account they have to give.

Skin color, what is it? Destini did not analyze it or care. She just wanted to be accepted for who she was. She was sure each person would like that too. For now, all Destini knew was the pain that people inflicted on her.

In time, it will prove that thoughts and actions are what really matters, not skin color. It couldn't cook, laugh, make love, or praise God. She would know in time that you will not experience the true meaning of freedom if the mind is held captive.

Orphan Home

*T*hree years after the plane crash, Grandma *Harris died, and Destini had no one to care for her. Her relatives thought the responsibility too much, and she was* sent to an orphanage. For the next three years, Destini jostled back and forth from foster homes to the orphanage. In some foster homes, she was not treated nicely. She was given heavy responsibilities to clean up and care for others. When she made mistakes or could not keep up with her responsibilities, she was scolded and sometimes beaten. There were times she just wanted to run away or die.

There was one foster family that treated her very nice, and they attended church weekly. The foster mother always hugged her and told her that Jesus loved her and He was going to bless her with a wonderful home one day. Destini wished she could stay with that family, but there were seven children in that home. She always kept in her heart what the foster mother said to her.

Even though Destini was treated unkindly at times, she always had something good and encouraging to say to those who were unhappy and feeling sad. People liked having her around to hear what good things she had to say. Destini loved to read the Bible. Her favorite story was about Joseph. He didn't have any of his family with him and God protected him. She prayed to God and asked Him to be with her and to deliver her. Destini learned much in school and by sneaking off to the library to bring home lots of books to read in the little spare time she managed to secure at night.

One day the orphanage had open house. A well-dressed, middle-aged couple and others came to adopt one of the children from the orphanage. The other guests remained in the waiting room while the middle-aged couple, Winston and Etta Taylor, met inside the office with Ms. Gates, the Director of the facility. Ms. Gates, a five-foot-two-inch, honey-colored woman, seemed so much shorter than the Taylors. She greeted them and thanked them for coming. As she spoke articulately, she smoothed the side of her nicely curled, dark brown hair that was glistening with hair oil.

"Thanks for coming," Ms. Gates said in her Texan accent. "The staff and I appreciate you taking the time to visit us." The Taylors glanced at each other and smiled with Ms. Gates.

"Now," said Ms. Gates as she continued to smooth her hair away from her face. "Mr. and Mrs. Taylor, make sure you look over the children's files very well because other parents will be here to adopt a child. We have lots of little ones for you to choose from."

"Thank you very much," Mrs. Taylor said calmly, her button nose twinkled as she talked, "and we will know what child we want when we meet him or her. You see, Ms. Gates, God sent us here." Ms. Gates stared at the couple, her smiling lips slightly curved upward. She noticed that Mr. Taylor, who was very nice looking with a dark brown complexion, was very calm and didn't talk much.

"Yea------------s," she sang slowly, "Tell me, do you want a boy or a girl?"

Mrs. Taylor responded, "A boy, a girl, doesn't matter. As I said, we will know what child we want when we meet him or her." The couple looked at each other lovingly.

"Yea------------s," with an expression of doubt, Ms. Gates responded, again, smoothing the hair from the side of her face.

Smiles and Sunshine

All the children were dressed in their best church clothes. They looked and acted like little angels on their best behavior mission. They sat quietly and waited patiently.

Thirteen-year-old Destini was intelligent with beautiful expressive brown eyes that evolved to a lighter shade in the sunlight; giving her lovely sun-lit brown eyes. Her soft elegant beauty with long curled eyelashes, smooth dark skin, and a glowing smile, attracted the Taylors immediately. She smiled shyly lowering her head and looking up at the Taylor. Destini introduced herself and did not give the couple a chance to talk, fearing they would leave. Her melodious velvety voice captivated them. They noticed that her beautiful brown eyes were a lighter brown in contrast to her dark skin.

"Hello, my name is Destini. It means good luck, good fortune or blessing. I'll be a blessing to you if you choose me. Well," she murmured nervously, lowering her head, "actually, that's what my parents said it meant. Anyway," she said looking up and smiling, "nice of you to come and visit us today. We appre . . . appre . . . ciate your presence." Fascinated, the couple was about to say thank you, but Destini chattered on. "I like your dress ma'am, and sir it's not that I don't like your clothes, but I am more familiar with women's clothes." She looked at Mr. Taylor with an air of innocence mixed with an expression of sincerity.

"But sir, you have a wonderful smile, you too ma'am." Destini continued, "I know how to cook, I sing very well, I am a good girl, I am obedient, I wash my own clothes, I read very well, I like school, I can even take out the garbage, and I don't cause any trouble. I don't take up much room. I don't eat a lot and . . . "

"Destini," Ms. Gates interrupted, "give Mr. and Mrs. Taylor a chance to meet the other children. Please forgive her. If you don't stop her she'll keep talking." Ms. Gates directed the couple to younger children. "Please, this way, I want you to meet two very special

11

children, a boy and a girl. Joseph is three and Cece is two and a half." Destini was left with the most disappointing feeling of loneliness. Finally, Ms. Gates came to Destini, "Destini, I'm sorry, but we don't want anyone to leave here today without a child. People usually prefer younger children. You're a big girl, you understand, don't you?" Destini sat motionless and watched the other children getting attention. She wished Ms. Gates did not stop her from talking to those people. She felt it was her last chance to get out of the awful cycle. She felt sad and unwanted. None of the other guests noticed her.

The next morning, under brightly shining sun, the Taylors came to see Ms. Gates.

"We've decided who we want to adopt," they announced.

"Wonderful!" exclaimed Ms. Gates. "If you'll just tell me which one of our little ones, I'll be happy to get the files and make all the necessary arrangements."

The couple looked at each other with joy and smiled, "We want Destini Pearson." Surprised, Ms. Gates looked at the couple, "Mr. and Mrs. Taylor," she began, "are you sure now. You realize the other children are so much younger and cuter . . ."

Mrs. Taylor stood up. "Ms. Gates," she said calmly, "Winston and I have both decided that we want to adopt the beautiful ebony girl with the gorgeous brown eyes and the million dollar smile. As I had said yesterday, God sent us here, all the way from Massachusetts, just for her. We will not leave here until we are sure she will be our daughter."

"Well," conceded Ms. Gates smoothing her hair with her fingers. "Yea------------s. As you know, there are standard procedures that I have to follow. But, I'll make all the necessary arrangements and get everything started."

When Ms Gates told Destini that the Taylors wanted her, she was beyond belief. She was excited that someone actually cared enough to adopt her. Destini thought since no one else had noticed her, there was no hope. She praised God for smiling on her and for answering her prayers. Finally, the Taylors actually wanted her as their very own daughter. She giggled, danced, and cried.

Destini's New Home

*D*estini *finally went to live with the Taylors in South Lancaster, Massachusetts, on a beautifully landscaped three-acre property. The scenery was spectacular.*

The property was decorated with tall trees, a perfectly manicured lawn with a large lake in the back yard. *"Oh, my goodness,"* she thought, as she rode up to the property, *"I've never seen anything like it."* She stepped out of the vehicle, and looked up at the gorgeous two-story, brick house. "Wow," she thought, "it is so big." She discovered that it was a four bedroom, three and a half baths, home. It also had a large family room, a den, and a lovely fireplace.

Destini was escorted up to her very own bedroom. On her bed, awaiting her, were beautiful new clothes and shoes. It was like Christmas in September. She was happy to take off the worn-out clothes that were small and out of fashion. She loved her bedroom. The pastel pink and white colored wallpaper gave life to the walls. A painting hung on each wall. The light-beige carpet gave the room a light feeling. She even had her very own bathroom. *"Ooo---oh,"* she thought, *"this is just too cute."* Destini got a panoramic view of the rolling hills in the near distance. She spent a lot of time sitting in her room, gazing through the window at the lake and enjoying the scene.

She noticed that her new family had an abundance of cranberries in the kitchen. She learned about the bright red fruit that her new mother used in making delicious jams, jellies, cakes, breads and cranberry drinks. Picking apples at an apple orchard was fun to her, especially after tasting the sweet and delicious apples right from the trees.

Destini loved the fresh scent of the beautiful flowers in the spring and the freshness of the air was like a healing to her being. Spectacular sights to her eyes during the fall were the red, yellow, orange, lovely multi-colored leaves. She loved all four seasons, but the spring and fall were her favorite.

Destini met a lot of new people, including three cousins, which were her new mom's niece and nephews. The mischievous boys followed her around, and the girl, Deloris, was a big show-off. She looked Destini up and down and twisted her lips as if to say, I'm better than you. Destini was happy to meet new family members however, when she saw their reaction she hoped she didn't have to hang out with Deloris and her brothers. Selina, Mrs. Taylor's sister, was not delighted about Destini, so she did not bring her children around much. Destini was very happy about this.

Destini went to picnics, retreats, parties and trips. She flew to New York and spent memorable times with her new grandparents, with whom she had so much fun. Destini felt like a princess with all of the attention she received. Her new grandparents sent her lots of gifts. They gave her shoes, clothes, books, numerous dolls to play with and a beautiful black doll for her dresser. She also received barrettes for her hair, a lovely penknife that included a fingernail shaper and a bottle top opener. It was quite unique and exquisitely decorated with a floral painting. Destini especially liked the doll for her dresser. She was fascinated with the penknife--so fascinated in fact that she carried it in her schoolbag.

Sometimes, she got into fights with some of the kids at school, who, teased her about her hair and skin. Some of the girls were jealous of her beauty, so they got the other kids to pick fights with her.

Destini fought very well. She had learned to defend herself while living in foster homes. So, the children stayed clear of her when they found out that she could beat them. The Taylors worked with her to guide her in the right direction and to keep her out of trouble. At times, she was grounded. Her new parents' rules were strict, but she didn't mind. She was happy to be in a caring, beautiful home.

When alone in her room, sometimes thoughts of the kids in her new school flashed through her mind. *"Oh,"* thought Destini, *"I wish my father were here. I wish that all the kids liked me and they thought I was a pretty princess just like my father said I was. I don't want to be teased anymore."* And while these thoughts passed through her mind, a teardrop wiggled down her face. "Oh Papa, I miss you so much."

Destini however, loved to read. She usually settled down in her room with the Bible or a good book to read. She chose a book she got online "Make Friends, be Popular," by, Joan Wright Lewis.
http://jvpublishers.com/H-t-b-P.html
She wanted to know how to make friends and to be popular. She read it happily being that it helped her to make friends in her new school.

Although Destini missed her Papa, she got along with her new father quite well. He was patient and calm. He taught her new things. She liked to hear him speak with his Jamaican accent. Mr. Taylor owned his business and he explained to Destini a little of how his business operated. Part of which included computer programming, building computers and fixing them. His customers were nationwide. He also rented mailboxes to customers.

The Barrontons

Destini attended the Christian Middle School and then graduated to the Church School Academy the following year. Both schools rested on a landscape of immaculate beauty. The children attending were of various nationalities, with European Americans being the largest in attendance.

A young man at the school, named Stephan Barronton, a year older than Destini, liked her the very first time he set his eyes on her in church. The Sabbath he saw her in the church corridor, she was wearing a gorgeous button down champagne colored dress that accentuated her long elegant legs as she strode gracefully towards him. It seemed as if everything disappeared around him as this charming new beauty entered his world.

Her smooth, relaxed and shiny hair, pulled back in a ponytail, emphasized her sparkling sunlit brown eyes. He stared at her in awe. He wanted to meet this lovely, rare beauty that appeared into his world and captured his heart. He accidentally bumped into her, hoping very much to get her attention. She lowered her head and then looked up at him shyly. Her gracious wide smile and enchanting, sexy brown eyes entangled his heart even more.

"Oh, ex, excuse me," he said staring at her. When the girls saw how Stephan looked at Destini, they were envious. Destini looked at him shyly and then looked away timorously, then back at him with a sparkle in her gorgeous eyes. Stephan's heart raced at the loveliness of her unassuming actions.

"Oh, I'm sorry," she said, as her velvet, melodious voice arrested his attention to a screeching halt.

"Oh no, please ex . . . excuse me," Stephan answered unhurriedly, "it was . . . my fault." Her smooth, dark chocolate skin glowed warmly against her dress. The contrast was a pleasant surprise to Stephan's

17

eyes. "Hi," he said, but before he could finish, annoying voices suddenly interrupted him.

"Stephan!" The two voices haunting at him were his sister, Shadae and her best friend, Tasha. "We are ready and Mom is waiting," Shadae said as the both girls looked disgustingly at Destini and rolled their eyes. Destini dismissed herself promptly to find her parents. Stephan stood and stared at the movement of her full exterior as she strode down the corridor. He wished she didn't have to go. He turned and looked at his sister and Tasha, shaking his head with disappointment.

Born in England, Stephan and his sister Shadae lived there until their early teens. However, their older brother Preston remained in England with his British wife. Their parents, the Barrontons met in England, and some years later, moved to the United States to set up and continue their businesses. Dr. Barronton's parents were born in Jamaica, but, he was born in the U.S. Being an American citizen, Dr. Wycham (Wic-kam) Barronton wanted to go back to the United States. Stephan looked like his father, Dr. Barronton. A proficient neurosurgeon at the main hospital in town, Dr. Barronton owned three other doctor's offices. Female patients made appointments just to see the tall, bronze, and incredibly handsome doctor.

Success filled Sophia Barronton with pride. She was very proud of her children, especially her younger son, Stephan. She gloated over her ivory complexion, noting what a blessing it was to be so fair. Carrying herself with grace and dignity, Sophia was always well dressed, wearing the latest designer fashions to accentuate her slim, shapely figure. She was proud of the fact that she was of Jamaican and English heritage.

Sophia's parents descended from generations of real-estate owners, and she carried on the legacy. She and her parents owned real estate in the US, Europe, Canada, Jamaica, and other countries in the

West Indies. The family amassed great wealth by investing in real estate. Although Sophia had her own real estate empire, Dr. Barronton along with his wife, invested in steel and commercial real estate. Sophia oversaw her husband's resorts and two retirement facilities.

She didn't like the fact that Stephan liked Destini. She did her best to dissuade him, but to no avail. Sophia had already coached her daughter and older son into dating and marrying whites or light skinned people. Destini did not care much for Stephan's mother. Sophia Barronton seemed too snobbish and she was not nice to Destini. When Destini was around she'd ignore her or say covertly to others, "You don't know anything about an orphan's background. Therefore, it's not a good idea to get mixed up with them." At home, Sophia and Shadae warned Stephan to stay away from Destini. They said Destini was too black. Sophia said she didn't want a "baboon" in the family. Sophia told Stephan to put his school lessons first, and if he dated any girls, he should date someone who looked like Yasmin, Tasha or his cousin LaVona. Stephan gently protested or ignored his mother's constant lectures.

Destini tried to ignore Stephan. She thought that a rich, popular boy like Stephan only wanted to make fun of her. However, she secretly loved the way he presented himself, as he was well mannered and extremely good looking. She had never met anyone like him before. When she saw him at church, she stared at him. When he caught her looking, she quickly looked away as if not noticing him. He would gently smile and nod his head.

Since Stephan was not allowed to talk to her, she found an attraction to another young man named Jim. He also attended her church. He was older and didn't seem as threatening as Stephan. Nevertheless, Stephan always made her feel nervous.

A lot of girls at the church and the academy also liked Jim. This included two of Destini's worst enemies, Tasha Grant and Shadae Barronton. Destini found out that Tasha liked Jim but was in love with Stephan Barronton. Both Tasha and Shadae attended the church school academy. Shadae was a year older than her brother Stephan and one grade higher than Tasha. Stephan and his sister were in the same grade because she had been left back one year. Shadae and Tasha were best friends and they both thought it was no big deal to make fun of Destini's skin, hair and weight.

New Friend

A year had passed since Destini was adopted. She had gained a little weight and was beginning to bloom. She always had something complimentary to say to everyone. Thus, she became popular. Her pleasant ways and beautiful smooth skin drew lots of kids and adults to her.

Destini met a very special person and they easily became best friends. Yasmin Michaels grew up in New York; however, she was born in Trinidad. She moved to Massachusetts to go to the church school academy. Yasmin's ivory skin and light golden-brown, long hair, received lots of attention from the boys and jealous stares from the girls. Yasmin reminded Destini of her cousin Crystal with whom she used to play when she was a little girl. Yasmin was nothing like Deloris who was stuck up and boring. Destini was thankful for her new-found friendship with Yasmin. She didn't have to listen to any more boring conversations with Deloris about her boyfriends.

The girls met in Sabbath school class. They found out that they lived down the lane from each other. Both girls spend a lot of time together. Destini always told Yasmin, "You're so pretty; I wish I looked like you. I wish my skin and my hair were like yours." Yasmin would respond, "And I wish I looked like you. You are so beautiful and you remind me of an Egyptian goddess. You have the prettiest features and the smoothest skin. You look like a dream or fantasy model. And you always have the sweetest things to say to people. I wish I were like you."

Sometimes when they were alone, Destini would refer to herself as a princess. She told Yasmin that her father always called her a princess. She reminded Yasmin that since God is our father and He is the King of the universe, we are all princesses. Yasmin would laugh and say she was a princess too and would tell Destini she had an interesting imagination.

Yasmin and Destini liked each other very much and they went almost everywhere together. They tried on each other clothes. The girls talked about many things, including boys, of course. They talked about their favorite celebrities that they hoped to meet one day. Their favorites were President Obama and First Lady Michelle Obama. Sleepovers were fun at each other's homes. They even dressed up in their mothers' clothes and makeup when their parents were not around. The girls had so much fun together. When they went out or were at school during sports practice and boys whistled at them, the girls smiled or giggled. Although the young men tried to get Yasmin's attention, she only wanted one particular young man's attention, but he did not notice her.

The Hayride

The academy sponsored an after-school hayride and bonfire for the students. This allowed new students to get acquainted with everyone. The teachers and students met in front of the school building after supper, chatting and laughing as they waited for the carriages. Yasmin spotted Stephan talking to a new girl.

"Who is that girl over there talking to Stephan?" she asked Destini.

"I don't know," Destini answered, "but she's cute."

"She's not all that. She's probably wearing hair extensions." Destini looked at Yasmin and saw envy in her eyes. "Well," continued Yasmin, "look how close she's standing next to Stephan. Look Destini, look how close she's standing next to him. Ah, and look, she's only wearing a sweater. Who is she trying to show off on anyway?" Destini looked at Yasmin.

"Well," Destini said, "maybe she doesn't have a coat. I heard her talking in school yesterday and she had a Hispanic accent. Maybe she just came here and she needs a coat. Or, maybe she didn't know it was going to be so cold this evening. It was kinda warm earlier."

"Well," said Yasmin, "she shouldn't be out here without a coat. And look, why is she following Stephan everywhere he goes?" Destini looked at Yasmin again, but didn't say anything.

The carriages came and everyone boarded. Stephan watched to see which carriage Destini was getting on. He helped the new girl, Maria, onto one of the carriages then got on the same carriage as

Destini. He sat to the left side of the carriage, without the girl's knowledge.

Yasmin whispered so the other students didn't hear, "I bet she's trying to sit real close to him."

"Yasmin," Destini responded, "it's cold out here and she doesn't have a coat on." Yasmin sat back and kept talking. Destini turned to her right and looked back to make herself comfortable. She noticed that the person behind, and to her right was Stephan. With sudden surprise she turned her head back to make sure it was him. She then quickly turned back around. Destini was about to tell Yasmin that Stephan was on their carriage but changed her mind. She will find out soon enough. Yasmin asked her what happened. She shook her head. Yasmin kept talking about anything she could find to talk about.

The students on one of the other carriages began to sing praises to Jesus and all the other students and teachers joined in. Destini joined in with her melodious voice, but she heard Stephan's voice and she paused to listen. She turned her head to look at him, and of course, he was waiting for her to look at him. He quickly winked and smiled. Not expecting him to do that, her eyes widened in surprise. Destini blushed and turned away quickly, and he laughed. Yasmin quickly looked around.

"That's Stephan," she exclaimed to Destini.

"Yea, I heard him. He's on our carriage."

Yasmin scrambled to see him and said, "How super, I like his style."

When they returned from the trip, everyone was laughing and talking. Destini looked over and noticed that the new girl, Maria, was sneezing.

"I'm gonna see if she needs my coat." Destini said. She excused herself from Yasmin's company and went to ask Maria if she was okay. She said yes but that she was very cold. Destini took off her coat and loaned it to Maria. Yasmin came over and asked Destini if she was crazy because it was cold. And of course, Stephan noticed what Destini did, and came over to the girls. He offered his jacket to Destini. At that point, she sneezed. Stephan quickly helped her to put on his jacket. Destini told him that it was very manly of him. He appreciated her sweet comment. Maria was trembling vigorously. Stephan suggested that they move closer to the building for warmth.

Finally, their families came and picked them all up. Maria's aunt arrived and Destini got back her coat and then gave Stephan his jacket. Yasmin stood and stared as Stephan accepted his jacket. She wished he loaned her his jacket. Destini was spending the night with Yasmin so Mrs. Vashti Michaels came to pick up the girls. On their way home Yasmin was quiet. Her mother asked her why she was so quiet because she was usually a talkative person. Mrs. Michaels asked her if anything happened during the hayride. Yasmin casually answered, "No." Vashti looked at Destini. She was not too happy with Yasmin and Destini's friendship, but accepted Yasmin's choice because Destini was very intelligent.

Impromptu Loss

*W*hen they got to the house, the girls had something warm to drink then went to bed. Destini wondered why Yasmin was not talking much but did not ask her. In the early morning, at about two o'clock, the phone rang. Yasmin jumped up and answered it. While her eyes hung onto the sweet sleep she was experiencing, her voice whispered softly.

"Hello?"

"Hello," the hurried response came. "Is this Yasmin?"

"Yea, who is this?"

"It's Mrs. Taylor, dear. I was just calling to see if everything was okay." Yasmin was confused.

"Okay, Mrs. Taylor?" she asked.

"Well, Destini didn't call and, ah... and I just heard... as long as everything is okay. I'll talk to her in the morning. Sorry to wake you, goodnight."

"Wait Mrs. Taylor," Yasmin raised her voice, "wait, what did you hear?"

Etta paused then said, "I'll talk to you in the morning. Goodnight."

"Goodnight," Yasmin responded. Destini woke up with sleepy eyes and scratched her head.

"Who called?"

"It was your mom, she was checking on ya to see if everything was okay." Destini suddenly remembered that she didn't call her mother after coming from the hayride.

"Oh, my goodness," she said softly, "I forgot to call home."

"Well," said Yasmin, "I told her everything is okay, so call her in the morning." Destini got up and decided to call home. Etta answered.

"Hello?"

"Hi mom, I'm sorry, I forgot to call. I'm fine and the hayride was fun. Is everything okay?"

"Yes, everything is fine, dear. I didn't mean to wake you. I just wanted to make sure everything was okay because I heard that one of the students that went on the hayride was in the emergency room at the hospital."

"What!" Destini blurted out. "Who Mom?"

"I don't know." She answered, "Just go back to sleep because you have to get up for school in the morning."

"Okay Mom, goodnight."

"Goodnight dear." After hanging up the phone, she stood and stared at the wall.

"What happened," Yasmin asked hurriedly, "what did your mom say?" Destini walked back to the bed.

"Mom said she heard that one of the students who were on the hayride is in the hospital."

"What! Who?" Yasmin gasped.

"I d'know." The girls sat up and tried to guess who it was. They wondered if it was Maria or another pupil. They wanted to call the hospital. Yasmin suggested they call Mrs. Anita Jones in the morning since she always knew everything.

In the morning, both girls showered and got ready for school. The phone rang at about six thirty, and Mrs. Michaels answered it.

"Hello," she sang. The girls listened to hear who called. It was early in the morning for someone to be calling, the girls thought. "Oh hi Mrs. Jones, how are you?" The girls sneaked near the door to listen. Mrs. Michaels continued on the phone, "No, hear what? Uh uh, no. How is she?" Suddenly Vashti Michaels's tone of voice conveyed astonishment.

"Oh my God, no, when? I don't understand. Mrs. Jones, how could this have happened so suddenly? Oh, my goodness, this is sad... okay, I'll tell the girls. Yes, Destini is still here. Okay. Uh-hmm, yea, okay, okay, thanks for letting me know. Yea, you too, bye." She hung up the phone and called Yasmin. Yasmin pretended she wasn't near the door and ran away quietly with Destini.

"Yes mother?" she responded.

"You and Destini come here."

"Okay," she shouted innocently, "coming mother." Upon entering the room Yasmin said, "Yes, you wanted us?"

Vashti looked at them sadly, "Do you know Maria Velasquez?"

They looked at each other and answered in unison, "Yes."

Then Yasmin continued, "She is one of the new girls in ninth grade, why?" Destini looked at Yasmin again and wondered why she pretended last night that she didn't know who Maria was.

Vashti looked at them and said slowly, yet softly, "I don't know if either of you were close to her, but she passed away about two hours ago." Both girls gasped in shock.

"What! What?" they exclaimed in disbelief.

"Mom, what are you talking about?"

"Oh my goodness, Mrs. Michaels," said Destini, "we, we just saw her last night at the hayride. She was really cold, but she seemed fine."

"Well," responded Vashti, "according to Mrs. Jones, she apparently got pneumonia and her body was too weak from being sick before, so she went into a coma and died. Mrs. Perez, her aunt, is not taking it too well. Maria was her sister's daughter and Mrs. Perez had offered to bring her to the United States to take care of her. Well kids, I have to go and see her. Mrs. Jones said the church committee asked me to go since I'm a psyche nurse. I'll ask Etta to come with me because she also knows how to deal with people in situations like this. Plus, we may have to help with funeral arrangements. So," Vashti took a breath, "if you want a ride to school now you are going to be very early, but if you prefer to walk let me know." Destini stood and stared with her fingers covering her mouth. She felt numb. Both girls looked at each other and didn't know what to say or do.

"Well," asked Vashti, "what have you decided?" Yasmin looked at Destini for an answer.

"Um," Destini finally responded softly, "I'll walk, if you don't mind."

"Okay, we'll walk Mom."

"Ah, well, um," Vashti said, "make sure you dress very warmly."

"Mother," Yasmin answered, annoyed, "it's not that cold out there."

"Well, just remember what I said, you too, Destini. Can't afford to lose any more of you because of the cold weather.

"Um, Mrs. Michaels," Destini asked, "does my mom know you are coming to pick her up?"

"Yes, Mrs. Jones already told her. See you later girls." She walked quickly towards the door. "Make sure you have your breakfast. Eggs are in the refrigerator; you know where everything is Yasmin. Bye." She blew two short kisses and left.

The girls prepared their breakfast, ate, and walked to school slowly. Sadness filled their heart.

"Oh, my goodness," Destini said, "I can't believe it. She died just like that. It doesn't seem real. It makes you wonder, suppose I got pneumonia. Would I be alive?"

"I know," Yasmin added. They both walked on quietly until Yasmin said, "I feel so guilty. I didn't treat her nicely. We can be so selfish at times." Destini agreed, and they walked on to school thinking about the events of the night before. Yesterday was fine. They were happy and thinking about nothing, really. Howbeit, today is sad. Life can be strange at times.

At school, everyone was solemn. The principal announced a moment of silence over the intercom system and prayed for Maria's family. Some of the students and teachers didn't know who she was, but they also felt sad. When Destini went home, she told her mom how sad it was in school that day and that she felt awful. Her mother hugged her and reassured her that everything would be all right.

The funeral service was held in the chapel near the main sanctuary. Mrs. Velasquez came to the United States for her daughter's funeral. She cried with such agony that seemed to come from somewhere deep inside. Mrs. Perez cried so hard that she almost fainted. Her body swayed back and forth as if about to fall. Her family members held her close while she walked. Destini and Yasmin stood and watched while tears filled their eyes and sorrow overcame them. Some students were crying while others looked numb. Destini looked over and noticed Stephan looking at her. She felt embarrassed, so she looked away. That evening, she went home, sat with folded arms, and gazed at the walls. She fell asleep on the sofa in the family room. Winston didn't bother to wake her. He simply carried her to her room and placed her on her bed.

11

Continued Dilemma

Three weeks later, on a windy, rainy day, Destini walked to school all alone. Yasmin had to go somewhere with her mother and Destini felt lonely. She said her morning prayers as usual and went on her way. School wasn't as exciting without Yasmin, especially since the day was gray and rainy. After school, Destini decided to ride home on the school bus instead of walking home alone. The bus passed near the road she lived. It was her first time on the school bus and she did not know what to expect.

As she boarded the bus, it seemed as if everyone was staring at her. *"Oh, my goodness,"* she thought, *"why are they staring?"* Destini looked around for a seat. All of the front seats were taken so she ventured toward the back. Destini thought, *"Why on earth am I taking the bus since I have never taken it before? Wonder if I should get off and walk home, but it's so cold."* She finally found two vacant seats and sat in one. A few seconds later, a tall dark-skinned girl came and demanded that Destini get up out of her seat. Destini's heart pounded as she moved over into the next seat and looked out of the window. The girl still demanded that she get up. Destini looked around to see if there were other seats available, but she didn't see any. She looked to see if someone was with the girl, but she was by herself.

"There are two seats here, why can't you sit in one and I sit in the other?" Destini asked.

"Because," the girl said loudly, "I don't wan' no ugly, black-looking beast sittin' next tuh me." Some of the kids laughed loudly while others stared at Destini. Destini refused to move, so the girl sat next to her and started to push her against the window of the bus. Destini felt as if her ribs were closing in. She told the girl to stop. Nevertheless, she laughed and continued pushing her, so Destini gave the girl a big push with her elbow. The girl flew off the seat and fell on to the floor. She got back up with a fury and punched Destini right in her face. Her face hurt badly. She screamed and her heart pounded faster. She started to look for the compass and the pretty penknife she carried in her school bag.

"Stand up and fight you ugly black nigger, you think you is all that. I'mma show you who's bad." Destini wanted to stand up and show her who was bad. She was very angry. She wanted to cut her up and teach her a good lesson--never to touch her again. Destini continued looking desperately for her penknife or her compass. The girl was big and tall compared with her slim and elegant stature.

Suddenly, the students at the front of the school bus screamed. They scrambled out of their seats and ran off the bus. The tall girl looked around to see what was going on. Now, the kids in the back got up and ran towards the front of the bus. Some were screaming, "What's going on?" The rush of students running towards the front of the bus almost trampled the tall girl. She ran with the crowd to see what was going on. Destini looked on with fear and amazement. *"I wonder what's going on,"* she thought. Destini sat and questioned if she should get off the bus too. Suddenly, as quickly as the students had left, they returned. They all asked each other what happened, but no one could explain what had happened. Some were asking if there was a fight out there. No one knew why almost the entire bus got up and ran out. The tall girl came back and gawked at Destini.

"You think you is so bad, don't you?" She said agitatedly. Destini ignored her. She was still looking for the knife but couldn't find it. Suddenly, a strong male voice sounded from the back of the bus.

"Yo! Nolita, leave that girl alone." Nolita looked over at the guy. He was her older cousin. "I said, go find another seat and leave her alone, now! Go pick on someone your own size, girl."

Nolita slowly walked away, sat down and stared at Destini the entire time. Destini told the guy thanks.

"Anything for a pretty lady," he said and sat down.

When she finally got home, she didn't say anything to her mother about the bus incident. She decided never to ride the school bus again. She thought it was more fun to walk home, even if it were cold or if she were alone. She went to her room to check her bag for the knife and the compass. To her surprise, they were right where she'd placed them. Destini wondered why she couldn't lay her hands on them. She sat on her bed and stared out of the window. *"If I'd found the knife,"* she thought, *"I was going to cut up Nolita because I was angry with her for slapping me in the face. Thank God I didn't find it."*

She thought about the incident repeatedly. She began to get angry again. She was angry with that tall, ugly Nolita, who had the nerve to call her black and ugly and to punch her. Nolita was very dark skinned herself. Destini was embarrassed to return to school. She said, "I wish I had found that knife. I would have shown her who was bad." Destini suddenly remembered the daily prayers she had been praying and her prayer that particular morning. She realized that God had answered her prayers. She did not get into any fights at school. God had protected her all this time, even today on the school bus. He actually kept her from finding the knife and the compass. Stabbing Nolita would have felt satisfactory at that moment; however, it would have landed her in jail. That would have been embarrassing for her parents. Her life could have changed forever. Destini felt better knowing that someone so great and mighty cared about her very much, that even though she got punched once, He kept her from getting into trouble.

"Oh, God is so great and loving," she said aloud. "Thank you, God, I'm not angry anymore. In fact, thanks for the experience. By the way, Lord, the incident with all the students running off the bus was funny. I don't understand what really happened, but thanks." Tears filled Destini's eyes as she thought about it. When Yasmin got home, Destini called her and told her everything that happened. Yasmin insisted that she tell her mother and the dean, but Destini insisted against it.

"Yasmin," Destini confided, "Nolita will never come near me again. God will see to that, and I trust Him. If she does, she has me to deal with because I'm not afraid of her." And in truth, Nolita never bothered Destini again. She only stared at Destini whenever she saw her.

12

Embarrassing Dilemma

ot long after the incident on the school bus, Destini and Yasmin walked into class one day, and one of the young men called out to Yasmin.

"Hey Trinidadian goddess, the fairest of them all, will you marry me?" Yasmin waived her hand and blushed as she seated herself.

Then one of the girls called out to Destini as she placed her long single braids behind her ears, "And heee-------re comes black spook, aaaaaaah," she screamed. The class roared with laughter. Then Tasha, who wore too much make-up on her brown skin, put her two cents in.

"I'd hate to see her in the middle of the night," she screeched, "would scare me half to death." The students laughed again.

"Don't worry your pretty little head Tasha," one of the dark skin boys said, "you'll never see her in the night," he then suddenly blurted out, "TOO BLACK AND UGLY!"

At that remark the class again roared with laughter, except for some students who did not think it was funny. They folded their hands and had a written disapproval all over their faces. Most of the white students misunderstood the reason for teasing her. They reasoned to each other that the students teasing had similar skin color. Destini pretended she did not hear anything. Stephan Barronton got up and addressed the class; his English accent rang through the room.

"That was not funny. All of you stop it now. How would you like someone to make fun of you?" Some of the students were still laughing. "And all of you have the nerve to call yourselves Christians. Jesus said 'If you do this to the least of my brethren, you do it to me.'" Some of the class started to jeer and make noise. "Oh

–, shut up," someone said, "we're just having some fun. He always has something dumb to say." Stephan looked intently at him as if to say, make me shut up. The boy lowered his head and looked away, fearing to confront a football athlete. While the noise was beginning to calm down, the teacher Ms. Anderson, a short, cocoa-skinned, full breasted woman, walked in to the room. She had heard the laughter and taunts. She raised her voice in a grand, melodious tone and with articulate pronunciation exclaimed.

"What is all this r-r-r-r-racquet? BE QUIET!" Everyone settled down immediately. "You all should set a better example to the lower grades." She started to pace the floor as she continued. "I know some of you are taking this class because you either missed it or failed it in your freshman or sophomore year. But that does not give you the r-r-r-right" she stressed, "to behave like five-year-olds." She glanced at Destini and saw the tears rolling down her pretty face.

"Now," she continued, "take out your textbook and tur-r-r-r-rn to page eighty-four."

Destini felt sad and ugly. The awful feeling, she felt inside kept the tears rolling down her face while she fumbled through the pages. *"When is all this going to end?"* she thought. *"I'm in high school now. When is it going to end Lord? Oh God, I can't take this anymore; I'm sick of this. I should get a gun and blow them all away. That will teach them not to mess with anyone again."* She was especially embarrassed because Stephan of all people had to be in her class. At the end of class, Ms. Anderson called Destini to talk with her. She seemed to feel the pain Destini felt. Being dark skinned herself, she remembered being teased mercilessly when she was a youngster. She wished she could take it all away. Yasmin waited outside the classroom.

"Yes Ms. Anderson, you wanted to see me?" Ms. Anderson looked at her tenderly.

"Destini," she calmly said, "sometimes in life we go through a storm." Ms. Anderson smiled, "But after the storm there is a rainbow." Destini stood with her head hanging, glancing at Ms. Anderson every now and then. "Now," said Ms. Anderson, "if there is anything you wish to talk to me about, please let me know dear, okay?"

"Yes ma'am," she responded softly.

"Destini," she continued, "your grades are excellent. You are one of my best students. Keep up the good work. The beautiful cocoa skin that God blessed you with is gorgeous and amazing. Always remember that."

"Thank you ma'am." Destini smiled slightly.

"You may go now."

"Thank you ma'am, goodbye."

Ms. Anderson smiled lovingly. "Goodbye dear." Destini walked quickly out of the room. Ms. Anderson decided to give the class a lecture on respect for others.

Stephan was waiting outside the school building to see Destini. He felt awful about what happened. He hoped Destini wasn't embarrassed. She was the prettiest girl with the smoothest cocoa skin and gorgeous brown eyes he knew. How could they be so cruel? Stephan loved the shy, sexy way Destini looked at him. When he saw her coming, his heart raced as he approached her shyly and apologized for the class' behavior. His English accent sounded very nice to Destini. She lowered her head, looked away shyly as he spoke to her. *"Wow,"* he thought, *"I just want to hold her in my arms and protect her."*

"Destini," he said, "please disregard the class' behavior. You are much too beautiful and intelligent to think what they say is true. As far as I'm concerned, you are a beautiful chocolate princess." Destini froze at Stephan's words. With widening eyes, she stared at him for a moment, but she was so embarrassed. She thanked him and walked away holding Yasmin's arm.

Yasmin looked at her surprisingly and asked softly between her teeth, "Why are you leaving so quickly? Let me go. The best looking and most popular guy in the school is trying to be friendly."

Destini responded as if about to cry, "Stay if you like, but I just have to get out of here, you don't understand." Yasmin followed complaining.

"Oh Destini, what is there to understand? I wish Stephan would look at me or just talk to me. Oh, my goodness, if he would, I'd just pass out. He is so-----o fine." Destini continued on her way home with Yasmin and left Stephan standing there thinking.

Destini looked at Yasmin and said, "Of all the classes I'm in, why did he have to be in that class with Tasha? Goodness, he's a sophomore. Why is he in our class anyway?"

"Because he didn't take that class in his freshman year. I heard he was happy to take it now because you are in that class." Both girls turned and looked at each other.

13

Shadae's Beau

*S*hadae *asked Tasha to meet her after school, right before cheerleading practice. She had something very important to tell her. Shadae, almost sixteen, was showing* her womanly curves. She slipped out of her spring jacket, draped it over her forearm to model her new sexy black dress. Shadae's natural tanned skin harmonized with her red, frosted strawberry blond, relaxed hair that flowed passed her shoulders. Her tresses gleamed in the sunlight as it blew gently in the cool breeze.

"Tasha," she said excitedly, tossing her hair with self-assurance, "I met this wonderful guy, he is so cute."

"Guy?" Tasha said as she looked at Shadae, smiling.

"Yes, he's cute. He has light brown hair and blue eyes and his name is Pete Silvers."

"Umm," Tasha gulped "light brown hair and blue eyes. Does he go to the academy?"

"No." she responded, as they started walking. "He goes to the public high school in Worcester."

"What about Jim, and does your parents know?" Tasha questioned curiously.

"Not yet, but they will love him. And I'm not interested in Jim anymore. He's too into himself." Tasha, fearing to ask the next question, looked back and forth at Shadae.

"Shadae," she finally blurted out, "please don't think this is a dumb question, but . . . is he white?"

"Why, yes, of course he is," she answered candidly. "And he has a car."

"White? A car! How old is he?"

"Seventeen," she responded.

"Seventeen! A car, white--are you sure your parents won't mind?"

"Tasha!" Shadae irritated by her questioning, stopped walking. "My mother herself said its better for me to marry a white man."

"What! You're kidding." Tasha responded surprised. "My mother would kill me. Well here comes your brother. Did you tell him yet?"

"Not yet."

"When are you going to tell him?

"Tasha," Shadae said irritated, "why do you ask so many questions? I will tell my brother when I feel like it."

As Stephan approached, he didn't seem pleased with Tasha. She stared at him as he walked toward them. He looked good walking in his jeans and leather jacket. He ignored Tasha and spoke calmly to his sister.

"Shadae, what time is cheerleading practice over this evening?"

"Why?" she asked. Stephan's expression was serious and he continued to ignore Tasha.

"Because Mom and Dad wanted us to attend our cousin LaVona's ballet recital."

"Uh," cried Shadae with her English accent, "I don't want to go. LaVona and Aunt Liz get on my last nerve."

"Well," said Stephan with a smirk on his face, while he emphasized, "We have to go. And, you can't get out of this one." Shadae pouted and folded her arms across her chest.

"Well," she replied, "I don't know what time cheerleading practice will be over. Mom never stops you from football practice." Stephan turned to leave.

"Don't be vexed about my football practice. Mom, or Cindy our maid, will be here to pick you up in about an hour and a half, so my lovely sister, you had better be ready. See you later." Tasha tried to talk to Stephan but he kept walking.

"Oooh, I wish my car wasn't in the shop. I hate when I have to be picked up. By the way, what's up with you and Stephan?" Shadae asked, as she looked at Tasha curiously. "He completely ignored you. And that's not my brother's style." Tasha hung her head as if in despair, while her healthy looking, shoulder length dark brown relaxed hair, blew gently in the wind.

"Don't look so drowned out," Shadae said. "It's not the end of the world. What happened?"

"Well," said Tasha, "I guess he's upset with me for teasing the ugly, black gyal in class today."

"I love the way you say 'gyal' for girl," chuckled Shadae. "You mean Destini?"

"Who else."

"Ha, ha ha ha ha," laughed Shadae. "It must have been pretty bad because Stephan really ignored you. Come, tell me what happened." The girls walked on to cheerleading practice as Tasha told her the details.

On their way home, Destini and Yasmin walked through the grassy pathway with the beautiful trees on either side. The whistling of the birds and the flow of the cool, spring air followed the girls while they continued home. Destini was still upset and depressed.

"Yasmin," Destini said sadly, "you don't know what it feels like to be called ugly names, especially by your own people. To be laughed at in front of a whole class just because of the way you were born. To be told frequently that you're ugly because you're dark skinned or too fat, too pale or even too skinny or perhaps you wear glasses or for whatever reason that makes you different. Also, you don't get invited to parties or events just because you're dark skin or African American. It's completely unfair and wrong. I can't help the way I was born. I hate being this dark, but I can't help it. I wish I was light skinned like you or even brown skinned." She started to cry. "Why should I be laughed at, teased and treated differently because I am darker than you are? That's evil and it hurts. It hurts," her velvety voice softened as she tried to hold back from crying again, "really hurts." Yasmin opened her mouth with confidence.

"Destini," she instructed, "all you have to do is ignore them like you did in class today. They'll get the message that you don't care what they say. They're all just plain stupid!"

"Yes, ignore them," Destini repeated. "I've been doing that all my life but, ignoring them does not take away the pain that I feel and the damage that it does to me mentally. Sometimes I feel so angry that I just want to kill them all; just get a gun and blow them all away." Yasmin looked at Destini with widen eyes. She was surprised at Destini's statement. *"Destini must be really hurting to say such a thing."* She thought. "But," continued Destini, "I know those thoughts are wrong and stupid. Plus, it wouldn't change the way they think. I love God too much to disappoint Him and mess my life up. I asked God to bless me and stop the madness. Sometimes it seems as if it is taking forever. And sometimes," she continued, as if about to pass out, "I just want to die. I don't want to look like this anymore." Both girls were quiet as they continued home.

14

Truth and Beauty

When Destini got home she ran up to her room and stayed there all afternoon. She couldn't wait until the school year ended. Etta called her three times to come to dinner. Finally, Etta went up to see Destini and found the door locked.

"Destini, open the door," she said in her usual calm voice. She waited and said more sternly, yet calmly, "Young lady, open this door now." Winston heard Etta calling to Destini and he inquired as to what was going on. Etta shrugged her shoulders and Winston came to the door and called Destini. Finally, Destini unlocked the door, then went and sat in front of the mirror. Winston left and Etta entered the room.

"Destini," Etta asked, walking to the bedside, "what's wrong?" Etta heard Destini crying. Her velvety voice rang through the room.

"I hate myself, I'm cursed. I'm black and ugly. I have no hair. My lips are too big. I'm skinny. They're right. I look like an ugly black spook on a bean pole." She calmed down slightly, sighed and then asked earnestly, "Why was I born this way? Why wasn't I born like my mother? She would have loved me more and treated me better. She was so beautiful." Destini turned and looked at Etta with tears in her eyes and anger in her voice. "Oh Mom, why wasn't I born with beautiful brown skin and gorgeous features like yours? You're so beautiful. I'm sure that's one of the reasons why Dad married you. The boys don't notice me and if they do, they are sorry for me or they think I'm ugly."

She finally stopped crying and softly said, "I sat here looking in the mirror, thinking desperately how to change my total appearance and I came up with nothing. The more I thought about it, the more I became angry. Oh Mom," she shouted in despair as tears rolled down her beautiful face, "I just want to die. I thought about killing myself because I just couldn't handle the way I was feeling. I am so sick and tired of being bullied and teased. It really hurts, Mom. My heart aches, my stomach hurts, my eyes are itching, and I feel ugly." The aching pressure of her soul caused her upper body to collapse on her dresser. The support of the dresser allowed her to feel a sense of security.

Etta sat on Destini's bed and extended her arms.

"Destini, come here." Destini slowly got up, not wanting to leave the secure feeling she sensed while lying there. She dragged herself over to the bed and sat on it, hoping to feel the same sense of security with her mom. The loving embrace she received from Etta, gave her a feeling of warmth and care. She held her mom as if hanging on for her life. Etta sensed her need and continued holding her warmly as Destini continued crying aloud. After holding her for a while, Etta took a tissue to wipe away her tears and noticed the swollen area surrounding Destini's eyes.

"My God Destini, what happened to your eyes?"

"Oh Mom, I thought if I penciled my eyes with black markers, I would look better. The black markers would let them realize that I am not as black as they think. Now, my eyes are swollen and itchy. I feel so stupid. I hate this world." Etta sat and stared with an expression of confusion on her face. She remembered penciling her eyes with markers when she was a young girl.

"Umm, you should never try to change who you are and what you look like for ignorant people. So, those kids are behaving evil again?" Etta asked.

"Yea, nothing I can't handle, Mom."

"Well, I will call and visit the school, and take care of this once and for all."

"No Mom, please don't. I can handle it."

"No, I will visit the school and put a stop to this."

"Um, okay, if you must. You may as well because, my goodness, this is getting old. It's about time they stop. Why are people so cruel for no reason at all?"

"Because they are insecure, and in order to feel better about themselves, they hurt or put others down to build themselves up. Older siblings beat up or bully younger ones. People treat their coworkers mean in the work place or even at church. Fathers and mothers are mean to their children. How sad. But they don't realize that God sees and hears all, whether they believe He does or not. He said, 'vengeance is mine.' You know, this may seem strange, but people always get back the good or evil they do. The bible does not lie. So, all the bad things that those kids did to you will one day come looking for them. It does not mean they will get it back the exact same way. However, they will feel the pain they caused you." Destini was still hurting inside and wanted to feel better. Etta looked at her and knew that her precious child was hurting.

"Destini listen to me, God sent us to Texas just for you. Winston and I were always talking about adopting a child for years. So, we prayed to God for guidance. We knew immediately when we saw this beautiful, dark skinned girl, that you were the one. The night before, Winston and I both had the same dream. We dreamt that we were looking for a Hebrew queen who was deep chocolate. She thanked us for coming for her and I think she said, 'I'm Queen Esther.' I don't remember, but we knew that we were going to adopt a beautiful queen."

A smile crossed Destini's pretty face. "Destini," she continued, "your skin is beautiful. It's the softest skin I've ever touched. You know, the darker the skin the softer it feels. It's smooth and silky. Maybe it's the amount of melanin, I don't know. Plus, you have no blemishes. Your lips are full, soft, and beautiful. And your almond-shaped eyes are like a work of art.

Girl, you don't need make-up. But if you wear it, you'll outshine even the most beautiful girl. Your legs are long and shapely. Your buttocks are full and round." Etta smiled, "Don't ever let anyone tell you that you are ugly. If they say you are black, thank them. Yes, let them know you are black and beautiful because God blessed you and made you that way, in His image. He knows you're beautiful. Be proud of who you are." Destini still felt sad inside. She remembered the awful, mocking words spoken by the kids in school and wanted to forget them.

"In the Bible," Etta continued, "we were known as Ethiopians, Hebrews, Midianites, Nubians, Judeans and Israelites. Stand tall and elegant my beautiful Hebrew Princess. The man who marries you will be happy to touch this soft, smooth, satiny black skin and kiss your naturally soft full lips. He will want only you because you are unique. Now, I want you to keep saying to yourself, 'I'm beautiful,' and put pictures on your wall of beautiful dark-skinned people. Now, say out loud, 'I am beautiful.'" Destini's eyes were filled with excitement, but she looked at Etta skeptically for a moment.

"You're kidding, right?"

"You better believe I'm not. Now say it," Etta directed. Destini was quiet for a while. She laughed.

"Okay," she laughed again, "Mom I can't say it. I feel weird."

"Do you feel weird to say you're ugly?" Etta asked.

"No because I'm used to that."

"Well," Etta said, as she stood up, "you'd better get used to saying out loud, 'I'm beautiful' and mean it. That is your homework assignment from me. You will start saying it now, during the summer, and for six months after that."

She looked into Destini's swollen eyelids as she held her shoulders gently. "I want you to realize something young lady. It's great to look good on the outside, but what really counts is what's happening on the inside. Develop your inner-self and it will reflect who you really are on the outside, and that's more important. So, young lady, you will visit the library a lot more and read lots of books. I want to see you reading books instead of being on your phone."

"Uh?"

"The library and the Internet is loaded with anything you want to know." Plus, you can use your phone to do research, to read books and the bible.

Etta sat down beside her, touching her arm gently. "Now, I want you to know this. You will always meet insecure people who are ignorant and jealous of you. They will try to hurt or drag you down. You must love you. God commands us to love ourselves. Free your mind from those evil people by forgiving them. Let go of all the negative stuff they say to you, because it's not true. Think about positive things, people and words. Know that you have the power through Christ to defeat every obstacle that comes your way. Darling, Destini," she continued, and touching Destini's pretty face gently, "remember that obstacles are stepping stones that God allows in our lives to take us to the next level of power. Invite Jesus into your life and you'll see you won't regret it. I'm talking from experience, Sweetheart.

"Listen, when I was a young girl in school, my dad told me not to fight in school. I wondered how on earth I was going to protect myself, because the kids were always fighting and arguing. He said 'to let God fight your battles for you. He did it for our ancestors. God just wants you to trust him.' I wondered if my dad knew what he was talking about, because, girl, *them* kids were crazy." A smile ran across Destini's pretty face. "Well, I decided to give it a try. I asked God to protect me and fight my battles for me. Not that I could not fight. I knew how to kick some butts. But, I was obedient to my dad. However, I did tell God that if someone was beating me up, that I was not going to stand there and take it. I told God that I would protect myself.

47

"Well, I can tell you many stories of how God protected me and fought my battles, just like he did for our people in the Bible. Even the very kids who bullied me, turned against each other and end up fighting each other. Ha, ha, God is funny." Destini smiled with tears in her eyes. She listened intently, hoping for the same experience. "You know why he protected me?" Destini nodded. "Because I asked for His protection and then I trusted Him to protect me. Yes, it was not all smooth. How else would I learn to trust God if it was all smooth sailing? However, He kept me out of danger and delivered me from trouble."

"Mom, um…" she lowered her head and tears rolled down her face.

"What is it love?"

"Um, I feel sad and depressed and I try to feel happy, but it won't go away. I don't know what to do. I pray and then I feel okay, but with the teasing and being sooo dark skin. Well, I'm so depressed," she cried. "I need help," she sobbed. "Please mom, I don't know what to do. I just can't take it anymore."

"Come here Destini," Etta put her arms around her. "I will pray for you and God will deliver you." They both closed their eyes, "Father God, Ruler of the Universe, I bring Destini before your throne. Forgive her of any sins, forgive me of any sins and deliver her from any and all sadness and depressions. Protect us from evil, Lord. Give her joy, peace and happiness always, coming directly from you. Give her hope and forgive any generational sins. I claim the blood of Jesus over her. Please let me see the answer to this prayer, in Jesus' Name, amen."

They opened their eyes and Etta hugged her. "God loves you more than you could imaging. He wants you to be happy. Trust Him and He will reward your trust."

"Now," Etta continued, "we are going to braid your hair and teach you how to grow it to a longer length. You know braiding helps your hair to keep its length. You fuss with it so much that it breaks off faster than it grows. Once you know how to allow your hair to grow, you will have the freedom to cut it as short as you want and grow it back to the length you want. Plus, if you keep it natural with no relaxers or chemicals, you will see; it will grow down your back. You're also going to take dance lessons, and voice lessons to strengthen your beautiful voice. You will enter beauty pageants." Etta stood up and walked towards the door.

"Beauty pageants!" Destini protested.

"Don't worry; you'll have more than enough time while you're out of school this summer." Destini followed behind her.

"Oh God, no! I'll never win. Everyone will think I'm crazy and that will not be too cute at all. Oh, Mom no, please." Etta ignored her plea.

"But before I go you will say, 'I'm beautiful.' Come on, say it." Destini held her head down.

"I'm beautiful," she said quickly.

"Say it again, I want to hear it plainly." Tears began to fill Destini's eyes again. This time she began slowly with her head still down. "Please look at me," Etta interrupted. Destini looked up and started again with her melodious voice trembling,

"I'm beautiful." Etta hugged her.

"Yes, you are indeed beautiful, smart, and intelligent. What's more, you're made in the image of God." Etta looked at Destini, "Oh my, I need to get some medicated cream for your eyes. Now come and eat." Destini felt like a burden was lifted that afternoon. She felt happier and lighter from that time forward. She thanked God from her heart.

Etta went to the school and met with the principal and her teachers. She wanted them to do something about bullying in the school. They agreed to meet with the staff, faculty, and parents to see what could be done. Ms. Anderson was very happy for this. She volunteered and presided over the entire operation. Many parents took part in it, and it was successful.

15

The Recital

That evening Stephan and Shadae attended their cousin LaVona's ballet group recital with their parents. Shadae was bored and jealous. The dance was beautifully performed, and everyone attending was proud to see his or her family and friends performing. At the end of the performance, LaVona, who was two years younger than Shadae, ran towards her aunt with excitement.

"How did I do? How did I do? Did you all like it?"

"Oh," said Sophia, "you were the best dancer up there and the prettiest one too." Sophia turned to her children, with her Jamaican-English accent,

"Wasn't she the best and prettiest one up there, children?"

"Uh, yes," Stephan readily said.

"Ha, ha ha," Shadae laughed.

"And" Sophia continued, "your lovely, strawberry blond hair just glistened as you moved." Shadae rolled her eyes upward, while her mother continued. "You look just like your grandma Fletcher." LaVona's parents, Sophia's sister Elizabeth and her husband Raymond Graham, came over to greet them. They all greeted each other with hugs and kisses.

"Oh, Liz," Sophia said joyously, "I am so proud of my niece. I am so happy she continued her ballet lessons. She is the best."

"Thanks Sophia," Liz said putting her arm around LaVona. "I want to thank everyone for supporting LaVona." LaVona smiled joyously as she looked at everyone. Shadae was not at all pleased. She did not want to be there.

"Mom," Shadae asked, "when are we leaving? I have things to do." Sophia was embarrassed by her daughter's rudeness.

"I'll leave when I am ready," Sophia replied. "If you had continued your ballet lessons, you would be just as good as LaVona."

"What does that have to do with me wanting to leave?" Shadae raised her voice "I don't like ballet and it's not for me." She turned away from her mother. Sophia was getting angry.

"You can make a career out of ballet," she continued angrily, "but you can't make a career out of cheerleading." With that remark, Shadae turned and looked at her mother furiously.

"I'm going to the car." She stormed out of the studio and everyone was quiet. Then Elizabeth broke the silence.

"So, Stephan, how are you?"

"Very well, thanks, Aunt," he replied.

"How is school?" she continued.

"Great," he answered.

"Stephan," she continued, "I hear you are doing very well in school and you're the star football player. You are growing to be such a handsome young man. I bet all the girls like you."

Stephan blushed, "Aunt Liz, I don't take much notice of those matters. I just try to do my best in school."

"You don't take notice," Sophia interrupted. She turned her head to her sister.

"He is simply crazy about this girl, and she is American. You should see her. She is ugly as a black toad." Stephan was getting angry. Why did his mother always have to say things to embarrass him he wondered?

"Mom stop it now!" he said sharply, "Look, Destini is the prettiest girl in school."

"Uh," cried Sophia, "as black as she is; can't even see her in the dark." Liz smiled and glanced at her husband. "Stephan, what is wrong with you?" continued Sophia.

"There is nothing wrong with me," he answered back. "But, there is something wrong with the way you think." Sophia's eyes widened and she gasped. "And she is just as beautiful," he continued, "if not more, than Shadae, Tasha, and LaVona." Stephan waved his arms up and down, "And all the others. She is also the sweetest person you ever want to meet. Her dark skin is awesome. It's a shame there is prejudice among our own people."

"Uh," Sophia angrily scolded Stephan. "I will not stand here and have you speak to me like this in front of family."

"Mom," Stephan interrupted, "I'm going to the car." He turned and left. Sophia looked at all three standing there.

"Please forgive my children for being so rude. I have to go. Goodbye, I'll call." She walked away quickly.

On their way home, Sophia scolded them both for talking to her, the way they did, in front of family. She scolded them for storming out without waiting for her. Shadae and Stephan sat quietly and rolled their eyes and glanced at each other now and then. Upon reaching home, Sophia looked at Stephan as he was getting out of the car and warned him,

"And I want you to stay away from that ugly black girl."

16

Surprise

ive months later, into the next school year, Tasha and a few friends were walking through the school's hallway. *They saw Destini and Yasmin approaching.*

Tasha whispered to the girls. "Watch this." As Destini and Yasmin approached, Tasha screamed and held her chest while they all passed each other.

"Aaaaaaah, oh my God, help. The black spook frightened me half to death." Tasha's friends laughed loudly.

"Not cute Tashee, trashee. You heard what the Principal said about calling anyone names. You keep it up and we will report you to the dean or principal's office." Yasmin then shouted after they passed. "If you have such a bad heart, you weakling, why don't you stay home?"

"Yea," Destini shouted. Then Tasha shouted back as she and her friends faced Destini and Yasmin.

"Shut up pale face, who's talking to you? If your friend wasn't so charcoal, I wouldn't be so frightened."

"Yasmin come on, let's go to class. She's not important," Destini said softly.

"If she keeps this up I am going to tell Ms. Anderson," Yasmin continued. Just then, Stephan and Shadae came around the corner behind Tasha and her friends. Stephan's presence surprised Tasha. He looked at Destini warmly and she returned a similar look, glanced at the floor, then back at him. She then turned and left. Stephan, still looking at Destini, questioned Tasha.

"What was all that about?" he then shifted his eyes to Tasha.

"What?" replied Tasha irritably, with nervousness, hoping that he did not hear her calling Destini those names. She was upset that his focus was on Destini. Shadae noted Tasha's bewildered look and interrupted.

"That's not important. Tasha, we have to talk."

"About what?" Stephan asked smiling.

"None of your business Stephan, this is girl talk," she responded in an unruly tone.

"Shadae, please don't talk to me like that," he said sternly.

"Okay, I'm sorry," she responded.

"Girl talk ay, I bet it's about Pete Silvers," Stephan said not smiling

"See you later Stephan," Shadae said. Stephan looked at both girls suspiciously and walked away. Shadae looked straight into Tasha's eyes.

"Tasha," she said, "I've got to go to class but I must see you right after school. It's very important."

"Give me a hint what it is."

"I've got to go. Later." Shadae hurried off.

In biology class, Destini sat in front of Yasmin. Yasmin tapped Destini on the shoulder.

"Destini?" she whispered. Destini turned to face Yasmin. "I saw Shadae Saturday night with her boyfriend and they were smooching really heavy."

"Really, where?" she whispered back.

"By Mike's Place in the parking lot. They were in Pete's car."

"She should take it easy. Well, her mom wanted her to date a white guy. Her older brother is married to a white woman."

"Yea, I know. And I heard Pete's parents don't like Shadae because she's not white."

"Really?" repeated Destini. "Where did you hear that?"

"From Mrs. Jones of course, she always knows what's going on."

"Uh, um," a voice sounded from the front of the room. Destini turned to see the teacher at the head of the class. He was tall, pale, and slender with frizzy salt and pepper hair. His crackly voice echoed through the room.

"Okay class, put your books away and take out a piece of paper, we are going to have a surprise quiz today." The whole class gasped, moaned, and groaned.

"Stop sounding like you are sick or dying," Mr. Solomon said. "Ready! First question."

After school, Yasmin and Destini met their friends at the front doors. On their way out, they noticed Shadae waiting impatiently by the door. Yasmin and Destini said goodbye to their friends and began to walk home.

"I'm so glad I don't have to take the school bus home," Destini said. "I just love walking home. The school bus gets so noisy at times, they try to pick fights with you and everyone just stares at you when you get on the bus. Remember that time when I rode the bus and Nolita tried to pick a fight with me?"

"Yeah, I remember you telling me about it, and I'm so glad I don't have to take it too," Yasmin responded. "And the reason they stare at you is because you are very pretty Destini, plus you're elegant. I love your braids; I wish my mother would let me wear braids. She said it's unchristian to wear braids."

"No, it's not." Destini looked at Yasmin and said. "So, God is gonna send me to hell for wearing braids? There is a command that Jesus gave. He said, 'Love the Lord your God with all your heart, with all your soul and with all your mind and your neighbor as yourself.' That's what we need to do instead of worrying about how people wear their hair."

"Whoa," Yasmin said, "please don't be so defensive. I agree with you. I don't think it's unchristian to wear braids, but I live in my mother's house and I have to obey her rules."

"I understand, Yasmin," Destini said softly, "and sometimes I feel like your mom doesn't want us hanging together; I d'know, maybe I'm wrong. You know I'm glad Mom lets me wear braids. She's always doing the best for me. That's why I thank God every day for Etta. She is the best mom in the world. Plus, she is gorgeous."

"Yea, Mrs. Taylor is pretty," said Yasmin.

"I'm grateful for the voice and dance lessons my parents got me to take. I've dedicated them to the Lord."

"You dedicate dancing to the Lord?" Yasmin knitted her brow and asked.

"Yes, I want to dedicate all my talents to God. I want all my talents to glorify Him." Yasmin looked at her with confusion written all over her lovely face as the gentle breeze blew her light golden-brown hair. Destini continued, "I pray," then noticing the look on Yasmin's face, "What's wrong, you look confused?" Yasmin was still thinking about dedicating dance to God.

"What do you mean 'dedicate dancing to God'?" she asked. "You can't do that. How is God going to accept dancing? We're not supposed to dance."

"Yasmin," Destini said, "where do you think dancing came from? It came from God himself." Destini moved rhythmically, "He gave us rhythm in our bodies so we can glorify his name with dances. The Bible said praise God with the dance. So, I want to praise God with dancing, okay!" She stopped dancing. "As I was saying," They both laughed "I pray..."

"Wait, where is that found?"

"In Psalms."

"Okay," Yasmin returned, "I'm gonna ask my Mom about that and look that up." Destini looked at her.

"Good, as I was saying," they both laughed as she continued, "I pray every morning and night that God will bless my Mom and Dad. I love them. They have really helped me a lot since I moved here." Yasmin abruptly changed the subject.

"How did you do on Mr. Solomon's quiz today?"

"I d'know, it was really a surprise quiz."

"Destini," Yasmin stated, "I know you, and I know you did very well on that quiz. Did you notice Shadae by the doors? She didn't look happy and pious as she usually does."

"I know, wonder what's wrong?"

"I wish I knew," said Yasmin, "but I'll find out. Mrs. Jones always comes over to gossip."

Shadae waited at the front doors of the school for Tasha. She paced back and forth. Finally, Tasha appeared, walking quickly towards her.

"What took you so long?" Shadae's said with voice raised slightly.

"Sorry I took so long, but Ms. Anderson was talking to me."

"Uh, she's always talking to someone. Anything wrong?"

"Well, she was talking to me about calling people names. But, that's not important. What did you want to talk about?" Tasha asked anxiously.

"Come, let's go outside," Shadae said. They walked outside. Shadae became very quiet as they walked.

"Well, what is it?" Shadae kept her head straight as if ignoring Tasha. Tasha held her arm so that it stopped her.

"Shadae, is something wrong?" Tasha asked with a slight Trinidadian accent.

"Yea," she said softly as she looked at Tasha.

"Oh no, you and Pete broke up."

"Nope."

"What's wrong then?" Shadae stopped walking and looked Tasha in the eye.

"You have to promise me you won't say a word to anyone, especially my brother." Tasha squinted her eyes curiously. "Promise I won't say what?" she asked.

"Tasha, promise me." Shadae squeezed her arm and raised her voice.

"Ouch, you're hurting my arm. Okay I promise." Shadae looked at her with a serious expression.

"I mean it Tasha, it's very important to me."

"Shadae, I said I promise, please, don't you trust me?" Tasha wondered what on earth could be so secretive because Shadae had never acted like this before.

Shadae continued walking. She paused before muttering, "Um, uh, I'm pregnant." She hung her head down.

"What!" Tasha incredulously exclaimed.

"I'm pregnant," Shadae repeated. Tasha stopped walking; she was shocked.

"My goodness, I thought that's what you said!" she screamed. Shadae pulled her and said with teeth pressed together and widened eyes,

"Shut up! What's wrong with you? I don't want anyone looking over here."

"Oh, my God," Tasha said softly at the highest pitch of her voice, "Are you sure?"

"Yes I'm sure," she answered.

"What are you going to do?" Tasha asked frantically.

"I don't know." They both walked quietly along the paved walkway. Tasha felt as if she was in a daze as she watched the students wandering home.

"Does Pete know?" Tasha asked.

"Yes," came the sad response. Tasha's eyes widened.

"He does? What did he say?" She muttered that he wasn't too happy. She didn't want to talk about it anymore.

"Wait, just one more question," Tasha insisted. "Does your mom know, and are you going to have an abortion?"

"No, my mom doesn't know yet," Shadae answered reluctantly, "and no, I'm not going to have an abortion. I'm going home."

"Home, aren't you coming to cheerleading practice?"

"Not anymore. You know they won't let me back in once they find out. I may as well stop going now." She paused then said softly, "Goodbye. See you tomorrow." With that, she left Tasha standing and looking confused.

17

Gossip

One *month later, on a cold windy Sunday morning, Yasmin came to Destini's home, ringing the doorbell anxiously and taking in the loveliness of the scene.*

The leaves on the trees, painted with the richness of red-orange and yellow, swung happily amidst the breeze. The dancing leaves chattered with each other as the wind glided through their pathway. The mist flowing from the lake in the yard looked enchanting and mysterious. The loveliness of the trees filled the area with beauty and serenity. Yasmin took a breath and closed her eyes imagining the loveliness of the scene, that it could resemble heaven.

"Who on earth is ringing the doorbell like that?" Etta shouted.

"I'll get it," Destini called out.

"No bother," her mother said irritably, "I'm right here, I'll get it." She opened the door, breaking Yasmin's thought of the glorious ambiance. Her eyes opened slowly to see Mrs. Taylor twisted lips and glaring eyes fixed on her. All of Yasmin's pearly whites appeared from behind her pink lips.

"Hi Mrs. Taylor, is Destini here? May I come in? Thanks." She walked in hurriedly; glancing at the floor, wanting to get away from Mrs. Taylor's disapproving posture.

"Oh, good morning Yasmin," Etta said still facing the outside. "I'm fine, please come in." She then turned slowly around and eyeballed her in a motherly way.

Yasmin smiled again nervously. She looked up at the ceiling and bit her lips. "Um, good morning Mrs. Taylor, how are you?" Then looking around she asked anxiously, "Is Destini up yet? I need to talk to her." Just then, Destini came out.

"Mom, who was at the . . . oh, Yasmin! Hi. What you doing here so early girl?" she said surprisingly.

"Hi, uh, see you later Mrs. Taylor." She put her arms around Destini and walked towards the stairs.

"Destini we have to talk. Let's go to your room." They left Etta standing on her shiny wooden floor with a spatula in her hand, shaking her head.

"Young people; what is so important that she has to come over here so early on a Sunday morning, ringing the bell like the house is running away? Um, um, um."

The two girls went up to Destini's room and closed the door to her bedroom. Her bedroom was clean and neat with a floral scent. The bed was dressed with a white comforter, accented with pink and red roses. On her cherry finished Queen Anne-style dresser were tiny bottles of perfumes. The perfumes were placed decoratively on two oval shaped gold-rimmed vanity mirrors. A beautiful doll, dressed in pink, white, and red satin accented with lace, separated the mirrors.

"Destini," Yasmin said while taking in the loveliness of the room, "I always love to come into your room. It's so . . . so . . . what shall I say?" She paused and thought, *"Um, how should I say this?"* She then said, "Always lovely . . . majestic . . . beautiful, really neat."

"Thanks, but you always say things like that when you come here."

"I know," responded Yasmin. She walked toward the dresser drawer. "I know. Take for instance this doll on your dresser, she's wearing a tiara. Is she a princess doll? She looks just like you. Where did you get it?"

"You know my grandma sent it for me. Yasmin," Destini said quickly, "enough already. What do you have to tell me that you couldn't call me? You had to come in person, on a cold, windy Sunday morning," she slowed down, "ringing the doorbell like you're mad."

"Oh, so now I'm mad," Yasmin responded.

"No. I mean, we-----ell on second thought." Destini looked around teasingly.

"On second thought," Yasmin teased. Destini reached out and squeezed her neck. Yasmin laughed.

"Okay, okay," she said quickly, "I'll tell you now." Yasmin walked to the window.

"Isn't it nice out today," she said softly. "Look at the way the trees are flowing gent . . . Aaaaaah," came a sudden scream from Yasmin. Destini was tired of waiting to hear what she had to say so she tickled Yasmin's waist. Threw her on the bed, then proceeded to tickle her some more. Yasmin laughed and screamed, "Sto-----p," between giggles, "sto-----p. Destini, Destini, okay. Shadae is pregnant." Destini suddenly stopped, then continued. Yasmin tried to get up. She didn't want to feel any more tickles.

"I'm serious," she screamed, "Shadae is pregnant." Destini jumped up from the bed in complete surprise.

"What?" she screeched. "Who told you that?"

"Mrs. Jones," Yasmin responded.

"Mrs. Jones told you that?" Destini's bewildered voice escalated.

"Shh-----h. Well not exactly, I overheard her telling someone else."

"Who was she telling and how did Mrs. Jones find out?"

"Okay, she was telling my Mom and she found out from Shadae's mother's friend. And the friend, who is a good friend of Mrs. Barronton, got the information from Shadae's mother."

"Oh, my goodness," Destini's voice softened, "Is Pete the baby-daddy?"

"I guess so. As far as I know he's the only one she's dating." Destini walked to the window and paused in silence.

"Oh, my goodness," she finally said. "Yasmin, this is not cute at all. Does Stephan know?"

"Gee, I don't know," Yasmin said as she sat up and scratched her head. "He is family. I guess he should. Dag, I wonder what she's gonna do?"

"Could you imagine," Destini said as if exhausted, "the embarrassment to her family? Their lovely and gorgeous princess gets pregnant by a white boy. That is not cute, not cute at all."

"I know," Yasmin responded softly. The girls sat in silence and stared at the walls as if the walls were talking to them. Destini thought about Stephan and she wondered if he knew. If he knew, she wondered how he was doing.

"Yasmin, I wonder how the high and mighty Sophia Barronton is taking this." The girls looked at each other.

"She's probably proud and happy that her daughter got pregnant by a white person." Yasmin stood up and said. They looked at each other again and sort of laughed.

"It's not funny." Destini concluded, "An innocent life is involved here." They both stopped and sat in silence again. Destini finally broke the silence.

"Oh goodness, I wonder what I would do if that were to happen to me." At that remark, Yasmin blurted out, "If that were to happen to you? Girl, what a thing to say. Whatta you talking about? Christian girls should not get pregnant outside of marriage."

"I know, but that could happen to anyone, Christian or not." Destini insisted while looking at Yasmin.

"I know that," Yasmin answered, "but it should not happen to a Christian girl because she should be taught to abstain from sex until she is married."

"Yea, that's all good and true," Destini went on, "but it doesn't always happen in today's society. The Bible does say we are not to have sex until we are married, but people today think it's okay to have sex before they're married. Plus, some kids become sexually active because they were sexually abused or have no parental guidance." Destini paused for a while shook her head then asked, "So, what are you saying, Shadae is not a Christian?"

"No silly, listen to me. I see Shadae in church every Sabbath. I'm saying, if you are not married a sure way to be safe from pregnancy is not to be sexually active. We should honor God by obeying His words and wait until we are married."

"I know, Yasmin, you're right. But, I'm just saying, don't judge Shadae because what happened to her can happen to anyone, Christian or not. None of us are exempted from temptation and sin. And at our most vulnerable time, we may be caught off guard."

"Yes, that's true, but," Yasmin said pointing her finger at Destini. "God made provision for us through Jesus Christ so we won't be caught off guard."

64

Destini pointed her finger back at Yasmin. "And God has made provision for us just in case we are caught off guard." They both agreed.

"Yea, yea, yea." They laughed.

"Yea, I see what you're saying," Yasmin said as she stood up and asked happily. "Say Destini, are you going to the Barronton's international holiday parties?" Still sitting on her bed, Destini looked at the floor.

"I wasn't invited last year and I didn't get an invitation this year, so I don't think I will be going. I'll just spend the time at home."

"Destini, it is now the end of November and you have a whole month to find out if you can go."

"Okay, but I don't think Mrs. Barronton wants me there."

"Oh Destini," Yasmin insisted, "you worry about everything. Don't worry about that stuck-up witch."

"Excuse me, it's her party," Destini blurted out, "and her house. What do you mean 'don't worry?'"

"Look," Yasmin said, "Stephan invited me and whomever the Barronton's children invite is okay with the parents. They don't say anything. Their parents told them to invite whomever they want, so we'll get Stephan to invite you."

"Na-------a," Destini said loudly, "Na, na, no!"

"Yes."

"No."

"Destini, what are you afraid of?" Yasmin asked. "You know Stephan would be glad to invite you. You know he likes you."

Destini looked at Yasmin. "Likes me? Yasmin, you are the one who likes Stephan and perhaps he likes you too. I see the way you look at Stephan when he's around." Yasmin was startled by Destini's statement. She knew in her heart how she felt about Stephan.

"Destini, I may be attracted to Stephan" she said half smiling, "be . . . because he's good looking and all, bu . . . but that does not mean I . . . I like him or I want to date him." Both girls became silent. Destini stood up and walked to the window.

"Yasmin, I'm sorry," she finally said softly while looking out. "I shouldn't have said that. It was a dumb statement."

"Um," Yasmin answered half-heartedly, glancing at Destini quickly, "that's okay."

"I don't think I want to go to either party," Destini said, "I'll stay home and help Mom wrap the gifts. Plus, we have family coming and I may have to stay home and help clean up."

"Oh, please come to the party Destini. I'm gonna be so bored if you don't come. Tasha will gloat when she realizes that you didn't come. It's gonna be really nice. There are two separate parties, one for the adults and one for our age group. There are usually lots of good-looking guys at the party. Besides, there are beautiful girls who are very much after Stephan." Destini half-smiled and looked at Yasmin.

"Good for them," she said and walked to the door. "Would you like some tea or hot chocolate?"

"Yea, thanks," Yasmin answered, following behind Destini. She opened the door and walked towards the stairs. "Destini, please come to the parties," Yasmin insisted.

"No," Destini held out, "and what would you like tea or hot chocolate?

"I don't care what you say Destini, I'm gonna ask Stephan about your invitations. And even if you don't come to both the holiday and New Year's parties, at least come to one, please," she begged. "Both tea and hot chocolate please," she finally answered. Yasmin grabbed Destini's arm as she was about to descend the stairs and begged again. "Plea-----se Destini, oh plea-----se."

"Okay, I'll think about it. I'll think about it."

"Great," Yasmin said exuberantly, "you're gonna go."

"I didn't say I'm going, I said I'll think about it."

With that, the conversation ended. The girls went to the kitchen for something warm to drink. On their way to the kitchen, Destini reminded Yasmin about her dance performance at one of the big churches in Worcester. Yasmin promised to support her if she'd go to the parties. Etta was in the kitchen finishing up breakfast--the girls had smelled the aroma from upstairs.

Etta looked at Yasmin. "So, Yasmin," she asked curiously, "is your urgent message delivered?" Both girls looked at each other and laughed.

"Yes, Mrs. Taylor," Yasmin responded brightly. "In seven months." Yasmin laughed at her joke and Destini's eyes widened and she looked at her Mom. She knew Etta was sharp and would figure it out. Mrs. Taylor was not smiling. She looked at Destini as if to ask what it meant. Destini tapped Yasmin on her back and Yasmin cleared her throat and looked around as if looking for something.

"Don't mind her Mom," Destini said, "she's hungry."

Mrs. Taylor looked at both girls and said, "Good. Yasmin, please stay for breakfast."

"Thanks Mrs. Taylor, I'm gonna call my mom and tell her." Yasmin walked quickly to the phone and Etta looked at Destini while continuing to put the food and dishes on the dinette table. Destini helped her mom put the rest of the things on the dinette table. Winston wandered into the dinette area. As the full aroma touched his nose, he exclaimed, "Hmmm that smells so good. Um, um, uum, my favorite!" He stared at the table with a smile and said, "Fried dumplings, avocado, callaloo, boiled green bananas, yellow yam, ackee and salt-fish." Winston looked up and said in Jamaican patois, "Unu ready fe eat?"

"Yes," rang a voice from in the bathroom. Yasmin popped out from behind the door joyfully.

"Good morning Mr. Taylor and how are you this morning?" Winston looked at her with surprise then at his wife.

"Good morning Yasmin," He smiled and said calmly. "Didn't know you were here. I am fine this cold morning. How are your folks?"

"Great," she responded as she looked hungrily at the table. Everyone took his place at the table. Yasmin sat next to Destini. Winston said grace and they all proceeded to serve their food. Yasmin whispered something to Destini and they both laughed. While everyone was eating and exchanging words, Etta watched the girls carefully. She seemed concerned about what the girls discussed upstairs. "So," she asked while looking at her plate. "Ladies, who's pregnant?" Yasmin's eyes and mouth opened.

"Yasmin," Etta said, "you can close your mouth dear; your food might fall out." Yasmin looked at Etta. "How . . . how did you know what Destini and I were talking abo . . . Destini!" Yasmin looked at Destini and shouted. "I can't believe you told your mom!"

"I didn't say anything Yasmin. It was you and your big mouth."

"What are you all talking about?" Winston asked, "Who's pregnant?"

Destini looked at her parents. "Don't look at me." She said and looked at Yasmin. Etta and Winston felt relieved at Destini's response.

Then Mr. Taylor gasped and with his eyes opened wide, he stuttered, "Yass, Yasmin, ah, um."

"Mr. Taylor," Yasmin interrupted, "I'm not pregnant nor is Destini. It's a girl at school. Nothing to worry about." Destini and Yasmin quickly glanced at each other.

"So," questioned Etta, still curious, "what friend at school is pregnant?" Yasmin quickly responded with food in her mouth.

"Itch, ahm Sha," she coughed, then held up her finger and coughed again.

"Are you okay?" Everyone asked. Destini hit her on the back.

"Are you choking?" Destini asked quickly. Etta got up quickly and came around, but Yasmin cleared her throat.

"Um, um, I'm okay. I must have been eating too fast."

"Are you sure, dear?" asked Etta.

"Yes, I'm sure." Everyone was relieved. Etta eyed Yasmin, realizing she was trying to get out of not saying anything. Etta pursed her lips but, said nothing.

Yasmin then asked Destini what she was doing for the rest of the day. Destini said she was going to cook, help clean up, and then study. After breakfast, Yasmin thanked Etta and dismissed herself quickly.

18

Trouble in the Hallway

*T*he following day at school, Yasmin shyly
approached Stephan and asked him about the
parties. Stephan looked masculine in his jeans and T-shirt. She
asked him if Destini was invited to any of the parties. He said she was
invited to both. He told Yasmin that he would personally invite Destini
because she did not attend last year. Stephan thanked Yasmin and
dismissed himself. She wished he would have stayed and talked with her.
He was so well-mannered and masculine.

As Yasmin walked to her class, she was met by Tasha, Shadae and
three of their friends. One of them was Nolita.

"Well," said Tasha, "look who is in the hallway and late for her class
too."

"Get out of my way," Yasmin said. One of the girls pulled her hair.

"Who ya talking to like that, goldie locks?" she said.

"Stop pulling my hair," Yasmin screamed, "and leave me alone."

"You're not so bad now that spooky's not around," Nolita said, who
was not dressed as well as the other girls. Yasmin wondered what she
was doing hanging out with Tasha and Shadae.

"Her name is Destini, thank you," Yasmin responded back, "but
you're too dumb to know the difference. And in case you haven't
noticed, you're just as dark skinned as Destini, so if I were you I wouldn't
call anybody spooky." Nolita dropped her books and shoved Yasmin.
Shadae came between them.

"Wait Nolita, there's something I want goldie locks to do and if she
refuses, she's all yours."

"I'm not doing anything for you," Yasmin shouted.

"Well, I know that you are crazy about my brother Stephan."
Yasmin's heart pounded and she looked away and then back at Shadae.

"Isn't that true, goldie?" Shadae questioned.

"No, you're wrong and my name is Yasmin, but then you're not
smart enough to know that. You all just get out of my way." Tasha
grabbed Yasmin's arm.

"Where you think you're going? We're not finished yet, goldie."

"Yea," said Shadae. "The deal is this. You keep my brother away from ugly duckling by trying to go out with him. And if you don't, you and she both will get your butts kicked." Yasmin got really angry and shouted in Shadae's face,

"Look here strawberry locks, who's gonna kick my butt? Pete or spooky here?" Yasmin asked, pointing to Nolita. Nolita moved around Shadae to hit Yasmin, but Yasmin moved backward, tripped over Tasha's foot, and fell. Yasmin was really screaming now.

"You all go to hell. I swear Shadae, if anyone of you so much as comes near me! You'd better watch your back because I will kill you. Nobody threatens me and walks free. Nobody! I'm not as nice as Destini, you better remember that." Yasmin looked right at Nolita when she said that. They all laughed.

"Girl, you don't scare me," Nolita said. Yasmin lowered her voice.

"You know spooky, the dead fear nothing. They don't know they are dead. The bible says when someone dies, his thoughts perish. So you will have nothing to fear. That is, if you don't touch me."

"Whoa---a," Nolita responded furiously. "I hate this, this little, oooo----oh." She turned to Tasha and the rest. "Get me outta here before I hurt her." Just then, Mr. Solomon came out of a room.

"Ladies, what's going on here?" He walked over to Yasmin to help her up. The girls walked off slowly, but Nolita kept looking back at Yasmin.

"Thanks Mr. Solomon. They were trying to pick a fight."

"Well," said Mr. Solomon, "we will report it to the Dean's office."

"Mr. Solomon, that's not necessary."

"I insist, no bullying in this school," he said. "Come let us go." On their way to the dean's office, Mr. Solomon related to Yasmin that he would be a witness because he overheard and saw everything that happened. Mr. Solomon reported the incident to the dean's office. Tasha, Shadae and their friends tried to lie their way out of it, but Mr. Solomon backed up Yasmin and they all got into big trouble. Sophia was not very happy. She tried to get Shadae from suspension but, was unsuccessful.

19

Dance

𝒯he church was having a special sundown Friday-night service. It was family week, and each family was welcomed to offer their talents. Yasmin decided to play her violin and Destini decided to perform a special dance to the Lord. She had performed for other churches on Sundays, and they loved it. So, she decided to perform at the church on Sabbath evening. Yasmin got a ride with the Taylors to the church. On their way, Yasmin tried to convince Destini to sing instead of dance, but Destini would not agree.

"Please, Destini, you know how those people are. They'll eat you alive, especially Stephan's mother."

"Yasmin," Destini said, "you told me that at the Barrontons' party last year, they were dancing."

"Yes, but that's different. It's a party, not a worship service, and this is the Sabbath." Etta looked back at Yasmin.

"Yasmin," she said, "I'd rather offer dance and praise to God on His holy Sabbath for His love and His wonderful care and protection towards me than dance for people or myself at a party, dear. I have a lot of praise in my voice, my heart and my body. The Bible says even the very rocks would cry out, so why shouldn't Destini praise God with her dancing? The very Bible says to praise Him with dance."

"Mrs. Taylor, I don't mean to be rude, but I beg to differ. When the Bible says to praise Him with dance, the Lord was speaking to the Hebrews because they didn't know any better. That passage of scripture was not referring to us today."

Destini looked at Yasmin with knitted brows. "Girlfriend, where did you get that information from?" Destini asked.

"It's in the Bible."

"Where?" asked Destini.

"Um, uh---m, well," she stuttered, "the New Testament never said anything about us praising God with dancing, so it's not for us. It was only for the Israelites back then because it was their culture."

"So, Yasmin," Winston butted in. "are you saying we should not believe in the Old Testament?"

"No Mr. Taylor, that's not what I'm saying."

"Well, what are you saying?"

"What I'm saying is that dancing is not necessary in these modern times to praise God. The world already uses it to praise themselves and it will seem worldly doing it in the church." Etta and Destini looked on as Winston continued. They knew Winston was a good Bible scholar.

"You know Yasmin," Winston said, "you have a very good point." Yasmin seemed very proud of herself. "But," he continued, "the people in the world sing, eat, walk, and dance. Am I to understand that you are saying, that since the world does all these things in these modern times, it is wrong or worldly for a Christian to do them also?"

Yasmin thought to herself *"Oh no, here goes."* "Mr. Taylor," she said with agitation, "you know that's not what I'm saying. You know we have to eat because that is necessary. Dancing is not. And we always sing in church services, and that's necessary. And yes, they also sang in the New Testament. Singing is a form of worship and praise."

"Well Yasmin, you have a good point again." Etta sat quietly and thought, *"I'm glad he took her on."* "Now," he said, "putting aside what your parents and the church taught you about praise, how do you know for yourself that singing is a form of praise?" Yasmin smiled.

"That's easy, from the Bible, Mr. Taylor."

"Great," he added, "and you're right." Yasmin smiled again as she looked at Destini, well pleased with herself. Destini looked on anxiously, trying her best to keep calm. Winston handed Yasmin a Bible, read Psalm 149, verse 1."

She found the verse and read, "Praise ye the Lord, Sing unto the Lord a new song, and His praise in the congregation of saints."

72

"What is it saying?"

"It's obvious; to praise God with new songs and praise Him in church." She emphasized songs as she looked at Destini. Destini just smiled.

"Now," Winston continued, "Psalm 147, verse 1 says about the same thing." Yasmin found it and read it also.

"See, we are to praise God in singing, not dance." She looked at Destini. They finally reached the church parking lot. Winston parked the car, turned to Yasmin and said, "Find first Corinthians, chapter 6 and read verses nineteen and twenty." Yasmin thought, *"Hmm New Testament, uh, oh,"*

"Okay," she said and jumped to it. She found it and read, "'What? Know ye not that your body is the temple of the Holy Ghost which is in you, which you have of God, and you are not your own? For you are bought with a price; therefore, glorify God in your body, and in your spirit which are God's.'" Yasmin took a breath as she asked, "So what does this have to do with singing and praise?"

"The Bible just read 'glorify God in your body'"?

"Yea----s, you use your voice to sing. Your voice box is in your body." she answered.

"Exactly, now Psalm 149, verse 3 it reads what?"

She looked at all three of them, and then proceeded, "Okay." She found it and read. "'Let them praise His name in the dance.'" She paused.

"Read on." He said. She glanced quickly at Destini's leg and continued.

"'Let them sing praises unto him with the timbrel and harp.'"

"Yasmin," Winston said, "you can read the rest at a later time. Now read Psalm 150, verse 4. She looked up at him.

"Sir, we might be late if we don't go now."

"Don't worry, we won't be late. Go ahead. Here." He found it for her.

"'Praise Him with the timbrel and dance, praise Him with stringed instrument and organs.'"

"Okay," Winston said, "you believe that the entire Bible was inspired by God?"

"Tse, of course I do, but . . ."

"Wait." Winston interrupted. "Since the entire Bible is inspired by the Spirit of God and we are asked to obey His word, do you believe you or anyone has the right to say otherwise?"

"No, but . . ."

"Wait young lady, you'll get your chance. Now, since the word of God tells us to praise Him with dancing and ah to glorify God in your body, this includes, eating, singing, talking, walking, dancing, etc. You're gonna tell God, 'Um, no Lord, I'm not gonna praise you with dancing because it's wrong; even though He asked us to praise Him with dancing also?" Yasmin was quiet. She looked at Etta, then at Destini.

"It just doesn't seem right," she finally said.

"Yasmin," Destini said, "if God asked us to worship Him in praise, whether it be singing, playing instruments or dancing, it seems perfectly right to me. I want to please Him. Just because it doesn't seem right to you does not mean it is wrong, especially if God said it is right in His word."

"Okay, okay, you've all made your point. I was just testing you, that's all."

Destini pushed her gently. "Yea, right!" She said. They all went into the beautiful church that seated over three thousand. Destini was beginning to feel nervous.

"You know, you don't have to do this," Etta said as she looked at her.

"I know mom, but I want to," she said softly. She watched all who participated. Some of them were so boring. She noticed some of the members sleeping. Right before she was announced to perform, Stephan came to tell her that Yasmin told him what she was going to do. He thought it was wonderful. Stephan's masculine presence made her feel safe. He told her "God be with you," and he smiled and squeezed her hand. She looked soft and feminine. He really wanted to hug her. The announcement came.

"Next, we have Destini Pearson Taylor. She will praise the Lord with her body and spirit." Some of the people were looking on and wondering what he meant. The music started, "Praise Him, Praise Him. Worship God in His sanctuary. May God be glorified and exalt His Holy Name together..." She danced out on the platform in her leggings and light blue-and-white flared long dress. The audience gasps. Many of the people, mainly the youth and young adults, were pleased to see someone dancing for God. They said, "Wow, it's about time."

"Oh my God, what on earth is she doing?" some of the adults asked. "This is ridiculous." Some people got up and left angrily. Others shouted out, "This is evil brought into the church." Mrs. Barronton was blue in the face with embarrassment. She had invited Elizabeth and her husband Raymond and her niece LaVona to the service. LaVona looked on with joy. She was excited about the performance. She wished it were her performing. She said she'd love to do that. Mrs. Barronton looked at her with a scolding expression and LaVona sat back in her chair. One of the elders went upon the platform and asked the audio person to turn off the music. Some young people shouted, "No, no, leave her alone." The young people continued shouting. Some members were surprised at the outburst in the assembly. Some got up and left. Poor Destini stopped dancing and tears filled her eyes. "Oh, Lord," she whispered, "I'm praising you from my heart. I'm not praising them. Why are they so angry?" While all of this was going on, she turned to see Etta who was standing backstage with her arms opened. Destini walked quickly to her.

The church elder who happened to be an elderly man, spoke with a Caribbean accent. "Dis is not a teata, dis is the house of God." Some of the adults shouted, "Amen!" He went on, "It is amazing how the young people of today treat the house of God. If dis was in times past dey would have been struck down." A few of the members shouted, "Amen."

While he was speaking, the pastor of the church, Pastor Edwards, mounted the platform. He walked slowly towards him and touched him gently on the shoulder.

"Thank you." the minister said in his baritone voice. The elder stepped back and the minister stepped forward to the microphone. "Brethren," he said, "I would like to apologize for any disruption.

When the spirit of God speaks to each of our hearts, we praise God in our own way as long as it is in accordance with the word of God. Brethren, I urge you to study His holy words." He paused for a short moment and looked out at them. "We will continue with the next item on the program." He quietly turned to the elder and put his hand on his shoulder as if to escort him off the pulpit. After leaving the pulpit, he went to Destini and shook her hand. His straight white hair looked full and healthy against his slightly wrinkled ivory skin. He looked at her with his bright blue eyes.

"Young lady," he said with a pleasant yet serious expression, "you have the bravery of the three Hebrew boys, the courage of David, the elegance of a swan, and the beauty of Queen Esther. I understand what you were doing and God appreciates it." Destini finally smiled. "Nevertheless," he continued, "some of us are not yet ready. I hope this does not mean that you are going to give up?"

Destini looked at Etta then back at the pastor and said, "No, sir."

"Great," he added, "and if you need anything, let me know."

"Thank you, sir."

"You're welcome." he smiled, turned and left. Destini felt so much better. "Here," she said, "a white person was kind to me and some of my own people behaved so mean."

"Destini," Etta said, "that's not true. It was fairly even on both sides. It's just that some of our people are a little more outspoken and it's an individual thing I guess."

Etta and Destini walked down the hallway and some members walked by expressing their disapproval. They shook their heads, while others applauded her. A teen wanted to say something to Destini and her disapproving mother called her back. A few more times other teens attempted to approach Destini and their families called them away. Etta encouraged Destini not to be worried about such insignificant things.

"Let's go," she said.

Stephan appeared from around the corner and shook Mrs. Taylor's hand. "Madam." He then looked at Destini, "Destini, you danced great. I would have loved to see the complete presentation. We all wanted to see it. We need to have more songs and dances to praise the Lord." Destini smiled shyly and looked at Etta. Stephan stared at her. She looked so enchanting to him, especially with her braids pulled back in a bun. Etta looked up and saw trouble with a capital B walking swiftly towards them.

"Well, well, well," she proudly stated upon reaching Mrs. Taylor.

"You, Madam, do not know how to train a child to follow the precepts of God." Stephan was so embarrassed. Why did his mother have to embarrass him like this? She continued, "I have called an emergency board meeting, to schedule a business meeting, to discuss awful things of this nature. The church will not allow this to happen again." Destini looked at her mother with fear in her heart, but Etta was calm as usual.

"I see," Etta responded. "You can call all the meetings you want Mrs. Barronton, you still can't stop the work or the word of God. God will prevail. Please excuse me." She looked at Stephan, smiled and said, "Nice to see you again young man, take care." Etta walked away holding Destini's hand.

"We'll see you at the business meeting," Mrs. Barronton said indignantly, then strutted off.

20

The Business Meeting

The business meeting was scheduled for that Tuesday evening. Etta called her younger sister, Selina, to come with her and Winston to the meeting. Even though Selina was a member of the church, she hardly attended. She knew a few of the members personally, but she was happy to go. She disliked most of the leaders and she loved a challenge.

More people showed up than was expected so the meeting was moved to the main sanctuary. The different ethnic groups made the sanctuary colorful even though the majority of the member were not present.

Pastor Edwards stood and started with prayer. He then addressed the problem in question. His concerned expression fell over the entire assembly.

"Brothers and sisters, I hereby call this meeting to order. Mrs. Barronton will open the floor for the discussion. The board is asking everyone present to conduct his or herself in an orderly fashion. Any misconduct will force us to close the meeting." He paused and looked around at everyone sternly. He continued, "We will be discussing one item only. The board met and made a recommendation. It will be open for discussion. Please do not bring up any other item."

"Excuse me," came a response from the audience, "You mean we can't talk about the amount of money missing from the church building fund?" a man of tall, slender stature asked. The pastor looked at him with a sigh. Mrs. Barronton rolled her eyes up and turned to give him the meanest look.

"No," Pastor Edwards said calmly, "this is an emergency business meeting and that item is not on the agenda and will not be discussed.

If you have any complaints, as we all should've already known, you need to give it to the church board members or to me."

He looked at Mrs. Barronton and smiled gently. "Mrs. Barronton will now state the item and open the floor for discussion." She stood up and proceeded, speaking in her Jamaican-English accent. Mrs. Barronton was always well dressed with matching accessories. Her well-tailored red suit sat on her perfectly slim figure. She looked around at everyone as if in command.

"Question!" she finally said. "Should dancing be allowed in any of our church services? Some of our church members seem to think it is godly, but our Church Manual states that it is improper. On November 30th, a young lady by the name of Destini Pearson performed a dance in our holy sanctuary. This was completely inappropriate and wrong according to the church standards. The floor is now open for discussion. Who will move?"

"I so move," a man stood up quickly and said, "that we discuss the problem in question."

"And I second it." Someone else said. Then one of the older women raised her hand and stood up. She spoke in a Caribbean accent.

"I was greatly disappointed the other day when I sat in church to worship the Lord and saw one of our, I must add, beautiful young ladies dancing in the holy sanctuary. As parents, we should not permit this to happen again." She sat down proudly. Many voices agreed enthusiastically, and other members got up and stated their displeasure. An old woman with an Irish accent stood up.

"As a child growing up in Ireland." she stated, "my parents taught me to honor the Lord, especially in His church. Where I am from, this would never be allowed." Some of the woman's grandchildren, who were present, rolled their eyes upward with displeasure and embarrassment. They wished she would sit down and say no more. She continued, "I was also greatly disappointed." She looked around. "Parents, we need to teach our children right." She finally sat down gracefully.

Etta finally got up. She was angry about their ignorance to the word of God. Winston sat and stared at his beautiful and intelligent wife. He loved the sexy-looking sweater that shaped her full round bosom and extended to her well-defined waist. He wished the meeting could be over so he could go home and run his hands over her voluptuous body. He thought this meeting was a waste of precious time. But then, he didn't mind being there with her to show her off. He sat quietly and fantasized on.

"Brethren," Etta said, "first of all my daughter's name is Destini Pearson Taylor," she emphasized Taylor, "not just Destini Pearson. To continue with the discussion, what does it mean in the Bible when it reads," and she read the Bible verses in Psalms 149 and 150, then went on. "As far as my understanding, it says to praise God with songs, instruments and dances. Why are we so stuck on having our own way and ignoring God's word?" The members, who were against dancing, complained noisily. Pastor Edwards stood up and asked the brethren to be quiet and to respect whoever was speaking.

"Mrs. Taylor, are you finished?" he asked.

"No, I'm not," she answered.

"Okay, please continue."

"She's said enough," a member in the audience shouted, "give someone else a chance." The pastor looked at him sternly.

"Mr. Miller," he said, "another outburst like that and I will ask you to leave or I will adjourn this meeting." It seemed as if the blood rushed to the pastor's face. The entire assembly was quiet. While the people were talking earlier, Destini and Yasmin sneaked onto the 2nd floor balcony. The pastor looked at Mrs. Taylor and asked her to proceed. Everyone sat in silence and listened as she continued.

"Thank you, sir. Some of you complained that it was part of the Hebrew culture to dance. But as far as I know, the Great God of Heaven does not take man's tradition and dictate it to us. The Bible says that holy men of God wrote the word through the power of the Holy Spirit." Some of the people started to grumble softly. Mrs. Taylor looked about and then asked, "I know that the Bible says to praise God with dances. Can anyone show me where it says in the

Bible that we should not praise God with dance?" The entire assembly was quiet.

Finally, Sophia got up to say something, and Etta sat down. Etta sat down and Winston put his hand around her waist, pulling her to him. She playfully slapped him. He removed his hand and then put it on her leg. She removed it. "Behave yourself Sweetheart," she told him.

Sophia looked around proudly, "Well," said Sophia, "in these modern times we do no such thing. The world dances in theaters, dance halls and parties; the Bible says we are not to do the things of the world." A voice came from the audience with a mild tone, "I guess you're worldly then." Those who heard, laughed. Winston kept whispering to his wife that he wanted to be with her and he wanted to go home. Etta smiled and quietly told him to stop and behave.

"Furthermore," Sophia stated proudly, "the Church Manual, says dancing is prohibited . . ."

"Excuse me," another voice blared out from the audience with a strong yet slow confident speech pattern. Selina stood up with her proud self, pointing her finger. "Excuse me, but we do not care what a little manual that man wrote has to say, especially when you're using it over the words of the Living God."

"Excuse me!" Sophia quickly snapped, "You are not a member here. Would you kindly leave?" At this point, the conversation caught Winston's attention.

"Uh oh," he said under his breath, "here goes." Etta was about to stand and say something, but Selina stopped her and continued speaking,

"Aaah, YOU are excused Ma'am, and YOU are free to leave. I am a member here, if you check your records, I am on the books and I return my tithes every two weeks faithfully. As I was saying," she went on as some folks in the assembly uttered, "Ooooh," "uh oh!" "Oh, my goodness."

"Some of us like to think," Selina continued, "that we are gods, trying to interpret God's word the way we feel is right." She continued slowly and articulately. Some of the people shouted, "Amen."

"And," Selina continued as proud as a peacock, "God . . . does . . . not . . . need us to interpret His word to suit us. All we need to do is obey and stop making fools of ourselves. What are you going to do?

Look into God's face and say 'Oh God you shouldn't have put anything about dancing or clapping your hands, because we don't want to do it.' Please, remember what the word says, 'If anyone adds to or takes out of God's word and teaches others to do so. God will destroy that person.'" she pointed her finger again, "how dare anyone put another book, no matter how traditional it is, over the word of God!" Selina felt that she'd said enough so she sat down.

The entire assembly was quiet. Winston looked on wondering when they were going to finish so he could get out of there and take his gorgeous wife home. Finally, Ilene Lynch, a stout ivory-skinned woman with straight sleek red hair that was pulled back in a bun, stood up. She looked around with her lovely green eyes.

"I have searched the scriptures thoroughly on this particular subject," she stated, "and the only thing I've found over and over again is that our creator loves when we praise him."

"Amen, Hallelujah," some people shouted as she continued.

"Whether it is singing, laughter, shouting, eating and drinking, or dancing, we as Christians need to set the example. We should be the head not the tail. God said in first Corinthians chapter 6 and verse 20, to glorify God in our body. And in Psalm 149, verse 3, the Bible says to praise Him with the dance. So, if we disagree with His words and then condemn His children, who are brave enough to obey Him, then our spiritual lives are in serious jeopardy. Of course, we are intelligent enough to know that certain types of dances should not be performed in God's holy presence. Just like certain types of songs are not to be sung in His presence. I say, if Destini Pearson Taylor was wrong and went against the word of God, then we need to reprimand, but in love. We then need to show her in the word of God where she went wrong. If we can't show her, we need to honor God's word and apologize to the Taylors. Thank you." She then sat down.

The entire assembly sat in silence and listened carefully. Some people got up and left without a word. It seemed as if the assembly was waiting for someone else to say something. Destini and Yasmin looked on from the balcony to see what would happen next.

Someone finally stood up. He was short and brown skinned with a receding hairline. Everyone waited to hear his comments.

"Ladies and gentlemen," he said, "it is all good and well to say all these things. But as Christians, who are called by the name of Jesus, we need to be very careful of the lives we portray. You see, we know that the world dances. They dance at parties, at theaters, at night clubs, in movies, and many other places that are not holy. And then we want to copy them and bring it into the church. If we do as they do, we are no better than they are. The Bible said 'be not of the world!' This means we should not do the things of the world and if we continue doing these things, we are going to hell," he said loudly. He looked around with a serious expression and asked, "How then can we witness to heathens when we accept their unchristian ways?" Stephan Barronton finally stood up and cleared his throat.

"Mr. Green, I disagree," he stated. "As was said earlier, the Bible gives us permission to dance, to worship God. Plus, the Bible says whatever we do, do it to the glory of God. Sir, that includes dancing, if it is done for the glory of God in a holy manner." Some people clapped and Pastor Edwards stood up and looked at the assembly. The clapping suddenly stopped and he sat down. "You see sir," Stephan continued, "God gave us that command in His word and you as a human being do not have the right to teach us differently." Suddenly the majority of the people clapped and cheered. Stephan was astonished. He didn't expect that kind of response. The pastor stood up again and looked at the assembly.

"Brethren, please," he said. He then looked at Stephan for him to continue.

"Also, sir," Stephan continued, but suddenly his mother stood up.

"Stephan," she said sternly, "that's enough. Give an adult a chance to speak." Pastor Edwards was about to sit, but he continued standing.

"Please, let us give our young people a chance to speak," he pleaded. "So far he is the only one brave enough to battle us adults." He looked at Stephan with a pleasant smile on his face and said, "Please, Mr. Barronton, continue." Stephan looked down at the floor then at his father. His father nodded affirmatively with a smile.

"Ladies and gentlemen," Stephan continued, "ever since I could remember, the world eats, sleeps, marries, laughs, helps the poor, sings and does many other good things we do. Are we saying that because the world does these things it's a sin for us to do them also? I know eating, drinking, sleeping and so on, are all necessary or we would die. Since the world sings, marries, dances and laughs, does this mean we are not to do those things? God is a God of love and He has appreciation for the arts. That is why He created dancing and then asked us, in His holy words to praise Him with the dance. He gave each of us talents. Some Christians have the talent to dance to His glory. I believe this. Dancing was created by God as a gift to man, to glorify His holy name. How would we know how to move our bodies in such rhythmic beauty if he did not create it? God is the one who put the rhythm in our bodies so we can praise Him. Please don't allow Satan to take away a beautiful art of expression and praise from us. I don't believe God is pleased with our behavior." Stephan looked at his mother and sat down. The whole assembly of about one thousand people stood to their feet, cheered and clapped. Stephan was so surprised. He looked at his father to see him smile, and Dr. Wycham Barronton put his hand on his son's shoulder proudly.

"Very good son, I'm proud of you."

"Father," he said, "I really don't know where that thought came from. I just asked God to give me what He wanted me to say." Wycham Barronton hugged his son.

"We have discussed this issue on both sides," Pastor Edwards finally said. "I know some of us were enlightened tonight and some of us were not. Now," he looked sternly, yet fatherly at the assembly, "we will vote. By a show of the right hand, dancing to the glory of God will be allowed during concerts and praise time. I don't believe some of us are ready for dancing during the divine worship." It seemed the entire assembly raised their right hand. The pastor continued, "Those opposed? The same sign." A few hands went straight up. "Well," said Pastor Edwards, "it's carried by the majority vote that dancing will be allowed in the church as long as it is done to the glory of God. And this will be only at praise time and concerts, such as the vespers we had this past Friday. Okay folks, do we move that this meeting be adjourned? I need a second. Thank you. This meeting is now adjourned, good night."

Destini and Yasmin were so excited they hugged each other. The whole assembly got up to leave, noisily chatting as they moved toward the exits. Winston was in his own little happy world. He couldn't wait to go home. Mrs. Barronton did not vote. She just sat there with an angry and disappointed expression.

People congratulated Stephan and the folks who were brave enough to speak up and challenge Sophia Barronton. Stephan went up front and sat beside his mother. She looked at him and started packing her books and belongings.

"Mother," Stephan said, "you taught us to speak our mind, to stand up for what we believe. I followed your advice."

"Well," she answered. "Satan has won again. In the long run we will suffer the consequences, won't we?"

"Mother," Stephan responded, "if o/beying God's word . . ." She cut him off quickly.

"Stephan, I don't want to hear another word about this. It seems as if that little black jezebel has won for now." She walked off and left her son standing there with a look--a mixture of disappointment and bewilderment.

On their way to the Taylor's car, Mrs. Lynch stopped the Taylors to ask if Destini could perform for a Christmas program in Worcester. Etta was pleased that someone from the meeting wanted Destini to perform.

"When is this program?" Etta asked Mrs. Lynch.
"It will be on the Friday night of December 14th. Mrs. Lynch thanked Etta for allowing Destini to perform in Worchester, and Etta thanked her for her wonderful comment during the meeting. They all went to their homes. Yasmin and Selina went home with the Taylors. At home, they all sat around and talked about Mrs. Barronton, Stephan and the meeting, until late in the night. Finally, they left and Winston was very happy. Selina dropped off Yasmin and they all retired to bed.

21

The Party

*O*ne afternoon, Stephan met Destini after school to *invite her to the holiday parties. He told her again that he loved her dance performance at the church the other night. She invited him to her performance at the big church in* Worcester. He promised to be there. He gave her two invitations, one for his international holiday party and the other for New Year's party. He told her he hoped to see her there. Stephan was calm and polite. He loved to stare at Destini. Destini took the invitations from Stephan shyly, thanked him and left. He watched until her and Yasmin, who, was waiting for her by a tree, disappeared. He wished she could stay and talk, but she was always rushing home.

Destini performed at the church in Worcester and got rave reviews. She was invited to come back, in addition she was invited to other churches. The international holiday party was coming up soon. Destini and Yasmin woke up early the day before the party. They did all of their chores and went dress shopping for Destini. They wanted to look their best.

Destini remembered that Yasmin and other friends had told her that the attires at the Barronton's party were exquisite and everyone was dressed to outshine the other. It was like going to a fashion show. Destini didn't want to feel out of place so she asked Yasmin to help her. Destini couldn't find any ethnic styles she liked, so she borrowed something out of Yasmin's closet. Yasmin's mom, Vashti Michaels, had traveled to Nigeria, Ghana and Egypt in the past. She had become familiar with their various styles of clothing. She made a few African dresses and head wraps for Yasmin. She had made Yasmin's outfit already. Destini was happy to choose one of the styles. She was excited about the party. Destini had attended holiday parties in the past, before she was adopted, but they were not so big and extravagant. She heard that there were going to be over three hundred guests at the Barronton's mansion.

The evening of the international holiday gala arrived. Yasmin got dressed at Destini's home. They were busy trying to look their best and Etta came to help them. Winston and Etta were not invited to the party, but Etta didn't mind. She didn't care to run into Sophia. She didn't want to see chatterbox Mrs. Anita Jones, and she did not care for all the fuss and competition in dressing up. In fact, she wanted to stay home and cuddle up in bed with Winston. He was looking forward to spending some sexy time with his beautiful wife. He always told her she had a sexy body.

The girls were dressed and ready to go. Yasmin looked elegant and lovely in an electric blue and gold colored Nigerian-style gown. Destini chose an ancient looking Egyptian style gown. It was ivory with touches of gold throughout, which accentuated her gorgeous shapely figure. She looked like an elegant Egyptian queen, especially since she still wore her braids. Her braids were accented with gold highlights. Her purse and shoes fell right into place with just the right touches of gold. Destini and Yasmin were very excited. They couldn't wait for Winston to drive them to the mansion. On their way, Destini thought about Stephan and the gentle way in which he invited her. He's such a gentleman, so much more than Jim is. But why did Sophia Barronton have to be his mother?

"Stephan is exceptionally different from his mother and sister." Destini finally said. She then turned to Yasmin. "Why is it that Stephan is totally different from his mother and Shadae? He is more mature than they are. He's such a gentleman. He's thoughtful and he's so cool. He's probably a lot like his father." Yasmin stared at Destini and smiled. Yasmin thought to herself, *"Destini is very beautiful. I know if she was light skinned all the boys would be lined up to go out with her."*

"Yea," Yasmin finally said, "I know. He's great isn't he?".

"Yea."

"Yea," Yasmin repeated, still staring at Destini.

The girls arrived at the mansion, with excitement running through their veins. Destini looked out of the car window.

"Wow," she exclaimed, "this looks like one of those gorgeous mansions you see on TV." It looked like a fairytale house to Destini. She had never been to the Barronton's Estate. She had been to different functions that Mrs. Barronton had sponsored, but the functions were not held at the Estate.

When they arrived, they saw other guests arriving and presenting their invitations. Destini felt the excitement in the air. It was as if she was a princess invited to a grand ball. She ascended the steps and entered the grand foyer. They were serenaded with classical Christmas music as they entered the mansion. The glistened floor was laid with rustic pink and cream colored marbled. The decorations were breathtaking.

The very tall Christmas tree to the right, was covered with imitation snow. Beautiful ribbons and lace adorned the tree along with many international glass ornaments depicting Christmas. On the floor was a toy train track with a train circling the tree. There were stationary electric toys with dolls turning and moving near the tree. The elevated ceiling had iridescent artificial snowflakes hanging from it. The snowflakes appeared to be floating in midair. In the center of the ceiling was an exquisite dazzling chandelier that lit up the entire foyer. Other chandeliers that were smaller and spaced equally apart, circled the main chandelier. Destini wondered how they reached the ceiling to hang snowflakes from it. She stood and stared at the grand staircase, *"Wow!"* she thought. *"It's beautiful."* The grand staircase parted as it ascended. A small waterfall cascaded in the center. Everything seemed like a dream--Destini was in a daze. *"Oh, my goodness,"* she thought, *"this is where Stephan lives? It looks like a grand hotel or a palace. No wonder his mother is so stuck up."*

Destini and Yasmin were directed down the hall to where the teens and young adults were gathered. She was fascinated with the beauty of the foyer. She kept turning her head back to admire it. Her eyes were then fixed on the height of the ceiling of the hallway as she walked on. She also admired the beautiful clothes of the invited guest. She saw some outfits similar to hers, but not exactly the same.

"Some of these clothes are incredible." Destini whispered to Yasmin. "Where did they get them?"

"Well," answered Yasmin, "some of the guests made theirs, some had theirs made by a friend, others bought from boutiques, and others traveled to Africa and bought them. In fact, believe it or not, one of the best vacation spot for the Barrontons is on the African continent." Destini looked at Yasmin in utter surprise.

"Get out, no way."

"Yep."

"Well I'm surprised."

"If you look around their home, you'll see an impressive art collection. Much of the artifacts are from the different countries of Africa, such as, Nigeria, Ethiopia, Ghana, Ivory Coast, Egypt, Kenya, Zimbabwe and others. Mrs. B. also has Italian, English, French, Russian, and Caribbean art." Destini shook her head in disbelief as she walked on.

"The Barrontons have a lot of rich friends, don't they?" Destini asked.

"Yea," answered Yasmin, "lots of them." The girls entered a very large room with a high ceiling where the music of the moment, played by a live band, was Christmas reggae.

"Oooh," sang Yasmin, "Reggae." She started to move her head to the music.

"Oh, I'm so nervous Yasmin. I'm not used to being around so many rich and important people."

"Don't worry," Yasmin said. "We won't be where the adults are, we'll be with our own age group."

"I know," said Destini, "but their children are the ones we'll be around, and I have found rich kids to be spoiled, show-offish and stuck up."

"Not all of them are rich. And look at Stephan, he's rich, but isn't he different?"

"Yea," Destini agreed, "but Stephan is one in a million, and . . ."

"Look," Yasmin interrupted, "here comes Stephan." *'Oh, my goodness,'* thought Destini. She felt a heat wave hit her and her heart raced. Stephan was so masculine and handsome in his three-piece white and purple gold-accented African suit. He looked princely. Both girls stared in awe as he approached them.

"Ladies," he bowed his head slightly, "welcome, happy holidays to you--and you both look lovely." Destini and Yasmin glanced at each other quickly, smiled, and thanked Stephan. Stephan was a little nervous himself, especially after seeing Destini. Yasmin stared at Stephan and then blurted out,

"Stephan you . . . look . . . great."

"Yea," Destini agreed softly, "you look . . . great, Stephan." He stared at Destini then said thanks to both ladies. There was silence for about five seconds; he then directed them to the buffet. As they made their way toward the food, Shadae showed up with Tasha. Yasmin noticed and alerted Destini.

"Yea, I know, I saw them," she said quietly. Shadae swished over to Stephan and said she wanted to introduce him to a girlfriend of hers. Stephan politely excused himself and left with his sister.

"I wonder who she is," queried Yasmin, "and look, she's White too."

"Yea, I noticed, but I don't know who she is and I don't care," concluded Destini.

"Well," continued Yasmin, "if you don't care why are you glancing over there ever so often?"

"Whatta you mean Yasmin? I'm just looking around to see who is here and stop watching me."

"Oh good, here comes Stephan again." Yasmin said joyfully. Stephan came over and asked the girls if they wanted to go into the dancing room to dance. Destini looked at him with surprise. She looked at Yasmin and questioned.

"Dancing room?"

"Told ya," Yasmin said. He escorted them into the dimly lit room. Others were on the floor dancing already. He asked Destini if she'd like to dance.

"Um, not really," she answered, "but I'd like to look around your home to see what it's like. That is, if you don't mind. You and Yasmin can go ahead and dance."

"I don't mind at all," he said happily. "I'd love to show you around." Destini tried to tell him she meant to go alone, but he looked at Yasmin.

"If you don't mind, Yasmin we'll be right back."

"Ah, oh, okay, see ya!" Yasmin said almost dryly. Stephan took Destini's hand and led her out. Destini turned and looked at Yasmin and beckoned her. "Come on," she said. But Yasmin was aching with jealousy. She turned away. Destini stopped and called Yasmin, but she pretended not to hear and walked away.

Stephan proceeded to show her around his parents' home. He took her arm and placed it around his. Destini felt the firmness of his muscle and she knew he worked out regularly. The beauty of the mansion overwhelmed Destini. She felt first-class being led by Stephan; he was quite manly. She loved the grand kitchen and the bathrooms. They were utterly exquisite.

"Destini," Stephan said warmly, "I really enjoyed showing you around. You look very much like a gorgeous princess or even a goddess tonight."

"Oh Stephan, you always have the nicest things to say. You . . . ." Suddenly, a sharp voice came from behind them.

"Stephan!" Shadae shrieked. "There you are. I've been looking all over for you," she said tartly. "Where have you been?" Her English accent rang through the hallway. "You know you are supposed to be helping me with the party. If mother knows you are not helping she'll be pretty angry."

"The hired help is taking care of the party. You know you don't need my help."

"Oh yes I do," she insisted. "If you would leave spooky here alone, perhaps I would not have to be hunting you down. Now, are you coming or not?"

"It's all right," Destini said softly with a sudden sadness in her heart. "You go on ahead. I'll find my way around." Stephan turned to his sister.

"Shadae," he said calmly, "that was totally uncalled for. Will you please apologize and say her proper name?" Shadae tried to interrupt, but Stephan raised his voice, "Or you and I will have it out tonight and you don't want to get me angry. How would you like to be called names everywhere you go?" Destini tried to speak to Stephan softly but his deep voice overpowered her soft voice.

"Well," he continued, "I'm waiting!" Shadae stared at Stephan, and then rolled her eyes at him.

"I'm leaving and I'm going to tell mother." She turned and left Destini and Stephan standing in the hallway.

"Ugh!" Stephan shouted and hit the wall. Destini jumped with fright at the loud thud on the wall. She had never seen Stephan so angry.

"Stephan," she said softly taking a backward step, "don't worry, I'm fine. I'm used to it." Calming down, he apologized.

"I'm sorry, I didn't mean to frighten you, but you should not be used to people calling you names. You're too good." He touched her face gently and whispered, "And much too beautiful." He came closer to her face as if to kiss her luscious lips. Destini moved away slightly.

"Stephan," she said, "I think we should get back before your mother comes looking for you." Destini did not get a chance to finish the tour of the mansion but she thought, *"I have the rest of the evening to enjoy the party."*

Shadae went and complained to their mother and a few minutes later Sophia was looking for Stephan. The maid, Cindy, approached him.

"Stephan," she called timorously, "your mother wants to see you now. She is in the large blue room on the east wing."

"I beg your pardon," he said, struck by the bizarreness of it. "What is she doing over there?"

"I don't know, but that's where she is." She then looked at the floor. Stephan eyed Cindy suspiciously.

"Destini," he said, "come let me walk you back to the..."

"Stephan," Cindy interrupted, "that's okay. I'll walk her back. Your mom wants you right away."

"Mother can wait! I'll escort her back, thanks Cindy. If you'll excuse us." Cindy looked at Destini and left reluctantly. Stephan escorted her back and then left. Destini started to look for Yasmin but, couldn't find her. Everyone was dancing, laughing, eating, drinking and playing games. Destini wandered off alone since she couldn't find Yasmin. She went out on the large balcony. The balcony overlooked a beautiful garden with a lovely manmade waterfall. There were colored lights surrounding the fall. It looked so romantic and majestic to Destini. Destini wondered how a waterfall ran in the cold and did not freeze. *"How amazing."* she thought. A few minutes later, a couple wandered onto the balcony, looked at the waterfall, then left. Two other couples walked out to the balcony. A few more couples joined them. As Destini was about to leave the balcony, she ran into Sophia. She was decked out in a multicolored, silk, Ghanaian gown accented with a beautiful head-wrap. Her sleek and shiny hair fell passed her shoulders.

"Oh," said Destini shyly, "excuse me Ma'am, um, hi. You look great." Destini's heart pounded as she looked at Sophia's cold, mean face.

"Well," Sophia said loudly, "I'm glad you think so. I'm sorry I can't say the same for you. Now, who invited you?"

"Excuse me," the confused response sounded from her velvety voice. "What do you mean?"

"Do you speak English, child?" Sophia asked furiously. "Now, where is your invitation?" Destini felt as if all eyes were on her. She fumbled nervously in her purse for her invitation and handed it to Sophia.

"Stephan invited me," she said softly. Sophia took the invitation.

"Stephan should have checked with me first to see whether he should have invited you. Now, I don't appreciate you throwing yourself all over my son and hogging him all night. He has more important things to do."

"Mrs. Barronton, I was not doing such a thing. I'm not like that. I don't . . ."

"Well," she interrupted, "this is what I know girls like you do. You try to trap a nice young man like Stephan. He does not realize the kind of girl you are. But I am not stupid.   So, you," she pointed her finger at Destini, "stay away from my son." Sophia turned to leave. She stopped and looked Destini up and down.

"And where did you get that ridiculous outfit?" Destini felt so embarrassed and belittled. *"How,"* she thought, *"can an adult in the church be so mean?"*

"I'm sorry if you don't like it." Destini responded. "I happen to like the way I look." Sophia stepped towards her. By now, more guests had gathered on the balcony.

"First of all," she stated, "the braids you are wearing are unbecoming and fake. That thing on your head, is it supposed to be an Egyptian crown? You could not pass the test to represent any kind of royalty so stop pretending to be one." Destini was hurt by the unkind words spat out by Mrs. Barronton. She wanted her to know that she was proud of who she was and she responded stately and with respect for an elder.

"I'm sorry if you do not approve of me being royalty. God is my Father and since I am His child, I am a princess. That makes me royalty in its highest kind; so, you have no say on the matter Ma'am." Sophia stepped even closer with an icy coldness, speaking directly in her face.

"You are black, ill-bred and baboon ugly. You do not belong with any of my family. And that ugly white dress does not match that black skin. And if I were you I'd stick to my own kind." Sophia turned and left the awful, unkind words stinging in the air. Destini heard whispers and snickering among some of the guests. She was so embarrassed. She wanted to mouth-off Mrs. Barronton. But she didn't want to embarrass Stephan. She walked quickly off the balcony and found her way out of the mansion. She did not care how cold it was outside. It was friendlier out there. She cried as she started to walk home, not caring about the distance. Tears rolled down her beautiful dark brown face. She was too embarrassed to stop and call her father. Even the night sky seemed friendlier.

Inside the mansion, Stephan was looking for his mother and Destini. He ran into Yasmin while she was talking to Tasha.

With a surprised and concerned look on his face he asked, "Have you seen Destini? I've been looking everywhere for her."

"No, you both left together earlier," Yasmin answered. "Where did you go?" He turned to leave and she grabbed his hand, told him she was sorry and asked him if he wanted to dance. She then put her arms around his neck and came very close so she pressed against him as one hand caressed his back. Stephan looked at her with disbelief. Looking around, he told her he had to go. He left her with a disappointed look on her face. As he passed by some teens, he overheard their conversation about his mother embarrassing Destini. Stephan started to look frantically for her. On his way to the grand foyer, he ran into his mother. She was looking for him.

"Stephan, there you are. I . . ." Stephan interrupted

"Mom, I was told you embarrassed one of my special guests. You took her invitation from her?" His mother looked sternly at him.

"She had no right hogging you all night."

"Mother, she was not hogging me. How could you embarrass me like this?"

"Well . . ." Stephan was angry with his mother for being so inconsiderate to Destini. But he dared not say it, because he didn't want to get into an argument with her. He had to find Destini as soon as he could.

"Mother, I have to go!" She held unto his arm.

"Where are you going?" she asked desperately. But he freed himself, backed away and left quickly.

"I have to go!"

"Stephan, come back here. Stephan, Stephan," she called frantically, but he was gone. He went to the doorkeeper and asked if he saw Destini. He said a young lady of the same description passed there fifteen minutes ago. Stephan ran and got his Jaguar and sped off into the night. As he drove, he wondered if she was all right. How could she leave by herself? How could his mother do such an awful thing to one of his guests? He breathed a small prayer.

"Please, Father God, let Destini be all right." He finally saw a figure up ahead. "Oh yes, that's Destini all right." He knew her elegant, sexy walk anywhere. She was stately and beautiful. He pulled up alongside her, but she kept walking.

"Excuse me," Stephan said jokingly. "Your majesty, why are you walking? Your prince in shining armor has arrived with his royal carriage?" Destini was awfully cold, but she pretended she didn't hear him. He pulled up the car in front of her, got out, and walked over to her.

"I know you are cold," he said. "Don't you want a ride?" Everything around was quiet including Destini. She stood there shivering and staring as if looking straight through his chest.

"Destini," Stephan said softly, "you didn't have to leave."
"Oh yes I did!" she shouted with quivering lips and tears gathering in her gorgeous eyes. "And I don't ever want to go back to your awful castle." Stephan was truly embarrassed. He didn't know what to say. All he wanted was to hold Destini in his arms and comfort her. He stretched out his arms to hold her.

"Don't you touch me," she yelled as the tears wobbled down her smooth dark skin. "Why don't you go back to your wonderful mother?" The tears gathered more and rolled down her soft beautiful face. Stephan reached out and touched her anyway. His heart ached to see her crying. He wanted to hold her in his arms and comfort her.

"Your coat is too thin for this cold weather," he said. "I don't want you to get sick or feel cold; therefore, you are going into this car whether you want to or not." He held her arm firmly and she pulled back, but she couldn't escape his strong grip.

"Let me go!" she screamed and pulled again. "You just let me go!"

"No, I will not." They both struggled and Stephan, who was athletic, and was much stronger than Destini, seemed to be having fun.

"Destini, please," he begged. "Let's stop this. Let me take you back to the house so you can call your father. That is, since you want to go home. Though I really wish you would stay. But since you insist, just come back and call your dad. You can't walk home from here. Anything can happen. Moreover, it's cold. Please."

"You expect me to go back there after what happened? I'm not going back there, I'm not going back." Destini quivered and continued, "Your mom is rude and mean. And she hates me for no reason other than I'm American and my skin is dark. And to dislike someone because of her color and nationality is utterly stupid, primitive, backward and evil."

"I understand Destini, but that's not true. She's just fussy."

"Fussy! Fussy!" she screamed. "If that's fussy, you have to give me the new meaning of the word fussy. Your mother embarrassed me in front of a lot of people. She took my invitation from me and told me that I looked awful and called me a baboon." Stephan breathed deeply. He felt his gut hurting. Destini continued, "And you call that fussy?" Stephan was so embarrassed; he wished he had not left her alone.

"Destini, I'm very sorry. I don't know what to say. The actions of my mother were very inconsiderate. I'm not saying what she did was right." He looked up at the sky and paused. He then looked at Destini lovingly, "But, please come back to the house. You don't have to go inside the mansion. We can go to one of the guest houses near the mansion. You may call from there." Destini looked at Stephan and agreed to go back.

"Okay, as long as no one sees me." She responded quivering and finally decided to ride back with him.

"No one will see us," he said warmly. He opened the door and she stepped into the warm car. He knew he could allow her to use his cellular phone, but he really wanted her to come back to the house. They drove to one of the guest houses that were not too far from the mansion. It was much smaller than the ten-bedroom mansion. Destini thought it seemed more safe and homely. When they arrived at the house, Stephan got out and opened the car door for Destini. *"He's such a gentleman,"* she thought. She looked at him timidly.

"Thank you, Stephan," she whispered softly. He held her hand as she exited the car. Stephan looked at Destini. All he wanted to do at that moment was to hold and hug her close to him.

"This way," he said. She walked quickly out of the cold and into the nice warm house.

"Hmmm it's nice and warm in here." She looked about the room. It was in fact cozy. "Wow, this is nice," she stated. "I could live here, I love it." Stephan still looking at her as he usually did, in awe, wished too in his heart, that she could live there.

"This is one of our guest houses and my favorite." He added, "I'm glad you like it."

"Why do you have guest houses? There's so much room in the mansion."

"Yea I know, but sometimes we have guests with children and they want privacy. Sometimes when family or friends get married, the newlyweds stay in one of our guest houses." Stephan took her by the hand and placed it around his strong arms. Destini felt the rock hidden beneath his sleeve and did not want to let go.

"Come, let me show you around. This time with no interruptions." She took a breath and he escorted her from room to room. She saw a dining room, living room, a family room, and an indoor pool. She walked around the large recreational room and noticed how fun the room was with its game arcade appearance, and she loved it. She also saw three exquisite large bedrooms. Each bedroom had its own full bathroom. She especially loved the huge bathroom with a Jacuzzi in the master suite. She also liked the fireplace and the kitchen; they seemed cozy.

"This is a nice big house with semicircular stairs. It's wonderful, I love it." She was finally smiling. Even though she felt a little sad inside, she felt a lot better being in Stephan's company. "Gracious me, I feel better." Stephan felt as if his heart skipped a beat as he took in the entire scene. The serene soft light from the lamps was flowing gently on Destini's intriguingly beautiful face and he longed to hold her and kiss her precious soft lips. He moved closer to her.

"Destini," he said softly, and started to kiss her lips. She pulled away quickly and looked at the floor. Stephan apologized quietly, "I'm sorry, I don't know what got into me."

"Um, yea. Where's the phone?" she asked looking around, not meaning to ignore Stephan. "That's okay," she said, "but don't let it happen again." They stood and stared at each other in loving admiration. Stephan moved closer to her and she laughed timidly.

"Come on, where's the phone?" she asked. Stephan stopped and pointed to it. She stared at the phone, "That's a phone? It looks like a toy car." He smiled because he had bought it for that house. She called home and her mother answered. "Hi Mom, can dad pick me up now?

I'm not having as much fun as I thought." Etta sensed something was wrong.

"What's wrong, are you okay?" Etta questioned.

"Yes mom, I'm fine. I just want to come home now."

"Okay, but you may have to wait a while because Winston is out at the moment. But as soon as he comes in, I'll tell him. He won't be long, okay?" *"Oh well,"* thought Etta, *"Winston went to get something romantic for us. There goes the rest of our evening together, but maybe we can continue where we left off and spend a half hour together before getting her."*

"Okay Mom. Mom!" she called. "Wait, tell him to meet me outside at the left side of the mansion. He doesn't have to come in and get me."

"Outside?" Etta questioned, "Destini, is everything okay?"

"Mom, I'm fine. See you in a little while."

"Okay, Love, see you in about an hour and a half." Etta said.

"Yea, bye Mom." She put the receiver down and sensed Stephan staring at her. Destini felt shy to look at him, so she said in a playful, quipped cartoon-like voice and a funny-looking face,

"Whom are you staring at young man?" Stephan's eyes widened and he laughed deeply as if tickled.

"You're funny. I didn't realize you had such a great sense of humor. And in answer to your question, I'm looking at a beautiful chocolate princess." Destini's lovely face became serious, yet curious.

"Chocolate Princess," she stated softly, "Why do you call me that?" Stephan came closer to her and took her hand.

"My favorite sweets are chocolate," he responded. "Your skin looks like a beautiful, smooth, delicious dark chocolate. I love to look at it. Do you know why those girls are jealous of you? It's because your cocoa complexion always looks deliciously tasty and powder fresh. Your skin feels silky soft and I love to touch it." Destini felt like her heart skipped a beat as he gently caressed her face and arms. Goose bumps covered her body as Stephan's words touched her ears. She felt a glowing sensation flowing through her body. She wanted his gentle touch to continue, but she was taught by her parents not to play with fire because one thing can lead to another. She gently pulled away from him.

"Thanks for your compliments," she said shyly. "I appreciate them very much. I'm gonna go ahead and wait out front for my Dad." Destini did not know what else to say or how to react to such sweet, beautiful words. No one had ever said such lovely things to her. She just wanted to hug him.

"I have a better idea," he said quickly. "From here, I can see when he drives up and it's cold out there. So, do you mind staying in here until he arrives?" She didn't mind at all, she loved to be around Stephan. They sat together, talking, laughing and staring at each other. Every now and then Stephan looked out the window, hoping Mr. Taylor would take a little longer. Stephan felt his cell phone vibrating. However, he did not answer it.

Stephan made some mint tea for both of them. Destini thought it was delicious. He asked her about her family and she explained to him about her parents' plane crash. They talked about school and their parents. Stephan wished his mother was kinder. He said he prays that she let Jesus into her heart. Soon Winston drove up and Stephan saw the car. He waited about a minute before letting her know her dad was outside.

"I believe your father is here." He stood up, looked at her then at the floor. He looked out of the window sadly. "Yes, it's Mr. Taylor," he said disappointedly. He wanted to spend more time with Destini. He wished he could have driven her home instead, but his mother would have had a fit. He never got to spend time with Destini. She was always busy or studying or hanging out with Yasmin. They both went to the car, and Destini thanked him and got in. He watched as the car drove away. He thought about the sweet time they had just spent together.

Stephan was very sad to see her leave. He wished she could stay all night. He wondered how he was going to enjoy the rest of the evening. Nothing seemed like fun anymore. He checked to make sure all was going well with the party and was told his mother was calling and looking for him. He acknowledged the message and then ventured to his bedroom. His sister came to his room and apologized to him for her rude behavior. She begged him to return to the party. He finally decided to go back because he didn't want to get into an argument with his mother. He talked to a few of his friends and then stood on the balcony and stared into the darkness with thoughts of Destini.

22

Confusion

*O*n her way home, she told Winston what happened at the party because he wanted to know why she left so early and had to be in a house alone with Stephan. Winston was furious at Mrs. Barronton's behavior. As soon as he got home, he called her. He told her how immature and unintelligent she was for a woman of her age and so-called high society. He informed her that she was rude and needed lessons on how to treat decent human beings. She tried to argue with Winston, but he said he'd rather speak to sane, intelligent people, and he hung up.

Winston was quite angry. His wife tried to calm him down, but when she heard what happened she too was upset.

"Destini," she said calmly, "we will discuss this in the morning and by the way, you look gorgeous tonight."

"Thanks mom, I really needed to hear that. Stephan thought so too." Destini noticed that Etta was looking very nice, but she didn't mention anything to her since she was in her red satin night robe. Destini went up the stairs and thought, *"Etta always has the sweetest things to say, unlike Mrs. Barronton."* As Destini began to undress, the phone rang. She wondered who was calling.

"Destini!" Etta called. "It's for you." Destini went back downstairs to answer the phone. "It's Yasmin," Etta said quietly, "and she is not happy." Destini took the phone with a worried look.

"Hello?"

"Uh," came the response, "What are you doing home?" She continued at the high tone of her voice. "Why didn't you tell me you were leaving? And how am I supposed to get home?"

"Yasmin, I'm so glad you ca . . ."

"I'm extremely upset with you."

"Yasmin, let . . ."

"We came to this party together and you spent the entire evening with Stephan and then left."

"Yasmin, let me . . ."

"Some friend you ar . . ."

"Yasmin," Destini shouted, "can you just listen?"

"Okay, I'm listening."

"I'm sorry I left you at the party but, there's a perfectly good explanation as to why I left. When I returned from the tour of the mansion I looked everywhere for you but I couldn't find you and I . . ."

"Well, I was at the party but you weren't," Yasmin spat. "Destini, you just went off with Stephan. In the first place, why didn't you ask me if I wanted to come on the tour of the mansion? You know why you didn't ask me; because you wanted to hog Stephan all for yourself. Just because your Papa called you princess does not make you better than me Destini." Destini was getting upset. She thought, *"Why is Yasmin acting and talking like this, and I did ask her to come on the tour."*

"Yasmin," she asked, "why are you speaking to me like this? You know I don't think I'm better than you. What's going on? And I did too ask you to come on the tour." Yasmin ignored the question.

"What's going on?" Yasmin shouted, "You ditched me tonight and I'm supposed to be your best friend."

"Yasmin, wait, calm down. You're accusing me of silly things. Why don't I ask Winston to pick you up and we'll talk about this face-to-face." Etta was looking at Destini with amazement and curiosity.

"That's okay Destini, Mr. Taylor doesn't have to pick me up." Destini was still bewildered by Yasmin's attitude.

"Is your mom still at the party?" Destini asked.

"No, she's gone, and what does my mother have to do with anything?" Destini was stunned by Yasmin's response.

"Ah, um," Destini stuttered, "I just wanted to know if she is dropping you here, that's all. Yasmin what's gotten into you? Why are you so defensive with me? I'm sorry I left without telling you."

By now, Destini sensed something was wrong. "But I didn't know where you were. Where were you anyway?"

There was complete silence. Then Yasmin continued sharply. "Destini, I have to go."

"Wait, how are you going to get home?"

"Don't you worry," she responded sharply. "I have friends here that care enough about me to spend time with me. They will take me home. Goodbye." With that, she hung up without waiting for a response. Destini tried to talk, but Yasmin had hung up.

"I knew I shouldn't have gone to that party," she muttered. Still confused, she walked slowly away from the phone with the receiver still in her hand. While Destini walked away, Etta took the receiver from her hand. They sat in the living room together and Etta asked Destini if she was okay.

"What happened?" Etta asked curiously. "How is she going to get home? Does she need Winston to pick her up?" Etta waved her hand and softly said, "Hello." Destini snapped out of her daze.

"Ah, Um, no."

"Well, how's she gonna get home? Is she coming here?" Destini stared into space.

"No, she's not coming here. She got a ride from her..." Destini squinted her eyes as she questioned, "Her friends? What friends? Who was she talking about?"

"Well," said Etta, "maybe it's some friends from school. She'll call you in the morning. Now, why don't you go to bed? We have a long day tomorrow with your grandparents coming." She got up to go to her room. Etta watched Destini going up the stairs as if she was carrying a load on her shoulders. Etta sensed that something wasn't right with Yasmin, but she didn't know what it was. She felt sorry for Destini and wished she could make her happy.

23

Tears and Smiles

*T*he following morning, Destini woke up to hear Christmas melodies coming from downstairs. Her eyes wandered out the window to see snow clouds floating in the sky. *"Oh,"* she thought, *"why do I have to feel so sad on Christmas morning? It's supposed to be the happiest day of the year."* A faint thought of the night before with Stephan floated through her mind. A pleasant smile crossed her lips. "Just thinking about Stephan makes me feel so much better. Thank you, God. I needed a lift to get out of bed." But as she got up, she remembered Yasmin.

"Uh," she uttered loudly as she walked around her room. She thought she'd better call Yasmin to see what was up. She called Yasmin but Mrs. Michaels answered and told her that Yasmin was asleep. Destini went downstairs and helped her mother fixed breakfast. She called Yasmin an hour later, but her mother said she was in the shower. After breakfast, she called Yasmin again. Destini asked her mother to have Yasmin return her call, because Mrs. Michaels said Yasmin was very busy. Destini was getting upset because Yasmin always came to the phone when she knew it was Destini calling.

Destini didn't feel like doing anything. She felt weak inside. She couldn't bear the thought of Yasmin being upset with her. *"Last night was a disaster,"* she thought. *"but then it wasn't so bad after all, because she spent much of the night with Stephan."* The phone rang and she sprang to her feet to get it, but Etta answered it. Destini ran to the kitchen thinking it was Yasmin on the phone.

"Yes," Etta said smiling, "we'll see you then. . . . Okay mom Taylor. Uh ha.... How far away are you? . . . Great; we'll see you in an hour then . . ., okay, bye." Etta hung up the phone to see the look of disappointment on Destini's face. "Sorry, that wasn't Yasmin; it was Winston's mom and dad. They're on their way. They started out about three hours ago. It will take them about another hour to get here."

Destini hung her head and absent-mindedly brushed the top of the chair with her fingers.

"Yea, I heard," she answered solemnly and walked away.

"Destini," Etta said, "come and help me in the kitchen. There's a lot left to be done. This can help take your mind off Yasmin."

"Oh mom, I'm not going to be of much help. I'll just get in your way and mess up everything. Can I go and visit Yasmin? Please?" Etta looked at Destini and felt sorry for her.

"Okay," she agreed, "if you promise to come right back to help me."

"Yes," she answered brightly. Destini felt a surge of energy running through her. "I'll be right back." She dashed to the closet and got her coat. As she walked quickly to the door, Destini remembered she had a gift for Yasmin and Mrs. Michaels. She ran and got them, scurried to find a plastic bag to carry them in. She leaped out of the door and hurried through the gate. Etta called out to her to remind her to dress warmly. Destini was too excited to think about dressing warmly.

The snowflakes kissed her face as she walked quickly down the lane. Yasmin's house was not far. The falling snow disappeared without sticking because it was falling lightly. *"Perhaps,"* she thought, *"the snow will stick later."* As she approached the house, her heart started to get excited. Her pounding heart seized her breath slightly. *"Why am I getting so nervous?"* she thought. *"Yasmin is my best friend."* She walked upon the front porch and rang the doorbell. Finally, Vashti opened the door and a phony smile opened her lips.

"Hi Destini, how are you?"

"Fine Mrs. Michaels, Merry Christmas to you Ma'am." She said trying to catch her breath. Vashti smiled rather sweetly.

"And the same to you love." Vashti looked back and then asked Destini to come in. Upon entering, Destini discerned an unwelcoming spirit in the atmosphere. She wondered why Mrs. Michaels took so long to invite her in. She had never done that before. Destini nervously took the gifts out of the plastic bag and gave one to Vashti.

"I got this for you Ma'am, hope you like it," she said shyly. Vashti took the gift with a spurious smile.

"Oh, Destini thank you very much. That's so nice of you." Destini wondered where Yasmin was and why her mother was being exceptionally nice. She was always standoffish. Something was definitely wrong.

"Is Yasmin here? I want to see her." Vashti put the gift down.

"Destini, Yasmin can't see anyone right now. She has some things that I want her to finish. She might come by later." Destini stared at her, in total confusion.

"Something to finish . . . might come later?" she said looking at Mrs. Michaels. Unable to contain her emotions, she blurted, "MIGHT! Can't I see her just for a few seconds, please? I just want to ask her something."

"I'm afraid not. I'll have her call you." Vashti stepped forward as if to escort Destini out, but Destini sidestepped the suggestion.

"Call?" she said desperately, "Call? I've been calling all morning and she has not returned any of my calls. Is something wrong? Why is Yasmin doing this? I would like to see her right now, Mrs. Michaels." Vashti was getting agitated.

"Look here Destini, I'll tell her for you. I'm really busy at the moment. Yasmin's father is coming from out of town to visit and I have a lot of things to do and . . ."

"I have a gift for her and I want to give it to her myself. May I please?" she said tearfully. Vashti stared at Destini. She rolled her eyes upward with an attitude.

"I'll be right back." She walked away quickly. Vashti knew within her heart that she'd rather see Yasmin and Stephan together. She came back in a few seconds. She said Yasmin might come by later, and that Destini could give her the gift then. Destini wanted to know why she couldn't see Yasmin right away.

"Yasmin is upset with me isn't she Mrs. Michaels?"

Vashti sighed, "Why don't you go home," she responded, "and when Yasmin is finished, she will call you. Okay?" A sudden anger burst through Destini's being.

"Bye." She said curtly and stormed out of the house without taking Yasmin's gift with her. Vashti tried to call her back to give her the gift, but Destini was gone. Vashti felt somewhat guilty. She closed the door slowly. Yasmin stood near the top of the stairs and watched through the window as Destini went home.

Destini walked quickly and jogged intermittently as tears ran down her face. She didn't notice that the snow was beginning to stick. Feeling colder, she pulled her coat tighter. *"Why,"* she thought, *"why do people treat me this way? Yasmin is supposed to be my best friend."* The closer she got to the house, the angrier she became. She stormed into the house, crying. She was about to ascend the stairs when Etta came running.

"My goodness, Destini what happened? Are you okay?"

"She didn't want to talk to me." Destini cried. "She didn't even want to see me, and Mrs. Michaels was acting very strange."

"What do you mean acting very strange?" Etta asked. Then as quickly as she asked it, she dismissed the question.

"Don't worry about it Destini. Maybe there was some misunderstanding. Maybe she'll call you later." Destini walked to the family room with tears still falling and her voice wavering.

"I don't think so. If she wants Stephan, she can have him. Why should she be mad at me because I spent some time with him?" A quizzical look ran across Etta's face; she followed Destini into the family room. "It's not my fault that Stephan's mother threw me out of the party. But Yasmin doesn't want to hear what happened. Yasmin hurt me, Mom, she really hurt me. Why couldn't she just come out and tell me herself why she's mad at me?"

"Um, talking about Stephan," Etta sighed, "he called while you were out, and . . . whatta ya mean -- you spent some time with Stephan?" Surprised, Destini turned and looked at Etta, pretending not to hear the question. She felt as if a cool breeze had lifted her spirit.

"He called me?"

"Yep."

"What did he want?" Destini asked softly, calming down.

"To talk to you. He said he will call back in twenty minutes, and that twenty minutes is about up." Destini stared at the phone. Somehow, a little spring of joy flowed into her heart.

"He didn't say anything else?" she asked Etta. As Etta was about to answer, the phone rang. Destini stood up and stared at it again. Etta shook her head and smiled.

"Talk about on time, twenty minutes to the tee," she said as she looked at Destini and went and answered the phone.

"Hello? Yes, just a minute." Teasingly she whispered, "Twenty minutes to the tee," and extended her arm to Destini. "It's him, here." Destini took the receiver. Her heart raced as she greeted him shyly.

"Hello?"

"Hello," he responded warmly. "How are you today my sweet chocolate?" Etta went back to the kitchen to continue what she was doing.

"Fine," Destini responded blushing. *"He called me his sweet chocolate."* She searched for something to say, but her mind went blank.

"Um, Merry Christmas," he said warmly, "and how is your Christmas day going so far?"

"Um, so-so."

"Just so-so?" he questioned,

"Yea, just so-so."

"Well," interjected Stephan, "maybe I can do something about that and spice up your day. Do you mind if I come over later?"

"Uh?" His question took her by surprise. *"Stephan coming here?"* "Um, sure, I mean I don't mind."

"Great, what's the best time or is three thirty okay?"

"I'd have to check with Mom first. Just a minute." She ran to Etta. "Mom, he wants to come over at three thirty. Is that okay?" Etta looked over at her. "Mom, I promise I'll help you in the kitchen happily and clean up." Etta took a deep breath.

"Well," she said, "dinner is at three o'clock and what about dinner at his home? Don't you think his parents want him there since it's Christmas?" Destini looked confused, *"Oh no,"* she thought.

"I d'know. I'll be right back." She dashed back to the family room and picked up the phone. "Hello?"

"Hello."

"What time are you having dinner at your home?"

"Mother and father have a lot of guests over and I don't want to be there. I've already asked to be excused and they have agreed. And I'd really love to spend the time with you." Destini was quiet. She was happy but didn't know what to say. *"Oh, my goodness,"* she thought, *"he just comes straight out and says what's on his mind."*

111

"Just a sec, I'll be right back," she said quickly. She dashed to the kitchen doorway. "Mom, he doesn't have to go to dinner they----y," she took a quick breath, "Um, have lots of guests over. He's uncomfortable, so his parents said he doesn't have to be there." Etta looked at Destini.

"Really! Well," she looked curiously at her, "tell him four thirty is a better time."

"Okay." she said quickly and dashed off again. "Hello Stephan?"

"Hello."

"Is four thirty okay?"

"Perfect, see you at four thirty."

"Okay, see ya." He hung up and Destini smiled. She really wanted to talk some more, but Stephan kept it short and sweet. *"He's such a gentleman,"* she thought. She felt so much better now. She remembered Etta telling her when one door closes, God will always open another.

"Yes, yes, yes," she screamed with joy and jumped up and down. One of the best looking guys in school was coming to her home. Even though he was from a very wealthy family, he was caring and he loved the Lord. She went to the kitchen and helped Etta cook and clean up. Destini decided that she was not going to worry about Yasmin because today was Christmas. The birth of Jesus is good news. Plus, she saw lots of gifts with her name on them.

"Now that you are settled," Etta asked, "when are you going to open your gifts?" With joy written all over her beautiful face, Destini looked at Etta, who noticed the difference in Destini's countenance. Gladness filled her heart. She thanked God for His goodness and for answering her prayers to let Destini feel happy. She decided that Stephan seemed like a very nice young man.

"That's right, Mom," Destini said, "the Christmas gifts. Okay, when I'm finished with this I'll be happy to open them." She went and hugged Etta and told her that she was the best mom in the world and that she loved her. Tears were welling up in Etta's eyes.

"You just go on and finish up what you are doing young lady," she said. Destini felt happy inside now. She decided not to let Yasmin spoil her holiday spirit. She thanked God for filling her heart with His love and for allowing Stephan to call her. She thanked God for the beautiful day He was about to give her.

24

Holiday Dinner

Winston's parents arrived two hours late. The snow had fallen two inches, so they drove much slower. Destini was hoping that their late arrival wouldn't set back her meeting with Stephan. Grandma and Grandpa had to talk, give their gifts and then freshen up before dinner.

It was about time for dinner. Winston, Etta, Destini, Grandma and Grandpa Taylor all settled in the living room. They talked about everything. They told Destini how lovely she was growing, but Destini wasn't focused much on what they were saying. She kept watching the time. Grandma Taylor loved her adopted granddaughter. Grandma always sent her money, new clothes, and books. Grandma Taylor enjoyed the weekends she spent with Destini.

When Destini first moved to Massachusetts, she told Winston that the lovely American girl was smart and intelligent. She was also humble and had a heartwarming spirit. She was thankful to God that they adopted her. They were about to dine, and Grandma was watching Destini very closely. She wanted to see how much Destini had changed as she grew up. Grandma Taylor spoke English very well, and sometimes she loved to interchange her English with Jamaican dialects. Sometimes she teased Destini and spoke in Jamaican patois. Grandma had taught Destini to understand and speak Jamaican patois. Destini learned very fast. Grandma had her eyes on Destini. And as everyone was enjoying the conversation, she noticed Destini's attention to the clock and asked in her strong Jamaican accent.

"Dear, weh yuh inna 'urry fi guh so?" Everyone stopped talking, and all eyes centered on Destini. Destini's eyes widened, and her expression was the picture of innocence.

"Huh?" she responded, with mouth opened and eyes searching from person to person. "I'm in no hurry to go anywhere, Gra'ma."

"Well," said Grandma, "yuh cud ave fool mi." Grandma looked at everyone and said, "Im a watch di clock, an den a koo pan im watch." She then looked at Destini and asked, "Destini, wahta young gyal like yuh wurry bout, uh? Yuh ungry or yuh 'ave wah bwoyfren a cum ya?" Everyone laughed and Destini looked at Etta.

"Looking at my watch? Gra'ma, I'm not worried, and I don't have a boyfriend. Yes, I'm a little hungry though," she said and looked at Etta again.

"Yea," Grandma said, "I'm ready to eat, too."

Everyone rose and Winston asked Etta if Selina was still coming. He hoped she had changed her mind. Etta said she was coming, but she said to start dinner without her because she might be late. As they walked toward the dining room, Grandpa Delroy overheard the conversation and wanted to know who Selina was. He forgot who she was.

"Who is Selina again?"

"Why, it's Etta's younger sister, dear." Grandma said.

Grandpa Delroy thought for a while. "Oh, I knew that." he added. She's coming with all those children."

"Don't worry Grandpa, they've grown a lot older now. They range from age fifteen to seventeen now," Etta said, as she put her arms around Delroy's shoulder.

"Ooooh," Grandpa said, "the troublesome age." Everyone laughed.

Destini frowned. "Excuse me Grandpa, but are you trying to tell me something?" she asked softly.

"Oh no dear, you are a very nice and lovely young lady." They all gathered around the dining table. Winston blessed the food and they all said, "Amen."

Then Grandpa turned to Winston, "I was wondering when you were going to finish your preaching. When I see food, I'm ready to eat." Everyone laughed and Winston looked at his dad and shook his head with a smile. Dad was always joking around.

The dining table looked exquisite. The embroidered white satin tablecloth was painted with sprinkles of tiny cream and red flowers. Each setting had its own silver platter with matching silver utensils. The decorative red napkins matched the place mats. The entrees consisted of jerk chicken, tasty vegetarian peppered steaks with green and red peppers, and curried goat. The curried goat was Winston's favorite for Christmas and holidays, and Etta had mastered it. Being American, Etta didn't know much about West Indian cooking at first, but she learned all about it after she married Winston. Destini had helped cook the rice and peas (red kidney beans and rice with coconut milk). She baked the sweet potato pie with marshmallows on top. She also prepared the cheesecake, baked potatoes, and salad. Grandma Rachael baked black cake, a traditional Caribbean fruitcake they have at special occasions. Etta's sister Selina loved lasagna, so Etta baked lasagna with ground turkey. Destini also prepared her favorite drink, Piña Colada, and everyone loved it. Etta mixed Winston's favorite drink, sorrel (hibiscus). The red flowers were put in boiled water, and then cinnamon and ginger were added. It was covered and set aside for twenty-four hours. The red drink was strained, sweetened with sugar and a little lime juice. The tasty drink was served with ice.

"Hmmm, this drink is delicious," Delroy announced. "I think I will take the entire jug back with me." Everyone laughed.

"You have to pass me first." Winston countered. They laughed again. The doorbell rang and Etta excused herself to open the door. It was Selina and her three children. Selina, who was about the same height as Etta leaned over and gave her sister a kiss on the cheek. Her red woolen knit suit was well tailored. She came in with a bright smile.

"Hello everyone," she said cheerfully. Grandpa smiled and quipped, "Hello, you' a kinda late. We have all finished the dinner."

"Well," she quipped back, "Grandpa Delroy, you sure have a lot left on your plate. I'll take what's on your plate and share it for me and my kids."

"You've gotta be very swift to get this one," Grandpa laughed and then everyone laughed.

Everyone was seated and eating. Destini felt a little out of place even though Etta always made her feel at home. Everyone there was related somehow, but she hadn't seen any of her blood relatives in years. Aunt Selina's fifteen-year-old daughter, Delores, was staring at Destini. When Destini smiled at her, Deloris shook her head to show off her straightened bouncy, shiny hair. She then looked away without smiling. Destini thought, *"There she goes again, dag. Why does she always have to show off? Just because she has swingy long hair, and she claims that the boys at her school always want to date her. Well I can shake my swingy long braids too."* Destini waited for Deloris to look at her again then quickly swung her braids. Deloris did a double take, and Destini laughed slightly.

"What's so funny?" Etta asked.

"Nothing, just something swingy shot through my head," she answered quickly and smiled.

Everyone was talking and enjoying the dinner. Destini was watching the time. It was about time for Stephan to come. Selina's two sons were staring at Destini. She wished they would stop staring. Jeffrey, the sixteen-year-old, was charmed by Destini's beauty. Tony, the seventeen-year-old was fascinated by her eyes, breasts and braids. Every time Destini looked at Jeffrey, he looked away quickly. When she looked at Tony, he stared and smiled enthusiastically. Destini said to herself, "Please hurry up and come Stephan." Finally, the doorbell rang. Destini bounced from her chair almost knocking over her glass and plate.

"Oh, my goodness," Grandma stated, "child be careful, you expecting someone, eh?"

"Oh, I'm sorry." Destini looked at Etta. "Sorry, Mom, I'll get the door."

"Well, you're up already, so you may as well." Etta smiled softly. Destini stopped and washed her mouth in the powder room as quickly as she could. She walked hurriedly to the front door. Destini straightened out her dress and wiped her face lightly. She looked in the mirror by the door to make sure she looked okay. Her heart pounded as she reached for the doorknob. She opened the door to see Stephan standing there with a beautiful bunch of flowers and a warm smile. Her heart raced as she lowered her head and stared. *"Oh, my goodness,"* she thought, *"he looks so masculine and handsome in his long coat and jeans with his classic haircut. Oh, my goodness, what beautiful eyes."* She realized she had not asked Stephan to come in and that she had not responded to his hello.

"Oh," she said shyly, "Happy Holidays, I mean, come in." Stephan smiled, stepped in and greeted her with a light kiss on the cheek. Destini felt his soft lips touch her cheek and she prayed that she wouldn't melt away. Feeling shy in his presence Destini did not know what to do.

"You look great Destini, I love your dress. I love to see a woman wearing lace. And I love what you did to your braids." Destini lowered her head as usual, and smiled coyly like a little girl would, with knees knocking and shoulder pressing as if about to meet. She thought, *"He said I'm a woman. He is such a man. Wow."*

"Thank you," she responded, while shifting her eyes away and then back at him. He noticed the little girl-like gesture and his heart skipped a beat. "Wow," she made him feel big and strong in her presence.

"Here," he handed her the flowers, "these are for your mom." Destini looked up at him with a surprise.

"Uh?" She took them. "Oh, thanks." Still surprised, she took his coat when he handed it to her. She said, "Everyone is in the dining room. Come, let me introduce you to them." As they proceeded to the dining room, she was a little disappointed that the flowers were not for her, even though she was glad that he was there. She thought, *"It would have been so nice to get flowers from Stephan."* As soon as they appeared in the dining room, Grandma was ready to say something.

"Oh my, now I know why you almost knocked over your plate. And who is this handsome young man?" She looked him up and down and everyone stared, especially Deloris. Destini noticed her stare and thought, *"I wish she would stop staring at him."*

"Everyone, I'd like to introduce to you, Stephan Barronton," Destini stated.

"Oh, my!" Grandma said again as she touched her face. "Not only is he handsome but he carries a classy name too." Everyone laughed.

"Stephan," Destini continued. "I'd like you to meet Grandma and Grandpa Taylor, Selina Davis and her three children, Tony, Jeffrey and um, Deloris." Deloris stood up, walked around and shook his hand. She flirtatiously swung her hair back.

"It's certainly a pleasure to meet you." She smiled with a look of 'I want him.' Etta and Selina looked at each other with an 'Oh, no' look. Destini was caught off guard and she forgot what she was about to say. Stephan smiled with embarrassment and looked at Destini, then said to Deloris,

"It's nice to meet you too," he said. Stephan thought, *"Oh no, not another forward girl."* Destini thought, *"I don't believe her."*

"Aunt Etta," Deloris turned to Etta, "is Stephan joining us for dinner?" Etta was now startled herself.

"Um," she looked at Destini, and Destini's eyes widened.

"Oh no, "Stephan added quickly, "I was just visiting, thanks anyway." Stephan looked at Destini, moved his eyes to the flowers and back to her.

"Mom, these are for you. They're from Stephan," she said.

"Oh, thank you," Etta said with delight. "These are beautiful. This is very special, Stephan." she stood up and kissed him on the cheek and he blushed.

"Uh, um," Winston cleared his throat. Everyone laughed.

"Are you sure you won't join us for dinner Stephan?" Etta asked.

"Thanks, but no thanks Madam. Perhaps I'll stop by for dessert a little later if that's okay with you Madam."

"Uh, um," Grandma cleared her throat. "What is this?" she said. "You come to visit the young lady but, bring flowers only for the mother." Everyone looked at Stephan then Deloris added her two cents.

"That was a very nice gesture on Stephan's part, right Destini?" she said with her eyes glued on Stephan.

"Definitely," Destini answered, thinking, *"I wish she'd mind her own business."* Stephan looked at Grandma and walked around to where she was sitting. He knelt beside her and took her hands. With his handsome face looking into hers, which did not show any signs of wrinkles, he charmed her kindly.

"Grandma," he said, "you are very intelligent, because with age comes wisdom plus beauty, and I will certainly take your advice, because grandmothers usually know best." With that, he kissed her hands and stood up

"Wow," she said, "not only is he handsome and has a classy name, but he is charming and intelligent as well." She looked at Destini, "Young lady, you certainly know how to choose your friends."

"Everybody," Stephan announced as he looked at them, "it was really a pleasure meeting all of you." He looked at Destini, "But I do not wish to interrupt your meal any further. If you will excuse us." He moved towards Destini.

"You're not disturbing us," Deloris blurted out. "You can stay as long as you wish." She looked at Destini, "Right Destini?"

Destini looked at Etta, "Um, Stephan may be back later, Deloris. Mom, I'll be in the living room, okay?"

"Okay dear," Etta returned. Winston looked at them with concern and then at Etta. They both disappeared through the doorway.

"Oh my," Selina said with envy in her voice. "Does he have an older brother?"

"Yea," answered Winston, "but he is married and lives in England."

"Figures," she said. "The nice ones are usually too young or married."

"You know his mother," Winston added, "Mrs. Barronton. He's the young man who spoke out at the meeting in opposition to his mother."

"Oh really; that was him?" Selina responded, "I'm surprised that he is here."

"I love his accent," Deloris said. "He speaks so manly."

Her brother Jeffrey pushed her head. "Oh, shut up and stop drooling over someone else's man," he said.

She slapped his arm. "Why don't you mind your own business?" she shouted. "I saw you and Tony staring down Destini as if she was the first girl you ever saw or that she's anything to look at."

"Okay children," Etta said sternly. "That's enough."

Jeffrey was embarrassed at what his sister said, so he lashed out at her. "And I saw you trying to flirt with Stephan. You were so rude and inconsiderate to Destini."

"Well," said Deloris, "at least I'm better looking than her. She's too black for him." Everyone gasped except Selina. Etta stood up with fire in her eyes. She didn't want to start an argument, so she calmed herself down.

"That's enough I said. Now both of you stop this instant," she calmly and sternly said. "Deloris, the true thing that really counts about a person is what's in here." She pointed to her heart and her head. "I do not want to hear you or anyone else mentioning anything negative about Destini's skin. She is a beautiful girl inside and out." Etta sat down and then asked, "Dessert anyone?"

"I would love some," Grandma said brightly. "Now, tell me all about the young man, Stephan."

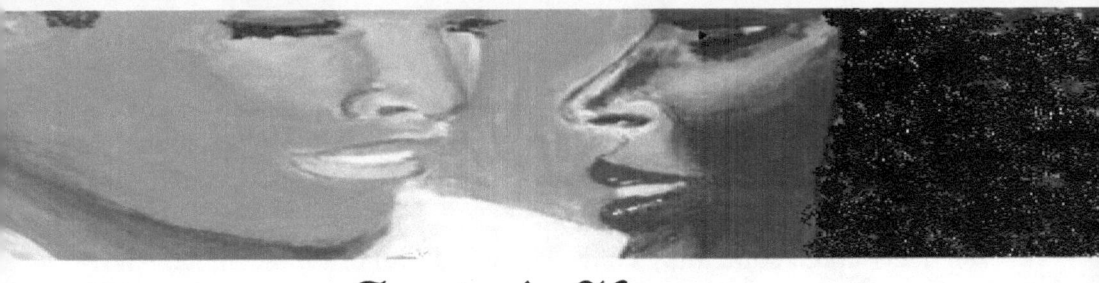

25

Stephan's Heart

*D*estini *was particularly happy to have Stephan Barronton over. She was happy to show him off, especially to Deloris. She always acted as if she was better* than Destini. She frequently bragged about all the good-looking boys in her school who liked her. Now the cards were turned and Destini did not have to brag. She had a good-looking guy, in the flesh, at her home, and she knew Deloris did not like it.

"Stephan, are you sure you wouldn't like something to drink or eat?"

"I'm sure. But I'll accept your offer later," he said, looking lovingly at her with a twinkle in his eyes. "I'm just so glad to be here with you. Food doesn't strike me now. I'm sorry to interfere with your dinner ..."

"Oh," Destini said gladly, "I'm glad you did. Here," she pointed to the sofa. "have a seat." He thanked her but offered her to sit first.

"Please, after you," he said politely. She looked at him and just wanted to throw herself on him and hug him, but she smiled shyly.

"Thank you," she said. They were both nervous and did not know how to start the conversation, but Stephan quickly thought of something.

"So, how has your day been?" he asked. She looked at him.

"Not so great, but great."

"Great, but not great," he repeated, looking away and smiling slightly, "Hmmm."

"Yea," she said.

"Well," he added, "tell me first about the not so great, then the great." They looked at each other and laughed.

"Excuse me," a voice interrupted. They looked around to see Deloris. *"Oh Lord,"* thought Destini, *"Not again."*

"Would you like something warm to drink?"

Stephan politely stood up. "No thanks, but I appreciate your asking."

"How about something cold? There is sorrel or Piña Colada. And by the way, Destini made the Piña Colada."

"Oh really, you didn't tell me." Stephan said, looking at Destini.

"So," insisted Deloris, "want some Piña Colada?" Stephan, still standing, wished she would leave.

"Thanks, but no thanks," he said calmly. "Perhaps later."

"I love your accent," Deloris smiled flirtatiously, "and your haircut is cool--real cool." He looked at Destini, and then said thanks to Deloris. A moment of quietness created a sense of awkwardness. Stephan looked at the floor wishing she would leave.

"Deloris," Destini said, "thanks for asking. Um, we'll let you know if we need anything, okay." Deloris looked at Destini with envy and reluctantly walked out. Stephan sat down and looked at Destini as if to say something, but he changed his mind.

"Now, what were we talking about?" he asked. They looked at each other. "Anyway," he said, "what's up with Yasmin?"

"Whatta you mean?"

"Well, she and my sister were on the phone for about an hour this morning, and I know they do not like each other." Destini half smiled with surprise.

"Oh! That's nice. Do you know what they were talking about?" Destini started to feel a little light headed. She wondered what was going on with Yasmin.

"I guess they were talking about the party this evening. I can give you a ride over there, that's if your parents don't mind." Destini was quiet and her face, a picture of puzzlement.

"What party?"

Deloris and Jeffrey passed the doorway and Deloris giggled and said, "Stop Jeff." They passed again and she giggled loudly.

"Um," Stephan said. "Is there anywhere else we can go where we won't be disturbed by our audience?" Destini was happy he asked.

"Um, yea. Let me see if it's okay with my parents." She walked quickly through the archway. Upon returning, she saw Deloris and Jeffrey trying to talk to Stephan.

"Um, Stephan, we can go . . .," Destini said.

"Go where?" Deloris quickly interrupted.

Destini looked at her and answered, "Deloris, Aunt Etta wants you."

Deloris sucked her teeth. "Uh," she exclaimed, "what does she want now?" Stephan and Destini walked through a hallway and into a cozy room with a sofa, two big chairs, and an office desk with a matching chair.

"This is Winston's office at home," she said shyly, "and at least this room has a door." Stephan looked around the office.

"Wow, and I thought my father loved to read."

Destini looked at Stephan. "Winston doesn't have half the number of books your father has," she said. He looked at her and smiled. Destini saw the same warm loving look in his eyes that she saw at the previous night's party. She started to get nervous again.

"If you don't mind," he said, "I have to go out to the car. I'll be right back." He left and then returned shortly. "You know," he said, "I like the smell of your house. It's nice." She looked at him, admiring his whole being.

"Oh really? What does it smell like?"

"I don't know yet, but when I do, I'll let you know." They both sat down on the sofa.

"So," Destini inquired, "tell me about the party."

"You talk as if you did not know about it," he said, looking at her.

"No, I didn't know about it," she answered. Stephan seemed puzzled.

"Maybe Yasmin is having it another time." He paused. "No, Yasmin said it would be today. It's a Christmas get together. I believe Shadae, Pete, Tasha, Kimmie, Tammy, Charles, Keith, and Nolita, are going." Destini was getting angry but tried to keep calm. She wondered why Yasmin was behaving like this. Especially, after all the things they had been through together. Stephan looked at Destini curiously. "Were you invited to the party?"

"No. I didn't even know there was one."

"Hmmm, I wonder if it is a surprise?" he questioned himself. "She didn't say it was." He then said aloud, "Let me call Yasmin." He took out his cellular phone.

"I'd prefer that you didn't call her," she said softly. He looked at Destini. He was puzzled as to why she said that. "Why?" he asked.

"Because, well, I don't think Yasmin is talking to me." Stephan looked at Destini with surprise written all over his handsome face.

"I don't understand. Why not?" he asked. Destini's eyes filled with tears, and she told Stephan the whole story, everything from the night before to the morning. Stephan was quiet. He didn't know what to say. He walked around the room in his manly gait, and then sat down.

"I am shocked. That explains," he finally concluded, "why Shadae was rather happy around the house this morning and what she said about Yasmin."

"What did she say about Yasmin?"

"Something to the effect that Yasmin finally got." They sat in silence. Then Stephan looked at Destini lovingly.

"Hey Sweet Chocolate," he said romantically and touched her hair. She loved when he called her 'Sweet Chocolate.'

"Yes?" she answered softly.

"I'm really charmed that you are spending this holiday with me. You know, I'm not going to that party after all."

"No?"

"Shhh," he touched her lips gently. "Nothing you say will change my mind. If you don't mind, I'd love to spend the rest of the day with you." Destini blushed. "Please take your mind off of Yasmin and the party and let us enjoy one another's company," he said. She smiled and looked into his handsome face.

"Okay, I'd love to spend the time with you," she agreed shyly. Stephan turned down his phone so he would not hear the ring tone. He got up and picked up something from behind the big chair.

"Close your eyes." She smiled and closed her eyes.

"You may open them now." Upon opening her eyes, she stood to her feet. There was a small dainty white basket with sprinkles of white baby's breath mixed with beautiful red roses and lively green ferns. Hidden inside was a small beautifully wrapped box of chocolate. The basket was lovely and delicate. Destini couldn't contain herself. With mouth wide open she exclaimed, "Oh, O my goodness, gracious me."

"For you," he said with a twinkle in his eyes. She took the flower basket.

"Oh, my goodness," she said. She thought to herself, *"And I thought he only brought flowers for my mother."* Tears filled her eyes.

"Oh, Stephan," she said softly, "no one has ever done this for me. And chocolate," she touched her chest gently with her delicate fingers. "Thank you very much. I really needed that." She gave him a big hug. Stephan was so happy for the hug that he pulled her closer. He wished he could hold her forever. When her soft body touched him, his temperature rose and he wanted very badly to kiss her.

From the first time he saw Destini, he loved her. He knew she was the one he wanted to be with forever. Stephan decided that he was going to follow through with his feelings. He lifted her face gently to his and kissed her. He was surprised that she didn't resist. A warm, strong gentleman holding her in his arms swept Destini away. *"Hmmm"* she thought, *"his lips are so soft."* She felt him pulling her closer and tighter. She was really starting to feel the heat, especially as he began to kiss her neck. Those feelings scared Destini and she pulled away.

"Stop, please, stop." she said desperately fearing to look at him. Her heart was pounding yet, she wanted him to continue holding her. Stephan didn't want to stop so he moved forward and Destini backed away and said a little louder, "Stephan, no, please." He stopped and looked at her. No, he didn't want to stop. He wanted to continue to touch her soft body and kiss her soft full lips. He took a deep breath, then looked away and back at her again. Destini wanted to feel his strapping arms around her again; but she knew she had to stop. One thing could lead to another.

"I'm sorry, please don't be upset with me," she said softly. "I didn't mean to lead you on. I . . . I was just so happy."

"That's okay," he calmly said. "You don't owe me any explanation. My heart pulsated with love in answer to your dangerous, ceaseless beauty. Not only are you beautiful on the outside, but inside as well." Destini wondered where he got such lovely words. He was so manly. He moved towards her and held her hand. Destini felt a tingly excitement going through her hand when he touched her. *"Oh, my goodness,"* she thought, *"what's happening to me? I feel so weak when he touches me."*

He touched her face with the other hand and continued. "Now I know and understand why Adam ate the fruit that Eve gave to him. He was overcome with fascination by her heavenly beauty and her womanly allure. You've captured my heart, Destini, and I will never be the same again." They stared at each other lovingly. Being alone with Stephan had weakened Destini.

He pulled her close to him again and kissed her gently and intensely. This time she didn't resist, because the words that he spoke made her feel like he respected and cared about her. Stephan felt her soft, warm body in his arms and wanted to caress her all over. His hand was reaching to caress her breast, but he asked God to give him the strength to resist the temptation. He gently pulled himself away. Destini felt his body next to her, and her mind flashed to what her mother had told her, and she knew he wanted her.

He walked away, turned his back to her and stood as if in a deep trance. She felt embarrassed and she turned away also. They were both silent for a little while. Stephan knew deep in his heart that he wanted to make love to Destini. He felt like he wanted no one else. But she was only sixteen and he seventeen. *"Why does life have to be this way?"* he thought. *"My sister didn't wait and even though she took precautions she still got pregnant. Moreover, how could he disappoint God?"* He looked at Destini, *"Oh my God,"* he thought, *"I love her so much. She's the most beautiful girl I've ever seen. She is so soft and feminine."*

126

"Destini?" he finally asked gently.

"Yes," her soft voice said as she turned towards him.

"Will you be my steady girlfriend?" Destini didn't know what to say; she looked at him in wonder, *"Stephan Barronton wants to go with me?"* She didn't know what to say.

"Um, I . . . I don't know. Winston and Etta would never allow that."

"Well," he stated, "let's ask your parents later when their guests are gone or tomorrow."

"Well, she told me that I'm not allowed to have a steady boyfriend until I graduate from high school, but I could have friends." Stephan looked at the ceiling then at her.

"And in the meantime," he softly and gently asked, "what am I to do with these feelings that I have for you? I love you, Chocolate." Destini had never had any young man say that to her, especially one like Stephan. She was dumbfounded. They stood and stared at each other, wondering what to do next.

"Okay," Stephan finally said, "I'll speak to your parents."

"No, it's okay. It's better if I ask them. And suppose they say yes; what about your mother?"

"We'll find some way around it," he said. Stephan sat on the sofa and asked Destini to come and sit with him. She wanted to sit with him, but didn't want him to kiss her again, at least not now. Those feelings were too strong for her to handle right now, and her parents might walk in. She stood and looked at him. He assured her he wasn't going to try anything.

Destini sat beside Stephan and he took out a little box.

"Here, Merry Christmas." She looked at him with surprise and admiration.

She took the gift and said, "Thank you." She held it out and looked at it.

"Well," he asked, "aren't you going to open it?"

"Sure," she said delightfully, still admiring the box. "It's wrapped beautifully." He smiled as she opened it. Inside was an exquisite, dainty, gold bracelet watch, with a face cover and small diamonds around the face. It was beautiful. She stared at it in wonder. She had never received anything so exquisite.

"Oooh, my, my goodness," she said delightfully. "Oooh, my goodness." repeated Destini excitedly. "This is so----o beautiful. Oh, Stephan." She hugged and kissed him on the cheek but pulled away quickly. "Thank you. This is precious. The gift I got for you is not nearly as elegant as this."

"Destini, you didn't have to buy me a gift."

"And why not? I wanted to." Stephan sat there, admiring the joy on her face and wishing that these precious moments would last forever.

"Look at the back of the watch." Destini turned it over and looked. It was engraved.

She read, *"To Destini, my Sweet Chocolate Princess, with all my love, Stephan."*

"Oh Stephan, this is very, very special." Tears filled her soft brown eyes. "Thank you. I really, really appreciate this. You sure know how to be a man. You're so strong and rugged and you are the best."

"Wow!" Stephan thought. He felt satisfied. Destini really made his Christmas a happy one. It was the best Christmas he had in a long time. Stephan remembered last Christmas when he stood staring through the window as the snow fell, thinking about Destini. He had wished then that he could spend the day with her. This year, his wish came true.

"What are you thinking about my handsome prince?" she asked. A boyish blush crossed his face.

"Handsome? Prince?"

"Yes Stephan," she said softly. "You are so masculine and a true man indeed. I love your gorgeous eyes. And you are quite handsome and since you are a son of God, you are a true prince." Stephan did not know what to say. He stared at her and wished he could hold her and kiss her all over. He then looked around the room shyly.

Destini stared at the flower basket with a pleasant smile on her lovely face. Stephan noticed her stares. He thought about the box of chocolate that was hidden among the flowers. He had brought the expensive chocolate for her while vacationing in Europe. Stephan wanted to see if she liked them. He asked her if she would like to try one of the chocolates and she agreed. Stephan opened the box and as she was about to take one out, he held her hands gently and proceeded to take the chocolate out himself. She looked at him wondering if he was about to eat one first. He slowly guided the chocolate to her soft, pliant lips. *"Oh, my goodness,"* thought Destini, *"this is so romantic."* She closed her eyes and opened her mouth to receive the tasty treat. Stephan sat and stared at her, admiringly. Oh, he wanted to kiss her again, but he controlled himself. He waited for her approval; and watched as she chewed the chocolate finishing with a long deep sigh of satisfaction. She opened her eyes and seemed to want more.

"Hmmm, Stephan, this is delicious. It's so good. Where did you get this?" He smiled. *"Wow,"* he thought, *"she really made my holiday a happy one."* She fed one to him also. He graciously accepted it. He told her he bought it just for her while vacationing in Europe. Destini thanked him and told him he was truly a prince. Stephan smiled and looked shyly around the room again, then stared at her.

Destini laughed and said, "I'll be right back." She went and got his gift. On her way back, Etta who was in the hallway, stopped her.

"Destini?"

"Yes mom?"

"Is everything okay?"

"Yes mom. Look what Stephan gave me for Christmas." Destini held up her hand and showed Etta her delightfully glistening watch. She hoped Etta wouldn't be upset at the expensive gift.

"Oh, my goodness; let me see. That's beautiful. I bet it cost a pretty penny. Why's a young boy like that giving such an expensive gift?"

"Mom, he works for his father after school and on weekends. And it's not the gift, but what's in his heart."

Etta peered at Destini curiously and asked softly, "So, what's in his heart?" Destini was startled by Etta's question.

"His heart?"

"Yes, his heart."

"Well," she paused, "I don't know." She looked at the floor quickly, then at Etta. Etta looked at her motherly.

"I'll talk to you later when he leaves, Mom."

"Then you'll tell me where his heart is?" Etta watched her reaction closely and Destini looked at her and smiled, then hugged her.

"Mom, see you later," she said softly. Etta stood and watched as Destini walked through the hallway, into Winston's office and closed the door. She was concerned about Stephan and Destini. She knew that young people could get themselves into trouble. She went back to the family room where the others were settled after dinner.

26

Circle of Color

*W*inston overheard Etta talking to Destini, and he preferred that Destini and Stephan stay in the presence of everyone.

"Was that Destini you were talking to, Love?" Winston asked.

"Yes Sweetie."

"Is everything okay? I don't like the idea of her being locked up in a room alone with a young man," he continued.

"Yea," Grandma butted in, "especially a rich, handsome young man. They think they own everything and they can get whatever they want." Etta interrupted, putting her hands on her hips.

"Excuse me, but Stephan is a decent young man and I trust Destini. Winston and I taught her well and she needs to know that we trust her."

Selina butted in, "Trust or not, young people should not be given too much freedom." Deloris looked at her mother and pouted.

"And you can keep looking at me like that young lady, but you know I am telling the truth." Etta was offended that Selina compared Deloris' behavior with Destini's.

"Well," said Etta, "each person has his or her own personality and I can't swear for anyone, including Destini, but in the past, she has proved that she can be trusted." Etta knew that Deloris caused much trouble for her mother. Destini was not allowed to keep company with her because Deloris was flirtatious and stuck up. Plus, she thought she was better than Destini. Etta looked at Selina and wondered where Deloris got that attitude.

"Furthermore," Selina said, "this is Christmas. Why are two young people locked up in a room all by themselves and the rest of us are out here?" Etta finally realized why Selina had been acting odd since Stephan arrived. She wanted her daughter to get a chance with Stephan because he was handsome and from a wealthy family.

"Well," Etta said, "if they wanted to be out here with us they would be here." Selina looked at Deloris then at Etta.

"Is he her boyfriend?"

"Really, Selina," Winston jumped in. "What kind of question is that? You know our rules around here."

"Well," insinuated Selina, as she pointed her finger at Etta and Winston. "They could be intimate friends and you wouldn't know." Everyone was silent. Selina continued. "Now, why would a rich, handsome young man, who probably could be almost anywhere he wanted to be, want to be here? You said his parents were having special guests, but he didn't want to be there. He decided he would spend the entire afternoon and evening with a girl like Destini."

Etta looked at Deloris then at Selina, *"Now,"* she thought, *"I know where Deloris gets her foolishness from. Oh, the nerve of Selina."* Winston focused his attention strongly at Selina.

"Let me explain," Selina said looking at Winston.

"Please do." he said sternly looking up at her.

"What I mean is, Destini isn't rich. Plus, she's not outgoing and she is an orphan. No one knows her real parents or relatives. And I'm sure his parents are not happy that he is here." Etta stood there as if stiffened at her sister's words. She wanted to slap her so hard.

"Come on, Etta, you know what I'm talking about. Don't look at me that way." Etta looked at Selina angrily. Here was Selina, her own sister, who knew about Destini's past. She knew about the hard life Destini had as a child. She was standing there with her puffed-up self, putting Destini down. Etta was afraid to open her mouth because she knew that when she did, what she had to say would not be very nice. She took a deep breath and sat back down. She didn't want to embarrass Winston in front of his parents.

"Etta, do you remember when we were kids?" Selina continued. "We had boyfriends and mom and dad didn't know." Everyone looked over at Etta as Selina continued. "What I'm saying is that Stephan must be getting something from Destini to want to be around her a . . ."

"That's it!" shouted Etta, standing up and pointing her finger. "We may have had boyfriends, but at least I didn't sleep with any boy, and you need to shut up. You don't know what you're talking about. Destini is a decent girl and she's outgoing and popular. And she does not have to be rich for any red-blooded young man to notice her. I saw your sons staring her down." Etta pointed to the nephews as she spoke. Winston stood up and calmly walked over to his wife.

"Love, that's okay," he touched her arm gently. "It's okay Love, come on calm down."

"No, I will not. She comes in here accusing my daughter of acting the way her daughter does."

"UH," Selina shouted, "Deloris is not like that. She is my blood." Deloris was enjoying this disagreeable conversation. "My daughter is beautiful. She has a beautiful complexion and she is outgoing."

"Destini may not be my blood, but since adopting her, it's like she is a part of me and Winston. So, it's like she is my blood. In reality we are all blood anyway because Adam and Eve were our first parents. So, there! And for your information Destini is beautiful. She has a beautiful complexion and is popular," Etta shouted.

"Destini," shouted Selina. "She's so black!" Winston was not very happy with her statement. He really wanted to throw Selina out, but that may cause a world of trouble. She had a lot of nerve condemning someone else's looks. She was not half as pretty as Destini. Plus, she had the nerve to talk about Destini that way. She had always made passes at Winston, but he ignored her advances. Even at dinner, she gave him an alluring look.

"Yes, you are so right," Etta added. "She is so black and beautiful with the smoothest skin and the most beautiful sparkling brown eyes. She has class and she is a wonderful person to be around."

Grandma interjected, "Oh yes, I can attest to that."

"You are just jealous. God in his love," Etta continued, "created that color skin and the Bible says God's skin looks like bronze burnt in the fire." Etta wasn't angry anymore; she was excited as she continued. "So, that makes God a dark-skinned being. And in Genesis God said, 'Let us make man in our own image.' So, Adam and Eve were dark-skinned people. So, don't bring all that to me about Destini being s—o black. It doesn't matter what color you are, it's all beautiful." She pointed to Selina and Deloris. "So, go tell God that you don't like black skin. I bet He'll tell you a thing or two. See, He doesn't play that. You know, Selina, you all need to get rid of that

133

stupid slave mentality about which color is better. It's about time we all stop this foolishness. I am sick of it." She sat down. "Sick of it." Grandma and Grandpa clapped their hands delightfully.

Selina shoved her palm towards her sister's face and said, "Whatever."

"Well said, I like that Etta," Grandpa Taylor said, "I've never heard it quite said that way before."

"Tse, well," Selina said, "God shouldn't have created black skin and white skin. They are opposite and very unbecoming. I'm brown skinned and proud of this color. It's the best natural tan there is. Everybody wants it. Pale people cram the beaches to get it and even pay millions of dollars for tanning each year. Dark people use skin whiteners to get it. What can I say, there must be something special about my beautiful brown skin." Grandma was quite agitated. She looked at Selina with pity.

"Young lady," Grandma said, "first of all, you have no right to tell God what color skin He should have made. Furthermore, I am very happy that you are proud of your skin color. We need a lot more people to be proud of the way God has created them." Then Grandma pointed to herself, "But, look at me. I am dark skinned. My son Winston and our three other children are dark skinned too and none of us use skin whitener to lighten our skin to look like yours."

Selina interrupted, "But Gra'ma, you're not as black as Destini."

"Doesn't matter," responded Grandma. "It's still black skin. We are proud of what God has made and, excuse me young lady, I would not want to be your color. If I were to be born again, I would like to come back this color. But if I were pale, as you put it, I would still be proud of my skin color."

"But Gram-ma..."

"Excuse me young lady, I am not finished. You, young lady, do not have the right to condemn anything or anyone because of the way they look or what color they are. You are not the Creator. Everyone is beautiful in his or her own way. And if you do not like the way dark skin and white skin look, I am advising you to shut up or go away somewhere where you won't see anymore black or white skin." Selina said, "Whatever," and her eyes widened as she sulked with twisted lips. She tried to interrupt, but Grandma went on.

"Wait, wait, wait; you had your time to talk. Now it's my turn." Selina pouted, and folded her arms with an attitude.

"People like you go around and hurt innocent, beautiful people. You poison the air with your unwanted hate and selfishness. Just because someone is "unbecoming" to you, does not make him or her bad or promiscuous. So, if you have nothing good to say, I'll say it nicely this time, close your lips."

Selina was waiting to respond, "Gra'ma this is a free country and I have the right to say what I think."

"Well, young lady, what you think stinks." This time, Winston and Grandpa Delroy were making faces and glancing at each other. Winston was thinking, "Uh, oh, I think I'd better stop this before it gets out of hand."

"See," Grandma continued, "this is a free country and I have the right also to say what I think. You are rude, and you have the nerve to talk about my beautiful granddaughter that way." Grandma got up from her chair. "And let me tell you something else young lady. I am sixty-nine years old, and I have traveled the world--Europe, Africa, the Middle East, the Caribbean, Asia, and the Americas." Wonder filled the minds of everyone present, including Selina. "And the best looking persons I have seen are not black, or brown or tanned, neither were they white. The best-looking people are those who were kind, pure and loving. Now, if you want to talk about color; the black skin has a powdery, smooth satin finish that glows with a mysterious elegant beauty and resembles polished ebony. The white skin has a certain glowing freshness of soft beauty that is like a lovely spring day. The brown skin is like gold or smooth bronze that won't quit." She pointed to Selina, "Now, you try and figure that one out." Then Grandma sat down. Grandpa was sitting there nodding his head affirmatively.

Grandma then concluded softly, "But you see, it does not really matter how we look on the outside. It is what is in here." She gently touched her head and her chest. Selina turned away and went for her coat. "But notice I said really matters, because we should care about our outward appearance." Selina looked with embarrassment at everyone, then at her sister.

"Thanks for a lovely dinner," she said. Her children got up to get their coats, but Deloris was not ready to leave yet. She wanted to see Stephan and try to talk to him again. She wanted his phone number. Selina continued as she put her coat on, "It was very," she paused in slight anger as she struggled to put on her gloves, "interesting being here, but I have to go." Winston was joyous; Selina was leaving. *"Yes!"* he thought, *"Everything will get back to normal. She's argumentative and always thinks she is right. It's such a joy to see her leave. Please leave, hurry, hurry."*

~~~~~~~~~~~~~~~~~~~~~~~~~~~~

*W*hy does each generation adroitly and unknowingly teach the next to hate themselves, and to prefer others above their precious own? Ignorant folks never stop to think about the priceless minds that are messed up.

Could skin color be an accumulation of melanin in varying degrees for each person? Na—a, it couldn't be that simple with all the backward primitive fuss. Skin color would not be emphasized out of context if people stopped to ponder the beautiful things of life. Therefore, why do some folks spend all of this undue attention to something that is insignificant? Is there something hidden that is not taught or spoken of? Makes you wonder.

Each human being was born with an outer covering (skin). God in his love allowed many shades of skin color. We ought to teach our children to accept these variations and stop spreading lies.

According to The Book; one day we all have to give an account to the Great God of the Universe for all the things we say and do. Ecclesiastics 12:14.

136

27

Etta's Concerns

*D*estini *went back into the office and gave Stephan his gift. He was happy and proud to get a gift from the girl he loved.*

"Destini, I will always keep this pen. It is lovely." He looked at her, kissed her on the forehead, wishing he could hold her, and kiss her soft, full lips again. "Thanks." He breathed softly. Destini looked at him shyly and didn't have to wonder if he liked her small gift. He was so appreciative.

"You're welcome," she answered shyly. They sat and talked about lots of things. After a while, she decided to go and see if anyone was calling her or discussing her. She thought she had heard her name a few times. Stephan decided to go also. At the arched doorway entrance, they saw the back of Selina with her coat on.

"I think my aunt is leaving," she whispered.

"Yes," Stephan said as he put his thumb up. Destini looked at him and smiled. Stephan continued, "Now I can come out and socialize without being clawed by your cousin." Destini looked at Stephan again Chuckling.

"Ooooh," she said and growled. They both laughed. Destini appeared at the open archway, smiling.

"Leaving already?" Selina looked at her and half smiled. Everyone was quiet. Destini wondered what happened. Everyone except Winston seemed solemn. Deloris tried to talk to Stephan, but he said that it was nice meeting her and stepped inside the family room. Selina and her children were out, and into the cold, and on their way home.

"So," asked Grandma, "what were you two up to?" Destini hung her head down and smiled as she looked up at Grandma.

"We were exchanging Christmas gifts and talking about school Grandma."

"Christmas gifts?" Winston butted in.

"Yes, Christmas gifts dad. Look what Stephan got me." She showed her gorgeous watch first.

"Whoa," Winston's eyes widened.

"Hmm, young man, you do have taste." She ran back to the room and got her beautiful flowers.

"Thank you, Sir." Winston looked at Stephan with curiosity.

"Look what else he got me." She showed them the flowers. Oh, she wished Deloris was there to see them.

Grandma said, "Oh, I see you did not forget the flowers after all. Young man, you are good. You were trained well." Stephan smiled.

Etta sat and stared. Stephan looked over to catch her glaring eyes. He smiled and looked away in his usual calm manner. He was beginning to feel a bit uncomfortable. "You saw Destini's watch, Love?" Winston asked, but Etta was in another world far away. "Etta?" Winston repeated, raising his voice a little. Etta seemed to return from her trip with a puzzled expression.

"Uh?" she said and stood up. Winston stood up and walked over to her and held her arms gently and said in Jamaican dialect,

"Ooman, whey you'd de?" Etta looked at him and put her hands on her hips.

"Really," she stated. "I haven't been anywhere. I've been here just thinking." She then looked at Stephan and asked him if he would like something to drink.

"Oh Mom, that's okay. I'll take care of that," Destini said.

"No, that's okay Destini," Etta insisted. "Come Stephan." Etta walked quickly into the kitchen. Stephan stood up to go.

"Uh, oh," he thought. *"Lecture time. I wondered why she was staring."* He walked slowly towards the kitchen. Out in the kitchen Etta was getting something light for Stephan, but she was studying him closely.

"Stephan," she asked, "why such an expensive watch? Destini is young and I want her to finish school. She doesn't have time for this male-female relationship. She is busy with pageants, voice lessons, music, dance lessons, church, and her family." She showed him various cookies, fruits and cakes. "Which would you like, please?"

"The cookies and the grapes, please. Thank you, Madam."

"You're welcome." Destini walked in with the most gorgeous smile on her uniquely beautiful face.

"Oh, Stephan everyone loves the gifts you gave me." Stephan was drowned in her beauty and her smile. It seemed like she floated over to him. Etta watched them and Stephan felt awkward.

He glanced quickly at Etta and said casually, "Great."

"Destini?" Etta asked, "are you going to have any dessert?"

"Sure Mom."

"Here Stephan, you can sit here."

"Thanks Madam." Destini sensed something wasn't right. She looked at Stephan then asked him if he was okay. She looked at Etta, hoping everything was alright and sat at the table with Stephan.

The rest of the evening was spent with everyone together telling jokes and laughing. It was eight o'clock when Stephan excused himself. He told them it was the best time he'd had in a long time and he was glad to have spent the Holiday with them. Destini was very excited. She thought her day would be wrecked, but Stephan made it beautiful. *"God is so good,"* she thought. *"He really blessed me today. Thank you, God,"* she prayed in her heart.

When Stephan got home, his mother wanted to know where he had been. He told her he visited one of his friends. She scolded him and said his sister had been calling him to come to Yasmin's party all evening. She wanted to know why he didn't answer his cellular. He calmly said, "I must have turned it off. Um, thanks mom," and excused himself to his room. Late that night Shadae came home and confronted Stephan for not showing up at the party. Stephan left the mansion and drove into the city to look at the huge lighted Christmas tree. He stood and stared at the lovely decorations. He wished that Destini was with him. He thought about the two of them there together, arm in arm. He hoped that one day that will happen.

28

Sophia's Wrath

*S*chool started two weeks later after the Christmas dinner at Destini's home, and Yasmin discovered that Stephan had spent Christmas with Destini.

One of his friends who knew his car saw it parked at Destini's home. Yasmin was exceptionally jealous, but she felt badly about the way she treated her best friend. She allowed Shadae and Tasha to talk her into having that party and to stop talking to Destini. At times she was lonely even though she hung with Shadae and Tasha. They didn't pay her the attention she wanted and their conversation wasn't much to listen to. Now, Yasmin wished that she and Destini were friends again. They used to have a lot of fun together. They had two classes together but during classes Destini sat by herself. She did not feel she could trust Yasmin anymore. Yasmin wanted to apologize desperately, but she didn't know how to approach Destini. At different times during the day, she saw Stephan and Destini staring at each other and smiling.

Destini asked Etta if she and Stephan could go steady. Etta said no, but he was allowed to visit. They were also allowed to talk to each other in school. Stephan drove Destini home every afternoon after school. Tasha and Yasmin were jealous, especially Tasha. She wanted to pull Destini's braids out. Yasmin still liked Destini very much and preferred her company to Tasha and Shadae.

When Stephan came home from school one afternoon, he was summoned to the library. *"Darn,"* he thought, *"wonder what this is about."* Upon entering the library, he saw his mother sitting in the large cushioned swivel glider, rocking chair.

"You finally reached home!" she said softly in a cold manner. "What took you so long to get home?" she asked calmly.

"Mother, I always come home at this time."

"It should take you only," she raised her voice, "ten minutes from school."

"Mother, I stop and talk to my friends. What is this, only Shadae is allowed to stop and talk to her friends?" His mother stood up and looked him straight in the eyes, her very being surrounded by an atmosphere of ice.

"Don't you dare talk to me like that," she declared. "And you will stop, starting today, taking that black baboon home. I don't want you to call her or speak to her in school." Sophia walked closer to him, placing her hands on her hips, all decked out in her checkered baby blue, and white woolen business suit.

"Stephan," she shouted, "Do you take me for a fool? You thought I wouldn't find out that you spent Christmas day at the wench's house?" Stephan was furious because of the names she was calling Destini.

"She is not a wench or a baboon. Her name is Destini." he shouted. With that statement his mother walked up to him and slapped his face.

"Don't you dare speak to me like that! Where do you think you are, at LaVona's recital, in front of my sister?" she screamed.

"Well you need to stop calling Destini Pearson Taylor names. How would you liked to be called unbecoming names? I am sick of you and Shadae calling her names."

"Now you listen to me and listen very carefully. Don't you tell me how to talk! If you continue to disobey me, I will send you to one of the academies in England or to a private school in Sweden, and I will take that car from you." Stephan loved his car. It seemed like it was the only independence he had.

"Take my car?" Stephan was still angry but reserved. "That car is mine. I paid for it from my own money that I earned." She looked at him and came even closer.

"You are my son. You are under age." Stephan wished this conversation would end. Why did his mother have to be so overbearing? She raised her voice. "You live under my roof.   You

142

eat my food. My signature is also on the Jaguar. Do not push me. You know I can get ugly and you know how I feel about that ugly girl." Stephan looked his mother square in the face.

"Destini is not ugly."

His mother looked at him while placing her hands on her hips, "She is ugly, ugly, ugly, like a gorilla." Then walking away slowly she said, "No son of mine is going to get mixed up with that. Now, go and do your homework."

Stephan looked at the time because he knew his father would be waiting for him.

"Mother, I've already done my homework and father is expecting me at the office..."

"I've already spoken to your father and he does not expect you today. By the way give me your cellular."

"Mom . . ."

"Now!"

"Mom, I'm the one who pays the bill for this . . ."

"Now!" she screamed. Stephan reluctantly handed the phone to her and walked out quickly. Stephan was hurt and angry. He wished he had a place to run away. But he went to his room and thought it through. He had to find some way of letting Destini know what was happening. Meanwhile, at the Taylors, the phone rang and Destini answered.

"Hello?" There was no answer so she repeated, "Hello?"

"Yes, may I speak with Mrs. Taylor." Panic struck Destini upon hearing that voice. "One moment please." She placed the receiver down and wondered why on earth Mrs. Barronton would want to speak to Etta. She went and got Etta.

Etta cautiously answered. "Hello."

"Good afternoon," came a solid greeting. "I am asking you," she stated coldly, "to keep your little black orphan child away from my son."

"Excuse me, orphan child?" Etta asked, "You wouldn't be referring to Destini?" There was complete silence on the other side of the line. Destini stood by listening and wondered what was going on.

"Don't you have an orphan that you adopted Mrs. Taylor?"

"You must be referring to Destini because she's the only daughter we have." Etta said emphasizing Destini's name.

"Look here," Sophia said sarcastically, "you just keep your orphan from Stephan."

"Mrs. Barronton, I can't stop your son from seeing or talking to Destini. They are in the same school and they have some classes together." Sophia cut Etta off sharply.

"You bet I can stop my son from seeing or talking to her. I have already. You need to do your part." Etta got upset and told Sophia she did not take orders from her and then scolded Sophia about her behavior to Destini at the holiday party. They argued back and forth and Sophia made it known that she did not invite and would not invite someone like Destini to her home. She said that Destini was black, sneaky and untrained. Etta let her know, if Destini was so sneaky, how was it that her daughter, Shadae, was the one who was pregnant? Sophia was furious. She screamed and forcefully jammed the receiver down. Then she took the phone and threw it across the room. The maid came running in to see what was wrong. Mrs. Barronton screamed her out of the room.

Mrs. Taylor hung up the phone and calmly said, "Wow, for a lady in high society she certainly behaves uncultured." Destini's despondent face watched Etta carefully. She knew Etta was angry, especially since she was very quiet. Later that evening, Etta called Destini to the family room to speak with her. Etta's serious expression told her something was not right.

"I do believe," she said, "you understand the gist of the conversation I had with Mrs. Barronton earlier. She doesn't want you hanging out with her son. And I prefer that you do not keep company with Stephan. I want nothing to do with that rude and insulting woman. I don't want to get into any more squabbles with her. So, I am asking you," Etta noticed Destini's shoulder's drooping and the dreadful expression overshadowing her. Etta stopped her sentence quickly.

"Well," she stood up and walked away thinking deeply. She remembered how much fun they all had whenever Stephan was around. Etta finally said, "Stephan is always welcome in my home. I won't stop him from coming here." She turned and looked at Destini. "But perhaps for his sake it's probably best that you stop any kind of friendship; especially at school, and at least for now. Mrs. Barronton says she has already stopped Stephan from talking to you. I don't know what she has threatened him with. But she is rich and powerful, and you don't know what she will do. You are both under age and if Stephan really cares about you like you told me he does, well, he will wait until you're grown." Destini was very disappointed. She lowered her head and stood up quietly.

"Okay mom, if that is what you wish," she said trying to contain herself. She asked to be excused and walked quickly out of the room and ran up the stairs and straight into her bedroom. She threw herself on her bed, which was comforting, and she cried and cried. She had finally found a guy who cared about her. He didn't even ask her to have sex. He was such a gentleman and he wasn't phony. He reminded her so much of her real father. He was gentle and loving, yet strong and masculine. How could someone like him be related to Sophia Barronton? Destini felt much hate for Mrs. Barronton. She was so evil. How could someone like her go to church every Sabbath, call herself a Christian, and sing praises to the Lord? The phone rang and a second later Destini heard her name called. She jumped up and opened her door.

"The call is for you," Etta called out from the room.

"Who is it mom?" she asked with a stuffy nose.

"A friend of yours from school probably. She said her name is Jenny."

"Jenny, I don't know any Jenny. I don't want to talk to anyone."

"Okay. Hello, I'm sorry she can't come to the phone right now." Destini listened and then closed her door. She heard her name called again.

"Oh," Destini wailed. "What now!" she said to herself.

"Destini," her mother shouted. "She won't hang up until she talks to you." Destini finally went and got the phone in her parents' bedroom.

"Hello?"

"Hello," said the unfamiliar voice. "Is this Destini?"

"Yes, who's this?"

"Oh, hi; my name is Jenny. How are you?"

"Fine, can I help you?"

"Just a minute," she said. Then Destini heard his warm and friendly voice.

"Hey Chocolate."

Destini's heart raced. "Oh, gracious me, Stephan?" she said, as her fingers gently touched her chest as if stilling her heart. "How are you and where are you? And who is Jenny?" Destini felt jealous about another girl being around Stephan.

"She is Keith's cousin. And how is my princess?"

"Fine, now that you called." Stephan wished he could be with Destini to touch her and to smell her lovely hair and hold her close to him.

"I need to see you, and soon," he whispered. "Can you meet me after school around the back near the farmhouse?" Destini was so happy she wanted to scream.

But she calmly and happily said, "Sure, see you Monday." Stephan then realized that he had to take Shadae home on Monday. Her mother didn't want her driving to and from school. He had to work early on Tuesday. He decided that Wednesday was a better time to meet. Destini knew she'd see him during the school hours even if they couldn't talk, but she waited anxiously for Wednesday.

"I know my mother called your mother" he said sadly, "and she is not very happy with Mrs. Taylor. She said your mother called Shadae a whore." Destini knitted her brow together and shouted.

"What? I was standing right there. Etta only said if I am so sneaky, how was it that her daughter, Shadae, was the one who was pregnant?" At that moment they both did not know what to say. Stephan knew Mrs. Taylor wouldn't have said such things about his sister.

146

"I thought as much," Stephan said. "Somehow I couldn't see your mother saying something so crude. I have to go. Destini, I wish I could stay longer but I'm at Keith's home and he doesn't want his parents to see me on the phone because they're close with my parents. Bye my beautiful chocolate queen."

"Thank you, and goodbye my handsome prince," Destini exclaimed while smiling. They both laughed because it sounded corny, but they didn't care. They wished they were together.

Etta was not very happy when she heard from Destini and Anita Jones, that she was said to have called Shadae a whore. She wanted to slap Mrs. Barronton. Before Destini left for school Monday morning, Etta told her she could invite Stephan over. She told her "I wouldn't stop you from being friends with Stephan as long as nothing intimate develops and you keep up with your school work."

29

Confrontation

*D*estini was filled with joy. Etta was allowing *Stephan to come over their house whenever he could make it. At school, she and Stephan passed each other in the hallway* without saying anything. They just stared at each other. He knew his sister and her friends were spying on him. He couldn't wait until Shadae left to live in Sweden with a relative, to have her baby.

Wednesday, after school, they met in the back of the school. He was so happy to see her. He hugged her so close to him. They made sure no one saw them. Destini told him that Etta was allowing him to come over whenever he wanted. Stephan was happy to hear such good news. He couldn't stay with her that day because he had to go straight to work. The next day he had to go to his cousin LaVona's recital. Saturday, he had to go to church with the family and spend the entire day with them. Destini and Stephan just smiled and stared at each other at church. On Sunday he had chores to do. Destini noticed that Stephan's mother was keeping him busy. He promised he'd try to see her Sunday evening or Monday, and he'd try to come over after school.

Sunday evening Stephan went to the shopping mall with some of his friends. He took one hour out to visit with Destini. They didn't get a chance to be alone because Winston and Etta were with them. They were all seated in the family room discussing different topics when Stephan turned to Etta.

"Mrs. Taylor," Stephan asked, "are you going to open night, Tuesday?" She looked at him.

"Yes, why do you ask?"

"Just curious," he said and hung his head down. He continued, "I believe my mother will be there also." Etta was still looking at Stephan.

"Why are you telling me this? I think that as a parent of two children at the school your mother would be there."

"No reason Madam. Just thought you should know."

"Why?" insisted Etta. He looked at her with a worried face.

"My mother can be rude and mean at times Madam. I just know that you are a sweet and wonderful person and . . ." he paused, then continued, "just thought that you should know Madam." He stood up. "I think I should be getting back now. Thanks for allowing me to park my car around the back and to visit with you lovely people." They all stood up and Destini accompanied him to his car. He looked to see if anyone was watching, then pulled her quickly to him and kissed and hugged her. He wished they could hold each other forever. He then kissed her on the forehead and said he would see her Thursday evening. It would work out perfectly, because he had to get something for his father this side of town and would stop by. Destini felt peaceful after seeing Stephan. He was gorgeous and well mannered.

Back in the family room, Etta wondered why Stephan had brought up the topic about his mother.

"I don't know Sweetie. Maybe Stephan was trying to warn me that Mrs. Barronton had something up her sleeve for Tuesday evening."

"Well," Winston concluded, "you'd better be on guard for the wicked witch of Barronton's castle."

"Oh, my goodness," said Etta, "I thought this was over."

Tuesday afternoon on her way home from school, Yasmin tried to talk to Destini but failed. Destini ran almost all the way home. She wanted to go home, shower, eat and put on something nice to go back to school with her mother. She didn't want to argue with Yasmin about anything, so she pretended she didn't hear Yasmin calling her.

Yasmin wanted very much to talk. Finally, she made up her mind and called Destini. Destini told Etta to tell Yasmin she was busy and that she would return her call later when she returned from open night. Yasmin was not going to open night but when she heard Destini was going, she decided to go. Mrs. Michaels was surprised because Yasmin swore she was not going to open night.

Destini and Etta arrived early. Etta wore a frilly white blouse and black slacks. Etta did not want to run into Mrs. Barronton, so she went and talked to each of Destini's teachers as soon as she arrived. Even though Etta arrived early so she could leave early, Sophia Barronton scouted around to find her. She came dressed in a peach silk suit with gold and white trimmings on the pockets and collar. Etta wanted to slap her face for her actions towards Destini at the Christmas party and for saying that she called Shadae a whore, but she controlled herself. After Etta finished talking to the teacher, she decided to go to another class.

Etta said to Destini, "Let's go to another classroom. I don't care to see this woman and her family." Destini didn't want to go because Stephan was there.

"Let's go Destini."

"Okay Mom." On their way out, Shadae bumped into Destini.

"Watch where you're going, whore." she hissed. Destini was embarrassed and angry. How much more should she endure from Shadae Barronton? She looked her straight in the eye, then at her belly.

Destini said assuredly, yet with shyness, "It takes one to know one." Shadae's English accent rang out as she quickly glanced at her mother then back to Destini.

"Who are you talking to like that? I am not a whore." Everyone present looked on in astonishment as she continued. "After all, I was not the one all over Stephan at the party." Stephan and Etta interrupted. He told Shadae to stop bothering Destini.

Etta said, "Young ladies, stop this right now. This is ridiculous." With Etta's interruption, this gave Sophia the chance she was waiting for.

"I don't appreciate," she said rather loudly and with great pains to pronounce her words clearly, "you," pointing to Etta, "or anyone in your forsaken family addressing my daughter as a whore. She is from a well-bred family and a decent home." Etta looked at Sophia with pity and touched Destini on the shoulder.

"Come on, let's go," she said and turned to leave. Sophia was offended that Etta ignored her.

She shouted, "Excuse me; I'm talking to you Taylor. I deserve an apology from you." Etta just wanted to get away. She and Destini walked out of the door. Mrs. Barronton followed along with the other nosy families who were anxious to see the outcome. They admired the Barrontons.

"I said I want an apology," she shouted. Stephan was so embarrassed.

"Mom," he said, "can't you give it up." She turned and slapped his face and spoke between her teeth, "Don't you be rude to me boy." Stephan was doubly embarrassed, especially since Destini was there. Mrs. Taylor answered, "How can I apologize for something I didn't say?"

"You did say it," Shadae shouted. Etta looked at Shadae and felt sorry for her in her state of mind and condition.

"And when did you, Shadae, hear me say you are a whore, dear?" At that moment Yasmin and her mother approached the scene. Destini and Yasmin stared at each other. Yasmin lowered her head and looked at the floor with disgrace. Shadae looked at her mother and then looked at the floor.

Mrs. Barronton answered. "You said that to me the other day on the phone and I don't appreciate you referring to any of my children as anything bad." Etta put her hands on her waist and walked toward Sophia.

"Mrs. Barronton, you know that you are lying," Etta said. Sophia's mouth dropped open and Etta continued, "You know very well what I said. I'll remind you then. I said . . ." Mrs. Barronton quickly interrupted. She didn't want anyone to know, as if they did not already know, about Shadae's pregnancy.

"Please don't call me a liar, and I don't have to be reminded of your words. You and your little black orphan had better stay out of my way." At those words spoken by his mother, Stephan turned and left. Yasmin tried to talk to him, but he raised his hand as if to stop her and continued toward the exit stairway. Mrs. Taylor was totally disgusted with Mrs. Barronton's constant throw down remarks about Destini. She came at Sophia with fire in her tongue. Dr. Wycham Barronton approached in time to hear.

"For a supposedly well-bred woman, you sure come across as an ignorant fool." Sophia's eyes and mouth popped open. Etta continued, "You strut around here as if you are queen of this city; and everyone has to bow to the queen. You claim that you are of African descent yet you are embarrassed of your own people. You are not better than Destini because of your peachy bright skin. God created all skin colors. If you don't like the dark brown ones, tell Him about it when you're in hell, because that's exactly where you are going if you don't change your nasty, stinking attitude, and stop lying." Someone in the hallway shouted, "Amen!" Mrs. Barronton tried to interrupt, but Etta continued.

"I'm not finished yet, you evil woman." Wycham scratched his head and Sophia turned to see him looking up at the ceiling as if nothing was going on.

"How can you stand there and let her speak to me that way?" Sophia demanded. Wycham looked at her. He knew his wife somehow got herself into this mess. He stated quickly, yet calmly, "Woman's quarrel. Where's the teacher?" He disappeared into a classroom.

Sophia shouted as she looked at Etta, "I don't have to stand here and take this."

"You are the one who started this," Etta said, "so if you dare leave, I'll pull every hair out of your head and tear your clothes off." Everyone started to whisper and talk. "Since you don't know, how to behave like a Christian woman," Etta continued, "I'll show you how to be a worldly, market woman, because I'm not afraid of you." Stephan came back at that moment and noticed the expressions on the faces of the people. Sophia turned and answered firmly, "And I am not afraid of you either."

"Good!" Etta shouted as she walked closer. "It's much more decent to pick on someone your own age."

Destini looked at both women and said softly to Etta, "Mom, come on let's leave now, please." Etta ignored her. "You asked me," Destini said quickly, "not to fight in school. How come you're doing different?" At that, Etta stopped and looked at Destini. She saw worry, pain, fear and such innocence in her beautiful face. Etta looked at Sophia and wanted to slap some sense into her but, changed her mind.

"I don't have time," she said, "for your foolishness because if I follow you, I'll sin and disgrace my God. Come on Destini." Sophia found a good opportunity to gloat as Etta and Destini turned and walked away.

"That's right. Go ahead and leave. You know it's better for you to leave, because I have what it takes and you don't." With a sudden stretch of anger in her voice, Mrs. Taylor turned and exclaimed.

"Why don't you wake up out of your fantasy world? You behave like an insipid little child. Just because you are light skinned and rich does not mean anything. You're on your way to hell and don't even know it." Everyone standing around gasped again, including Sophia. Sophia tried to interrupt. She was quite embarrassed.

"Who do you think . . ."

"I'm not finished yet," Etta spat out the words with fire as she stepped towards Sophia. Destini and Stephan were looking back and forth at each other with embarrassment on their faces.

"It's people like you who disregard other people's feeling and teach their children to be oppressors. You keep your own people down. You're supposed to be intelligent? Huh! Just because this little girl here," Etta placed her hand on Destini's shoulder while continuing, "has one of the most beautiful skin colors and complexions in the world, and it's smooth and soft, you envy her. You call yourself a Christian and you think you're intelligent?" Sophia tried to interrupt a few times but she could not get a word in. Etta's voice overpowered hers. "Go back to the rock you crawled from, you wicked witch."

"OH!" Sophia screamed, "You B--!" Etta had turned again to leave, but she stopped as Sophia was about to call her a female dog. Everyone around gasped again and Sophia caught herself. Sophia was considered a high-society, important woman in the church and the community. Her husband was an elder in the church. It would be a scandal, calling a church member a dog. Sophia was steaming, and she wanted to fire back at Etta with something that would hurt. She screamed out to Etta and Destini as they walked down the school hallway.

"You both go to hell, where you belong." With that remark bellowed at them, Etta turned and answered, but this time much calmer than before.

"Please, do not send us to your home when you're not there." Destini's eyes widened. *"Oh, gracious me,"* Destini thought. *"I didn't know Etta had it in her. Wow!"* Sophia was dreadfully upset and embarrassed at the remark. She placed her hand on her hip, stomped her foot and proceeded down the hallway after them. Etta had turned and walked out of the building. Stephan ran after his mother.

"Mother, come on, give it up."

"You get away from me," she screamed, trying to push him away.

"I'm not going to let you go; even if you punish me later. I'm not going to let you continue to make a fool of yourself." Sophia had not thought about it much until then, but Stephan had grown a lot taller and he was much stronger than she thought. She tried to loosen his grip but could not. She turned and looked at him. She finally noticed the hurt and embarrassment on his handsome face. When Stephan saw that Destini and her mother were not in sight, he let her go. Sophia was embarrassed, especially in front of people passing and standing. She looked at him and slapped his face. Stephan being much taller than his mother looked at her with love, hurt and pity.

"Mother," he calmly said, "I'm going home and if you wish to talk to me, I'll be in my room." Sophia at that moment felt she lost something in her son. She wanted to reach out and hug him, but her pride stopped her. She blocked out everything around her as she watched him walking with his manly stride, down the hallway and through the doors. She felt awful. She just wanted things to be normal again. *"Oh,"* she thought, *"it's entirely that little black whore's fault."* Sophia wanted her out of their lives, and she was determined to do something about it.

30

Goodbye My Darling

hat night seemed awkward. Friends were calling each other and talking about what they saw or heard. Destini said nothing to Etta. Etta was very quiet as she went about the house. Destini saw that Etta was still very upset. At about nine-thirty, the doorbell rang. Etta went to open it and Yasmin was standing there with a look of embarrassment.

"What do you want?" Etta's cold, fierce voice rang, which was so much unlike her usually calm and warm personality. Yasmin wanted to disappear. Her stomach ached, but she wanted to talk to Destini desperately.

"Um, is Destini here?" she asked timidly. "May I speak with her please?" Etta was not very happy with Yasmin. She asked her to leave. Yasmin wanted to cry. She couldn't take the mean, facial expressions that Mrs. Taylor was showing her.

"Please, Mrs. Taylor, I really need to speak to her, please."

"Do you remember when Destini came over Christmas holiday to see you and you refused to see her? We don't need a two-faced hypocrite around here. Destini needs a true friend." Tears gathered in Yasmin's eyes as she looked at the floor. Then a soft sweet voice was heard behind Etta.

"Mom, it's okay," she said and touched Etta's back gently. "Really Mom, it's okay. I'll speak to her. Jesus said forgive and you shall be forgiven."

Destini looked at Etta, "Is it okay," she asked, "if I invite her in?" Etta's lips were tightened and pressed together. But she managed to answer.

"Ten minutes and no longer." They both stood in the foyer. Yasmin hugged Destini but Destini didn't feel comfortable hugging her back. Yasmin apologized for her past behavior. She asked if they could continue walking home together again. She said she wouldn't be so stupid and selfish again to give up such a wonderful friendship with such a wonderful person. Etta appeared exactly ten minutes later and said firmly, but calmer this time.

"Ten minutes!" the two girls looked at Etta, then at each other. Yasmin smiled, but couldn't get the same kind of smile from Destini. They both said good night and she left.

Etta asked Destini to come to her bedroom because she wanted to talk to her before she retired. When she walked into her parents' room, Etta seemed very serious and Destini felt uneasy. She thought, *"Oh please don't tell me that I can't be friends with Yasmin."* Etta looked at Destini and asked her to come and sit on the bed next to her. Winston was already in bed with his glasses on, reading a religious book. Her parents' room was always warm and cozy. Etta held Destini's hand gently.

"Destini," she said. "What I'm about to ask you to do is very serious." She paused then continued. "Destini this is best for you and all of us. Winston and I have discussed it and we feel that it is best that you stop seeing Stephan." Destini felt like her whole world came to a screeching halt. What was she going to do?

"But Mom," she belted out, "he's the only friend I have right now, that I can trust." Destini removed her hands gently and stood up. "Why," she continued, "should we fall to Mrs. Barronton's every wish?"

"We're not following her every wish. But, right now it's best…."

"Best for whom? Surely not me; best for Mrs. Barronton!" Destini then shouted, "Oh, God I hate her!"

"Destini!" Etta exclaimed then turned and looked at Winston. His head was deep in his book. Destini went around to his bedside.

"Dad, please," she cried, "I really like Stephan, I mean as a friend. Please, can't you all discuss this again, please?" Winston looked sadly at Destini, then at his wife. Etta was looking to him for an answer.

"Destini," she said finally, "we have already made up our mind and it's for the best. This will keep that wicked woman out of our lives. I want nothing to do with her. And furthermore, you're both under-age and I don't want any trouble. If you were older, it would be different because Stephan is such a remarkable young man. But our decision is final." Destini looked at Winston and he concluded that he agreed with Etta. Without a word Destini stormed out of the room. She dashed into her bedroom and threw herself onto her bed. Her tears soaked her pillow as the night moved on. Finally, she couldn't hold back the sound of her crying. Etta and Winston heard her sobbing, and they could not sleep. Etta felt awful but, decided not to go back on her words. She went into Destini's room to comfort her and held her gently as she said softly, "Destini, I know it seems like the whole world is against you. But, remember what you told me your teacher said, 'that after the clouds, comes the sunshine.' God knows and hears what you're going through. He will work things out. Just ask Him and trust Him, you'll see. I have trusted Him and He has always come through. One day you will be friends with Stephan and no one will be able to stop you." Destini's head rested on Etta's lap and she fell asleep after hearing those comforting words. Etta laid her head gently on the pillow and quietly went back to her room.

Early the next morning, the phone rang. Etta was already up and she answered the phone to hear Stephan's voice on the line. She told him that Destini was still sleeping and that it was best not to call her anymore. Stephan asked Etta to relay a message to Destini. He said his mother was sending Shadae to Sweden and he had to go also. He could be leaving that night or the following night, and that he wished to see her before he left. Etta asked him to call back later, but Stephan said he couldn't. Etta decided to wake Destini. When she went to Destini's room, she was already up. Etta told her this was the last time she would accept calls from Stephan. Destini dashed to the phone.

"Hello?"

"Hey Sweet Chocolate; how are you?"

"Well, okay I guess."

"I wish I could be there with you to comfort you. I guess your parents don't want us to continue seeing each other."

"Um, we can talk about that when I see you," she answered.

"Destini, I'm going away and I don't know when I'll see you again."

Surprised; Destini's heart sunk as she exclaimed, "Away? What do you mean away? Where?"

"To Sweden with my sister. There is a private school that mother wants me to attend." Sadness filled Destini's heart.

"Oh, my goodness, Stephan I'm not gonna get to see you anymore." Tears filled her eyes. "When are you leaving?"

"Tonight or tomorrow."

Destini screamed at the top of her voice, "What? What?" There was complete silence. They both couldn't say anything.

"Destini?" he called but she couldn't answer. "Destini?" he called again. She was trying not to let him know she was crying.

"Um . . ."

"Destini? Are you crying?"

"I'm okay." She answered with a stuffy-sounding nose.

"Oh, Destini my love," Stephan said. "I don't want you to cry. I've only brought you grief and sadness since I came into your life. Can you please forgive me?"

She finally caught her voice. "Oh Stephan, there's nothing to forgive. On the contrary, you've brought me love and happiness. You and Winston have shown me that there are good, strong, patient, loving and caring men in this world. Thank you." Stephan felt an ache in his heart to be with Destini at that moment. He wondered how he was going to survive without seeing her.

"Destini, I need to see you later after school, because I don't know when we're leaving. I have to finish packing my suitcase today and I'm not going to school either. So, can I meet you about six o'clock over by the big willow tree near Mike's Place? They're having some kind of party there and mother wants us to go. I have to take Shadae, Tasha and LaVona to the party. I was planning on coming over, but I got the feeling that Mrs. Taylor does not want me there." Stephan heard someone coming. "Destini, I have to go. I'll see you later. I will pick you up after school, so wait for me outside around the back near the farm house." He was gone, but Destini sat in silence with the phone still in her hand as if still listening. When she finally hung up she looked out of the window and saw that it was going to be a cloudy or rainy day. It drizzled on and off all day. School seemed like such a drag. Stephan told Keith to tell Destini he couldn't meet her after school.

Destini and Yasmin walked home together but Destini did not feel as close to Yasmin as she used to feel. They didn't talk much. Yasmin talked more and Destini tried to listen, but her mind was on Stephan and the fact that he was going away. She wondered if Yasmin knew. She didn't say anything to Yasmin just in case Yasmin would tell Tasha and Shadae that she knew Stephan was leaving. Yasmin was trying very hard to get their friendship back the way it used to be; but Destini was not showing much interest. The girls reached Destini's home first, as usual. Destini said goodbye and walked quickly to her front gate and up the walkway. Yasmin stood in the cold as the rain pattered lightly on her umbrella. She watched Destini until she was inside. She felt very lonely. The best friend she had ever had and she blew it. How could she have listened to Tasha and Shadae? Why couldn't she see that they only wanted to use her to divert Stephan's attention from Destini? Yasmin felt foolish because Stephan did not even notice her. She only opened the door for Stephan to spend more time with Destini, because she wasn't around. Yasmin lowered her head and walked home slowly.

As the afternoon carried on into the evening, the rain strengthened. Destini looked out the window from the living room and thought, *"Why does it have to rain? It's winter. It's supposed to snow not rain."* Soon the phone rang and she dashed for it.

"Hello?"

"Hey, Chocolate?"

"Hey."

"Sorry but I cannot meet you at six o'clock. Sorry I did not get a chance to see you after school. I now have to go somewhere with my mother. We're leaving tonight. The weather doesn't look so good. I don't know if any airplanes are flying tonight."

"You mean I'm not going to see you before you leave?" she asked desperately. Stephan felt awful. He didn't know what to say. "Stephan, what are we going to do?"

"I don't know my love. I have to go. I'll call before I leave." He hung up his line and was gone. Destini walked through the entire house, pacing the floor, waiting for Stephan's call. She sat down, stood up and paced again.

"Have you finished your homework?" a voice from the den yelled. Etta heard her walking around.

"Um, in a minute Mom," she returned. It had been three hours since Stephan called, and the rain was pouring on and off. Finally, the phone rang. "I'll get it," Destini shouted." She dashed for it. "Hello?"

"Hello Destini. Are you finished with your homework yet?" Destini was disappointed.

"Oh, Yasmin, no. Can I call you back? I'm really busy, okay."

"Okay," a disappointed response followed. Destini hung up quickly and continued pacing the living room. The rain was pouring again. It had tapered off, but it started to rain again even harder. The phone rang again and this time Etta got up, and she heard Destini shouting.

"I'll get it." She dashed for the phone. "Hello?"

"Chocolate."

"Hi Stephan--what's happening?"

"I will be leaving in two hours or sooner," he answered quickly. "I need to see you before I go. Is it raining heavily over there?"

"Yes."

"It's raining heavily here too," he said. "Destini, I know this is asking a lot of you because of the pouring rain, but can you meet me now near..." Destini didn't wait for him to finish.

"Yes, yes, where?" she answered quickly.

"Um, over by the big red barn. You would be out of reach so your parents can't see you."

"Okay, I'll leave now." She hung up and walked hurriedly to get her rain gear. Etta was still in the den, and she wanted to know who called.

"Destini, who was on the phone?" she shouted.

"Yasmin had called mom."

Etta was not enthused, "Oh," she responded in a lowered tone and voice. Destini put on her outer garment and shouted to her parents without hearing what they had to say.

"I'll be right back. I'm gonna see Stephan." And she dashed out the front door. Etta listened and she finally realized what Destini had said. She jumped up from the couch and ran out of the den towards the front door. She threw it opened and stepped into the charging rain. It was pouring with such strength. She barely managed to go out on the front porch. But she screamed with all her might.

"Destini, Des-----ti--ni----i, Destini come back he----re." She saw the shadow disappear in the darkness. "Destin-----i," she screamed. "Uh." Etta ran back inside because of the force of the rain. She was dripping wet. "Oh my God, Winston," she gasped as if out of breath. Winston was by the foyer looking bewildered. "Winston, she just ran out into this crazy weather in the darkness to see a boy." Etta started to cry. Even though her face was already wet, tears were gathering in her eyes and wiggling down her bewildered face. Winston kissed and hugged her quickly. "Oh, Winston I have to go and find her. It's an awful storm out there."

"No, love. I'll go and find her." Winston was worried about Destini out there in the awful rain; but he kept cool. Etta was puzzled as to why Destini would go out in such weather, even if it was to see Stephan.

Stephan was already there when she arrived out of breath. They saw each other and ran into one another's arms. It seemed like the rain stopped, while their arms cling to each other. However, after a few moments they felt the showers. He moved closer to the barn for shelter from the rain. The light from the barn shone on his handsome face. She was so happy to see him and to look at his gorgeous smile. Stephan couldn't wait to kiss her soft full lips. Their lips touched and glided with love on each other.

"Oh, I'm so glad to see you." Destini said softly as Stephan looked deeply into her eyes.

"And I'm glad to see you too, princess." They held each other close. They finally pulled apart.

"How did you get here so fast?" she asked

"I called you from Mike's Place." he said.

"Your mom still has your cellular phone?"

"Yes." He answered. Destini turned and looked back slightly.

"Oh Stephan, I have to get back very soon. I heard Etta calling me as I ran through the shrubs." They both looked intently at each other. He loved touching her soft, smooth face gently.

"Oh Destini, I'm gonna miss you so much," he said as he held both her arms. He looked up in desperation as the raindrops washed his handsome face and with a sudden cry of anguish, he closed his eyes tightly.

"Oh my God," he wailed, "why, why does my mother have to be so------o wicked?" Destini was startled by his outburst and by what he said.

Stephan looked at her as he continued to hold her arms firmly. Destini didn't know what to say. She suddenly noticed that Stephan was crying. His face looked so bewildered. *"Oh, my goodness."* she thought, *"What do I do?"* Destini knew she had to go home very soon because her parents would come to look for her. Now, she was crying. They both held each other and cried and her heart felt like it was about to break. Winston heard their voices and went in the direction of the sound. He didn't want to interrupt them. He stood back and tried to listen as they continued speaking.

"I have to get back," Stephan said solemnly. "My mother will be wondering where I am." They started walking back toward Destini's home as the patter of the raindrops splattered on the ground.

"I take it that your parents don't want me to come around anymore?"

"No."

"See Destini, no one wants us together. It's probably for the best that my mother is sending me away because I couldn't bear to see you and not talk to you."

"I know," she said softly, "me neither." She looked at him lovingly and said, "Stephan I have to go. I know they are worried."

"I have to go too. I just didn't want to leave without seeing you." They paused and stared at each other as much as they could see in the darkness. "Oh, my darling." he said as they embraced, "I will miss you." They finally released each other. Destini walked backwards towards her home. She suddenly stopped. They both raced into each other arms as if they were going to be separated for eternity.

"Oh, Stephan I don't want you to go." she cried. They held each other for a while until they slowly released each other. Destini turned and started to run towards home. Stephan stood and watched as she disappeared into the darkness. On her way back, she ran into Winston. His presence surprised her. She walked back with him and he did not say anything, as usual.

When she got home, Etta was waiting at the front door. The rain wasn't pouring hard anymore.

"Young lady!" Etta met her with fury. "What is the meaning of this? How could you scare us like this? You could've been hurt." Destini couldn't hold it any longer. She burst into uncontrollable cry and told Winston and Etta about Stephan leaving that very night and how she knew that she wasn't going to see him again. Destini told Etta that she knew that they wouldn't let her go to see him, and how they didn't want him near the house. Winston and Etta looked at each other, feeling guilty. Etta thought Stephan was bluffing when he said he was leaving. Destini's final words were that she was ready to be punished. Etta realized that she was at fault for laying down such an overbearing rule. She thought about not being too different from Mrs. Barronton.

"Okay then," she finally said as she looked at Destini, "go up to your room we'll talk to you in a moment. Twenty minutes later Etta tapped on Destini's door.

"Come in," Destini answered humbly. Etta walked into the room and leaned against the wall. She looked at Destini motherly.

"Okay, seeing that you were in a desperate situation and didn't have anyone to turn to, Winston and I will show you some grace," Destini smiled. "But," Etta continued as she pointed her finger at Destini, "that does not mean you are off the hook. You have to help me in the kitchen when you come home from school. You have to clean all the doors and windows for the rest of the week and you have to show us that we can trust you again. Whenever you are in any situation, no matter, and I repeat myself, no matter what it may be, please come and talk to us. You could've been hurt. Next time you won't get off so easily."

"Thanks mom, and I'm very sorry, I didn't mean to scare anyone." Destini embraced Etta.

31

Friends Forever

*T*he next five weeks were miserable without Stephan. February was a cold month. Snow was everywhere. The girls were winter padded from their heads to their toes. Destini and Yasmin were in the swing of friendship again. Yasmin apologized continuously until Destini finally told her to stop, stop, stop. Destini finally told Yasmin she knew about Stephan leaving for Sweden. Yasmin now realized that Stephan truly loved Destini, and she wished she hadn't listened to Tasha and Shadae. The girls saw Tasha looking lonesome though she had other friends.

Destini and Yasmin told each other a lot of things that happened while they were separated. Yasmin told Destini she felt like such a fool because she allowed herself to be manipulated by Tasha and Shadae. She promised Destini to be an ever-faithful friend.

One afternoon after school, the girls went to Destini's room to do their homework as they'd often done in the past. Destini gathered her books and sat on the floor and Yasmin got comfortable on the bed. About thirty minutes into their homework, Yasmin kept glancing at Destini.

"Did you notice," she finally said, "that Shadae wasn't showing that she was pregnant?"

"Yea," Destini said casually while still looking at her books. "I was wondering if she had an abortion."

"Oh no, she didn't. Mrs. Barronton wanted to send her away before her belly started showing big so people here wouldn't find out or see her lovely daughter pregnant." The girls continued doing their homework; but Yasmin kept glancing at Destini.

"You know Destini," she finally said again. "Please don't get me wrong, but I miss seeing Stephan around." Destini looked up at Yasmin and smiled, while studying Yasmin closely.

"You like him don't you Yasmin?" Destini asked playfully.

"Oh me? Only as a friend." she scratched her head and answered as if it wasn't an important question. "It's been about what, three months since they've gone, right?" Yasmin asked. Destini shrugged her shoulders as they continued their homework. Destini started fidgeting and Yasmin kept glancing over at her. Destini finally looked up at Yasmin again, as if studying her. They looked at each other and smiled as they continued their homework.

"Yasmin," Destini, finally asked, "how much as a friend do you like Stephan?" Yasmin was caught off guard.

"Well, what? Destini what kind of a question is that?" Yasmin asked. Destini paused as if thinking deeply.

"Yasmin," she finally stated, "you have never mentioned anything about the Christmas party you had and I know you had a Christmas party. Plus, you didn't invite me. You invited Stephan, Tasha, Shadae and, oh my goodness, Nolita of all people." Yasmin hung her head down.

"Okay, I did have a Christmas party and I didn't tell you because I didn't want any trouble."

"Trouble?" Destini questioned. Tears were gathering in Yasmin's eyes.

"Worst of all," Yasmin said, "I didn't even enjoy myself. Oh, Destini I'm so sorry." Destini looked away.

"Yasmin," she asked again, "Tell me the truth. How much do you like Stephan?" They both sat and stared at each other.

Yasmin looked away as if embarrassed, then finally said, "I don't want to talk about this anymore because it's not important." Destini was determined to know so they argued back and forth until Yasmin said she had to go. Destini got up and blocked the door so she couldn't leave.

"Yasmin," she shouted with tears gathering in her eyes. "You really hurt me last Christmas. I trusted you so much." Destini was feeling the pain in her gut again. The very same feeling she felt when Yasmin stopped talking to her. She continued, "You were the only supposedly, true friend I had. And you somehow turned against me. Why? Was it all because of Tasha and Shadae or the fact that you're in love with Stephan?" Poor Yasmin didn't know what to say; she just wanted to get out and go home. Destini continued, "Out of the blue, you decided not to be my friend, after all we had been through together, and for what-- a boy who hardly noticed you?" Yasmin was very upset, she finally shouted back at Destini.

"Just because," she said furiously, "Stephan was showing attention to you, you are going to throw all of that in my face?"

"Yasmin, you know exactly what I'm referring to. What could make you give up a great friendship, unless of course, only I thought it was a great friendship?" Yasmin didn't want to go through any more interrogation.

"DESTINI," She screamed, "I was wrong okay, and I said I am sorry. Isn't that enough?"

"NO!" Destini screamed back, "I want to hear it Yasmin. Are you in love with Stephan?" Yasmin turned and walked away. She picked up her belongings and walked to the door. Both girls were standing by the door. Yasmin wanted to get out of there quickly. How could she tell Destini how she really felt about Stephan?

"Let me out of here Destini," Yasmin stated.

Destini looked at Yasmin, "And," she said softly yet sternly, "if you leave like that, don't ever come back."

Yasmin started to cry. "Destini just let me out of here because if that's the way you feel, I can't force you to be my friend."

"You're right Yasmin. You're so right. See I don't know if I can ever trust you again. And I wouldn't want to force anyone to be my friend." Destini raised her voice, "I can't even trust you enough to tell me if you love Stephan." Destini opened the door with a sudden force. "GET OUT AND GO!" she shouted. Yasmin walked slowly out of the room. Etta heard shouting and screaming and was on her way up to find out what was wrong. She was mid-way up the stairs when she saw Destini shouting Yasmin out of her room.

"Um, um," she cleared her throat. "What is happening up here? Why are you screaming at each other?

"She leavin'," Destini said abruptly and closed the door. Yasmin stood at the door with her head down. She walked slowly to the stairs as she kept looking back at the door. She felt so disheartened. She had tried very hard to bring back their friendship and when it seemed like everything was fine, this had to happen. Why did a boy have to cause them to break their friendship? It was all so stupid.

"Is everything okay Yasmin?" Etta asked, "What happened?" She looked quickly at Etta.

"Nothing Ma'am, just a little disagreement." Yasmin suddenly stopped and turned back to Destini's room. She didn't want to lose friendship with Destini again. She was about to reach the door when

169

Destini opened it. Destini stood by the door. They both stared at each other, trying hard to fight back the tears.

"Yasmin," Destini finally said in her soft melodic voice, "I'm sorry."

"Me too," Yasmin responded, "I'm so sorry. Everything is my fault." Etta was standing on the stairs watching them. She could only smile and shake her head and return down the stairs. What seemed like disappointment went out of the door. The girls had reached some form of maturity.

"May I come back in, please?"

"Sure," Destini opened the door wider as Yasmin walked in and she closed the door.

"Please," Yasmin said in desperation, "Destini don't be upset with me. In answer to your question, I really like Stephan a whole lot. And I guess, well, I guess I was jealous because he was always showing you all the attention. I'm sorry Destini. That was very selfish of me. Can you find it in your heart to forgive me for what I did and for lying to you all those times?" Destini stared at Yasmin then walked slowly and sat on her bed in silence. She didn't know what to say or do. Things didn't seem the same anymore. How could the girl she trusted so much lie about liking a guy she knew Destini was in love with?

"And," Destini continued softly, "why couldn't you tell me this before?"

"Because I knew how much you liked Stephan and I didn't want to hurt you. But now I know Stephan really likes you. So, it doesn't matter anymore."

"Yes, it does matter. You're my best friend and I don't want to see you hurt either. If and when Stephan returns, I'll stay away from him."

"No Destini. You can't do that." Destini looked sternly at Yasmin. "It's settled now. Let's finish our homework. And I don't want to talk about it anymore." After Yasmin left, Destini did not eat much supper. She went to bed and cried herself to sleep. She prayed a small prayer to God and asked Him to let her get over the bad feelings and to continue to love and care about Yasmin. She also asked Him to protect and be with Stephan while he was in Sweden. She prayed for Stephan to come back soon.

32

More Confrontation

*E*arly Sunday morning, Destini woke up to a freezing room. Coming from under her comforter, she wondered why it was so cold. She wanted to jump right back under her blankets. *"Ooooh,"* she thought, *"why is it so cold?"* She threw on her housecoat and a pair of sock. She went to her parents' room to tell them that the boiler didn't trip on, but they weren't there. She ran down the stairs calling as she shivered.

"Woa, woa, Ma, Mom?"

"Yes," a response came from the kitchen." Destini thought, *"I knew she would be in the kitchen."*

"Wh, why is it so-----o cold?"

"Well," said Etta, "the boiler broke and Winston is fixing it. Come and warm yourself by the stove." Hmmm, this was so much warmer to Destini.

"How long has he been at it Mom?"

"For about an hour."

"Oh no, does this mean that it's broken badly?"

"I d'know," Etta answered, "but here is some warm Coco with whipped cream."

"Thanks Mom. Hmmm, this is tasty. I'm sure glad the stove isn't connected to the boiler."

"Yea, I know. We have to get rid of that old thing and make everything electric. Mrs. Jones called earlier. She needs her large baking pans that I borrowed to bake the cakes. Winston was supposed to take them, but he's busy with that boiler."

"Mom," Destini said quickly, "I can take them over to her." I'll just run upstairs and get ready." Etta looked at her.

"You know I don't like you driving alone, especially when it's so cold outside and snow is on the ground."

"Come on Mom. I can do it. I'll be extra careful. I drove home alone from the mall when Dad had to go with Mr. Chan to the hospital, didn't I?"

"Yes, but he was not supposed to let you do that. You're supposed to have an adult with you."

"Please Mom. Why do I have my driver's license if I'm not allowed to drive?" The phone rang and Etta answered to hear Anita saying she needed the baking pans as soon as possible. Etta responded affirmatively and then hung up.

"Mom, you know," Destini quipped, "you need to get your own large baking tins."

"I know that, but I have to order them and you know I don't like to mail order."

"Please Mom let me drive them over there. I need more practice anyway; and Mrs. Jones doesn't live too far." Etta looked around then said, "Let me see if Winston can stop and take them." She was back with a disappointed look.

"Mom, I promise I will drive slowly and very carefully. Mom, I used to practice with Stephan when he was here and he said I drive very well and safe. Moreover, you said I drive well."

"Okay, it's not you that I'm worried about; it's the other dumb drivers out there."

"Mom, I promise I will look out for them." The phone rang again. Etta looked at it but, didn't answer.

"Okay," Etta said, "um, promise me you'll drive very carefully."

"Mom, I promise."

"Oh, I wish I'd learned to drive," Etta said as she went and got the pans.

"You still can," Destini shouted, "and I can teach ya."

Etta turned and looked at her, "Yea, right!"

"No, really Mom." Destini tried to convince her but to no avail.

"Okay, go get ready." Destini ran and got ready. She was back in no time.

"I'm ready," she sang.

"Here are the keys and the pans. Now be very careful and come right back. I can't have Anita spreading all over town that I borrowed her baking pans and didn't return them." Destini looked at the huge pans.

"Whoa, where did she get these things from?" Etta helped Destini carried them to the car. Destini drove carefully and took the pans to Mrs. Jones. She was brown skinned, medium height and chubby. Her small full lips were always ready to mind someone else's business. She invited her in and Destini accepted. Destini liked the Jones' two-story, Victorian styled home. The living room was huge and spacious.

"Would you like some hot chocolate, or herbal tea, Destini?"

"I'll take some hot chocolate Ma'am." She brought her a cup of delicious hot chocolate with whipped cream and marshmallows. "Thanks Mrs. Jones; hmmm that looks tasty."

"You're welcome dear." Mrs. Jones looked at Destini in her inquisitive manner. "So," she asked, "how are things with you and Yasmin?"

"Great," she responded. Destini knew Mrs. Jones very well and she knew she just wanted information so she could call others and gossip. Mrs. Jones continued to watch Destini very closely.

"Too bad Stephan is gone." She looked at Destini closely to watch her response. Destini knew what she was up to so she was very careful of the things she said. She knew Mrs. Jones and Mrs. Barronton were close friends, so she answered cheerily.

"I hope he's happy where he is. So, Mrs. Jones what are you baking?" Mrs. Jones wanted to find out more about Stephan and Destini, so she answered quickly and continued to ask more questions.

"A cake for Mrs. Barronton. Um, Stephan is a very handsome young man isn't he?"

"I think he favors his dad, right Mrs. Jones?" Mrs. Jones was becoming frustrated because she wasn't getting any response she really wanted to see and hear. She was about to ask another question when the doorbell rang. She excused herself to answer the door. A few seconds later, Destini felt someone staring through her. She turned quickly to see Mrs. Barronton standing there with a smirk on her face. Destini's heart raced as she tried to compose herself calmly.

"Hello Mrs. Barronton." Mrs. Barronton stared at her then responded sarcastically,

"So, now I know the reason you are so black. You drink too much hot chocolate." *My goodness"* thought Destini, *"she couldn't even greet me. What a witch!"* Destini just wanted to tell her the most horrible things but she kept cool. She thought of something quickly.

"Mrs. Barronton, have a good day," and she turned to leave. She didn't feel like drinking hot chocolate anymore. Mrs. Jones came back out of breath.

"Oh," she sang. "I can't find it anywhere Sophia. I have to look some more." Mrs. Barronton completely ignored Anita. She stared sharply at Destini.

"Oh, leaving already? I see you're just like your so-called mother, afraid . . ." Destini cut off Mrs. Barronton's sentence sharply.

"Excuse me Ma'am, but Etta is my mother and she is not afraid of you or anyone. Furthermore, she knows how to behave like an adult, unlike you, who acts like a child. Mrs. Barronton it's about time you grew up."

Sophia was extremely angry. She moved towards Destini with vengeance as she screamed, "Don't you think I'll stand here and take any freshness from an ugly little black American whore." Destini felt a sudden pang of anger that reached to her gut. She wanted to take up a chair and smash it over her head. Destini stared at her with spite and suddenly all fear of this woman was gone. Mrs. Jones broke the silence by telling Destini thanks for bringing the baking pans and to tell her mother thanks. Mrs. Jones quickly looked at Sophia as she said "her mother." Destini ignored Mrs. Jones and broke her sentence before she concluded.

She pointed at Sophia and spoke sharply, "You, you are an evil, wicked person. You prey on the innocent to boost yourself. You are so full of pride and it's going to kill you someday if you don't change. And, for your information, I am a Black Hebrew," Destini emphasized 'Black,' "American Princess. I am," she repeated, "a Black American Princess. I am proud of this black skin that God in His love and mercy granted me." Tears gathered in Destini's eyes. "It's adults like you who cause young people to hate ourselves; but I thank God that I have a redeemer, Jesus. I don't have to depend on people like you to like myself. It's too bad Stephan had to be born to an evil person like you. He must have learned to behave like a normal human being from his father." Sophia couldn't listen to anymore and she shouted for Destini to shut up. She walked up to her and slapped

174

her face. Destini and Mrs. Jones screamed. Destini felt like her face was shaken.

"How dare you speak to me that way? You untrained little, black wench." Destini picked up a chair swiftly. Mrs. Jones was so frightened she screamed, "Oh my god, child!" Destini held up the chair for a few seconds, as if to hit her with it. She then put the chair down slowly. She fixed her eyes on Mrs. Barronton and started to laugh, shaking her head. Destini got her coat, glanced at Sophia and continued laughing.

"You must be crazy," Sophia concluded with embarrassment. "You keep laughing and I will give you something to laugh about." Destini continued laughing, especially remembering the petrified expression on Mrs. Barronton's face when she picked up the chair. Destini stopped laughing and with a serious expression on her lovely face, she looked at Mrs. Barronton.

"Mrs. Barronton, "she declared looking straight into her eyes with assurance, "don't you ever put your hands on me again." Destini continued in a softer tone while on her way out, "You are a beautiful woman, but because you are so mean it subtracts from your beauty. You think you are better than others or me. I didn't mean to disrespect you, and I apologize. But you say some awfully mean stuff." With that, Destini went to her car and drove off. Mrs. Barronton tried to tell her that she was ugly and stupid; but she didn't get a chance. She wanted to hurt Destini, because Destini had gotten the better of her. Mrs. Jones tried to calm her down, but she went away upset and embarrassed.

The house was warm when Destini returned. She told Etta the entire episode and how angry she herself was when she left. The only thing that kept her from hurting Mrs. Barronton was to laugh at her, particularly after she saw the expression on Mrs. Barronton's face. She didn't want it to spread through the community that she hit Stephan's mother with a chair.

Winston and Etta were proud of Destini, yet they were angry because of the incident. They decided to go to the Barrontons and straighten this out once and for all. Upon arriving, they saw an employee outside and asked to speak to Dr. Wycham Barronton and his wife. Dr. Barronton was looking over one of his guest houses, but he was willing to stop what he was doing to speak with them. He called to the mansion and asked his wife to join him. She came over reluctantly. Sophia did not like the fact that her husband was involved. Dr. Barronton was surprised to hear all that had taken place. He was disappointed about what happened at the holiday party. He apologized for everything with seriousness and kept looking back and forth at his wife. The Taylors left feeling satisfied. They had the feeling Dr. Wycham Barronton was going to take care of everything.

Two weeks later, Stephan called his father. He told him that he refused to stay in Sweden any longer and that he was coming home immediately. He said if they didn't want him to live at home anymore, he would quit school, work, and get his GED. Wycham didn't want to see his son out of school. He also did not want his son in Europe. His other son Andrew was in the UK with his wife and children. Shadae was also in Europe. He loved his children very much, and he missed them.

"Father, I really miss you and all my friends. If you prefer that I stop talking to Destini, for now, I will."

"Son, I miss you too and I don't care if you want to talk to Destini. She is beautiful and intelligent. You know, it's your mother who has the problem. But, as long as Mom doesn't find out that you're talking to Destini, I guess everything will be all right. And, I'll make arrangements for your ticket, and inform both schools of your departure and arrival." Stephan laughed with joy.

Wycham informed Sophia of his decision, and she quarreled with him. She was very upset, but he answered her with firmness, "Our daughter got pregnant by a white boy. Our other son is married to a white woman, because of your interference. If Stephan prefers a black woman, I certainly have no problem with that. I am a Black Hebrew, Jamaican, American, and I am proud of my roots." He looked at her sternly, "Discussion closed. And I do not wish to talk about this anymore. If you do anything to cause any more problems, you will be sorry." He excused himself and went about his business. Sophia knew her husband meant business when he put his foot down. She dared not interfere with his decision.

176

33

Answered Prayer

*D*estini was not successful at winning a crown in the beauty pageants she entered. The judges thought she was poised and beautiful, but they gave the awards or crowns to other girls. Sometimes Etta would walk away disappointed. She and others thought that Destini should have won. It would have seemed fair even if she were one of the finalist, or first runner up.

One Sunday evening after a pageant, Yasmin visited the Taylors. She rang their doorbell hurriedly. Destini opened it in an unhappy mood. Yasmin was at the doorway smiling with enthusiasm.

"Guess what?" she whispered. Destini didn't seem enthused. She walked away from the door.

"What?" she answered casually

"Gue---ss," Yasmin said impatiently. Destini looked at Yasmin as she came in and closed the door. Yasmin was getting impatient. "Stephan is back," she finally blurted out.

"Very funny Yasmin," Destini said calmly.

"I'm serious. He's back, but I don't think Shadae came back with him." Destini's heart raced. She didn't know what to do. She felt happy inside, yet not so enthused.

"When did he get back?" Destini asked.

"Last night I think."

"Oh."

"Come on Destini show a little more spirit. I thought you would be happy to hear this." Destini looked down at her fingers as she played with them. Yasmin was hoping to stay for a while and talk about Stephan.

"I know Yasmin. I am happy to hear that." Destini did not know how to react in front of Yasmin.

"You're unhappy about the pageants aren't you?" Yasmin asked. Destini continued looking at her fingers.

"Yea," she answered sadly. "The judges are always ignoring me." She then looked up at Yasmin. "If it were you, they would have noticed you a long time ago. It's not fair Yasmin. Why does the color of our skin have to matter? How would they like if someone judged them the same as they judge me? They would not like it." Yasmin looked away then back at Destini. She felt guilty because even though she envied Destini for her soft, beautiful, smooth skin and her overall beauty, she felt Stephan should have liked her over Destini because of her light skin. Even Stephan's best friend, Keith, told him that Destini was too dark. But then, he was trying to date Destini also. Destini finally dismissed herself by telling Yasmin she had some homework left that she had to finish.

"Thanks for letting me know Yasmin. I really appreciate it."

"Are you gonna call him?"

"No," she answered softly. "I'm not allowed to, plus, I told you I'd stay clear of him. Thanks. See you tomorrow." Yasmin left, but wished their friendship were the same as before. She ran home in the cold and ran up to her room. She fell on her knees and cried. She begged God to forgive her for what she did to Destini and to let their friendship return to the way it was before.

"Here I am Lord," she continued. "I could have any guy that I want and the one guy that I want, Lord, wants Destini. And now she's gonna stay clear of him just for me. God, please help me. I don't know what to do because I really like Stephan a whole lot and I'm so jealous of Destini. She is the best friend I ever had. Please dear Jesus," she cried. "Please help me, please." She wished she felt good inside.

Destini retired to her room to think about how she was going to face Stephan. *"What am I going to do?"* she thought.

"Oh Father in heaven," she prayed, "what am I going to do? I really care about Stephan and Yasmin. God please work this out for me. Thank you. In Jesus' name, Amen." The phone had rung and she heard her name. Destini jumped up and opened the door.

"Yes mom."

"It's for you. A school friend."

"Oh, thanks Mom." She ran downstairs to the living room.

"Got it Mom. Hello?"

"Hey Chocolate," came a warm and friendly male voice. Destini's heart seemed like it stopped. She froze with unbelief. *He called me? How did he get past my mother?* " she thought

"Hello," he continued. Destini wanted to scream, but she kept her cool.

"Hello," she answered.

"Do you know who this is?" he asked.

"Of course, I do. Who else would call me 'Chocolate?'" she responded.

He smiled and then asked, "And how is my chocolate princess? Destini just wanted to cry. Tears were gathering in her eyes. She choked slightly.

"Fine," she responded.

"Destini," he said gently, "are you alright?"

"Yea."

"I'm here in Lancaster, my darling," he continued. "I'm at Keith's house. He called your home for me so your mother wouldn't recognize my voice." He paused and then continued. "I really missed you my love."

"I missed you too," she responded.

"Did you get in trouble when you got back home that night?"

"Almost, but I was forgiven."

"You know," Stephan smiled, "you have the neatest parents."

"Well," said Destini, "I heard your father is pretty cool too."

"Yes, he is. He is the one who got me back here."

"Really?"

"Yes." Stephan felt an urge to be with Destini. He missed her so much.

"Oh, Destini I want to see you. I thought about you every day when I was away. I wanted to write but my mother told me not to write. Plus, I knew your parents didn't want us to keep in touch. I didn't want to get you in trouble." Destini didn't know what to say.

"Destini are you okay?" Destini had started to cry quietly. Her head felt stuffy. She was very happy to hear his warm sexy voice again. She tried to control herself but couldn't. He heard her sniffling. "Destini what's wrong? Oh, my sweet chocolate, I really want to see you now. Can I meet you on your porch at the side of the house?" he urged. *"Suppose Etta found out, I'd get in trouble,"* she thought.

"Oh Stephan, I d'know."

"I promise I'll talk softly, and I will park my car down the road and walk up. Please Destini, please.

"Oh Stephan, I d'know."

"Please my princess." She paused and thought. Finally, she got brave.

"Okay, but how will I know when you are here?"

"I will go by your window. Just keep looking for me. Then meet me on the porch." Destini remembered the auto night-lights on the house.

"Stephan, the auto lights...."

"Don't worry; I'll stay out of their range. See you in five minutes."

"Okay." Destini was vastly happy. She had forgotten what she said to Yasmin. She couldn't wait to see him. She ran up to her room and turned down the lights so she could see him. *"Keith didn't live too far so Stephan should be here soon,"* she thought. Destini suddenly remembered something Etta had asked her to do and she reluctantly went down stairs to talk to Etta. Etta was busy folding the laundry clothes.

"Mom," she said softly. Etta turned and looked at her.

"Hmm?" Etta answered. Destini said it as quickly as she could.

"I won't do this again, and I promise to do as you say from now on. Please, Mom! Stephan is coming over in the next minute and I haven't seen him for a few months. Please, I just want to say hi and to see him, please." Etta looked at her in a state of shock and disbelief.

"Excuse me," Etta calmly said, "what are you talking about?"

"Mom, Stephan is here in town. He's back. His father sent for him and he just wanted to say hi. Please Mom, please. I promise I won't see him again after this, please!" Etta put down the clothes and took a deep breath. She looked away with concern on her face.

"Mom, you said if I ever had anything to tell you that I should never be afraid to tell you. And I don't want you to think I'm sneaking around behind your back."

"Oh Destini," Etta answered as if frustrated, "I just don't want any more trouble from that woman." Destini was getting desperate because she knew he was outside by now.

"Oh, please Mom," tears were in her eyes and Etta looked at her and felt sorry for her.

"Oh, girl you always make me feel this way. Go ahead; tell him to come on in."

"That's okay." Destini ran off, got her spring coat, and dashed outside. She went around to where her room was and the automatic light lit up the yard. Stephan was standing there waiting for her in his long spring coat.

"Destini, get away from the lights." She told him it was okay, because Etta knew he was there, and was allowing them to see each other. Stephan was surprised. He thought her parents would never want to see him again. Especially after what happened with his mother and their last meeting before he went to Sweden. They hugged each other and headed back to the porch. She asked him if he wanted to go inside, but he refused.

"No, I just want to feast my eyes on you and only you."

"Stephan," she responded gently as she smiled coyly and blushed. The cold night air was flowing softly as they walked towards the porch. It felt so nice walking beside him. He was tall and had the manliest walk.

"I missed you princess. I really missed you. It was boring there. People just stared at me. I just wanted to come home. The girls were bold and Shadae was nagging. I couldn't take it any longer, so I called my father. I'm very happy I did, because here I am." I also wanted to be here before your birthday." Upon reaching the porch, they continued walking around to the back porch. He turned and held her arms firmly yet gently.

"My Princess," he said, "I thought about you every day. I was so miserable without you." He caressed her face gently. "I really need to be around you Destini. I'm glad your Mom is allowing us to see each other." Destini looked down, and then looked up at him.

"Stephan," she said with a gentle smile and her usual soft tone, "I'm only allowed this once to have you over. I'm still not allowed to see you." Stephan stood and stared at her then up at the night sky. He gently pulled her to him. His presence felt strong and powerful to Destini as they snuggled into each other arms. It was a pleasant feeling, especially since it was cold outside. They continued snuggling.

"Destini," he said, "it's not fair. Why is everyone trying to keep us apart? My mother is still at it. She's considerably angry with my father." Stephan wanted to hold her forever. He gently pulled his head away to kiss her soft, full lips. He only got a chance to touch them slightly when he heard the backdoor opening. He separated himself and looked at Destini with such a longing in his heart that brought pain of being separated from her. He heard a pleasant voice; it was Etta.

"Hello Stephan." He turned to see Etta who had a look of worry, but a sweet smile as always.

"Hello Madam," he responded. Etta sensed unhappiness. She realized that she was interrupting, but it was cold out there and she didn't want them getting sick.

"Please, come inside," she said. Stephan didn't know what to say. He felt awkward.

"Madam," he responded, "I was not planning to stay long I just wanted to say hello to Destini. I didn't mean to interrupt anything."

"You're not interrupting anything, sweetheart." She opened the door wider, "Please, come in. It's a cold spring night."

"Thank you, Madam." and they both went inside.

"Would you like some tea or hot chocolate?"

"I will take some tea, please Madam."

"Did you want something warm to drink Destini?" Etta asked.

"Sure Mom, I'll have some hot chocolate. I'll fix them Mom. You don't have to bother yourself." Destini felt guilty since she knew her parents didn't want her to see him, but she felt happy to have Stephan there.

"That's quite alright," Etta said cheerily. "You all go into the family room. I'll bring your beverage in." Stephan and Destini were so happy to be inside in the warmth. Etta and Winston joined them a few minutes later and they laughed and talked about Sweden and the happenings when he was away. Stephan told them he heard what happened at Mrs. Jones' home with his mother. He congratulated them for talking to his father. He said his father was a wonderful, hard-working man. He told them his father was the best in the whole world. He promised to bring his father around more so they could see that not all of the Barrontons were evil people. Stephan didn't want to leave because he knew once he left he wouldn't be allowed to see Destini so freely. He tried to linger on as much as he could. It was getting late and he finally decided to go.

"Well," he said as he stood to his feet. "I believe I have over stayed my welcome and I must be going." He looked at the Taylors. "Thanks for allowing me to visit. I really appreciate it." Destini told her parents she'd be right back and went outside with Stephan. "Well," he said as he gently held both of her arms. "I guess this is it, because with your parents and my mother against us being together, I . . . guess . . ." Stephan didn't want to finish his sentence. He looked up at the sky, then at Destini. He put his hands gently on her waist.

"Chocolate, may I kiss you goodbye?" he asked. Destini loved when he called her 'Chocolate.'

"Yes," she answered softly. He pulled her closer to him and lovingly kissed her with all he had. Destini felt something that night. She stood by the door and watched him go. She felt the pain he felt and wished it would go away. But somehow, in her heart she knew God would work everything out someday.

34

Pathway to Sunshine

*A*s time went by, Destini continued to bloom into *a fascinating young woman. She grew with grace and beauty. Her delicate elegance and beauty captured the eyes* of many. People were fascinated by Destini's beauty. They stared at her. Sometimes Destini was embarrassed because of the stares. Many of the girls in school said they wished they were as pretty as Destini. Stephan tried to get her to go out secretly on dates, but he did not succeed. She stayed clear of him because of her parents and Yasmin. Destini was not allowed to date steadily until she was seventeen. She went to summer school, passed all of her classes, and was skipped to the twelfth grade. Yasmin wanted to be around Destini so she did the same and was skipped also.

Destini had worn her braids until she was seventeen. With much care, her hair grew down her back. By the time Destini turned seventeen, Stephan was dating Tasha. Mrs. Barronton was elated. She treated Tasha better than she treated her own daughter. Even though Sophia loved her grandson, she was embarrassed given that he was born to her unwed daughter. Destini continued to enter several pageants and only came in the finals or first runner-up, but Destini did not give up. Etta continued to work very closely with her to give her confidence.

Destini loved Stephan and she ached to be with him. She was unhappy with him for dating Tasha, so she pretended to ignored him. Stephan would often stare at Destini as if looking at a beautiful goddess. When Destini noticed his stares, she became nervous and looked away or at the floor. When he wasn't looking, she also stared. When he caught her eyes, he looked lovingly at her and she'd blush.

Once in a while, Stephan would purposely bump into Destini to get her attention. They would stare into each other's eyes lovingly. Tasha saw the way Stephan looked at Destini. She was filled with jealousy and it would drive her to make fun of Destini and tell lies about her.

Destini tried not to feel the pain of seeing Stephan with Tasha, so she dated Jim. He had been secretly trying to date her, and she dated him twice. One of her date was at a school function and the other at a church service. Jim discovered that Destini was in love with Stephan and he desperately tried to discourage her about Stephan. She could not deal with the fact that he was conceited and he was putting down Stephan. Jim wanted to make love to Destini. He tried in his slick ways to manipulate her, but Destini always trusted God to guide and protect her. When she found out what Jim was up to, she stopped dating him and avoided him. She found out he was having sex with other girls and she didn't want to be among his conquests. Plus, she wanted to honor God. Etta didn't like him nor did she trust him at all. Etta warned her to keep her focus on school, on God, her voice and dance lessons, and on the pageants. Sometimes they argued, and Winston would smooth out the problems in his strong yet gentle, loving way.

Destini was scheduled to enter a teen pageant in the next three weeks. One Sabbath, during the month of March, the weather was like a warm spring day. Everyone shed their coats and decided to sport their spring clothes. Destini was walking through the church lobby and she ran into Jim and two of his friends. She candidly asked for his support during the pageant. Jim looked her up and down with desire and her shimmering, midnight hair flowed with curls down her back.

"Wow, Destini," he said, "you're looking beautiful girl. And I see you took them braids out. Now don't tell me you're still trying to win in those pageants girl," he said as he looked at his friends. He then looked back at Destini, as he continued to talk in his slick way. "Can't you see girl? They'll never choose someone with your color."

"Excuse me," Destini stated. "Someone with my color?" Jim was tall, brown and good looking. He was egocentric and always liked to show off in front of his friends.

"Destini," he said, "remember we've talked about this before. You're beautiful and smart. I can see that, and so can the judges; but, you're wasting your time. I want to be honest with you. I don't know if I'd marry someone like you because you're too dark. You should marry someone light skinned so, you know, your children won't be so dark. But, coming back to the pageants, the judges won't choose you for the same reason. Look, at least I'm being honest and I'm not saying this behind your back." Destini felt as if Jim had punched her. A sudden anger ran through her being. She was sick and tired of people talking down her beautiful, blessed dark skin. When would they realize that it is awesome to have different colors and types of people in the world?

I'm sorry," she calmly stated in a quiet voice, "for someone like you." Her voice escalated. "And for your information, I wouldn't marry someone like you either; who is egotistical, a womanizer, and a stupid attention-seeker. And for your information, I am black and beautiful. I'm proud of how God made me. Now, please don't speak to me anymore. You are not worth my time." With that small speech, she turned and sashayed outside into the sunshine. The peach dress she was wearing accentuating her gorgeous, shapely figure. Jim watched with embarrassment and surprise as she went through the doors. He wished he could be brave enough to date Destini steadily in the open. She was absolutely gorgeous. He was afraid of what his friends would say, because of her dark complexion.

"Ooo----oh," Destini said to herself. "The nerve of that . . . that idiot!"

"Chocolate," Stephan said warmly as she strode by him. She turned to see the handsome love of her life.

"What do you want!" she shouted. Stephan paused and looked at her with surprise and concern. His picturesque bronze skin dazzled in the sunshine. He'd never seen Destini so upset. He wanted to talk to her and spend time with her.

"Is everything okay Chocolate?" She stared at him. She really wanted to put her arms around him and talk to him; but she looked at the floor.

"You are still angry with me for dating Tasha?"

"Stephan!" Destini exclaimed. "I'm not in a good mood at the moment and yes I'm still . . . well . . . I'm disappointed with you." Her voice softened finally, "But, I forgive you. Goodbye." She glanced at him and tears began to form in her gorgeous baby brown. She then ran off. Stephan tried to tell Destini he had something to say, but she was gone. He dared not stop her with the kind of mood she appeared to be in.

Three weeks later, she entered the teen pageant and won the crown. The judges loved her. She was poised, elegant and intelligent. Some of them wondered why she had never won before. Destini was elated. That Sunday evening, Stephan came by her home to congratulate her. She was much calmer than when he had tried to speak to her three weeks earlier. She apologized for her behavior. He told her he had stopped dating Tasha four months ago, and that it was still Destini he wanted. They sat on the front porch and talked a good while until the sun softly went to sleep. They watched the snow as it sparkled on the ground.

"This weather is crazy," Destini said softly. "You wouldn't believe it was warm, almost like summer three weeks ago. Now there's snow on the ground."

"I know," Stephan agreed, "and it looks like it's about to snow again tonight." Destini was feeling chilly even with her jacket on, but she didn't want to go inside. Stephan finally got up the nerve and held her hands. "I knew you would win the crown," he said as he looked at her. "Destini, you are the most beautiful girl I've ever seen. You have the sweetest personality and the most gorgeous features." He gently touched her hair. She lowered her head and looked up at him shyly. "Your hair is ebony rich. It's soft and it always has a fresh delicate scent. Destini, you are very smart and your smile, well, it takes my breath away."

"Oh, Stephan you are so sentimental," she said smiling.

"Destini," he continued, "I am serious. Please, I'm asking you again to be my steady girlfriend." Destini was quiet and she felt uncomfortable. She was afraid to look at him. She knew the way his mother felt about her. She knew her parents didn't want her to date anyone now. She told Yasmin she'd stay clear of him. What could she say to him? She moved back a little from him.

"Stephan," she answered, "I want to finish high school before I think about a boyfriend." Stephan squeezed her hands gently.

"Destini," he said softly, "you're so soft and delicate." He looked deeply into her gorgeous brown eyes and touched her hair gently. Stephan moved slowly to her face as if he was about to kiss her. He wanted to touch her soft full lips again, to feel their fullness against his. "Please give me a chance." Destini didn't know what to say. She stared at him as if in a trance. She then started to pull away slowly. He continued, "I'll wait for you as long as I have to." Just then, Etta opened the screen door. "Destini you have a call." They both stood up.

"Thanks Mom." Destini looked at Stephan and gently pulled her soft hand from his strong big hands. "Thanks for your compliments, Stephan . . . um, goodnight." They stood and stared at each other wishing they didn't have to part. She then quickly disappeared through the doors and left him standing there.

35

A Case of Emergency

*W*hen Destini came inside, Etta was waiting for her in the family room.

"*After you finish with your call, I need you to take* something to Anita for me."

"Okay Mom." Destini took her phone call and to her surprise, it was Shadae and Tasha on the line. They began threatening her to leave Stephan alone or else they would cause trouble for her. They told her she needed to go out with her own kind. Destini was sick and tired of their continued nuisance. She didn't want to hear their threats, or their voices.

"Listen," she blurted out angrily, "you pale face parasites. Leave me alone; and it's the pot calling the kettle black, Shadae. Haven't you noticed you have a white child? If you'd stick to your own kind and mind your own business, maybe, you wouldn't have a white boy's baby."

"You leave my son out of this you ugly black baboon!" Shadae shouted.

"Shut up," Destini shouted back, and she jammed the phone down. Etta came in when she heard the shouting.

"Oh, my goodness child. Who on earth were you shouting at and telling to 'shut up?'"

"It was Shadae and Tasha. They were threatening me again to leave Stephan alone." Destini stormed to her room so Etta would not get a chance to say anything to her about talking to Stephan. She went and finished her school project until Etta was ready for her to go to Mrs. Jones. One hour later, Destini was on her way to Mrs. Jones' house. When she got there, she checked to make sure Mrs. Barronton's car was not parked there. *"Good,"* she thought, *"I'll stay a little while."* Destini really liked Mrs. Jones. She was really a nice

191

person. She only had one problem, gossiping. Destini spent an hour listening to Mrs. Jones while she baked goodies. She was really waiting for Mrs. Jones' homemade candies and cookies. Meanwhile, Mrs. Jones tried to get information from Destini, but Destini artfully changed the subjects. Anita finally gave up. Mr. Thomas Jones, her husband, was in the next room reading the newspaper and smiling every time he heard Destini change the subject.

Mrs. Jones finally finished making her famous candies and cookies, and she gave some to Destini. Destini was glad she'd waited. The phone rang and Anita answered it. When she was finally finished with her phone conversation she came back to talk some more. Thomas Jones came into the kitchen and told Destini that it was probably best that she leave because it was snowing heavily. They told her to call when she got home. Destini said goodbye to the Jones' and was off.

On her way home, she decided to take the back road. It had less traffic and was much faster to her home. About ten minutes from the Jones' home, she noticed fresh skid marks going off the road. She drove very slowly up to the tire marks. She looked ahead, and then in her rearview mirror, but there was no car in sight. *"Well,"* she thought, *"a lot of people aren't out in this weather and they wouldn't drive this route."* While Destini was passing the skid marks, her heart raced and she sped up a little. She decided to look again and she saw the top of a car down the hill. She stopped and turned her windows down slightly to listen. She thought, *"Umm, skid marks? I wonder if anyone is hurt?"* She didn't know what to do. Finally, she decided to go and get Winston. Home was ten minutes away in the snow and ten minutes back. Maybe I should go to the nearest house and call the police. She started to drive again and stopped suddenly, because she thought she heard a sound coming from down the hill. She heard it again. Her heart started to race again and she drove off. As she was driving down the road she felt a rush of excitement and fear, but she also felt guilty. She drove to the nearest house, ran up to the door, knocked on it and rang the doorbell hastily, but there was no answer. The lights in the house were off except for the nightlights outside.

"Oh, my goodness," Destini thought looking around. *"What am I going to do?"* she looked at the other houses in the distance. Their lights were off also.

"Dag, where is everyone?" She looked up to the sky and asked, "Oh God, what should I do? I'm scared to go back." She slowly walked towards the car and wondered what to do. "God please give me the strength to do what you want me to do," she uttered. She suddenly felt a strong urge to go back to the scene. She ran, jumped into her car and drove back. Reaching the skid marks, she stopped and turned her headlights in the direction of the car down the hill.

"Oh, dear Jesus," she said, "it looks like a car crashed." She wrapped her coat tighter around herself and moved down the hill cautiously. It looked like the car slammed into the huge rocks down the hill. The closer she got, the more the car looked familiar. She got close and looked inside. To her surprise, she saw Mrs. Barronton and Shadae. They were unconscious and covered with blood. The car seemed like it rolled on its way down the hill. She didn't know what to do.

"Oh my God," Destini screamed, "oh my God. Oh no! Dear God, please help me and show me what to do!" She stared at the entire scene while her hands covered her mouth. She composed herself and finally opened the back door, which was already partly open. The front door was locked. *"How strange,"* she thought.

"Mrs. Barronton?" she called. "Mrs. Barronton! Shadae!" Shadae moaned softly and her eyes opened slightly. Destini bent over the seat and checked Mrs. Barronton's pulse. "Shadae!" She called again. "Can you hear me?" Shadae tried to move but Destini asked her not to move. Destini placed her hand into Shadae's hand.

"If you can hear and understand me, squeeze my hand." Shadae squeezed her hand weakly. Mrs. Barronton's pulse was faint and then gone. Destini tried the front doors again, but they were jammed. She climbed over the front seat and realized there was not enough room. She then tried her best to get herself out of the awkward position she found herself in. Destini placed her left leg near the passenger's seat and her right leg against the seat. She put her butt against the dashboard close to the passenger's side for support, so she could work with ease. Destini tilted Mrs. Barronton's head back and gave her

CPR. She finally felt a pulse. She looked at Shadae and she looked awful.

"Dear God," Destini prayed. "Please, I beg you to keep them alive, I have to go and get help." She struggled back over the seat and saw Mrs. Barronton's mink coat on the back seat. She took it and covered Mrs. Barronton to keep her warm. Destini dashed out of Shadae's car and struggled through the deep snow. On her way up the hill, she glanced to her right and saw a small figure in the snow.

"No," she shouted. "Oh, gracious me. It's Shadae's son. Oh no, oh no; dear Jesus. No!" Grappling towards him, she saw little Pete lying in the snow, as if dead. He seemed icy cold. She fell to her knees. "Oh goodness. Please don't be dead, please. Oh, oh, please be alive." Destini checked his pulse and felt a faint beat. She scooped him up and struggled up the hill to her car.

At home, Etta was frantic because Mr. Jones called to find out why Destini had not called them back yet. Etta was pacing the floor and looking out of the window. Meanwhile, Destini drove back in the direction of Mrs. Jones' house. There were gas stations and the houses were closer together. She got to a gas station and called the police. She told them exactly where the accident was located.

Mrs. Jones heard the sirens far in the distance and started to worry. She and her husband looked at each other. In the meantime, Destini called her parents and told them what happened. She then went back to the accident scene to see if she could keep them warm. Winston and Etta dashed out of the house to find Destini.

Even though Destini's car was warm, little Pete seemed very cold. So, she took off her coat and covered him. She went back down the hill and checked their pulses again. Mrs. Barronton's pulse was faint, and Shadae's pulse was becoming fainter. Destini tried talking to them to see if Mrs. Barronton would wake up. She said things like, "You'd better wake up or else I'm gonna marry Stephan." Mrs. Barronton was beginning to wake up. Destini heard the sirens coming. She had parked her car with the engine running to keep the baby warm and had left the lights on so they wouldn't miss the spot. Destini continued talking to Shadae to keep her awake. Mrs. Barronton was awake, but she was having problems breathing. She tried to move, but Destini told her not to move. The medics and the fire department came. It seemed like the entire area lit up. She showed them where the baby was in her car. They went to Shadae's car and tried to open the door but couldn't. They decided to take out the car seats to get them out as quickly as possible. They finally got them out and were off to the emergency room.

Etta and Winston finally arrived. They dashed out of their car to find Destini. They saw her trembling even though the police loaned her a blanket. She was talking to the police. They both ran towards her.

"Destini, Destini," Etta said. "Are you alright?"

"Sure, she is," responded the police. Winston took his coat and threw it around Destini's shoulders. "Hi," the police shook their hands. "I'm Officer Amato. Is Destini your daughter Ma'am?"

"Yes Officer."

"Well, Ma'am, Sir, you both should be very proud of her. She may have saved the lives of three people tonight." The police looked at her and smiled. "You are a brave young lady. She insisted on waiting for you. She said you would be here soon. Well, we got all the statements we need. If we need anything else we will contact you." He looked at each one and excused himself. "Have a goodnight, Destini, Mr. and Mrs. Taylor."

"Officer Amato, thanks for everything and here is your blanket. I appreciate it."

"You are quite welcome young lady. Goodnight." They all said goodnight to the officer and he joined his fellow officers. Destini ran into her parents' arms.

"Oh Mom, Dad, I was so scared. I'm so glad to see you. I hope they'll be alright." Etta looked at Destini with admiration. She was very proud of her.

"So," Etta said, "the very same people who mistreated you, got another chance to live because of your help. Ha, ha, ha, ha. Life is so funny." Etta and Winston went over and looked at the Barronton's car. "I wonder how it all happened?" Etta asked. "It's weird how they just skidded off the road."

"Who knows, Love," Winston said. "The evil that people do in this world, have a way of coming back. Even though I can't stand the woman, I pray that she'll be alright."

"Mom, Dad, may I go home and call Stephan?" Etta looked around to see Destini standing near them, hugging herself to keep warm. Etta looked at Winston and assured Destini that the authorities would get in touch with the family.

"Come, Destini," she said, "let's go home. You look cold."

"I know Mom, but I know Stephan loves his Mom a lot, and I want to be there for him if he needs me."

"I know dear," Etta said, "but Stephan has his father. Come, let's go home and call the Joneses. They were very worried about you." Destini walked with her head down wishing she could be with Stephan. Destini felt secure with her parents' arms around her as they walked to the car.

They went home and called Mr. and Mrs. Jones and told them about Destini's brave actions. Mrs. Jones went on and on about how proud she was of Destini. After Etta hung up, Mrs. Jones called as many people as she could. She told them to pass it on. As the night moved on, the Taylor's phone rang continuously until Etta couldn't take anymore calls. Winston disconnected the phone so they could get some sleep. Destini wanted very much to call Stephan to see how he was doing. She knew that by now the entire community knew about the accident.

About twelve o'clock when everyone was retired, the doorbell rang.

"I don't believe this," Etta stated. "Who on earth could that be at this hour?" She looked outside to see whose car was there, but no car was insight. Destini got up and stood by the stairs. She couldn't sleep anyway. The doorbell rang again. Winston got up and turned on the front door lights, and looked to see who was ringing the doorbell. He opened the door slowly, and was neither surprised nor amazed at whom he saw. Winston stood and stared at her.

"Hi, Mr. Taylor" she said with a huge grin.

"Young lady, do you know what time it is?" he answered seriously.

"Well Mr. Taylor, actually, when I saw that I couldn't get through on the phone, I became very worried. I just wanted to make sure everyone was okay." Winston looked at her as if he wanted to put her across his lap and give her a good spanking.

"Does your mother know where you are?" he asked with a look of concern.

"Well Mr. Taylor, I didn't want to disturb her so I left a note and . . .

"Okay, okay," he said swiftly. "Yasmin . . ." Winston turned and called Etta.

"Honey, can you just come and take care of this problem." He walked away shaking his head from side to side and headed up the stairs. Destini had quietly descended the stairs and leaned on the wall, facing the front door. She looked at Yasmin in a motherly way and folded her arms. Yasmin came in and closed the door. Meanwhile, Etta came down the stairs. Yasmin looked at both of them and tried to convince them.

"Really," she said, "I wanted to make sure everything was alright." Etta came closer to her.

"As you can see," she stated, "we are alright. I'd like to thank you for your concern. Now that you know we are okay, who do you suppose will accompany you home? Surely not Destini, because she is not walking back by herself, and she is up way past her bedtime, thanks to you."

"I can walk back by myself Mrs. Taylor; that's no problem."

"Not from this house you are not," Etta stated, "and there's no one here to walk you back. So, young lady you'd better come up with something real quick, because I'm tired and sleepy." Yasmin looked at Destini who was still leaning on the wall with her arms still folded and looking at the ceiling.

"Well, Mrs. Taylor I'll just call my mother," Yasmin said.

"Why don't you just go and do that." Yasmin walked slowly to the phone with her head down.

"Mom." Destini said. Etta turned and looked at Destini.

"Yes, dear?"

197

"Do you suppose," Destini said with her hands on her hips and partially smiling, "that since it's kinda late and Mrs. Michaels may not want to come out in the cold . . ."

"Uh ha," Etta answered. Destini walked away from the wall and continued.

". . . perhaps Yasmin could spend the night?" Yasmin stopped short of dialing and looked at Mrs. Taylor with a look of hope.

"Please Mrs. Taylor," Yasmin begged. "I promise I'll go right to sleep and I won't cause any problems. Please-----se." Etta glanced at Destini.

"Um, I d'know. It's pretty late and I know if I let you two up in that room you will talk until daybreak." Destini went up to her mother, hugged and kissed her, and walked towards the stairs.

"Mom, I don't know about Yasmin, but I'm sleepy. If she's not ready to sleep, she's gonna be up talking to herself. Goodnight Mom." Etta finally agreed that Yasmin could stay for the night. "By the way Yasmin," Destini stated as she continued up the stairs, "don't forget to call your mother so she knows where you are." Yasmin looked at Etta, and Etta pointed to the phone. She had reconnected it so Yasmin could call her mother. She called her mother and Mrs. Michaels was not happy with her. She told Yasmin she would deal with her in the morning.

Stephan and his father were at Mrs. Barronton's bedside. She was bruised and her left arm was broken. She asked continuously about Shadae and little Pete. They decided not to give her much information about their condition. Little Pete had hit his head and somehow wandered into the snow.

Pete Silver and his family heard about the accident and came to see little Pete. They found out that his condition was very bad. Pete was tall, handsome and fairly muscular.

"What caused him to get pneumonia?" Mr. Silver, Pete's father, asked. He was tall, good looking and slender.

"Well," said the doctor, "according to the report, he was found lying in the snow."

"In the snow?" Pete blurted out as his father turned and looked at his distraught son. "How on earth does a baby open a car door and crawl out of a car?" Pete continued.

"I'm sorry sir, but we don't know." Pete walked around thinking deeply, while his parents talked to the doctor. He then asked the doctor if only Shadae and her mother were in the car, and who was driving.

"I believe," said the doctor, "according to the report, the driver was Shadae Barronton. Folks, if you will excuse me I must get back to other duties."

"Please," Pete continued. "Sir one more question." His blue eyes glanced at his parents quickly before asking.

"Um, how is Shadae doing?"

"The last I heard she was still in a coma. I'm sorry I must go. If you need anything, the attendant at the front desk will be more than happy to help you. Please excuse me," and he left.

"A coma," Pete kept repeating, "a coma, a coma." He hit the wall with an open palm. His parents looked at each other and then at him.

"Pete," his mother said, as she flipped her short blond hair, "she'll be alright. You'll see." Pete turned and looked at his mother. Her white sweater and black slacks fit nicely on her slim figure.

"Mom, I really care a lot about Shadae; and that little boy dying in that room is my son; but you don't want me to have anything to do with them and it's only because they're Black. The Barrontons are decent people. They work hard for their living. That's why they're so rich. You're wrong. They don't sell drugs." Mrs. Silver's mouth dropped open. "Why do whites usually think blacks are bad or are doing something bad? We are no different from them. Black people must think we are backwards or stupid to regard them like that all the time. Mom, just because the Barrontons are black and rich, does not mean they are selling drugs."

"I, I never thought they sold drugs," she exclaimed. "And, and I know they are decent people or else I wouldn't be here. You know I care about our grandson."

Pete interrupted his mother. "Mom, you did say that they sell drugs and you only care about little Pete, but you care nothing about his mother. I know I can't force you to like her, but at least let me have a chance to be with her and my son without threats."

"Pete," Mrs. Silver said firmly, "you know how I feel about that girl. There are other decent girls in our own neighborhood and church. These girls are not walking around getting pregnant."

"That's because," Pete shouted, "you don't know about the birth control pills they're taking, and all the abortions they do. And by the way, it takes two for conception." Mrs. Silver's eyes widened and she flipped her short blond hair back.

"Uh," she said, "I don't believe those disgusting untruths," she turned away from him, but Pete continued.

"Why wouldn't you believe me? You should, because I know you and Dad made love even before you were married."

"That's enough!" his father shouted. "You have no right speaking to your mother this way. You should be ashamed of your se. . ." Suddenly, they noticed someone was standing there.

"Excuse me, Pete, Mr. and Mrs. Silver." Pete embarrassingly stepped forward and greeted Stephan.

"Hi, Stephan." Stephan shook his hand and looked straight at him. Stephan's voice sounded soft and sad.

"Um, hello. Dr. Chen is asking you to come to little Pete in the ICU. They don't think he's going to make it." By the time they walked to the room the doctor came out to meet them.

"I'm sorry, but he didn't make it."

"Oh no!" Stephan shouted and ran into the room. The Silvers looked at the doctor and went into the room also. Stephan stood and stared at little Pete and tears rolled down his face. The Silvers came closer to little Pete's bedside, and Stephan moved away. *"Oh,"* he thought, *"why?"* From his heart he asked God *"Why?"* Pete was crying silently with flushed eyes. Pete's mother, Marcy, felt guilty. Now she wished she hadn't tried so hard to keep them apart. Stephan turned around and walked out of the room quickly without looking at them. Mrs. Silver followed him with tears in her eyes.

"Stephan," she called out to him, but he kept walking. "Stephan, please," she repeated desperately. He stopped with his back to her. "I know you won't believe me," she continued, "but . . . I really loved him too and I'm sorry for all the things I said and did. Please,

I'm sorry about little Pete. He's my grandson too." Stephan finally turned and looked at her. He then looked at the floor as if thinking deeply. He looked at her again.

"Don't you think," he answered angrily, which was unlike Stephan, "it's a little too late to be sorry? He's dead! Goodnight Mrs. Silver." Mr. Silver came out to hear the end of Stephan's comment. He and Marcy looked at each other as he placed his arm around her shoulders to comfort her.

When Stephan got back to the floor where his mother's room was, the nurse at the nurse's station relayed all the messages from people who had called him. He checked to see if Destini was one of them, but to his disappointment she had not called. Stephan was angry, grieved, and feeling anxious. He paced the floor waiting to hear if his sister was going to be all right. He waited to hear from Destini and waited to hear what his father was going to do about little Pete. Destini's phone was disconnected. He really needed to speak to her.

"Excuse me, sir," said the attendant, "you have another call, and I think it's the person you said you were waiting for. She said her name is Destini?" He thanked the attendant and walked swiftly to one of the guest phones.

"Hello?"

"Hello," a soft and sexy voice entered his ear.

"Destini, what took you so long to call? I've been waiting for your call all night." He sounded frustrated and agitated. "I'm so happy that you called. Thanks for saving my Mom and sister's lives. I owe you a lot, princess." He was beginning to sound less irritated.

"Stephan, you owe me nothing. I just praise God for His wisdom and care. It was He who sent me on the back road and led me to your family. The reason I couldn't call was because my parents disconnected the phone because too many people were calling us. Everyone's asleep now, but I came downstairs quietly to call and see how you're doing." Stephan felt so much love for Destini. He wanted her to be by his side. He sounded a whole lot calmer, yet troubled.

"I really miss you Chocolate, especially now." Destini wished she was there with him. She didn't know how to respond.

201

"I wish I could be there Stephan, but Mom said I couldn't." "How are your Mom, Shadae and little Pete?"

"Um, Mom is awake. She broke her left arm. She had a little trouble breathing, but she's gonna be all right."

"Good, how are Shadae and little Pete?"

Stephan took a deep breath. "Shadae is pretty banged up. She hasn't awakened since she came out of surgery."

"Surgery?" Destini shouted. She looked up the stairs and covered her mouth hoping her parents hadn't heard her.

"Yes," he continued, "the doctors had to stop the internal bleeding. You should see her. She's three times her normal size. I'm really worried about her."

"Oh, Stephan that's awful. I'm so sorry."

"Destini, I'm so worried," he said. "I don't know if she is going to make it either." Destini thought, *"either? What is he talking about, 'either?'"*

"Destini, I wish you were here. I really need you here with me now." Destini wished Stephan wouldn't say that. It made her feel guilty because she wished she were there with him. She didn't know what to say.

"Stephan," she finally said. "I wish I were there too.

"Destini?"

"Yes?"

"I didn't really want to be the one to tell you; but I think I should before you hear it on the news."

"What?" she asked cautiously.

"Little Pete didn't make it." Destini was quiet. She didn't know what to say or do. "Did you hear what I said?" he asked. She had started to cry silently. The tears washed her eyes as they rolled down her lovely face.

"Um, ah, yes?" She responded crying.

"Oh Destini, I didn't mean for you to cry, I'm sorry." Stephan himself started to cry. "Oh Princess, I wish you were here so I could hold you and comfort you. This is so heart breaking." Wycham saw his son crying and he approached him, rubbed his back and placed his arms on his shoulder. He then told him his mother was asking for him. He told his father he'd be right there and said goodnight to Destini. She tried not to let him know she was still crying. Before she hung up the phone he reminded her to remember to disconnect the phone in her parents' room.

"Oh, thanks," she said gratefully because she had forgotten about the phone, especially in their room. She told him that she was praying for his family. He said thanks and bid her goodnight. She disconnected the phones, went back downstairs and sat in the darkness while tears streamed down her face. Everything seemed still and quiet as she sat with the receiver in her hand. After sitting and thinking for a while she went up to her room quietly and stared out of her window. Sleep wasn't important at that moment. After peering through the window, she turned to look at Yasmin who was asleep. *"Oh Yasmin,"* she thought, *"you are my best girlfriend and life is too short to be holding anything against you in my heart."* She looked out of the window again. *"Father,"* she said in her heart, *"please forgive me for holding anything against Yasmin, Shadae, and Mrs. Barronton. Please let me be the best friend Yasmin has ever had. Father, please heal Shadae and Mrs. Barronton. Please change their attitudes and forgive them of their sins Lord. Let this be a new beginning in their lives. Thanks for answering my prayers. I appreciate it. In Jesus' name, Amen."* She got into bed, and the rustling woke Yasmin. She rubbed her eyes and looked at Destini.

"Destini," she said with a sleepy voice. "What's up?"

"Nothing; sorry, I tried to be as quiet as I could." Yasmin rubbed her eyes and looked over where Destini was.

"Destini, I can't see you that well, but you sound like you're crying. Is everything okay?"

Destini started to cry again. "Oh, Yasmin," she said crying, "little Pete is dead."

"What!" Yasmin exclaimed, "What! Are you sure? How did you find out?"

"I called the hospital."

"Oh my God, oh no." Yasmin sat up in the bed and stared at the wall. Tears filled her eyes so that they ran down her face. They both sat in silence.

"He was so young," Destini said. "He didn't even get a chance to live. Why?"

"It's not fair Destini, it's not fair. How are Shadae and Mrs. Barronton?"

"Um, Mrs. Barronton is okay, but Shadae underwent surgery and . . ."

"Surgery! Oh, my goodness. Why?"

"She had internal bleeding, plus she's still in a coma."

Yasmin was beside herself. "Oh, my goodness," she exclaimed. "This is serious. This is awful. What can we do?"

Destini looked at Yasmin. "I d'know," she answered as she shrugged her shoulders. "But we can pray that Shadae and her mom will make it through."

"Yes, yes," Yasmin answered quickly, "that's the answer. Oh, my goodness. This is awful. Poor little soul. I wonder how Stephan and Mrs. Barronton are taking it." They both prayed, and then talked about Shadae's pregnancy, her stay in Sweden, and some of the episodes with Mrs. Barronton and Destini. "Yasmin," Destini yawned and said, "God works in mysterious ways." She stretched and yawned again as she looked at the time. "Oh, my goodness Yasmin, it's four forty-five in the morning, and I have to go to school. Goodnight," and she slipped under the covers and was out like a light.

Later that morning, Etta knocked on the door. Destini covered her head and wished Etta would go away. Etta came in and looked at the girls.

"Okay girls, time to get up."

"No----o," Destini let out a whimpering sound.

"Come on girls. It's seven o'clock and you should've been up earlier, but I let you sleep one hour extra."

"Mrs. T," Yasmin answered, "I mean, Mrs. Taylor, I'm not going to school today. I'm going to the hospital to see Stephan and the Barrontons. You know, to visit them in their time of bereavement."

"Well," Etta said, "that's between you and your mother child, now come . . .what bereavement?" Etta asked. She looked at Destini.

Destini was somewhat awake now, but her eyes felt like they were burning. She squinted and looked at Etta.

"Um," she answered, "little Pete passed away last night." Etta covered her mouth in shock.

"Oh no. Are you sure?" How did you find out?"

"I called the hospital last night and Stephan . . ."

"Stephan?" Yasmin interrupted.

"Yes, Stephan," she answered as she looked at Yasmin. "He told me that little Pete died, and that Shadae was in a coma. He said that Mrs. Barronton was having problems breathing, but that she'd be alright." The phone rang and Etta went out to answer it.

"You didn't tell me that you spoke to Stephan." Yasmin kept pushing. Destini was really awake now. She looked annoyingly at Yasmin.

"Yasmin, why are you still harping on that note? Yes, I spoke to Stephan. So, what if I didn't tell you? I . . ." Etta came back in with a surprised look on her face.

"Destini," she said while looking at Destini with concern, "it's Mrs. Barronton. She wants to talk to you." Destini raised her head high and with eyes wide open she stared at Etta as she pointed to herself.

"To me? Did she say why?"

"No dear. She doesn't sound so high and mighty as she usually does. In fact, she spoke rather nicely." Etta looked at her, "Well, come and hear what she wants." Destini got up, still surprised. She looked at Yasmin and got her robe.

"Oh lord, I bet she found out that I spoke to Stephan last night. Uh, I can't take any more of this woman's attitude."

"Well, your Mom said she was nice on the phone. Maybe she wants to thank you." Destini was silent. She then laughed, "Ha, ha! Right!" Destini went to the phone in her mother's room and sat on the bed.

"Hello?" she said softly and cautiously.

"Hello," a shattered voice sounded through the phone. Destini looked at the receiver then at her mother who was staring anxiously at her.

"Destini?" Mrs. Barronton said softly.

"Yes Ma'am?"

"How are you?"

"Um, I'm fine Ma'am and how are you feeling Ma'am?"

"Well I am somewhat bruised and hurting."

"I'm sorry to hear that Ma'am. I wish there was something I could do to ease the pain. I know it's no fun to feel pain." Mrs. Barronton became quiet. The quietness of the moment made them both uncomfortable. Destini didn't know what else to say. She didn't want to put her foot in her mouth. "Um," she finally thought of something to say, "if there's anything you need or want me to do, please let me know Ma'am." Etta placed her hands on her hips; her face an expression of grave disapproval. Destini looked at Etta with confusion on her face. She finally turned away from her mother's disapproving gaze.

"Thank you dear," Mrs. Barronton quietly said. At the moment that Mrs. Barronton said 'thank you dear,' Destini was astonished at the way Mrs. Barronton was speaking. "But," Mrs. Barronton continued, "that's alright. I just wanted to thank you for saving our lives. I appreciate your concern and help. Um, ah, as far as you're concerned, we didn't deserve it from you." Destini's eyes and mouth opened wide, and Etta looked on intensely with curiosity. Mrs. Barronton continued softly. "The doctors told me that you gave me CPR and if you hadn't, I would not have made it. I guess I will be forever indebted to you."

"Not really Ma'am," Destini said. "Only God deserves the glory and our debt." Sophia didn't know what to say. She now realized that Destini was a very special girl. Destini didn't have to stop and help them, especially since unbeknown to her they were on their way to hurt her. And even though she stopped, she didn't have to apply CPR. She now remembered Destini putting the fur coat over her to keep her warm. Sophia felt so guilty.

"Um, Destini dear?"

"Yes Ma'am?" Destini answered, still, in disbelief.

"If you, uh, um, don't mind, I'd love to see you today to thank you in person. That is, if you don't mind?"

Destini looked at Etta, and then said, "Oh, I don't mind, but I have to come and visit you after school." Etta demonstrated her disapproval by shaking her hands and head. Destini did not know what else to say and she looked at Etta in confusion. "Um, okay Ma'am. I have to see how much homework I'll have later, and I have to check with my parents first. Maybe I'll see you later. Um, goodbye." Destini hung up the phone and looked at Etta with a worried look on her beautiful face.

"Well," Etta said with her hands on her hips, "what was all that about?" Destini got up from the bed.

"Mom, she was thanking me for saving her life and she asked me to come to the hospital to visit her."

"Na, na, na, na, NO-------O, you are not going anywhere to visit that evil woman."

"But Mom, I promised."

"Well young lady, you should've checked with me first." Etta walked out of her bedroom and headed for the stairs with Destini following behind her. Yasmin was dressed and ready to go home.

"Please Mom, please."

"No!"

"Can I go just to see how they're doing?"

"Call the hospital," Etta said as she went down the stairs, "to see how they're doing." Yasmin walked towards them wondering what was going on. She wanted to find out so she asked while looking on. "What's going on?" Destini stopped at the top of the stairs and looked at her.

"Would you believe it? Mrs. B. apologized and asked me to come and visit her."

"What!" screamed Yasmin, "Are you serious?"

"Yes." The girls followed behind Etta as she continued down the stairs.

"Can I come when you're going?" Yasmin asked. That gave Destini more incentive to ask again.

"See Mom, Yasmin wants to go with me. See, pleas-----se." Etta, who was now in the kitchen, turned and looked at Destini,

"Look here young lady, no! And that's final." Etta turned and started to take out plates, pots and utensils as she talked. "Ooo-----oh the nerve of that, that! . . . She's embarrassed because you saved her life. She knows the whole community is going to be talking about, how the person she treated like a dog saved her life. Huh, I wouldn't

207

give her the time of day." She turned to Destini and then looked at Yasmin. "It's time for you to go home and get ready for school. Now go." Yasmin looked at Mrs. Taylor's stern face and shot out of the kitchen and to the door. She grabbed her coat and told Destini bye and that she'd see her later, and she was out and on her way home.

Etta was not happy about Mrs. Barronton asking Destini to visit her at the hospital, because she didn't trust Mrs. Barronton.

"There's one thing you should remember," Etta continued pointing her finger. "That woman did everything she could possibly do to stop you from going out with Stephan. You must realize that no matter how nice she is to you now, she does not want you going out with her son. She just wants her conscience eased. That's why she called. Now go upstairs and get ready for school--end of conversation." Destini turned sadly and reluctantly headed up the stairs to take her shower and get ready for school.

Destini was distracted the entire day at school. Her thoughts retraced the accident, Mrs. Barronton's phone call, talking to Stephan the night before, and little Pete's death. Additionally, many of the students were congratulating her. They tried to ask her how she did it, but Destini was not in the mood to answer their questions. She tried her best to be nice. In some classes, the teacher interrupted the class to congratulate her. Destini was embarrassed from all of the attention she was receiving.

One of the students passed by and said, "And to think, Shadae treated you so badly, not to mention her beast of a mother."

"Yea," someone else added, "if I were them I'd be ashamed, but grateful."

"You're good, oh so---o good. I wouldn't even look at them much, less help them; especially after the way they've treated you, uh, uh." Some of the boys wanted to ask Destini out on a date but were too shy to ask.

36

Apology

*D*estini couldn't wait to get home to get away *from all of the attention. Yasmin wished she got some of the attention too but she was happy for Destini's recognition. At* the end of the school day, the girls hurried home. On their way, one of the boys in Destini's class drove by and asked to give her a ride. Although she was cold, Destini refused. He asked if she was sure. Yasmin stared at her as if to say 'Are you crazy, turning down a ride?' Destini looked at her and said to the boy, "Thanks, but no thanks." He said okay and drove away.

"Destini it's freezing. Why didn't you accept the ride?"

"Because I don't want to give any guy the idea that I'm interested in him. First, they ask to take you home, then they want your body. Na, uh, uh. I'd rather beg Winston to borrow his car."

"Then why don't you?"

"Because if he has to meet with any of his clients, he drives that car, and he uses his pick-up for his business." The girls were getting cold so they walked home quickly. When they finally got to Destini's home, Yasmin said, "You know, when it's cold like this we need to take the school bus. At least it seems shorter than walking."

"Not really. The bus takes a long route," Destini responded. She then asked Yasmin if she wanted to come inside and warm up before going home. "Sure," she responded.

When they got inside, it was warm and cozy and the house smelled wonderful.

"Hmmm, your house always smells very nice. It has a certain scent." Destini took off her coat and took Yasmin's coat.

"Scent?" she asked. "What kind of scent?"

"Um, I d'know. Your house just always smells good." Destini stopped and looked at Yasmin.

"Funny," she responded, "Stephan said the same thing." Yasmin looked quickly at Destini and asked, "He did? When did he say that?'

"I d'know. He always says that." Destini quickly changed the subject. "Want some hot chocolate?

"Sure," responded Yasmin. They went into the kitchen and saw Etta there. Yasmin opened her troublesome mouth again.

"Oh Hi Mrs. T. You're always in the kitchen. You must love it."

Etta turned her head and looked sternly at her, then asked nicely, "Yasmin dear, would you like some homemade cookies with your hot chocolate?"

"Sure Ma'am," she responded.

"And would you like some dinner? We're having jerk chicken with rice and beans, corn, salad and dinner rolls." Yasmin's mouth was watering,

"Hmm, sounds delicious. I'd love to stay Ma'am. I will call my mom?" Yasmin took out her cellular and called her mom.

"Sure," a slow response uttered from Etta's lips. Destini knew Etta was annoyed at Yasmin's remarks about her being in the kitchen all the time. After Yasmin got off the phone, Destini led Yasmin up to her room.

"Oh Destini, I just love your room."

"Okay Yasmin," Destini said quickly, "I know you love my room, believe me, I know you do. Okay listen up. Why do you have to open your mouth and say things without thinking sometimes?

"What's wrong with me saying I love your room?" questioned Yasmin with a puzzled look.

"I'm not talking about my room; I'm talking about what you said to my Mom." Destini repeated what Yasmin had said earlier, "'Oh Mrs. T. You're always in the kitchen. You must love it.' As if Etta spends her whole day there and does nothing else." Yasmin continued to look confused.

"Destini, I was giving her a compliment. I didn't mean anything."

"Okay Yasmin, what was the compliment?" Yasmin eyes wandered around with expressions of uncertainty. "Well?" Destini said as she waited. Both girls were silent. "See, Yasmin," she continued, "you don't even know. I'm asking you to be careful what you say. Etta is very sensitive when it comes to domestic work. She didn't have a formal education. She is the oldest of her siblings. She helped to rear them; she never got a chance to go to high school. She always wanted to get her GED, but she's afraid she might fail the test. But even though Winston went to college, he married someone who didn't, and they're happy. She makes the perfect housewife. I mean perfect "domestic business woman," she said as she touched her chest gently. "And sometimes she wants to do other things, but she's afraid to venture out.

Being in the kitchen is one of the things she's good at. She gets a lot of joy being in the kitchen, cooking and baking for charities. She is happy doing the laundry, cleaning up the house and helping others. Furthermore, she has a lot of common sense unlike some educated, degreed fools I know. They are only book smart in their particular studies. So, don't let it seem like you're mocking her. Just because your mother has a formal education with degrees and eats at up-scale restaurants or orders out, doesn't mean that what my Mom does isn't important too. One last thing, her name is Mrs. Taylor, not Mrs. T. Only when we're among ourselves we say names that way. How would you like me to address your Mom, 'Yo, Mrs. M?'" Yasmin laughed, but she felt awful about what she did to Mrs. Taylor.

"Okay Destini," she said, "I'm sorry, okay."

"Don't apologize to me. Mrs. Taylor is downstairs." Yasmin scurried to the door and then stopped.

"Can you come with me?"

"Nope, you got into this all by yourself. You get yourself out." Yasmin moved away from the door and sat on the bed.

"Okay," she said. "I'll wait until dinner time."

During dinner, Etta was quiet. Yasmin didn't say much either. Winston kept looking at his wife, but she ignored him.

"Darling," he finally said, "this food is so good, hmmm."

"Well," Etta said seriously, "one has to be in the kitchen to make some good home cooking." Winston was about to respond when Yasmin butted in.

"Yea, that's right." Destini looked at her and kicked her foot. Etta looked at Yasmin and if looks could kill, Yasmin would have been in trouble. Destini thought, *"Oh goodness, can't Yasmin think before she speaks."* Yasmin looked at Etta, then quickly at her plate. Winston looked at all three women suspiciously. He felt something was going on that he knew nothing about.

"Is there something that I missed?" he asked. Yasmin blurted out before anyone could say anything, "Mrs. Taylor, you're the best cook, and Destini is very lucky to have you as a mother. I want to apologize for what I said earlier, about you being in the kitchen all the time. I meant it as a compliment. Well actually, I'm," she paused, then went on. "Actually, I'm jealous. You always have a delicious meal ready for Mr. Taylor and Destini when they come home. And on weekends you have good tasty meals. You always have the best tasting breakfast. Your house always smells so lovely, and it's always warm and cozy." Tears were gathering in her eyes as she went on. "I just wished my mother would do the same things, at least sometimes. If I don't cook, we order out. And when we order, it's pizza or Chinese and I don't like Chinese food. Plus, I get sick of eating pizza all the time. Well, sometimes we have microwave dinners. I don't like them either. If I don't eat here sometimes, I just go home and eat ice cream, or a cookie, or I try to cook. Mrs. Taylor, I don't even know how to cook. If I sound ungrateful, I'm not. I just want you to know that there is a difference when, at least, one of your parents is at home when you get there. I just wish, well, I wish both of my parents were there, and I wish they were happy just like you and Mr. Taylor."

By now tears were rolling down her smooth, lovely face. Etta looked at Winston who was engrossed in what Yasmin was saying. Then she looked at Destini who was looking at the table. She then looked back at Yasmin.

"Yasmin, honey," she said softly, "your apology is accepted. And if your mother doesn't mind, I'd love to teach you how to cook, and you know you are always welcome here."

Destini smiled and clapped her hands. "Oh, good lord, she needs some teaching." Yasmin looked at her and threw a paper napkin at her. Everyone laughed. Winston asked if everything was okay now. Everyone turned and looked at him.

"Hey." He added, "I was just asking, and I'm outnumbered three to one, so, don't look at me. All I wanted to know was, if my darling is okay. That's all." Etta smiled pleasantly and she told him all was cleared. Destini looked at Etta and saw the love and relief in her youthful-looking face.

After dinner, Etta saw that Destini had finished her homework. She told her that she had a long talk with Stephan and she'd decided that Destini could go and see Mrs. Barronton. Surprised, Destini was happy to go and visit. The Taylors and Yasmin decided to visit her also. Mrs. Barronton didn't look as grand and dignified as she usually did. They found out that Shadae was still in a coma. Destini saw the hurt and pain on both Stephan's and his father's faces. Mr. Barronton was grateful to Destini for her bravery, and he promised to repay her when things got back to normal. In fact, he promised to pay for her entire college education. Sophia seemed embarrassed, but Destini tried to make her feel good with comforting words. She told her that God loved her and that Shadae would pull through. She added that, the community and the Taylors were praying for her and that God answers prayers. The Taylors prayed for Sophia and Shadae then went home. No one said anything on the way home.

37

Concern

The following two days, while Destini was in school, two other boys asked to take her home. She refused again and walked home. She hoped Stephan would call, but he didn't; so, each day after she got home, she called the hospital to see how the Barrontons were doing. Stephan did not attend school for two days and Destini missed seeing him. The days were beginning to warm up and spring was flowing in the air.

At 2:30 Thursday morning, the phone rang--Stephan was on the opposite end with anticipation in his voice.

"Good morning, Mr. Taylor." Winston rubbed his eyes while lying on his bed.

"Is this Stephan?" He asked.

"Yes Sir," He responded.

"Son, do you know what time it is? Is everything okay?"

"Well, yes and no Sir, and I'm sorry to bother you so early in the morning, but I have an emergency on my hand. Winston sat up in his bed. Etta turned and looked at him curiously.

"What's the problem Stephan?" Winston asked.

"Shadae woke up out of her coma twice, Sir, and both times she asked for Destini. Dr. Chen wants to know if Destini could come to the hospital as soon as possible? I can come and get her Mr. Taylor if you can't bring her, but I really don't want to leave just in case Shadae wakes up again." Winston was quiet.

"Hello?" said Stephan.

"Um," Winston said as he finally got his thoughts together. "Um, just a moment Stephan." He looked at Etta who was already sitting up looking at him. He told her what Stephan said.

"This early?" She paused, then said, "Okay, let's wake her up and get dressed."

"Stephan?" Winston said, "We'll be there, son. Give us twenty minutes."

"Okay, sir. Thank you very much."

Etta went to Destini's room and woke her. She barely opened her eyes as she looked up at Etta and flopped her head back on to the pillow.

"Destini, wake up. Stephan just called." Destini's head popped up quickly. "I knew that would get your attention," Etta smiled. Destini rubbed her eyes and got up to answer the phone.

"Where are you going? He's not on the phone. He wants you to come to the hospital right away. He said Shadae came out of the coma twice, and each time she asked for you." Destini, being slightly disoriented, blinked her eyes and stared. She looked at Etta then sat on the bed. She wondered why Shadae was asking for her.

On her way to the hospital, she kept wondering why Shadae asked for her. What about Pete or little Pete or Tasha, why her? "Mom," Destini asked, "wonder why Shadae is asking for me?"

"Maybe because you were the first person that helped them at the accident before the ambulance arrived. You said you were talking to both of them while they were in the car, right?

"Yes, but that was just to keep them awake."

"You said you found her son in the snow, right?

"Yes."

"Maybe" Etta said, "she knew he was not in the car and she wanted you to look for him. You said the car door was opened right?"

"Yes, but who opened it? Maybe she tried to open it to get him but did not have the strength to do what she wanted to do, and he wandered outside into the snow. I d'know," Destini continued, "Everything seems weird." When they arrived at the hospital, Winston parked the car while Etta and Destini went up to the Intensive Care Unit. One of the nurses assigned to that unit went and got Stephan. He came and thanked them for coming. Destini was happy to see Stephan again and she noticed that he needed to shave. *"Poor Stephan"* she thought, *"he must be going through so much."*

"I would like to apologize for getting all of you up so early. I did not know what else to do." Etta looked at him with pity. She felt sorry for him.

"Oh Stephan," she said, "that's no problem. We're happy to do what we can."

"Thank you, Madam, you're the best. Father is resting; he's very tired. He had patients he attended to earlier, plus he was with Mom, and then with Shadae." He looked at Destini, and even though he was tired and sleepy, he just wanted to hug her. "Mrs. Taylor," he asked, "if you don't mind, I would like Destini to come with me into Shadae's room and stay by her bed until she wakes up again." As Etta was about to answer, the nurse called Stephan. He went quickly to Shadae's room. Winston finally came up to the floor. Stephan came back and called Destini. He asked her to come quickly. She looked at her mother and went quickly with Stephan. Winston asked his wife what was going on, but, she did not have much to tell him, other than that Shadae seemed to be coming out of the coma, and that it was an answer to prayer.

As Shadae laid in her bed, she started to call little Pete's name over and over again. She seemed to be frantic. Stephan tried to calm her down, but she kept calling. "Help my baby. Help my baby." Destini didn't know what to do.

Finally, in her usual calm voice, she said, "Shadae, little Pete is safe. He's alright." Shadae calmed down for a split second and then said desperately, "Destini, my baby, my baby." She then screamed frantically "Destini, save my baby, please, the door, the door . . . I open . . . Oh Destini . . ." Her eyes opened and she glanced around, as if looking for someone. Just then, Dr. Chen came in and cleared his throat.

"I'm afraid you have to leave."

"NO!" Stephan answered abruptly. He turned his head to his sister. Dr. Chen was about to speak again but Stephan hushed him. He looked at Destini.

"Please, Destini say something."

She gestured as if not knowing what to say. "Um, Shadae, little Pete is safe." She repeated quickly. Shadae turned her head slowly and looked over at Destini and tears began to build up in her eyes.

"Thank you." She said with tiredness in her voice. "Thank you. My baby is safe." Stephan and Destini looked at each other, then at the doctor. Destini felt tears coming on. She felt guilty. *"But I'm right,"* she thought. *"Little Pete is safe now, he's asleep in God."* She looked at Stephan.

"I have to go," she said quickly, and excused herself. With gratitude flowing from his heart, Stephan watched her. He moved away as the doctor and nurses took over. He went out and thanked the Taylors for coming and bringing Destini.

"Somehow," Stephan said, "I knew you would make things work out." Ten minutes later, Dr. Chen came out.

"Well, for right now," he said "she is critical, but in stable condition. By tomorrow morning we will know if she will be out of ICU. Young lady," he said, looking at Destini, "you seem to be a miracle worker. Keep up the good work. If you will all excuse me." He turned and left. Winston yawned and Stephan said reluctantly, "Well, I guess you all will be going home now."

"Yes, unless you need us for anything else," Etta said. Then she looked at Stephan and put her hand on his shoulder. "Young man," she said with concern, "you need to get some rest or sleep, okay. The doctors and nurses are doing the best they can. Besides, your aunt Liz is here." Stephan looked at her with tired eyes.

"I know Madam, but I don't want to miss anything, in case they need me right away." Etta, still looking at him with concern, noticed that he really needed some rest.

"Stephan, God is taking care of your mother and your sister and He won't let anything go wrong if you put them in His hands. He also knows you need the rest. Now as a mother, in your mother's place, I'm demanding that you get some rest." Stephan smiled and looked at Winston.

"Don't look at me," Winston added, backing away, not wanting to deal with the situation. Destini smiled her cute smile, and looked at the floor, then back at him.

"Okay," Stephan said calmly, "I'll take your advice Madam." He looked at Destini, "Especially, since I'm outnumbered."

"Good," Etta said. "Now go and get your belongings, and let's go." Winston, Destini, and Stephan stared at Etta, with surprised expressions.

"Excuse me, Madam?" Stephan responded.

"Stephan," her voice inflected, "do you think I was born yesterday? If I leave you here, you're not going to rest or sleep. And I know," she glanced at Destini, "you are more than willing to come to our house. Come on, get your belongings, come." Etta glanced over at Winston. "Winston honey, would you bring the car out front, while Destini and I wait for Stephan to get his coat and belongings?" Winston shook his head and smiled as he went down the hall and through the double doors. Destini could not wipe the smile off her face. And Stephan, he was stunned. He didn't know what to say.

"Stephan," Destini said, "let the doctors and nurses know where you are just in case they need you. Four or five hours of sleep will do you good, and I know you're hungry." He looked at her with love and kindness. She looked at the floor shyly, and then looked back at him.

"Well," he said, "can't fight two caring, beautiful women, now can I? I'll be right back." He went and got his belongings and they were off. On their way home, Stephan fell asleep on Destini's shoulder. Destini felt good as he leaned on her. She imagined that they were married and were coming home from a long day's work. Upon their arrival, Etta tapped him on his shoulder and woke him up. They all went inside and Stephan was escorted to the guestroom. Etta made sure he was comfortable, and she promised him that she'd call his father and let him know where he was. Stephan felt peaceful sleeping in a warm comfortable bed. Thoughts of Destini filled his mind until he fell asleep. Destini was so happy to have Stephan in her home. She thanked God for blessing her and went back to sleep.

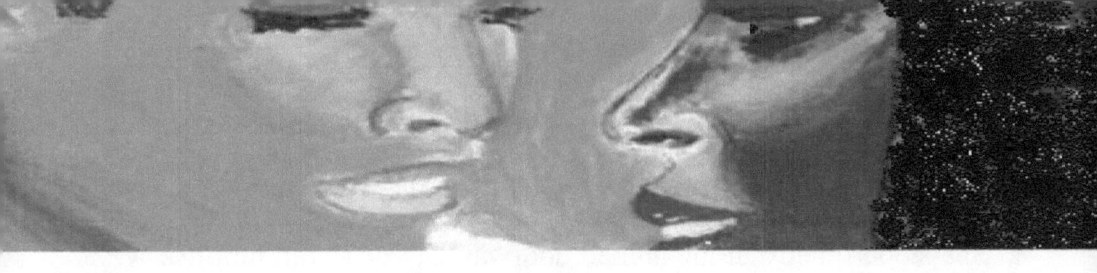

38

Strong Love

$\mathcal{D}$estini *was awakened by the bright sunshine beaming through her window. She suddenly remembered that Stephan had slept over. She jumped out of bed to take a* shower and get ready for school. *"I wonder if Stephan is up,"* she thought, while her eyes wandered to the clock.

"Oh, gracious me," she screamed, "I'm late." She wondered why Yasmin or her mother did not wake her. Destini dashed and took a shower, got dressed, and ran down the stairs. Etta was in the kitchen putting the finishing touches on breakfast.

"Oh, you're finally up I see," she said calmly.

"Mom," Destini asked anxiously, "why didn't you wake me? I'm late and you know how I hate going to school late. Did Yasmin come by?" Her mother looked at her calmly.

"I wanted to make sure you got your proper rest, especially since you haven't gotten much rest from the recent events. Yes, Yasmin stopped by, but I told her you weren't going to school today. And I've already called the school and told them you'd be out for the day." Destini was quite happy to have a day for herself. She was always busy with school during the week and on Saturdays she was at church. On Sundays, she did her chores. She jumped up and down.

"Yes, yes, thank you Mom." Etta looked at her as she said, "Now, this does not excuse your homework or your studies, young lady.

"Yes, I know, Mom. Destini looked around to see if Stephan was nearby. "Did Stephan leave yet?"

"No, he's in the living room. His father told him to stay and eat some breakfast before going back to the hospital." Destini was so happy that he was still there.

"I'll go and see what he's up to." Etta looked at her as she walked out of the kitchen. Destini walked quietly around to the living room. She stood quietly in the arched doorway and observed him. He was standing and staring at one of her pictures on top of the fireplace. She noticed that he had shaved. He looked strong and masculine to her innocent eyes. She watched him for a while, until he sensed someone there. He glanced quickly at the floor. He then turned to see the love of his life standing in the doorway, looking at him in her shy sexy way. She was a perfect picture of a dream goddess. Stephan noticed her smooth, round bosom from the top of her white, short sleeved blouse. Her long dark legs contrasted nicely against the pink skirt. As he looked on, his heart pounded and it seemed like the blood rushed throughout his body.

They stood and stared at each other as if the whole room had disappeared. *"Oh,"* thought Stephan, *"God knew exactly what He was doing when He created woman."* She was the complete opposite of him. Destini was soft and graceful. She did not have an attitude like some of the girls he knew. She had a freshness and purity about her that made him nervous. Oh, what a most pleasing sight standing in his presence. He wanted to hold this soft, delicate beauty in his arms and never let go. Her sunlit brown eyes seemed to pierce deep into his soul, and he could no longer meet her gaze. Destini felt the same rapture and they both looked away shyly.

"Um," she broke the silence, walking towards him. "You must be hungry." He looked at her, transfixed.

"Yes, I am hungry," he earnestly replied. She smiled and he whispered, "Hungry to be with you." Her enchanting smile had already entangled his heart into wanting to reach out and touch her. His hands touched her face gently and he moved closer to her.

"Destini," he continued earnestly, "I love you." He pulled her with a sudden force into his arms and kissed her intimately and passionately. She felt the strong impression of his manhood as he held her tightly. She wanted to say, "Please, never let me go, Stephan." His hands wandered over her back and continued gently towards the full roundness of her buttocks, then stopped suddenly. He wanted so much to pursue, but he respected her very much.

"Why," he thought *"did she have such a tempting, curvaceous figure that it stirred up his manhood?"* Destini felt the same strong feeling emerging. *"Oh,"* she thought, *"he's turning me on."* Stephan was gentle, yet forceful and strong. Her body melted with the firm muscles of his arms wrapped around her. *"Oh, he feels so good. If I don't stop him I don't know what's going to happen next."* She tried to pull herself from him, but he became more determined not to let her go. She tried to speak, but her voice was quieted by his demanding lips. He finally pulled away slowly and held her arms. He then looked deeply into her satin brown eyes and said intently, "That's how much I want you to be mine. I'll do everything I can to have you." Destini was amazed. She felt delicate and weak. She never realized he was so overpowering. His serious expression was making her nervous. He was looking at her intensely.

"Destini," he said again, "I love you, why can't we go steady? I want you and only you. I've loved you for five years. I know I've told you that I'd wait, but it's getting harder to wait, especially when I see you." She couldn't meet his gaze. His deep penetrating eyes sent chills up and down her spine. She loved him, but she promised Yasmin she'd stay clear of him. And Etta and Winston told her to wait until she finished high school. "I would also love to escort you to the Senior Banquet." She was about to answer when Etta called out to them.

"Destini? Stephan? Breakfast is ready. Aren't you coming to eat?" They looked at each other as they heard again. "Destini! Stephan!"

He released his grip slowly and gently. "Yes Mom, we're coming," Destini shouted. She turned to leave and he grabbed her hand gently.

"Destini," he said softly, as if waiting for an answer. She looked at him. He seemed vulnerable at that moment. She didn't want to hurt him anymore, especially since his mother and sister were in the hospital.

"Stephan, I'll let you know," she said softly as she held his hand firmly. "Come, let's go eat. I know you must be very hungry." They looked at each other, and she said quickly, "I mean for food." They laughed and went to eat.

Stephan ate and went back to the hospital. But before leaving, while standing at the doorway, he kissed his finger then placed that finger on her lips gently, and said softly, "I'll be waiting for your answer." Destini stood by the door and stared at him. She wished he didn't have to go. Winston dropped him off at the hospital and then went to his place of business. Destini stayed in her room most of the day. She studied and daydreamed about Stephan as she peered through her bedroom window. The snow was melting rapidly as the spring temperature was making its way in. The frozen lake in the yard was also beginning to melt. Yasmin called her from school on her cell phone to let her know that most of the boys were asking for her. She also told Destini she had something very important to tell her. Stephan finally called Destini before school was finished. He told her that Shadae was out of the ICU and was in critical but stable condition. He said he didn't know how or when they were going to let her know that little Pete didn't make it.

39

Change of Face

On her way home from school, Yasmin stopped by to see Destini. She was anxious to carry some news to Destini. The doorbell rang and Etta opened the door.

"Hi, Mrs. Taylor, may I see Destini please?" Etta told her to come in and that Destini was up in her room. Yasmin dashed up the stairs and knocked quickly on Destini's door.

"Come on in, Yasmin."

Yasmin walked in and placed her hands on her hips, "How did you know it was me?" she asked quickly as she walked towards her.

"Because I know the way you knock, and I heard your famous doorbell announcement. So, how was school today?"

"Great," came the anxious response, "except," she continued as she waved her hand with expression, "all of the boys are asking for you."

"Right," Destini answered in disbelief, "all of the boys are asking for me."

"Okay," Yasmin looked at her and stated, "a lot of the boys were asking for you."

"Okay, who and why didn't you text me their names?" Yasmin eagerly sat on the floor to dish out all of the information.

"Thought you wouldn't ask. Plus, I wanted to tell you in person." she responded. "Johnnie Taylor.

"Right, no way!" Destini blurted out.

"Yes, Johnnie Taylor, and he asked three times, then he had the nerve to ask for your phone number."

"Get outta here, no way."

"Hold up," Yasmin said, "Mark Anderson, Joey, John Wong, Antonio, Stanley, Malik, Ch . . ."

"Wait--Malik Sanders?" Destini shouted at the top of her voice.

"Yep." By now, Destini was beside herself with wonder. Malik talked only to White girls. "Also, Charles Michaels, buck toothed Peter, Jay, tall good-looking Tom and Anson. And there were more, but I don't remember." Then Yasmin suddenly burst out, "O yes I do. You wouldn't believe who asked for you, and he said he'd call you later." Destini sat up straight.

"Call me? Who has my cell number? Because I know I didn't give my number to any guy."

"Well," said Yasmin, "this guy may have your number." Destini wondered who would have her number. "Okay," Yasmin finally said, "its Keith, Stephan's best friend."

"Oh," Destini said smiling. "He's cool. He always talks to me and asks me how I'm doing. He's cool, he can call." She looked at Yasmin who looked a little surprised at her response. Yasmin knew that Keith had tried to keep Stephan from going out with Destini. He told Stephan that Destini was too dark for him. But Stephan thought Keith was probably checking Destini out himself.

"I can't believe all these guys are asking about me, or maybe they just want to ask me to the Senior Banquet. What on earth happened? Just because I helped the Barrontons? I don't believe this. How strange." She shook her head. "So, Yasmin," Destini asked, "what else happened in school today?" Yasmin paused, then looked at Destini.

"Well I heard some juicy gossip today. I overheard Tasha talking to one of her good friends, Kim, about the accident."

"Really, what about the accident?"

"Well, Tasha was telling Kim that it wasn't the Barrontons who were supposed to be in the accident that night. It was you."

"Very funny," Destini laughed.

"I'm serious. Tasha said that she was supposed to go with them to help run you off the road, but she said that as much as she didn't like you, she couldn't do it. She thought it was wrong and she said she didn't want to be responsible for you getting hurt like that or getting killed." Destini stood up and looked at Yasmin.

"I don't believe it. That's a lot of bull."

"She also said," Yasmin continued with a surprised expression; reviewing in her mind, '*bull,*' "that when she heard about the accident, she thought at first it was you who was hurt, but then she heard it was them and she thought you ran them off the road instead."

"What!" Destini shouted. "What? This is crazy. Oh Yasmin, first of all the Barrontons didn't know I was out that night. And, even if they did, they didn't know I was going to travel on the back road." Yasmin was ready to tell some more. Destini sat on the edge of her bed.

"Yes, they did know you were out, and they knew where you were. Mrs. Barronton had called over to Mrs. Jones, and she mentioned that you were there." Destini remembered that while she was visiting Mrs. Jones, there was a phone call and Mrs. Jones did speak to someone.

"Well, like I said before, they didn't know I was going to drive on the back road." She waited to hear what Yasmin had to say, because she was beginning to get angry.

"Uh, huh, Mrs. Jones somehow told them you usually take the back road. So, they took the chance that you'd travel that way because it was faster to your home and had less traffic. But instead of meeting you, they somehow skidded off the road before you passed by." Destini sat in silence and disbelief. She got up, went to the window, and stared outside. Yasmin, still sitting on the floor, looked at Destini and wished she could say something happy to make her laugh. But she couldn't think of anything.

"You know," Destini finally said, "Yasmin, if all of this is true, God's word is so true. In Galatians 6 verse 7, He said, 'Be not deceived; God is not mocked,'" Yasmin joined in with her, "'Whatsoever a man soweth that shall he also reap.' So, if you hurt someone," Destini continued, "don't think for a moment you won't get it back somehow. It will be either right away or later when you least expect it." She turned to Yasmin. "Well, it seems like Sophia and Shadae Barronton got what they were planning for me and they got it right away." She walked towards Yasmin. "This is so sad. I'm extremely disappointed and angry that a woman, supposedly of such

227

high standards, could stoop so low, just to satisfy her own selfish plans."

"Yeah," Yasmin responded, "I know. I wonder what Stephan is gonna say when he finds out." They both stopped and stared at each other. Destini broke the silence.

"Well, he won't find out from me, and I know you're not going to tell him or my parents, right Yasmin?"

Yasmin stared at Destini then said, "Are you kidding? Why not?" Destini told her not to worry, because she would take care of everything. Yasmin tried to find out what Destini was up to, but Destini dismissed the thought, as though it was nothing.

"I have to finish my homework."

"Homework?" Yasmin asked surprisingly. "You didn't go to school today. How you got homework?" Destini went back to her desk and sat down, and told Yasmin she called the school, because she didn't want to be behind even if it was one day. Destini told Yasmin she had to finish her homework and that Yasmin was allowed to stay or leave. Yasmin looked at Destini and wondered what she was up to. She was so calm, especially after hearing such disturbing news. Yasmin finally went home, and Destini was happy. She wanted to finish up her homework and go to the hospital to visit her enemy, Mrs. Barronton.

Destini got permission from her mother to visit Mrs. Barronton at the hospital. She went straight to her room. Destini wanted to get there before the visitors came. Mrs. Barronton was reading a book when she entered. Destini walked in quietly with a soft smile. She asked her how she was doing. Mrs. Barronton's smile was not warm and caring as it was earlier when Destini visited her. She looked much better than the other day. She was more alert and her movements seemed stronger.

"I'm feeling better than before. Did you see Stephan out there?" she asked. Destini shook her head.

"No, I didn't see him."

"Oh, you mean you came to visit me? How nice of you." Mrs. Barronton's smile was warmer.

Destini walked closer to her bedside. "Yes Ma'am, I came to visit you, and I'm happy to know you are feeling better."

Mrs. Barronton looked down at her book then scratched her head. She felt awkward.

"Um," she finally said, "I heard what you did for Shadae. Thank you."

"You're quite welcome Ma'am." Destini didn't know how to start. She just stood there and stared at Mrs. Barronton. Mrs. Barronton asked her how her parents were and to thank them for looking after Stephan for her.

"My parents are fine, and yes, I'll relay your message to them." Destini knew that visitors would be coming soon, so she gained the confidence that she needed. She walked around the bed and began to talk. "Mrs. Barronton, I heard a rumor going around that on the night of your accident, you were on your way to run me off the road." Destini stopped and looked at her to watch her reaction. Destini said that she didn't believe it and didn't know why anyone would spread such an awful lie.

Mrs. Barronton's heart raced as she exclaimed, "What? Where did you hear that ridiculous lie?"

"From a good source," she responded coldly.

"Well," said Mrs. Barronton as she looked down at the sheet, "that's utterly ridiculous. I, I didn't even know where you were much less to think about such an awful thing." Destini turned away and thought, *"Oh God, could I be wrong to just walk in here and accuse her? Oh God, please, I need your directions, please."* A thought came to Destini right away.

"Okay," she said as she spun to face Mrs. Barronton. I'm gonna tell Stephan so he can find out why this ugly rumor is going around." Destini turned to leave.

"No!" Mrs. Barronton said hastily. "Why would you bother him with such foolishness?"

"Because he ought to know that someone is passing ugly rumors around about his mother," Destini insisted, "and I want to get to the bottom of this. Furthermore, Mr. Barronton should know too." Sophia's eyes widened as she looked down at her book. She didn't know what else to say. She looked up into Destini's piercing eyes.

"Why have you come to the hospital to provoke me?" she finally said. "Leave now!" Destini stared at her then said, "Sure, good evening Ma'am." She turned to leave and Sophia stopped her.

"Wait," she shouted, "wait, um, I hope you will not say anything to Stephan or my husband about this ridiculous rumor."

"I think it's best that I do, unless you tell me the truth," Destini said.

"Are you calling me a liar?"

"No," Destini answered, "but if you did plan such an escapade, I just want you to know that I forgive you and that God is my army and bodyguard. If it's true that you tried to hurt me, your family got hurt instead. Poor little Pete would be alive. Sin doesn't pa . . .

"What are you talking about?" Mrs. Barronton asked anxiously.

"I'm talking about the fact that Jesus protects his children, and you would be much happier if you let Jesus into your life and . . .

"No," Sophia screamed, "what do you mean little Pete would be alive?" Destini stopped immediately. She looked at Mrs. Barronton.

"I'm saying little Pete would be alive if you and your daughter were not trying . . ."

Suddenly, Sophia felt like the room was spinning. "Wait, wait," Sophia shouted. She put her hand out, "wait, what do you mean 'would be alive?' What are you talking about?" She said with trembling voice. "What do you mean," Sophia screamed, "would be alive?" Destini was confused as to why she was harping on about 'be alive,' Sophia rang the nurses' station consistently without stopping. One of the nurses came running in.

"Where is my grandson?" Sophia cried." Where is my grandson?" The nurse looked at Destini and then told Mrs. Barronton to calm down. "No!" she continued, "Where is Stephan?" Stephan was near the nurse's station when his mother called. He quickly walked to the door when he heard her frantically asking for him. The nurse was trying to calm her down when Stephan came in.

"Stephan," his mother asked desperately, "where is little Pete?" Stephan looked stunned, because he and his father had not told her yet about little Pete's passing away. They were planning to tell her tomorrow, after the funeral service was scheduled, because they didn't want her to worry. Stephan came to her bedside, held her hands and looked into her eyes.

"Mom," he said, "if you don't calm down, I will ask everyone in here to leave, and I will leave too. You will be given some medication to calm you down. Now, I want you to lay back and calm down so we can let you know how little Pete is doing." Sophia looked at him. She felt weak and anxious. She was about to say something, but, Stephan sternly said, "Mom!" She finally decided to lay back.

She glanced over at Destini and then at Stephan. Stephan wondered what had happened. He looked around to see the other nurse who had come with a needle. He told her that it was not necessary. Sophia looked at Stephan. He seemed so mature and in control of the situation. He was much like his father. Destini turned to leave, and Stephan stopped her without looking at her.

"Destini," he said, "please stay." Destini stopped immediately. He looked at the nurses and politely asked them if they could leave. One of the nurses asked Mrs. Barronton if she was okay, and she replied that she was fine. The nurse told Stephan that if he needed her, she would be right outside. She closed the door and returned to her duties.

After the nurses left, Stephan looked at Destini, and he wasn't smiling. Destini felt uncomfortable. Stephan looked at his mother and she asked him how little Pete was doing. She said that she wanted to see her husband at once. Stephan didn't know how to tell her about little Pete. He was about to answer when the door opened and his father walked in. His eyes swept around the room as he asked in his serious calm manner, "What's going on?" His melodious baritone voice controlled the stillness of the room. He continued, "Sophia, can't I leave you for a few minutes? I'm on duty, and one of the nurses called me to let me know that my wife was frantic about something."

"Dad, Mom is asking about little Pete." Wycham looked sternly at Stephan, then at Destini. She looked at the floor. He stepped closer to Sophia's bed and looked into her eyes.

"Hon," he said, "little Pete did not survive the accident." Sophia wrinkled her face as she said,

"What . . . and when did this happen?" Tears began to roll down her pretty face, "and why am I just finding this out?" She raised her voice as she cried, "And I had to find it out from her." She pointed to Destini, hoping to cause a dent in the relationship between Stephan and Destini. She continued, "a non-member of the family." Tears continued to flow as she looked at her husband. "Oh my God," she cried out, "and when did you plan to tell me?" Wycham walked around to her bedside.

"First," he said calmly, "hear me out. I thought it best to wait until you were strong enough. I was planning to let you know tomorrow morning. You see, the wake is scheduled for tomorrow and the funeral service is on Saturday after church service." Sophia clung to her husband and cried. He hugged her lovingly and tears gathered in his eyes also.

"After the church service," Wycham said, "the folks are coming to the hospital. The funeral is being held in the big chapel because you are not released yet. Now, I don't want to hear any fuss about it. Shadae doesn't know either. We're hoping she'll be strong enough so we can tell her tomorrow." Mrs. Barronton was still crying. She felt guilty and had a pain that made her feel as if she wanted to die. Wycham hugged her close. Destini did not know that Mrs. Barronton could cry. She stared at her in wonder. Destini felt guilty. She wished she had not come to the hospital. Stephan looked at Destini with sadness in his eyes. Destini couldn't bear him looking at her, and she left the room quickly. Stephan started to follow her and his mother called after him. He told her he would be right back and went after Destini. He walked quickly through the hallway so he could reach her before she got on the elevator.

"Destini!" he called. "Wait." She was so embarrassed. She didn't want to see him. He reached up to her and held her arm.

"Destini, I need to talk to you." She turned and looked at him,

"Stephan," she said quietly, "I'm sorry, I thought she knew already." He looked around for an empty room, and they both went in.

"I'm sorry," he apologized. "I should've let you know that we had not told her. I just did not know that you would visit my mother, of all people. Did she call you?" She looked into his eyes and answered,

"No, I just wanted to visit."

"Destini," he said, "I'm flattered, no, happy, well, no I'm elated that you would visit my mother after all she's put you through. Thank you." He looked at her lovingly, "That is one of the reasons I love you so much. You are one of the sweetest persons I know. And don't worry about little Pete. It's our fault for not telling her earlier and . . . um, for not letting you know." Stephan touched her chin gently, "Okay?"

"Okay," she responded still feeling guilty. He hugged her lovingly.

"Are you coming to the wake and the funeral services? It's gonna be held in the hospital chapel."

"Yes." She said, and he escorted her out to the parking lot and watched her drive away. When he returned to his mother's room, his father was gone. Sophia watched him very closely to see his reaction.

"Where is Destini?"

"She went home." He answered, and then said, "Mom, wasn't that nice of her to visit you?" She watched him very closely as she responded.

"Yes, very nice," she answered sniffling.

"Where is Dad? Did he go back to work?'

"Yes, he's getting off work soon," she responded. Just then some visitors knocked on the door. Sophia straightened up herself, her hair and wiped her eyes and nose. Stephan let them in and was about to leave when Sophia asked him where he was going.

"I'm gonna be outside Mom, I'm not going anywhere, and if I'm not outside I'll be with Shadae.

40

Unlikely Revelation

On the day of the funeral, Wycham decided to tell Shadae, because Sophia insisted that she should know about her son. Stephan went with him. Shadae wasn't strong enough to go to the funeral, so she was not permitted to go. When her father told her about her son, she screamed and cried. She somehow found the strength to call out little Pete's name and kept repeating, "I want my baby, my baby." The guilt was too much to endure, and she cried until she went into shock.

Wycham knew something like this could happen, which is why he didn't want to tell her, but Sophia insisted that she had to know her son was going to be buried that day. Now his daughter was in shock. He had to go to the funeral and leave her. Stephan told him to go with Mom and not to let her know what had happened until the service was over. He asked his father to tell Pete what happened and to allow him to come and see Shadae if he wanted to. He said that he would remain with Shadae just in case she revived, and he assured his father that he would text him if an emergency arose.

Wycham looked lovingly at his son and was proud of him. "You know son, you are truly a man. I've watched you these past few days and you have toughed it out without any complaints. I'm proud of you Stephan, and I want you to know you're the best and I love you." He reached out and hugged Stephan. Stephan was happy to have his father showing him some fatherly love. Even though his father loved him, he was always busy.

At the funeral service, everyone wondered why Stephan was not there. Dr. Barronton called Pete aside and told him the situation and asked him not to say anything to anyone. He told him that he would like him to visit Shadae's bedside as soon as the funeral was over. Pete agreed to go and see her. At the end of the funeral, Wycham mentioned Shadae's state to Sophia just before he went up to announce it. Everyone, including Sophia, was surprised, and he asked them to pray for her. Sophia started to cry, she felt guilty. She wished she had gone home that night, instead of planning to run Destini off the road. She also hoped Destini didn't say anything to Stephan or Wycham. Pete went to see Shadae. He loved her very much and prayed in his heart asking God to please make her well.

When Sophia was wheeled back to the room and was finally alone, she cried and begged God to forgive her. She wanted relief from her guilt. When she finished praying, her door opened and Stephan came in. His countenance recounted anger and grief. He was quiet as he walked slowly into the room and stood facing the windows. Tears were still in Sophia's eyes. She saw the strain and anguish on Stephan's face.

"Stephan," she asked anxiously, "what's wrong? Is Shadae alright?" There was no response. Still peering through the window, he finally responded.

"No, Shadae is still in shock, but stabilized. Mom," he continued, "why couldn't you just let it go?"

"Because," responded Sophia, "Shadae had a right to know that her son was dead and was going to be buried." Still looking out the window, Stephan moved away. Without looking at his mother, he repeated his statement.

"You just couldn't let it go. Why couldn't you just leave Destini alone?" Sophia looked at him with a puzzled face.

"What are you talking about?" Stephan looked directly at his mother and asked her without being disrespectful because he loved his mother very much.

"Mom, why did you and Shadae go on the back road, with the baby," he paused as if searching for words; "with the baby," he repeated in a stronger tone, "to run Destini off the road that night?" Sophia's eyes widened with surprise, then anger.

"O----h," she said with her eyes wandering around angrily. "That little black wench and her lies. She just couldn't wait to tell you, could she?" Stephan's eyes squinted.

"Why," he said loudly, "do you always have to call people names? Why can't you address them by their name, especially if they are supposed to be your friend? How would you like Tasha to call you a black wench?"

"I was not talking about Tasha," she screamed. "I was . . ." she suddenly stopped, her eyes wandered around again as if thinking deeply. She stared at her bed. Stephan stood there waiting for a response. "So," she finally said softly, "that's how Destini found out."

"Found out what, Mom? You're not making any sense . . ." Stephan suddenly stopped talking and wondering if Destini knew.

"Are you saying that Destini knows about this? Oh God, no!" He rubbed his head and walked towards the door.

"Where are you going?" She asked desperately.

"I've got to go."

"Stephan," she screamed, "come back. Stephan. Please come back here. I'm your mother, listen to me. You come back here now. Ste----phan." As he walked to the elevator, he kept repeating to himself that he couldn't believe that she knew and did not tell him. He was very embarrassed.

Destini was at home helping her mother clear the dining table. Their guests from the church were in the family room discussing the sermon that was preached that day. They also touched on the funeral service at the hospital and the events surrounding it. The doorbell rang, and Etta wondered who it could be.

"Oh, my goodness; was there anyone else coming to dinner?"

"Not that I know of, Mom." Destini went to answer the door. To her surprise, she saw Stephan standing there. She stood and stared at him with tender love in her gorgeous eyes. She noticed that he looked troubled. Destini took his hand and asked him to come in. He walked into the house slowly and said in a slow unhappy voice, without smiling, that they needed to talk.

"Where can we go?" he asked.

"In here, in the living room. Stephan, is Shadae okay?" Stephan was not his usual self. He just plainly answered, while he walked into the living room.

"Shadae is fine, she will pull through, evil people usually do." Destini's eyes widened and she stared at him.

"What? What are you talking about?" He turned and looked at her steadily.

"Why," he asked, "didn't you tell me, that you knew about my mother and my sister's plan to run you off the road the night of the accident?" Stunned, Destini stared at Stephan and then sat down and looked straight ahead. She then rolled her eyes to the side.

"Ah---m," she stuttered, "ahhh, I, how did you find out?" she asked.

"That's not important," he said softly. "Destini, I trusted you, and I thought you trusted me enough to come to me about something so serious. Do you know the police are investigating the accident, especially since my nephew died? They want to know what could have caused the car to slide off the road; and why little Pete was lying in the snow. My Mom and sister can get into serious trouble." Etta came from behind the wall near the doorway. Stephan was surprised by Etta's presence. He didn't realize she was behind the door.

"I trusted you too," she said, "to come to me about this, Destini. But what I really want to know is," she looked at Stephan, "if what you said is true? Because, if it is, *that's the last straw to the camel's back.* I'm taking no more foolishness from your mother Stephan, no more. Destini could've been killed. Then what would she have done?"

"Madam, I didn't realize you were by the doorway."

"Well," said Etta as Destini stood to her feet, troubled. "After sundown I'm going first to the police station, and then I'm going down to the hospital to see Sophia Barronton."

"Mo---m," Destini said, "wait, let's talk this over." Destini felt awful, and even though Mrs. Barronton was trying to hurt or scare

238

her, Destini didn't want her to get into trouble with the police. "Please Mom," she begged, "before you make any hasty decisions please let us all discuss this." Etta placed her hands on her hips.

"And what is there to discuss? A wrong is a wrong. And she has done many wrongs to you. I will not stand here and listen to you protecting an evil enemy. There is too much evil going on in the world today, for a Christian woman to behave in such an insulting manner." Etta looked at Stephan, "Sorry son, I don't mean to hurt you or your family, especially because of what they've been through, but I'm sick of this." She then turned to leave, and Stephan tried to stop her.

"Mrs. Taylor," he began, but Destini interrupted him by putting out her hand. She then spoke to her mother earnestly.

"Mom, please listen and wait just a moment, for my sake, please." Etta stopped and turned to her and folded her arms.

"Okay," she said, "Speak."

"What Mrs. Barronton did in the past is inexcusable," Destini said as she continued. "Naturally, those things hurt me. But, Mom you taught me about God, that He's a loving, forgiving, protecting, and also a vengeful God. He said, 'vengeance is mine,' so leave it all to Him."

"As you can see, God protected me because I trusted Him. That is what you asked me to do. And He's true to His word where He said 'Whatsoever a man soweth, that shall he also reap.' Mrs. Barronton has reaped and is reaping the seeds that she sewed the night of the accident. Mom, she lost her grandson and her daughter is very sick. Mom please, Jesus asked us to forgive one another." Destini stepped forward. "Mom look at me, I'm not hurt. I praise the God of heaven. He protected me, and I'm healthy and on my feet. Mom, if you go to the police station, it's gonna stir up a lot of things and things will never be the same again. Mrs. Barronton may be charged with murder for little Pete. Stephan and his dad do not deserve this kind of publicity. Mom, please put it in God's hands and let Him take care of it. I know He will. I think Mrs. Barronton has learned a good lesson. I'm not saying you shouldn't go and talk to her. After all, she needs to hear from someone like you who's not afraid to put her in her place."

"Yes," Stephan said, "I very much agree, Madam, indeed I do." Etta looked unhappily at Stephan with concern.

"Has your mother learned anything from this? And what else do you think she has up her sleeves to hurt or humiliate Destini?" Questioning him, Etta noticed Stephan's bewildered look and she pitied him.

"Stephan," she said, as she looked at him, "for your sake and for your sake only, I'm taking this to your fathers." Destini and Stephan looked at Etta in confusion, "Uh?"

"Don't you have two fathers, Stephan?" Etta asked with a slight smile on her face. Destini and Stephan looked at each other. Stephan finally smiled.

"Certainly Madam." He said. "Mrs. Taylor, in fact I will be happy to come with you when you go. That is if you don't mind." Destini looked at both of them curiously. "Destini," Stephan continued, "Father." And he pointed upwards.

"O---h, okay, God the Father and your dad. Okay, so I'm a little slow."

"No, you are not." Stephan answered as he looked at her lovingly and put his arms around her shoulders. "Thanks," he said warmly as he looked into her gorgeous eyes and squeezed her shoulders gently. Stephan was also grateful to God for working everything out.

The Taylors and Stephan went and talked to Dr. Barronton. Again, he was very unhappy with his wife. Etta went to the hospital and confronted Sophia, and at first, she denied it. But, Etta threatened to let the police investigate it. She told Sophia that she and her daughter could be charged for the death of little Pete. She told Sophia that she had a good witness who heard her saying what she was planning that night. She also told her that the back road was a distance from her mansion and was completely out of the way from where she visited that night.

Sophia finally confessed and cried. She asked Etta to forgive her and said that she wished she were in little Pete's place. She asked to see Destini to apologize. Sophia was so embarrassed, especially since her husband and Stephan knew about her malicious plan. Her husband lectured her thoroughly when she was released the next day from the hospital.

Winston had sat and listened while Etta talked to Sophia. He figured that Etta could handle the situation, which she did. It was dark when Etta and Winston finally got home. Destini was home pacing the floor. She heard the car pulled up in the driveway and then the keys jiggling in the door. She dashed to the front door. It opened, and Destini anxiously questioned them.

"So, how did it go?" Her parents walked in calmly and closed the door. Etta went into the living room and Destini followed behind, anxiously.

"Well?"

"Well," Etta responded, "Mrs. Barronton denied it at first, then she finally confessed. Only when I told her what I intended to do. She apologized and asked for forgiveness and said she wanted to see you to apologize for all the wrongs she has done to you." Destini smiled.

Winston also told Sophia that she had to apologize to Destini in person. In addition, she had to ask Destini to forgive her for all the wrongs she had done to her in the past. Dr. Barronton agreed and invited Destini and her family to the mansion, about a week after Sophia was released from the hospital. The Taylors agreed.

"It's about time," Destini said, "that Mrs. Barronton learned to humble herself. Thank you, Jesus."

41

The Invitation

*D*estini *dressed exceptionally beautiful to go to the Barronton's Mansion. She knew Stephan was going to be there, so she wanted to look extra lovely.*

The Taylors were ready and waiting downstairs. Mr. Taylor wore a navy blue and white sweater with gray woolen pants, and Mrs. Taylor wore a silk, red suit that accentuated her gorgeous full figure.

"Destini!" Etta shouted. "Come on girl. What's taking you so long?"

"I'm coming, Mom!" she returned. "Just a minute, I'm coming. Here I come."

"Well, stop coming and come on . . . Oh, Destini," Etta looked up at Destini as she descended the stairs. "Child, you look great. You go girl. You need to give Sophia Barronton something to talk about so she can see the reason why Stephan adores you."

"Oh Mom, thanks. You always have the nicest things . . ." Destini stopped in the middle of her sentence and repeated, "Stephan adores me?"

"Girl, you know he adores you. Come here . . ." Winston strolled out of the living room.

"Okay, ready," he looked up to see Destini coming down the stairs. "Oh, my goodness," he said, with a wonderful look of surprise. "I have the two most beautiful women in Massachusetts. I hope the Barrontons are ready for Mrs. Universe and Miss World." They both laughed.

"Oh sweetheart," Etta said.

"Oh dad, you always say such lovely things."

The Taylors got into the stretch limousine that was sent for them and were off to dinner at the Barrontons. Destini thought about Stephan the entire ride. When they finally got there, her heart started to race. *"Why am I so nervous?"* she thought, *"I can't believe that the Barrontons invited us to dinner and sent a limo to pick us up. Mrs. Barronton is going to apologize to me. Wow, this is unbelievable."*

They finally reached the mansion. They looked outside and saw someone waiting to escort them inside. *"He must be the butler or something,"* thought Destini. He escorted them inside. *"Wow,"* thought Destini, *"the mansion is still awesome."* She noticed that the Christmas tree and decorations were not there and the foyer seemed even larger.

The Taylors went in and looked up at the ceiling. They looked around in awe. It was breathtaking.
"I'm impressed," Etta said. "I'm very impressed. Wow, this is gorgeous, superb. No wonder she is, is so-----o." Her husband and Destini looked at her. She closed her mouth and decided not to say anything else.
"This way please," said their escort.

Stephan had told his mother earlier that he was going to meet the Taylors when they arrived. Mrs. Barronton did not want him to meet them. She asked him not to go. She told him to let the servants do their jobs, but Stephan insisted, and disappeared before she had a chance to stop him. Stephan was excited that the Taylors were finally invited to his home. The butler called and told Stephan that they had arrived and he was escorting them to the meeting room. Stephan quickly walked to meet them. As he approached the Taylors, his eyes sparkled when he saw Destini. "Oh my," he said to himself, "she is simply beautiful." It was as if she glided towards him in a decelerate motion. Her gorgeous ivory and gold colored dress accentuated her curvaceous body, and of course he noticed her long shapely chocolate legs showing from the off centered, delicate split of her dress.

Stephan greeted them in his usual manly style.

"Mr. and Mrs. Taylor" he shook their hands, "Destini." He took her hand gently and kissed it. "Good afternoon. It's certainly a pleasure to have you here with us today." Destini loved the feel of his soft, warm lips on her hand. The Taylors returned his greeting and they were all escorted to a huge room. The ceiling was a high cathedral like ceiling. The room was spaced by four columns, which were situated in a square, twenty feet apart from each other. The off-white color of the columns off set the three-dimensional painting of small golden leaves winding their way around each column. The gold trimmings at the top and bottom made the look complete. The Taylors stopped and stared in awe at the columns. Their attention was drawn to one of the walls. It was glass; well, at least it looked like glass to them as they stared outside.

Destini noticed the waterfall she saw the night of the party. The beautiful colored lights were not lit, but the water was flowing. To her, it was still very beautiful. The beige and peach curtains with hints of brick red throughout. It encircled the walls and windows, and made the room feel alive.

Stephan stared at Destini while she looked in awe at the room and outside. The scenery was nothing to him, because he grew up in that environment and it didn't distract him either way. He was just excited that Destini was there.

Dr. and Mrs. Barronton finally came into the room. "Good afternoon," they said simultaneously as they shook hands with the Taylors.

"Good afternoon," the Taylors replied. Destini stared at Mrs. Barronton with a half-smile. Wycham stretched out his arms and walked towards Destini. "Destini, my dear! It is certainly a pleasure to see you, and you are looking gorgeous as usual," Destini didn't know what to say, she was dumb-founded. She looked over at her parents and finally mustered up something to say as she looked back at him.

"Um, thank you sir . . . I mean . . . good afternoon, and it's really nice to be here." She then looked at her parents again. Sophia was watching her steadily. She stepped forward and took Destini's hand.

"Yes" she added, "it's certainly a pleasure to see you dear," she said as she kissed her on the cheek. Etta and Winston glanced at each other as if to say "hypocrite." Sophia glanced slightly at her son and she motioned for Destini to have a seat.

"Please, have a seat." Wycham also motioned for the Taylors to sit. The atmosphere seemed somewhat stiff.

"You have a beautiful home, Ma'am." Destini said shyly.

"Well, thank you dear. I appreciate your compliment," she said and then looking down at her lap and then looking up at her.

"Yes, thank you Destini." Wycham added. "Everyone please," he points to the sofas. Everyone sat. Destini sat in a sofa chair with cabriole legs, and her parents on a matching loveseat. Sophia asked if they would like something to drink. They didn't want to spoil their appetite by drinking prior to their meal, so they declined. Wycham then continued, "Well, uh, we invited you here to apologize to you." He glanced at everyone, and then looked at Destini, "especially you Destini. We apologize for certain wrongs that were done to you. I am a no-nonsense type of man, and as you can see, I get right to the point." Sophia fiddled with her fingers and glanced around the room as her husband spoke. Destini noticed the cast on Mrs. Barronton's arm. Even though Stephan was listening to his father, he could not stop staring at Destini. Sophia noticed Stephan's gaze. She thought to herself, if only Destini was not so dark. Why couldn't she be a few skin shades lighter? Destini was such a beautiful girl. Sophia also wished she was not a Black American.

"And," Wycham continued speaking, "I am really sorry for what happened. Now," he turned to his wife, "Sophia has something she wants to say to you and your family. Honey, go ahead." Sophia looked at everyone and mustered up a rubber band smile.

"Um, well," she said. "Um, thanks for coming. Um, Mr. and Mrs. Taylor."

Winston interrupted her with a smirky smile. "Please, Winston and Etta."

"Oh, um, Winston, Etta, and of course Destini." Sophia glanced up at the ceiling, then back at Destini. Destini sat like a proper lady with her hands on her lap, her head slightly lowered, and her gorgeous eyes looking up at Sophia. "Um, I would like to apologize to all of you for my unruly behavior. And ah, Destini dear," Sophia eyes could not meet Destini's steady gaze. "Um, I have been awfully unkind and non-Christian in my behavior to you. I apologize. I am deeply sorry and I am asking for your forgiveness." Destini was totally surprised. She looked at her mother and father and then looked backed at Sophia. Sophia continued to smile with the rubber band smile. Destini didn't know what to say. She realized all eyes were centered on her. Finally, Etta broke the silence. She cleared her throat.

"Um, Sophia, I'm deeply touched by your apology, but as Destini's mother, I need to feel secure that the things of the past won't be repeated. Because, . . ." Etta paused, thinking, and then continued, "for instance, I know, and you know the reason for your past actions against Destini. It was because you didn't want Stephan and Destini to date each other. Now, I know that you have not miraculously changed your mind on that matter. So, how are we to be sure that history will not repeat itself?"

Sophia felt insulted by the interruption. She looked at Etta with a straight face trying her best to speak nicely.

"Etta um, I understand your concerns, and I will admit, I prefer that Stephan and Destini finish high school first, before anything happens between them. But, I am sitting here in front of all of you apologizing. Therefore, I do not plan to cause any kind of mischief from this point forward." Etta twisted her lips in disbelief and thought to herself, *"sure."*

Sophia looked at Destini with discomfiture wishing she didn't have to be there and that it was all over with. Destini looked over at Stephan. Everyone was quiet, and all eyes were on Destini. She looked at Sophia and finally said softly,

"Um, I accept your apology Ma'am. I just want to say something if you don't mind. I know we all have faults. However, as professed Christians we should be like Jesus Christ. I choose to follow in His footsteps and learn through His word to be loving, kind, forgiving, and accepting of each person as God's wonderful creation. It doesn't matter how anyone looks. It's all beautiful. God created us individually. Some of us have green, blue, brown or hazel eyes, or light, brown or dark skin. God wanted it that way. He is artistic. I am happy to accept your apology Mrs. Barronton, and I hope we can be friends." Sophia hung her head down in shame. Before her, sits a gorgeous young lady, telling her, an adult, about Christ.

"Well, Destini, thank you, and you're absolutely right," Sophia agreed. She was troubled in her spirit and needed to get something else off her chest. She wanted to say it to Destini but, was embarrassed. Finally, Sophia decided to say what was on her mind.

"Destini," she continued, "I have something else to say to you." She paused and cleared her throat. "Um, during the holiday party last Christmas, I behaved rather childishly and I was wrong. Destini dear, you looked wonderful that night. In fact, you were the most beautiful girl there that night. That is why I was so nervous to see you and Stephan together." It seemed like tears were in her eyes. Sophia stopped and tried her best to hold back the tears. She succeeded and then continued. "I was worried about my son getting into trouble. But I guess if I had taken the time to get to know you, I would not have judged you so harshly. I am very sorry for my behavior. Please forgive me."

Etta stared at Sophia in disbelief, with her mouth open. She turned and looked at Winston. He was looking at Sophia in astonishment. *"Could this be the same person who spoke to him so rudely on the phone that night? God certainly has His ways to humble us,"* he thought. Destini sat and stared at Mrs. Barronton. She seemed more peaceful and motherly now, not threatening. Destini's gorgeous smile brightened her beautiful face.

"Of course, I forgive you Mrs. Barronton. I did that a long time ago. I gave it all to the Lord, and asked him to make me love you, and He did." Sophia was more ashamed. *"Oh, my dear Father,"* she thought, *"a child has made me look stupid and selfish in front of my husband and my son. How can I face them?"* Sophia then heard a gentle voice calling her.

"Mother," he said, "you are the best mother in the whole world and I love you. I'm so proud of you." Stephan had moved over to his mother. He pulled her gently towards him and hugged her tightly. Tears were in both their eyes as they embraced.

"I love you too, my darling," she responded. "I love you very much." Wycham stood up and looked at them lovingly. He felt especially proud of his wife. He looked at the Taylors who were sitting and looking at Sophia and Stephan. Destini stood up also.

"I am proud of you Sweetheart," Dr. Barronton said, holding her hands and then squeezing them lovingly, and smiling. "Well, are we all at peace now, because I don't know about anyone else, but I'm hungry. So, can we pray and ask God to seal this?" The Taylors stood up; they were hungry also. Everyone agreed, and Dr. Barronton prayed and thanked God for the apologies. Wycham asked that God would bless everyone and let His will be done in all of their lives. He also asked God to bless the food that they were about to devour. They all retired to the dining room. When Etta entered the room, she looked around. She loved the elegant touches. Sophia certainly had a talent and flair for design.

The Taylors and the Barrontons conversed as they sat and enjoyed the delicious meal that was prepared. Mrs. Barronton looked at everyone enjoying the meal. She knew deep within her heart that she did not want Stephan and Destini to date or see each other, but she agreed to put aside what she felt inside. She stared at Destini, *"How,"* she thought, *"can such a beautiful girl be so dark skinned. If only she were lighter."* Destini's skin was smooth and beautiful. In fact, as Sophia stared at Destini, she realized that Destini was far more gorgeous than even her own daughter, and Tasha. She stopped staring when she realized Destini noticed her stares.

Mrs. Barronton wondered why she felt the way she did about Destini. Perhaps it was her parents' influence about skin color. She thought, *"Since my parents influenced me against dark skin, why wasn't Stephan influenced by me?"* She looked at her son. She felt such love for him. She wanted the best for him. He was quite intelligent and handsome. Her husband was busy talking to the Taylors, but he was also watching his wife. He noticed she was paying much attention to Destini and Stephan. He decided to break her concentration.

"Sweetheart," he called, "is everything okay?" She looked over at him. "You're so quiet," he continued, "are you feeling okay?"

"I'm feeling great, dear," she responded. She smiled politely and looked at everyone. After dessert, they all assembled in the family room.

Stephan wanted to spend some time alone with Destini before she and her parents went home. After assembling a few minutes in the family room, he asked if they could be excused. Etta answered quickly before anyone had a chance to say anything.

"Okay, kids, you have approximately twenty minutes, because we have to leave soon, so scurry on outta here now." Mrs. Barronton looked at Mrs. Taylor with a look of surprise and disappointment. She preferred that they stayed with everyone. A half smile ran across Sophia's face.

"Are you sure," Sophia added, "you wouldn't want to spend the rest of the time with us boring adults?"

"Thanks, Mom," Stephan kissed her lightly on the cheek. "See all of you in a bit." Winston was looking at Destini, proudly. How lovely she had grown. She was tall and elegant. He looked at Sophia and smiled to himself. By the look on her face, he figured she disapproved of them going off alone. Sophia tried to pretend she didn't mind them going off alone, but she was distracted. Her husband noticed her reaction and thought of something that could bring her attention back.

"Hon, why don't you tell the Taylors about our trips to Italy, Egypt, Greece and Kenya." Wycham was smart. He knew that she loved to talk about herself and her accomplishments. Her travels opened the door for this. It was difficult for her to get started, but she finally got into it.

Stephan was elated to be alone with Destini. They went out to the balcony. Stephan stared at Destini. He wanted to hold her close in his arms. He told her how gorgeous she looked and that he was happy to have her at his home. He gently held her hand, and he noticed she was wearing the watch he gave her.

"The gold and diamonds look awesome against your gorgeous dark brown skin," he said softly.

"Thank you," she answered shyly lowering her head and looking up at him with a smile. She was very happy. This was like a dream come true.

"You're quite welcome," he said as he stared into her eyes with a look of love. They both smiled. "Destini?" he said.

"Yes," she responded.

"Why do you have the most beautiful, gorgeous, sexiest brown eyes?" he asked as he stared into them. Destini smiled and looked away. *"Oh, my goodness,"* she thought, *"why does he have to say those things, and then look at me that way? I just love it."*

"You're funny, Stephan," she answered.

"No, I'm not. Really, I'm serious. You have the most gorgeous, sexy, satin-brown eyes I've ever seen. I love to look at them. It's like you have a twinkle that attracts me every time I look at them. God has truly blessed you with beauty; the beauty of a Nubian Queen. You're well-endowed with a curvaceous figure that won't quit." He said and tapped her lightly on her buns as he moved closer and continued to look into her eyes.

Destini laughed, "You are so funny, Stephan." She glanced at him then looked away. "You sure know how to make a woman feel special. Thank you." They both gazed steadily into each other's eyes as their lips pressed together. Stephan held her closer to him and she snuggled into his arms, wishing to stay there forever. She felt soft and warm to him. He wanted to continue, but heard the maid calling him as she cleared her throat.

"Stephan, the Taylors are ready to go and they need Destini to come now." Stephan told her thanks, and she turned and left. Destini turned to leave. He pulled her back to him kissed her again, and then said, "You are mine, and I truly love you." He gently ran his finger across the top of her breast to feel its softness. She took a deep breath, gently moved his hand and looking into his eyes.

"I have to go Stephan."

"Wait," he added, "I'm still waiting for your answer. May I escort you to the Senior Banquet?" They stared into each other's eyes lovingly.

"I'd love to be your date for the Banquet," she responded. They walked hand in hand as they went to meet their parents. Destini was excited to be Stephan's date for the Senior Banquet.

Everyone hugged, kissed each other on the cheek, and said their good-byes. Sophia was happy that it was all over. She even felt at peace. Stephan was happy to have Destini as his date for the Senior Banquet. The Taylors were escorted back to the limousine that brought them to the mansion.

On her way home, Destini wondered how she was going to explain to Yasmin about being Stephan's date for the Senior Banquet. Well, Yasmin told her not to stop seeing him for her sake, but she thought, *"I told her I'd stay clear of him. Oh God what am I going to do?"* Yasmin was her best friend. *"Well,"* she thought, *"maybe I'll tell Stephan I can't go. But he'll want to know why? What will I tell him? Oh God I really want to be Stephan's date for our Senior Banquet. Please give me wisdom about this situation, please."*

After getting home, Destini told her mom and dad that Stephan asked her to be his date for the Senior Banquet. Etta told her she was waiting to hear that announcement and she was hoping that it was Stephan that would escort her to the Banquet. Both parents agreed and said after graduation, she was free to go steady with Stephan; but they wanted her to put her college education first and foremost. They advised her not to allow romance to keep her back. She accepted their guidance and promised to get a college education first.

Three weeks later, Shadae was discharged from the hospital but returned weekly for physical therapy. She hated the therapy because it was so painful. She had counseling with both the pastor and a psychiatrist because of the loss of her son. Pete, her boyfriend, continued to see her. He finally asked her to marry him when she graduated, and she accepted.

Shadae gathered her nerve to go and visit with Destini and to thank her for saving their lives. She also apologized for being so nasty and rude to her all those years. Shadae was embarrassed, especially since she knew that Destini knew about their plan to run her off the road. After she left, Destini was surprised at how humble and sweet she had become.

Shadae went home and told her mother that Destini was one of the nicest persons she knew. She wished she had taken the time to get to know her instead of judging her, because of her color and nationality.

42

Assertiveness

$\mathcal{T}$asha was upset because Stephan, Jim and Shadae no longer associated with her. She called Destini and asked to meet with her after school. Destini agreed to meet with her, wondering what it was all about. She saw Tasha in the distance, pacing back and forth. Destini approached her cautiously and Tasha walked towards Destini with venom. She coldly accused her of trying to take Stephan, Jim and Shadae from her. Tasha promised Destini that she would never succeed, and she was going to give her a good butt whipping, especially since Destini was stupid, black and baboon ugly.

Tasha walked around Destini snaking her neck, venting and pointing her finger like a lioness waiting to devour its prey, shouting, "West Indian men don't like Black-American dogs, especially ugly ones like you." Destini stood and listened as if in combat, waiting for the attack and being prepared at any time to protect herself. Tasha continued to vent her anger towards Destini, "And your sleazy type will never take the place of us West Indian women. We have class, dignity and beauty unlike you." Destini looked at her with pity. "I hate you, you black, stinking ugly baboon." Tasha vented. Destini was upset, sick, and tired of the name calling. She looked at Tasha and return strongly, yet with dignity.

"Please, stop talking about yourself, and for your information, I would never want to take the place of any woman, West Indian or American. And I don't have to try and take Stephan," Destini stated, "because I can have Stephan at the snap of my fingers because he loves me. And if West Indian men do not like African-American women, how is it that Etta, who is American, is married to Winston Taylor, a Jamaican?" Destini continued with a sudden burst of anger. "I am not going to allow you to intimidate me anymore. You are jealous, condescending, and in need of some darn good discipline. Since I'm more gorgeous than you, you can't deal with it." Destini snapped her fingers and swished away. She suddenly stopped and turned around. Calming down, she walked back slowly.

"And if I were you," Destini raised her voice, "I would have someone teach me how to wear my makeup so I would look pretty instead of looking like a clown." Tasha's eyes and mouth opened wide. Destini continued, "By the way, Jim loves clowns. Why don't you give him a call?" Calming down, Destini said while walking around Tasha, "You claim to have dignity, yet the words that slid from your mouth are embarrassing and un-lady like."

"Destini, you are nothing, you come from nowhere. You don't belong with good, normal people" Tasha spat angrily. "You are so darn black and spooky ugly." Destini looked Tasha straight in the eyes and said, "And is that all you can say? Well guess what, I am proud to be black. I thank God for showing me His loving mercy by giving me this beautiful, velvety, satin, black skin. It is His creation, and just as He is proud of it, so . . . am . . . I. I do come from somewhere. God is my Father and I am His child. Therefore," she pointed her finger on Tasha's chest, touching it and pushing her slightly. "I am a princess of the most High God." Tasha tried to interrupt and pushed Destini's hand away from her, but Destini pushed her back, knocking her to the ground. Destini continued with fire on her tongue.

"Wait, I am not finished yet. Your vocabulary needs an upgrade. You need to do more English and grammar homework after school, girl." Tasha had never seen Destini behaved in this manner. She got up and cautiously approached Destini as if to hit her, but Destini stopped her.

"I'm not afraid of you so don't even think about it. I will stomp you if you dare touch me," she said, glaring at her. Tasha, knowing that Destini fought well, backed away. Destini was about to say something else that was not nice, but she felt sad inside that she had to talk to Tasha that way. She just wanted to make peace. She paused and then changed her topic. "Tasha," she said, "as a people, we should learn to love and care about each other instead of putting each other down. It doesn't matter where we are from. Whether I was born here, or you were born in the Islands, I am your sister. We are the real Hebrews. Maybe we are related from way back. We don't know. The slave buyers separated our families during slavery. As a family, we should try to build one another up and stop acting like crabs. Crabs don't have the intelligence we were blessed with--they grab and pull down. I'm sorry to snap at you like that, but I'm sick and tired of you and others being ugly to me. I'm sick of the name-calling. Is there any reason we can't be friends?"

"No!" Tasha shouted, "Some of our ancestors were never slaves. They came here free just like some Whites. The free Blacks also owned slaves. So, we may not be related."

"I know that Tasha. But, we all still came from the continent. So why can't we be friends?

"Never, not with you--you b----. I'd be too embarrassed to be seen with someone as black as you." Destini stood there spaced out, staring at her in disbelief.

"I'm sure," Destini said, "if Jim and Stephan heard the names you just called me, they would be greatly disappointed in you, this brown-skinned beauty, who's supposed to be a Christian, and who thinks the world of herself. Yea, maybe I should tell them."

"Huh, it's your words against mine. And they wouldn't believe you any way," Tasha said with a snickering laugh. Destini continued playfully, yet serious.

"Yea, maybe I should. I'll tell Mrs. Jones, and she'll pass it on to the whole community. What would your mother say? Yes, Tasha it will be your words against mine, but seriously, who do you think the whole community would believe?"

"You wouldn't," Tasha said sheepishly, calming down.

"Who knows, maybe you can leave home and join a circus." Destini shouted and walked away.

"You know," Tasha shouted at her, "Stephan loves me. He made love to me when we were dating." Destini stopped, squinted and gnashed her teeth. She didn't know what to say. She was stunned. She felt that her world was turned upside down, but she kept calm as she turned and looked at Tasha, pausing.

Then she said, "Even if it is true, it's your loss."

"Well," said Tasha, "it is true and at least I'm his first." Destini looked at her with pity.

"Tasha, she said, "wake up out of your dream world. Stephan is a man. Do you really think you're his first? But, that's not important. More importantly, please understand this, some men use women for sex, to quench their desire and need for a sexual release. When they get what they want, they move on to the next woman, leaving you to think about what you gave up, or they leave you with a baby or some kind of disease. You need to think before you willingly spread your legs. You are the one who will be hurt, not him." She turned and went home, leaving Tasha to contemplate the words.

Yasmin was waiting for Destini. When Destini approached her, she looked at Destini with concern.

"What's the matter? You look very upset." Yasmin asked.

"Oh," said Destini, "it's Tasha and her foolishness again. She asked me to meet her."

"Next time don't go alone."

"Okay."

"What did she do this time?"

"She accused me of trying to take Stephan, Jim and Shadae from her. She said that the men wouldn't like me because I'm a Black American."

"Uh," Yasmin shouted with a burst of anger, "Tasha gets on my last nerve. Oh Destini, she is so jealous of you. Believe me I know, I remember the things she said when I went to her house last year. Oooooh, I just want to pull her hair out, and, and send her somewhere."

"Don't worry, I told her to join a circus," Destini said calmly. Yasmin laughed.

"She needed to be told about her make-up." The young ladies looked at each other and laughed.

"I feel so guilty though, telling her about a circus and laughing at her. But I was angry with her."

"Destini," Yasmin said with widened eyes. "Tasha deserves what she gets. Ever since you came here, she has been teasing you and causing trouble for you. She tried to break us up, and almost succeeded. What you said to her is nothing. In fact, she should be kicked off the planet. Evil people deserve what they get. I mean, Shadae gave up, why can't she?"

"Maybe I should just try to be her friend," Destini said softly.

"Friend!" Yasmin screamed, "Are you crazy? She'll eat you alive. She's like a barracuda. No, no no, that will never work."

"I d'know Yasmin," Destini continued. "Maybe she needs a friend."

"She has a friend," Yasmin stated, "her one and only buddy."

"You know Shadae has not been the same since the accident, plus she is stuck on herself. I heard Shadae is mad at her for telling what really happened the night of the accident, plus Shadae is engaged to Pete now. So, maybe Tasha has some problems we don't know about and she needs someone who truly cares. You know what I mean Yasmin?"

"No, I don't know what you mean. But you are right. She definitely has a problem. And she needs more than a friend for help."

The girls walked home along the grassy pathway. They took in the beautiful scenery. Spring always brings such beauty and loveliness. Destini felt better admiring the loveliness of the scenery. The majestic trees flowed gently in the breeze. The colorful flowers along the grassy sidewalk were breathtaking. The girls, with books in their hands, continued on enjoying the cool gentle breeze. Destini loved the beautiful scenery, but her mind was centered on Tasha. She wanted to be her friend, and let the past be mended. She wanted Yasmin to understand what was going through her mind. Maybe if I remind Yasmin that Jesus asked us to forgive.

"Yasmin, Jesus was kind to others even though they were mean to Him. Remember what the minister said in church on Sabbath? Jesus blessed those who hurt Him. I'm gonna follow His example and ask for His advice."

"I d'know Destini. I'd think twice before trying to be friends with someone like her. Jesus was angry when he came at those stupid people with a whip. And at His death, there was an earthquake that I'm sure, it frightened the daylights out of the evil people. At

His resurrection, there was another earthquake and a very bright light that knocked out the soldiers who were guarding His tomb."

"I know what you mean Yasmin, I know."

43

Tasha's Confession

*W*hen Destini got home, Etta, who seemed excited, handed her an envelope.

"Destini," Etta said, "look, an envelope came for you from Model Society, hurry open it." Destini opened it and learned that her photograph was chosen for a model search contest in New York City. She was one of the forty finalists chosen from among one million photographs to compete in August for Ms. Belle Model U.S.A. Destini was very surprised, because she did not send any photographs. No one knew who sent in the photos. That night Destini called Tasha and talked to her. Tasha was still cold and rude.

"Tasha," Destini said, before hanging up "I'm trying to be your friend even though you have treated me badly ever since I've known you. I've tried to be nice to you. I've apologized for anything I did or said to hurt you. I did what the Lord asked me to do. Tasha, I am here if you need a friend to talk to. But I want you to know that I will not take any more foolishness from you. Thanks for listening and have a good night."

One afternoon, two weeks before graduation, Tasha came to see Destini. The doorbell rang and Etta opened the door.

"Yes?" Etta said, looking at Tasha quite sternly.

"Um, is Destini here, Mrs. Taylor?" Replied Tasha nervously, especially because of the look she received from Etta.

"Yes."

"May I speak to her please?" Etta stared at her, and then stepped back into the house to call Destini.

"Wait here," Etta said. Destini came to the door and invited Tasha to sit on the back porch. The girls sat together and Tasha apologized for all the bad things she did and said in the past. Destini listened and tears swelled in Tasha's eyes as she spoke. Destini noticed that Tasha's makeup was toned down considerably.

"Destini, I don't know why I did what I did, but it was awfully stupid. You're such a nice person. You are the only one who treats me with respect and had the decency to call and apologize when I should have been the one to call. I really appreciate the things you said to me the other day. I thought about it, and you're right." I went online and did some research about the Hebrew slaves in the Western world and it's true." Tasha wiped her nose with her hanky and continued. "I wish I were like you. You're so beautiful and strong. Your skin is smooth and pretty. I guess I was very jealous because Stephan always showed so much attention to you." They sat quietly for a while and listened as the birds whistles sounded through the trees. The gentle breeze blew over the rolling hills in the distance. The lake rippled gently to the breeze. Etta came out with some cool lemonade.

"Would you ladies like some cool lemonade and a piece of my delicious apple pie?"

"Sure, thanks Mom," Destini said gladly.

"I'll just have some lemonade," Tasha said. "Thank you, Mrs. Taylor.

"Tasha, do you eat apple pie at home?" Destini asked.

"No."

"Well," said Destini, "you have to try this. I promise you will love it, especially with some whipped cream or ice cream. Hmmm, it's delicious." Tasha looked at the pie, then at Etta. She noticed that Etta had a more pleasant face than when she first came to the door.

"I'll try it," she said smiling. She took a piece and ate as Etta and Destini looked on. Tasha smiled and shook her head. "Hmmm, this is good. May I have some more, please?" They all laughed. Etta left the lemonade and the pie on the serving tray and went back inside.

"Destini, I'd love to be your friend. I feel so happy inside now. I don't know why, but I'm really glad you called me that night. I didn't mean to be so rude. In fact I am very sorry I was so rude. Can you forgive me for all the things I did to you? I know that is asking a lot. And I know I don't deserve it, but . . ."

"Tasha," Destini interrupted, "sure, I'll forgive you. And I'd love to be your friend. By the way, your makeup looks beautiful."

"Thank you so much, I needed to hear that. And thanks for accepting me," Tasha said smiling. "I appreciate it." Tasha

262

embraced Destini and Destini returned the same. Tasha decided she wanted more pie.

"Hmmm, this pie is delicious. May I have some more please? And I'd love to have the recipe." They both laughed.

44

The Senior Banquet

That same evening, Destini visited Yasmin at her home. She couldn't wait to tell Yasmin about Tasha's apologies. She also told Yasmin that Stephan asked her to the Senior Banquet. Yasmin was displeased. She did not want Destini and Tasha to be friends. She wished Stephan had asked her to be his date for the Senior Banquet. How was she to discourage Destini from both relationships? Yasmin didn't know what to do or say. She hung down her head in despair. Destini noticed her disappointment.

"So, um, whatta ya think?" Destini asked hesitantly, looking keenly at her.

"Um," Yasmin walked away, cautiously eyeing Destini and trying not to let her see her reaction. "Well, um, I think you made a terrible mistake by talking to Tasha. She only wants to be friends with you so she can get close to Stephan. She really likes him a lot, and she hates you." Yasmin spun around and faced Destini, looking directly at her. "Have you forgotten all the rotten things she did to you? Why would she change suddenly? People are not like lizards. They don't change overnight or at the snap of a finger, especially someone like Tasha."

"You are right Yasmin, and I've already put everything in God's hands and asked Him to take care of it. She will never be my best friend like you are. She told me she was sorry for all the bad things she did, and I accepted her apology, just like how I accepted yours. I believe that it is the Christian thing to do. I believe Jesus would have done the same thing, because that's what He admonished us to do."

"Okay," she answered irritably, "if that's what you want, but I know I wouldn't." She looked at the floor and sat down. Destini waited to hear what else she had to say, but she was quiet.

"Well, um," said Destini, "has anyone asked you to the Senior Banquet, yet?"

"Yea," she answered hurriedly almost cutting Destini's question off. Destini looked at Yasmin and realized that she was upset.

"Is everything okay? Do you want to talk about it or do you want me to come back another time?"

"No, why did you say that?"

"Because you are acting strange. Does it have to do with Stephan asking me to the Senior Banquet?"

"No, why would you say that?" Destini was beginning to feel some degree of tension. She squeezed the back of her neck, rolling her head in a circular motion, attempting to relieve the tension in her neck.

"Because . . . I don't know? What's wrong with you Yasmin?"

"Nothing." Yasmin responded irritably.

"Yes, something is wrong. Listen to you. You are snapping at me. Yasmin, I know when you are upset. Why can't you ever come clean with me? What's wrong?"

"Nothing is wrong, okay." And she walked off and went out to the backyard. Destini sat and waited inside for ten minutes. Yasmin did not come back inside. Destini decided to go outside.

"Yasmin, I'm leaving. I'll see you later?" But Yasmin did not answer. "Yasmin, Yasmin? Yasmin, I'm talking to you, would you stop being rude. What is your problem?" Yasmin spun around and faced Destini angrily.

"Problem, problem, what is my problem? What's your problem? You come over here showing off. '*Yasmin, Tasha and I are friends now, she apologized. Isn't that great*?' Wow, wup ti do. After all the evil that was done to you, how can you be excited about her friendship?" Yasmin shouted. "An' then to make matters worse, you're all up in my face, '*Stephan asked me to be his date for the Senior Banquet.*' Oh goodie, that's nice Destini. I'm happy for you. Have fun. Okay, goodbye, you can leave now." Destini stared at Yasmin, and Yasmin turned away from her glare. Destini shook her head in disbelief and walked towards her.

"Okay, I'm sorry. I didn't realize I was . . . showing off, and that I was all up in your face. I figured that with you being my best friend, I could tell you things that I'm excited about, and are happening in my life. I'm sorry if anything I said upset you." Destini scratched her head. She was beginning to get angry at Yasmin's behavior.

"There you go again," Yasmin shouted, "with your self-righteous attitude, like you're always right. *'I'm sorry, I didn't realize,'* acting all innocent. You act like you're better than me and everybody else, just because Stephan likes you and because your hair grew down your back. You come round here swinging it all up in my face. Destini, once upon a time when you had no hair, you were totally different from the way you are now." Destini stood there listening to her supposedly best friend. She looked at Yasmin and wondered where all of that anger and jealousy were coming from. Yasmin had long hair down her back too. Destini felt bad. She decided not to argue with Yasmin. She knew it would not get them anywhere. Tears were beginning to gather in her eyes.

"Yasmin, all I wanted to do was to share something with you. I thought . . . , well, um, I know I told you I would stay clear of Stephan. I'll just tell him I can't go to the Senior Banquet. I gotta go, um goodbye. Hope you have fun with your date." Destini walked from the backyard to the front yard. She felt sadness in her heart. She wished she had a caring and loving friend who was happy for her. Why are girls always jealous of me? Do I really show off like Yasmin said? She was glad she didn't say anything to Yasmin about Ms. Belle Model U.S.A. Yasmin would have probably kicked her out of her house. Why couldn't she meet someone who is genuine, kind and caring? She then remembered Etta. Aside from Jesus, Etta was the best friend she had on earth.

When Destini returned home she saw Etta outside in a swing under a tree. She ran to her. Etta noticed immediately that something was wrong. She stopped swinging.

"Destini dear, what's wrong?"

"It's Yasmin. She's accusing me of showing off in her face, just because I told her about Tasha coming over here and apologizing. She's upset about Stephan asking me to the Senior Banquet. I don't understand it Mom. She's supposed to be my friend. Isn't she supposed to be happy for me?"

"Not if she's jealous of you. That's the bottom line, honey."

"Mom, I told her I'd stay clear of Stephan, just for her, and she had said I didn't have to. Now I've got to tell Stephan that I can't go to the Senior Banquet with him. I know he is going to be very disappointed."

"Yes, he is."

"Mom, what would you do if you were in my shoes?"

"First, I would thank God for making me so pretty." Destini smiled. "Then, I would go to the Senior Banquet."

"You would?"

"Yes, and why not? Is Yasmin gonna live your life for you? Stephan is interested in you, not her. Isn't there any other boy at the school who could escort Yasmin? She is a pretty girl."

"Yes, she is very pretty. I remember when we first met I wished every day I looked just like her. But thank God you taught me to love who I am. And yes, she said she has a date."

"See, now you go on with Stephan."

"Mom, I promised her. I d'know, I'll see? Thanks for talking to me. I feel a little better already. I'm going inside. Thanks Mom." Destini's confounded thoughts bared heavily on each step as she walked into the house. With rounded shoulders she plopped herself down on the sofa, sighed and called Stephan. When she told him what her decision was, he didn't hesitate. He got into his car and drove straight to her house. Destini was surprised at how fast he got there. The doorbell rang and she answered it. Upon entering he told her he liked the smell of her house. She told him he always said that. He smiled and asked her to explain what was going on. When she told him what happened at Yasmin's, he was furious. Destini tried to calm him down. She finally calmed him down enough so they could sit on the back porch and talk.

"Destini, I've already bought my suit. I told my parents and they both agreed." Destini sat up straight.

"Your mother agreed?"

268

"Yes." Destini was stunned. *"I really have to go now,"* she thought.

"Stephan, I'll let you know later." He hung his head in obvious disappointment.

"Destini," he said holding her hand, "please don't let Yasmin spoil this for us. I really care about you and if Yasmin really cares about you, she would be happy for you. Besides, I wasn't planning to tell you this, but she called me and asked me to escort her to the Senior Banquet." The sudden silence gave recognition to the chirping of the crickets.

Then Destini screeched, "She did what? You're joking, right?"

"No, I wouldn't do that." Destini shook her head and squinted. She wanted to knock the mess out of Yasmin.

"That little, uh! When did she ask you?" she said tightening her grip.

"Two weeks ago."

"Two wee . . . okay, that's it. Um, . . ."

"Keith asked her to go with him and she accepted." Stephan said. "As a matter of fact, I know of seven different guys who asked Yasmin." Destini sat in silence. Yasmin told her nothing about this. Of course not! Stephan looked at Destini and then asked, "Um, about how many guys asked you to the Senior Banquet?" Destini assumed control of her emotions and gathered her thoughts. She took in a deep breath and then breathed out slowly.

Destini smiled, "How did you know I was asked?

"Believe me Destini," he said with love in his eyes, "you are very beautiful and I am not the only young man at school who noticed. Besides, I know there are quite a few seniors who are in love with you. So, who asked?" he questioned her again with a twinkle in his eyes.

"Okay," she answered smiling. "Antonio, Stanley, Charles Michaels, Anson, Jay, Malik Sanders, Tom and um . . ." She looked at his handsome face and decided not to say the young man's name. That's it." Stephan shook his head and half-smiled.

"Well princess, what is your answer?" The confusion that had settled in her head flew away. Destini decided to go with Stephan to the Senior Banquet and to stay away from Yasmin.

Destini asked Etta to go shopping with her for the Banquet dress. She was excited to go on her first formal date with Stephan. She wanted to look her best. Etta gave her a facial and helped her with her makeup. She also helped styled her hair. Destini felt beautiful with the fashionable hairstyle that was sleeked back, with soft bouncy curls on top as it flowed down the back of her head. Her silver tiara sat in the right spot. Long tendrils cascaded at the sides and back. Her stunning baby blue, one-shoulder, georgette gown was lined with satin. Destini's shapely curves accentuated the shape of the dress in the right places. The off centered split in the front of the gown showed off her gorgeous chocolate legs, while the back of the skirt elongated to the floor.

When the door opened and Stephan saw Destini standing at the top of the stairs, he gaped in awe. He felt like he was immersed in a beautiful dream. He was beside himself. *"She is absolutely glamorous,"* he thought. He couldn't believe that he finally got a chance to take out the love of his life without anyone stopping or saying anything to him. He took her hand as she descended the last two steps, and then proceeded to pinned the corsage on her gown. He tried his best not to show his nervousness.

Destini stepped outside to a sleek white limo waiting for them. She wondered how excited a person could be. Tonight, she was quite excited beyond words, to spend the evening with Stephan. And to think she was about to turn him down because of Yasmin. She looked up at Stephan; he was so manly. *"I'm proud to be with him,"* she thought. On their way to the Banquet, Stephan held both her hands in his and stared at her. His gorgeous brown eyes were warm yet, piercing. She wondered what he was thinking. He's making me nervous. Every time she looked at him, he smiled shyly. They didn't talk about anything much. It made him feel good inside just looking at the precious beauty sitting in front of him. Stephan told her twice that he was proud to have her as his date and how gorgeous she looked. Destini didn't know how to accept such wonderful attention from someone she cared so much about. She wanted to hold him close to her and kiss his soft tender lips, but she sat like a lady and thanked him kindly for his compliments.

When they arrived, he held her hands to escort her out of the limo and into the Banquet hall. She looked at him and told him he was an awesome man. It stirred his heart to hear such inspiring words from the girl he loved. The live band was sounding out some great tunes. The banquet hall was beautifully decorated. Many of the students stared at the couple and whispered as they entered the hall. Stephan handed their names to the guide at the door. They were announced and were then escorted to their table. Four students were seated at each table. Keith and Yasmin were the ones to be seated with Stephan and Destini. However, Stephan called the attendant and requested that the seating arrangements be changed. He explained the reason to Keith, who objected at first. Nevertheless, Stephan insisted and Keith finally agreed.

Destini noticed Keith and Yasmin seated at a table. She saw them looking over at her. In fact, Keith was staring at her. She was hoping Stephan did not notice his stares. Destini tried to say hi to Yasmin, but she turned her face away. Destini wanted very much to say hi to Yasmin and to be friends again. She hated to be at such a nice gathering with the man she loved and her best friend sitting at another table looking unhappy. Stephan noticed what was happening and he gently touched Destini's hand and told her to relax and to enjoy herself. He told her not to let anyone or anything bother her. She told him it was hard not to notice Yasmin. He advised her to ask God to let them have a wonderful time tonight. She agreed and decided to try and enjoy her food.

The master of ceremonies announced that winners of the king and queen titles for the Senior Banquet would be chosen. It would be announced within the next thirty minutes. He also announced that everyone was allowed to mingle and to make their way up to the ballot and vote for the new king and queen.

Destini decided to go to the powder room to freshen up. On her way back, she ran into Yasmin.

"So," Yasmin said, abruptly, "you still went with him even though you promised." Destini looked at her sadly.

"Good evening and nice to see you too Yasmin. By the way, you look great. Can't we just get over this and make up? You have a very nice date and I have mine." Yasmin looked her straight in the eyes.

"You know Destini, we both want the same guy, and I'm not going to hide the way I feel anymore. I really like Stephan a lot. No, actually," she said looking up and then back at Destini, "I'm in love with him. And you didn't even care about me enough to stay clear of him. And yes, I'm very angry with you for that. You show up here all up in my face with him. You're wrong Destini and I don't know if I can forgive you for that."

"Forgive, forgive!" Destini raised her voice. "You have a lot of nerve talking about forgiveness, when you had the audacity to call Stephan and ask him to escort you to the banquet. An' and you ask about forgiveness! You wanted to go out with him and would have if he had said yes; yet you are asking me not to." Yasmin was surprised that Destini knew about her asking Stephan. "How dare you," continued Destini with tears gathering in her eyes, "come up in my face acting all innocent and you . . . you going behind my back and asking the man, you know I love and who loves me--not you . . .!" Destini pointed her finger at herself and then at Yasmin almost touching her. Yasmin slapped Destini's face for claiming Stephan. Destini was beside herself with anger and she instinctively returned the slap, grabbed Yasmin by the throat strongly, pushing her up against the wall. She then held both arms with force against the wall. Yasmin screamed as Destini muttered between clenched teeth, "Don't you ever touch me again because I will knock the mess outta you." Yasmin tried to loosen Destini's grip, but could not. "Do you hear me?" Destini stated angrily squeezing her arms. Yasmin did not answer and Destini repeated the question shaking her, "Do you hear me?" Yasmin looked into Destini's face and felt afraid.

"Yes, I hear you. Destini stop you are hurting me. Sto----p." Destini finally released her grip and stepped away. Some student passing by looked on with astonishment.

"Let me tell you this Yasmin Michaels," Destini unleashed. "You stay away from Stephan Barronton. If he wanted you, he would have been with you. I would have respected that and stayed clear of him for your sake; because you are my friend. But Yasmin, you don't respect me. The funniest thing about all this is that I care about you very much." Tears were gathering in her eyes again. "I have to get back inside because if I stay out here any longer, I'll stomp you. Good night." With that, she left Yasmin standing there feeling upset and foolish. Stephan was talking to Keith when Destini approached. He looked at her and knew something was wrong. He excused himself from Keith.

"Excuse me Keith. Princess, what's wrong?"

"Nothing, why?" He gazed in her eyes and she looked away and hung her head.

"Okay," she conceded softly, "I ran into Yasmin and we got into it, but I straightened it out. Oh, Stephan I just want to be friends with her. I hate this."

"Chocolate," he said gently with concern in his sexy eyes, "there are times in your life when you have to let things or friends go. When Yasmin is ready she'll come around. Frankly, I prefer not having her around, because I want all of your time, especially when you decide that we'll go steady." She looked at him. "Yes, I'm still waiting for your answer," he concluded lovingly.

"I told you, my parents said after graduation."

"Okay . . ." The master of ceremonies interrupted the conversation to announce the king and queen.

"Okay ladies and gents. The votes are in and have been calculated. I will announce the winners and you will make your way up to the platform to receive your crown and your prize. Now remember the winners do not have to be a couple, but if they are a couple, great." The drums played. "Our new queen for this year is

273

Destini Pearson Taylor." Destini eyes widened with surprise as she covered her mouth.

"Stephan, oh my goodness. I, I didn't expect that any of the students would have voted."

"Destini Pearson Taylor, please make your way up to the platform." Destini walked up to the platform and was crowned queen of the Senior Banquet. The students clapped and cheered. Stephan felt a slight tinge of jealousy. He was hoping that no other guy would win. He didn't want any man touching his woman. "Now," came the announcement. "our new king is Stephan Barronton." The cheers of the students soared higher. Stephan was excited, only because he did not want any other guy near Destini. He made his way up to the platform and took his place beside her. He was crowned king. Everyone cheered except Yasmin. Destini was happy to be with Stephan, and to be at his side as his queen. They were both to open the dance floor, which was similar to a step dance, march with attitude. The master of ceremonies led them onto the floor. The music played and all of the couples held hands and the dance began. Everyone stepped forward, stepped to the side, dance in place, clapped their hand, moved backwards, raised hand in the air; repeated it and marched around the hall, etc. They danced, laughed, and had fun until it was time to go home.

Stephan's Confession

*G*raduation arrived and the students were all in *their caps and gowns. All the parents showed up to see their children graduate. The sun shone brightly on the well*-manicured lawn as the graduates walked to the beat of the music. The Taylors were happy to see Destini in her gown. They sat and reminisced about the beautiful chocolate girl with the million-dollar smile and elegant long legs that they saw at the foster home facility. Tears filled their eyes as they watched. She was now tall and elegant with a twinkle in her eyes and dance in her steps. They thought she was the most beautiful girl there.

Mrs. Michaels and Yasmin's father were both proud to see Yasmin walking down the aisle. The Barrontons and Pete were proud to see Shadae and Stephan in their gowns. Stephan was chosen to give the Valedictorian farewell speech, which was very welcoming and very encouraging. His speech included loving one's self, trusting in God, and caring about others no matter their appearance. The graduates were challenged to move forward with all their might, develop their talents to serve humanity and to own their own businesses. Sophia, proud as a peacock, looked around to see how everyone was enjoying her son's speech. With her nose up in the air and lips pouting, she seemed so properly stuck-up. If she could only see herself. Mrs. Jones was pointing out Sophia to the other parents and imitating her. Some of the parents found it amusing and chuckled, while a few expressed displeasures.

After graduation, friends gathered to congratulate each other. Winston and Etta looked on while Sophia and Elizabeth watched Destini and Stephan very closely. Sophia did not mention anything to Stephan about Destini. Wycham hugged Shadae, Stephan and

Destini. He reminded her about paying for her entire college tuition. Destini thanked him and assured him she would not forget to remind him. He smiled, went and told Stephan that Destini was a very good choice. Yasmin stood afar off and watched until she left with her parents.

"I need to talk to you, Destini," Stephan said, looking lovingly into her eyes, "but not until I return from England, Nigeria and Zimbabwe. I will be traveling with my parents on a business trip and will be away for about three to four weeks." He hugged her, and when some of the other girls saw, they quickly ran over to get a hug from Stephan. Sophia and Liz exchanged glances and smiled.

A month after graduation, when Destini was about to leave for New York for the contest, Stephan confessed that he was the one who submitted her pictures. He said he wanted to tell her at the Senior Banquet but decided not to, so he could surprise her right before she left. He revealed to her that she was the most beautiful girl he knew, inside and out, and he believed she had a chance to win. They both took a walk in the yard. Destini hugged him. He thanked her again for saving his mother's and sister's lives. He also confessed that the reason he went out with Tasha was to get her jealous because she always ignored him or shied away from him. He declared, she would always be his first choice.

"I'm sorry if I hurt you," he said, "but I was hurt also, especially when you paid so much attention to Jim, that self-centered show-off. I wondered every night what on earth you saw in someone like Jim."

"I wondered myself," she smiled, "but back then I was so insecure, that I thought being around Jim would make the other kids like me and stop teasing me. He seemed so sure of himself."

"Well," Stephan nodded his head, "Jim is too sure of himself. He seems very egotistical, but guess what, we all have faults. I'm just happy that you are not seeking his company anymore. He had his way with the girls he went out with."

"Like the way you had with Tasha?" Stephan stopped walking for a while and closed his eyes. He finally looked at the ground, and then he looked at Destini.

"I did not mean to hurt you," he said softly. "I don't know why I did what I did. I know that I really missed you then and she kept coming on to me, and I pretended it was you I was with. I am sorry for making love with Tasha. I feel really bad about it, but it meant nothing to me. I was wrong and I've already apologized to her." Stephan held her hands gently, but firmly. "Can you please forgive me?"

"Yes. I forgave you a long time ago," she said.

"You didn't say anything to me about it before or at the Senior Banquet," he said.

"I know. I figured we would talk about it sooner or later, and I didn't want to spoil a perfectly lovely evening at the banquet."

"Thanks," he said. Stephan was taller and had grown even more handsome than when she first met him. His beautiful bronze skin was a treat for the eyes. She stared with pleasure at his toned, muscular, body and his gorgeous woolly dark hair, which was always properly shaped. She wanted to run her hands over it. Stephan looked at her and asked again if she would be his girlfriend. She told him she'd answer him when she returned.

Destini's Triumph

Destini's arrival in New York City, created much attention from the media and the contestants. The people were fascinated with her skin color and beauty. In spite of this, nervousness permeated her mind, especially after seeing the beautiful contestants of different ethnic backgrounds. A few of the contestants said that she wouldn't reach the top ten because she was so dark. One contestant reminded them that she was chosen from millions of photographs, and she was elegant and beautiful. The contestant concluded--she may have a good chance. Regardless of their conversations, Destini emerged with beauty and elegance. She performed superbly in the competition. Destini's years of involvement in past pageants pushed her ahead and she won the crown. The grand prize included a car, a book store gift card, clothes, a computer, a daily schedule book, perfumes, vacation for two to Jamaica and Hawaii, hair and skin products, and a modeling contract, that included a trip to Paris for a photo session.

The appealing television production caught the interest of many. Some of the people at home, who watched, were surprised to see her as a finalist. Destini's relatives, who did not want anything to do with her, the pupils in school who called her names and the families from the foster homes who treated her badly, were equally surprised to see her on national television. They now wished they had not mistreated her. Her picture would be on magazine covers and she would be famous. Yasmin had tears in her eyes. She felt badly for treating her best friend dishonestly. She asked God to forgive her and to take away the jealous feelings she felt for her best friend. Even though Destini was mistreated, and bullied, she kept in her heart what her grandmother taught her when she took her to Sunday school, "No matter what happens to you, God is always with you; never leave Him out of your life. Take Jesus with you everywhere you go. Trust in Him always. Evil might try to control the battle, but God wins the war." Tasha and others who teased her realized Destini had overcome the crippling evil with which they'd tried to hold her down. Tasha was now very happy for her.

Destini arrived home from her tour and photo sessions. She strode towards the house wearing an ivory, v-neck, silk top and a red straight skirt. Tasha and Deloris walked next to her on either side. Destini looked elegant and gorgeous. Her long and beautiful midnight colored, woolly hair was soft and attractive as it flowed passed her shoulders. Waiting inside the house were some family members: Grandma and Grandpa Taylor, Ms. Anderson, her schoolteacher, friends, and one mysterious guest. They cheered, surrounded her, hugged, and congratulated Destini.

Etta interrupted and asked her to go into the library. Upon entering the library, she saw a handsome, distantly familiar face.
"Destini," Etta said, "I know this will be a shock, but this man is your father." Destini looked at Etta with a spark of surprise and asked what was she talking about.
"My father died in a plane crash eleven years ago. You know that." Jeff then explained that he was her father, and that he was arrested in Mexico by mistake and sentenced to jail for something he didn't do. They later found he was innocent after he finally got word to the United States government about his dilemma. The charges were dropped, and he was released four years ago. Since his release, he had been looking for his little princess. None of her relatives knew where she was located. He was very upset with them. He finally got a job and hired a private detective. The detective at last found the orphanage. However, at the same time he saw her on the model search and discovered where she lived. Jeff told her that her mother died in the plane crash when returning to the states. He didn't know at first that the plane had crashed. He thought his wife had deserted him.

Destini stood for a good minute and stared at her father. Could it really be him? He sounded and looked familiar.

"Destini," he said, "the last thing I remember saying to you was 'Papa loves you, my beautiful chocolate princess.'" Destini's fingers covered her mouth as tears gathered in her gorgeous brown eyes. Yes, she recognized him; that tall, handsome king who was her father. Tears rolled down her face.

"Oh my God," she cried as her heart ached with joy. "Oh, oh my God," she repeated. "Papa, Papa, oh Jesus. . ., Papa, oh Jesus, thank you God." With arms outstretched, she walked over to him, hugged him and her face fell on his chest. She cried and would not let him go. Her heart ached with joy as she held unto him. Etta stood watching and wiping her teary eyes as joy bubbled from within. Destini cried and cried. She told him that, one of the things that had kept her going before she met the Taylors, was what he said right before he left. She was about to say it, and he repeated it.

"You are my little heart. Your skin is so soft and beautiful. I love you my beautiful chocolate princess."

"Papa, all I could remember was that someone precious to my heart told me that he loved me and called me chocolate, one of the best tasting treats in the world, and princess which made me feel like royalty." Destini did not want to see anyone else. She spent the rest of the day with her father. She took him on a tour around the house and the beautiful manicured landscape until the sun disappeared. The Taylors wondered whether she was going to leave them now that her father returned. Destini reassured them that they were the best, and without them she wouldn't be where she is. She told Etta that she had three fathers now--God, Winston and Jeff, and that she did not plan to go anywhere except to college. When Selina saw Destini's father she wanted him. Somehow the color problem she felt earlier went out the window. But little did she know she would have a rival--Vashti Michaels lived down the lane.

Stephan, now back in town from a business trip in Jamaica, visited Destini, the next day. The evening sun was glowing softly through the dusky sky, though it seemed about to say goodnight. Destini introduced him to her father. Stephan told her he now saw where she inherited her beauty and her pleasant and caring personality. Jeff liked Stephan right away. He sensed something exceptional about the young man. After the exchange of pleasantries, both young people went off alone and walked hand in hand around the yard. His black and white shirt coordinated perfectly with his smoke gray dress pants. His stately presence and masculine manner were so impressive to Destini. He was tall and protective with his broad shoulders. *"Wow,"* she thought. They stood and stared into each other's eyes as if mesmerized by each other. He handed her a beautiful bouquet of red roses, and she accepted it most graciously. She quickly walked up to the porch and put the lovely roses in a vase, located inside the house and ran back towards him. He took her hand and looked at the soft, gentle beauty standing before him. He just wanted to hold her close, to protect her, and feel her soft sexy body next to his strength.

Destini heard Etta calling her. She looked at Stephan and wondered what happened. Etta opened the door, "Destini, you have a visitor, and she is begging to see you."

"Who is it Mom?"

"Yasmin."

"You 'a joking, I wonder what she wants," she said. "Mom, tell her, um, I'll be right there." Before she could finish, Yasmin came to the door.

"Destini, it's okay. You don't have to come inside. May I speak to both of you, that is, if you don't mind?" Stephan stared at her with a serious face and looked at Destini for an answer.

"Sure," Destini answered gently. She looked at Stephan, "you mind?"

"Yes, . . ." he responded and turn his face away. He then concluded with, "okay, go ahead, no problem." Etta went back inside and Yasmin stepped towards them. Stephan looked at her as if to say you are interrupting.

"Um, I'm sorry for interrupting, but I really want to apologize for acting a fool . . ."

"Yasmin . . ."

"Please, let me finish without interruptions. Please." They both agreed. "As I was saying, I want to apologize for acting like a jealous fool all those years. Stephan, I should have realized that there was no hope for us and backed off. Destini . . .," she paused and tears were in her eyes. "I'm so sorry," she said crying. "You've been an awesome friend." Jeff was sitting by an open window inside the house. He listened to everything that was said. He wondered what happened. He wasn't happy about anyone hurting his darling daughter. "You showed me patience," she continued. "You cared when no one else cared. You forgave me even when I did you wrong. I was so jealous of you and Stephan . . . Destini, I'm sorry for the way I've felt in my heart about you all along. I'm sorry I slapped you at the banquet." Jeff stood to his feet and folded his arms about his chest with a serious expression.

Stephan looked at Destini, "Slapped you?" Destini held his hand gently as if to quiet him. He understood the gesture, but he was not very happy about anyone touching Destini, even if it was Yasmin.

"But I deserved the way you handled it. Thank you, reality checked in." Jeff sat back down. It seemed that Destini could take care of herself. In addition, it appeared to Jeff that Stephan was very protective of her. *"Wonderful,"* he thought.

"I don't know if we can be close like we were before," Yasmin continued, "because I blew it twice. But I'll accept any kind of friendship. It's great to have a friend like you. There is more to be said, but I don't want to take up anymore of your time. So, could you both please forgive me?"

Stephan looked at the ground. He had one hand at his side and the other in Destini's hand. He shrugged his shoulders. Destini told Yasmin that she forgave her. She said that she loved her and cared about her. Stephan was still looking away from Yasmin. Destini squeezed his hand. He finally looked at Yasmin expressionless.

"I'll forgive you," he said, "because the Lord God said we ought to forgive. As for you hanging with us, I'll think about it and let you know." Jeff laughed. He thought Stephan had a great sense of humor.

"Well," Yasmin said while turning to leave, "good evening and I'll call you Destini." Destini motioned for her to wait, and she ran up to her and hugged her.

"I love you Yasmin. I'll talk to you later." Yasmin left and went home. Her heart felt better because the heavy burden was lifted. She thanked God for answering her prayers. *"Destini is such a wonderful person,"* she thought.

Stephan was happy that Yasmin finally left. He turned to Destini, "And why didn't you tell me that she slapped you at the Senior Banquet?"

"That was between Yasmin and me and I handled it. I don't think she will be doing that again."

"I don't want anyone, even it is Yasmin, touching you," he concluded. Destini smiled, leaned on his strong arm and then turned to walk with him away from the house. Stephan suddenly stopped. "Oh," he said quickly, "by the way young lady."

"Uh oh," she thought, *"he said 'young lady' instead of Chocolate.'"*

"What?" she asked looking at him innocently. Jeff had been listening from the window. However, he granted his daughter some privacy. He shook his head, smiled and went into the next room.

"I forgot to ask you about this. Is there a reason why you somehow . . . absentmindedly, forgot to tell me about Keith being one of the young men who asked you to the Senior Banquet?" Destini stared at Stephan, *"I knew somehow he would find out. He's so smart."* Then in a state of pretty confusion she answered, "By George, what do you mean?" He glared at her in a fatherly manner and folded his arms.

"How, um, did you find out?" she asked.

"Don't worry I have my ways."

"Um, okay, I didn't want any fight between the both of you. You guys are best friends. Please Stephan, I can't take anymore foolishness." She looked at him in desperation.

"You don't have to worry, I took care of it. I believe Keith will be minding his own business from now on."

"What did you do?" she questioned with eyes wide open.

"Keith and I have an understanding and it's between both of us. Can we change the subject?" he asked lovingly as they walked away from the house.

"Yes, I'd love to change the subject and concentrate on this gorgeous, strong masculine man standing before me." Stephan blushed, held her close to him, and kissed her soft, full lips gently, yet passionately. The feeling of her soft lips and soft body pressing against him set him aglow. He wanted her so much, and he said to himself, *"When I am through with college, she will be my wife."* He caressed her glorious curly, cottony-soft tresses. Hmmm, the fragrance of her hair always reminded him of a fresh garden. He caressed her face and looked deeply into her eyes.

"Destini," he asked, "would you be my girlfriend and we commit ourselves to each other?"

"O Stephan," she softly whispered, with tears in her lovely eyes, "if I didn't know better, I'd say you are an angel in disguise." She smiled and continued, "Yes, I'd love to be your girlfriend and we commit ourselves to each other." She thought, *"Well, later for his mother, Yasmin and anyone else."* With that, they embraced each other. Destini thought to herself, *"Thank you God for guiding and directing my life. Thanks for giving me love and the strength to go through all the evil that I went through, and for allowing me to meet such a wonderful man."* Tears began to flow as she recalled some of the foolishness that people in their ignorance had put her through, and how they tried to keep them both apart. Stephan heard a slight sniffle and gently lifted her face to see a tear drop gliding down her gorgeous face. He gently caressed her face.

"Princess, what's wrong?" He wanted to stop any pain that she was feeling. He just wanted her to be happy.

"Oh Stephan," she said softly, "these are not sad tears. Even though my mother died and my father disappeared, I now realize that God was with me. He has directed and guided my life all those years. He truly blessed me, especially when he opened the door for me to meet you. You have no idea what you, Winston, and Etta have done for me. Stephan, I love you." Tears were beginning to gather in Stephan's eyes also.

"Oh, Chocolate you have no idea how much I love you. I've never met anyone like you before. You brought life and excitement into my world. You actually showed my mother how to be a Christian. You forgave her for all the things she did to you, and you treated her with love and respect." Stephan paused slightly to hold back from crying. He quickly turned his head away, and then looked back lovingly at Destini. "You saved her life even though she was trying to hurt you. You say I'm an angel in disguise. You're the angel in disguise." He held her hands gently and spoke tenderly and lovingly to her.

"Chocolate, I love you very much. The love and care I feel for you are so deep inside. It's almost like an ache that I cannot explain. All I know is that I want no one else but you. You make me feel like a man. I don't have to fake or hide anything when it comes to you." She looked into his eyes and his eyes answered with love. He embraced her gently, yet firmly, and he kissed her lovingly again. Destini was swept away in the arms of Stephan Barronton. She thought, *"Not only is he a man of steel and compassion, but he's gorgeous as well."* The cool night air caressed their bodies with an atmosphere of love. They continued to embrace each other, both knowing that one day they would be man and wife.

The adventure continues as they go off to college.

Book 2
Destini

~~~~~~

Give a Gift to a Friend or Family Member
Place order for your school

CHECK YOUR FAVORITE BOOKSTORE OR ORDER NOW

☐ Yes, please send ____ copies of **Destini the Chocolate Princess** at $18.95 each, plus $4 shipping per book

☐ Yes, please send ____ copies of **Destini the Chocolate Princess** at $28.95 each, (hard cover) plus $4 shipping per book

☐ Yes, please send ____ copies of **How to be Popular Like a Celebrity and love it** at $16.95 each, plus $4 shipping per book

Indiana residents please add 7% sales tax per book. Allow 14 days for delivery.

My mailing address is:
Name: _____Address: _____

City: _____ State: _____ Zip: _____

Email address: _____

Order online:
Please pay by credit or debit card to:
JWANI Productions, LLC
Order online – Jo-Val Publishing --
Amazon
Barnes & Noble
Call for discounts on large orders for schools or
organizations
1-317-286-8759
Email: jo@jvpublishers.com
Visit our website: www.jvpublishers.com

287

1. Why do you think Mary was not happy about the skin color of her new born baby girl?

2. How would you describe Jeff Pearson?

3. Have you ever felt someone was too dark or too light skin skinned? Explain.

4. What would you have said to Selena about her beliefs regarding skin color?

5. Should Destini have meet Stephan in the rain or should she have told her parents?

6. What made Destini come to the conclusion that her biological mother did not like her skin color?

7. Was Destini justified in her thinking to bring a gun to school, and blow her bullies away?

8. What do you think Destini should have done when the class was mocking and laughing at her? What would you have done?

9. Would you forgive Yasmin and befriend her again? Why or why not?

10. If you had the chance like Destini, would you have hit Mrs. Barronton with the chair? If so, why? If not, why?

11. Would you have become friends with Tasha or would you ignore her for the rest of your life?

12. What would you have done when Nolita hit you on the school bus?

13. Did Destini do the right thing by confronting Mrs. Barronton when she found out that they had planned to run her off the road?

14. Should Destini allowed Stephan to kiss her when he visited her home for the first time?

15. Should Destini have stopped and saved the Barronton's when they were in the accident? Would you have helped them? Explain.

16. How do you feel about your skin color? Are you pleased with the color that God blessed you with? If not, why?

17. How do you feel about you? If you are not happy with yourself, why? If not read chapter 14 "Truth and Beauty."

18. Why do you think Sophia Barronton was prejudice? How did this novel help you to realize your pain or the pain of others?

19. Destini contemplated suicide? Is suicide the answer to life's problems?

More questions for discussions on Website: www.jvpublishers.com/questions.html

www.ingramcontent.com/pod-product-compliance
Lightning Source LLC
Chambersburg PA
CBHW031111030726
47496CB00002BA/484